Item
sho
bor
te!
bε
Th
Re
Fir
inc
be

r

WHO ARE YOU?

WHO ARE YOU?

Elizabeth Forbes

Cutting
Edge
Press

A Cutting Edge Press Paperback Original

Published in 2014 by Cutting Edge Press

www.cuttingedgepress.co.uk

Copyright © Elizabeth Forbes

Elizabeth Forbes has asserted her moral right to be identified as the author of this work under the terms of the 1988 Copyright Design and Patents Act.

This book is sold subject to the conditions that it shall not, by way of trade or otherwise, be lent, resold, hired out or otherwise circulated without the publisher's prior consent in any form of binding or cover other than that in which it is published, and without a similar condition, including this condition, being imposed on the subsequent purchaser.

The characters appearing in this book are fictitious, any resemblance to real persons, living or dead, is purely coincidental.

All rights reserved
Printed and bound by CPI Group (UK) Ltd, Croydon, CR0 4YY

ISBN: 978-1-908122-73-5
E-PUB ISBN: 978-1-908122-74-2

All rights are reserved to the author and publishers.
Reproduction in any form currently known or yet to be invented, or the use of any extract is only permitted with the written approval of the publishers.

For Y. J.

HOMECOMING

Alex walks up the street he's walked up every week night for the last twelve months. Lime trees, uniformly spaced, march up the wide pavement. Useless things that cover the cars with an irremovable stickiness and make the parking difficult especially as each house now seems to accommodate two cars, and sometimes even a third for the help. Litter escapes the street cleaners' suction machines by skulking beneath the trunks. Detritus from the KFC, McDonalds, lager tins, supermarket carrier bags and styrofoam cups mingle with the dead leaves. Alex scans the rubbish as he walks past it, searching for anything that looks unusual; anything other than the normal crap. There's a fresh lot every day because each morning between 5 and 6.00 a.m. the road-sweeping machine drones along the street, waking him up if he's not awake already, mawing and scraping and bleeping its health and safety warning. His ears are so finely attuned to the noises of the night that he can hear it coming from a long way off, and he can hear it going first down one side of the street fading into nothing, and then coming slowly back up the other, growing louder once more. The same movements every single day; a fixed routine that you can set your clock by. Alex never feels comfortable with fixed routines.

The street, which is actually an avenue thanks to the trees, is flanked mostly by semi-detached houses of the late-Victorian period constructed from mellow, reddish-orange brick. London brick. Each house shares the same footprint, apart from the grander detached ones nearer to Richmond Park at the top of the hill. They are all of a similar value, give or take the odd few thousand pounds for an added-on conservatory or remodelled kitchen. It's nearly half past seven and most of the inhabitants haven't yet got around to shutting their curtains, so when he looks up from the pavement he can see right into the elegant rooms. He sees silk-covered lampshades, collections of silver-framed family photographs, gilded antique mirrors over the Victorian mantelpieces, and tasteful pictures adorning the walls. Through some of the windows he can see small children in nightclothes talking animatedly to slim, chic, interchangeable women. Their hair, clothes, mannerisms, all seem to have morphed into an homogenous glob of same-ness. Alex prides himself in recognizing when things are the same, and sensing the danger signs when there is the slightest shift from the norm. In the same way that he watches the street, the houses and the people inside them, his hyper-vigilance picks up on anything that is out of place, and things are definitely out of place in his own home. It's just a matter of time until he'll have to act, or perhaps deploy is a better word. The irony is that he really does love Juliet and he wants to have a happy, perfect home with her and Ben. He wants to be able to look into the windows of his own house and see the same story-book scene of marital and material comfort. A genuinely happy wife and child waiting for his homecoming, instead of the caricature they have created. He's always looking in at them from behind his own walls, and there's nothing he can do to pull them down. If only ... If only they were different people, if only life had been different, then things would be different. Now they are just advancing towards the inevitable battle. Alex is so tired. Not just tired as in needing to get in, pour a drink, sit down and somehow put his mind on hold; he feels swamped by a thick mud of exhaustion that invades both his limbs and his mind.

Before he's within ten yards of the house he knows that something has happened. He feels a familiar surge of adrenalin. So perhaps this is it. This is what he's been preparing for. There is no light coming through the glazed door; instead just blackness receding far into the house. The sitting room to his right is also in darkness. He takes a step backwards from under the canopy of the porch and looks up to the first-floor bedrooms. They too are in darkness. He turns to see if Juliet's BMW is outside. His hand trembles but he manages to fit the key into the lock and pushes the door open, sweeping a pile of flyers across the doormat and onto the quarry-tiled floor. He closes the door and flicks the hall light switch. He puts his briefcase down, and then he squats to gather up the various takeaway leaflets, screwing them up into a tight ball. His footsteps echo across the floor, amplifying the silence of the house. He shrugs off his coat and puts it on the newel post at the foot of the stairs. He walks through to the kitchen. There is something that makes him pause before switching the lights on, knowing that this is a situation he has rehearsed in his head many times. His hand hovers over the switch, and he takes a deep breath. The room floods with light. It is all too tidy. There is nothing on the sink. All the work surfaces are clinically clean and clear. It is the way he likes Juliet to leave it if they are going away. He likes it to be tidy to come home to.

Propped up against the fruit bowl, on the island that occupies the centre of the kitchen, sits a white envelope marked ALEX. He picks up the envelope and stares at those four capital letters.

PART
1

A FIRM BASE

Juliet wanted their new house to be perfect; a new life, a fresh start. She wanted to live in the sort of neighbourhood where people like herself lived, so she didn't stick out like some sad, isolated sore thumb. She long ago got tired of their peripatetic lifestyle. Two years somewhere, just enough time to settle and get to know the people and, if you were lucky, make maybe one good friend, and then they would move on once again, all because of Alex. And now all that is behind them. She's got her little family unit just as she wants it. So everything about this house, and their new, settled life *is* perfect, because she tells herself it is so, and she believes that if she tells herself often enough, then it *will* be so. In ten years of marriage it is the first place that she can really think of as her own home and so she is determined that they will fit in, like *normal* people, doing *normal* things and that she won't let Alex fuck it all up. OK, so Alex would much rather be living in some isolated farmhouse in the Welsh hills rather than in the goldfish bowl of south-west London, and there's a big part of Juliet that is attracted to the picture-postcard idyll; it's just that there was something threatening about being in the middle of nowhere with only Alex. Alex's mother was so thrilled at the prospect of them living near to her after all the years of postings abroad, that she gave him a substantial gift of money to invest in the house. They could never have afforded it by themselves, *and* he found a good job. But she knows that he hates the transparency of suburbia. He hates being subjected to the sounds of other people, including their intimate moments, their rows, their children playing or crying; he says he can smell the scent of other

Leabharlanna Poiblí Chathair Baile Átha Cliath

Dublin City Public Libraries

people's lives drifting across their air space. He reminds Juliet of an alpha male displaced from his pack.

'No Alex?' Rowena Wood sits beside Juliet and unwinds a dramatically printed pashmina and removes her hat. 'Phew. Hot in here.'

'He couldn't get away from work. Ben's disappointed but what can you do?'

OK, so last night they had a row about the fact that he wasn't coming to the nativity play at Ben's school, but to be honest she's actually pleased. Juliet is very wary of him and his unpredictability, and lately he's become even more volatile. She never knows just which Alex she might get. When he left the Army he told her he was tired of having to be nice to people just because it was either in his job description or because they were of some, as he put it, artificially constructed seniority. He was perfectly capable of ignoring someone, of blanking them, if he thought what they were talking about was dull or stupid. He said he just didn't have the patience any more to suffer fools, that life was just too short to fill it with idiots.

'And Robert?'

'You must be joking,' Rowena says. 'My job is *just* as high-powered as his, and if I can bloody well get here, so can he. But you know, it's like a competition about who's the most important. It's so stupid because if he'd got any sense he'd realize that this is far more important. First nativity? I'm feeling sick with nerves.'

'What's Cordelia?'

'Mary, wouldn't you know it. How about Ben?'

'A sheep.'

Rowena laughs. 'Bloody pain in the arse. Last night I had to cut up a really pretty dress of mine because it was the only thing that was blue. And she's got one of my designer belts holding her head thing on. I'm so scared she won't look the part.'

'She'll look perfect, I'm sure.' Juliet nudges Rowena, dropping her voice to a whisper, 'Just look at Arabella. I *bet* Charlotte went to a professional fancy dress place. I'm sorry, but those wings, and the halo ... That dress is silk chiffon.'

'Oh. My. God. Oh, poor little Cordelia. I do hope that won't scar her for life. Perhaps she won't notice. Ben looks good.'

Juliet looks at Ben and waves. She spent most of last night sewing cotton wool balls on to a large white T-shirt. Then she found a woollen bonnet in the discarded baby clothes box and bunged on a couple of ears which she'd snipped off Ben's fluffy rabbit. He was getting too old for cuddly toys but when he cried she promised him she'd sew them back on afterwards. 'Aw, thanks. Yes he does look sweet, doesn't he?'

'So sweet. Imagine – Mary, star role. Do you think this means she's headed for the stage? RADA here we come?'

Juliet likes Rowena. She's about the only woman she's met since they moved who is becoming a real friend; someone she can trust enough to confide in. When they first arrived, Rowena turned up on the doorstep one Saturday lunchtime with a bottle of wine as a welcome present, and while they drank it Juliet was given the full lowdown on who was who and why and what. 'Of course I get all my intelligence from the nanny,' Rowena explained. And by 'intelligence' Juliet knew that it wasn't the bit between the ears kind. Rowena was VC or VCEO or some blah-blah senior person of a swanky bank, or investment company. Juliet had been told, but to be honest, it all sounded a bit boring and technical, and anyway the last thing that they ever discussed was her job.

'We can both take lots and lots of piccies so that our beloved absent husbands can flash them around their offices and show off their precious little ones ... How's Alex enjoying his job? Still finding it tough to adjust to city life?'

'I s'pose. You know what he's like – a caged animal most of the time.'

Rowena squeezes Juliet's arm and gives her a sympathy-filled smile. 'Guess it must be tough to adjust, after what he did before.'

Juliet and Alex never discussed 'what he did before', even between themselves. He didn't want to talk about it, and she knew he didn't want to talk about it, so it was a dead topic. Except what he did before made him into who he is now.

'I know. But the money's good, and he was lucky to get it.' Security advisor for ExCo, a major oil company, with special responsibility for the Middle East. Alex's knowledge of the Middle East and his fluency in Arabic opened many doors for him, but they weren't necessarily the ones he wanted to step through. Still, he'd been doing what he wanted for nearly all of their marriage. It was now time to settle down and give Ben as normal a life as possible.

'Oh Christ, look – it's the Hunts.' Caroline and Marcus Hunt are their neighbours higher up the avenue. Caroline sees Juliet looking at her, and so she smiles and waves, mouthing 'hello'. Juliet waves back but her smile is tight-lipped. 'Rupert's been bullying Ben. He put powder paint in the sandpit yesterday and blamed Ben. Ben was really upset.'

'Oh well … you know what kids are like.'

'I had to stay behind and be "talked to" by Miss O'Connor – I got the whole "is everything all right at home?" lecture. Little monster. She should have been asking the Hunts that question rather than me. That's one seriously dysfunctional family. When we first moved in I thought Caroline was really sweet. Like, amazingly welcoming. Then all that stuff … where are you from? … who do you know? … how much does your husband earn? … trying to work out if we were worth knowing or not … I really hate that.'

'It's insecurity. I feel rather sorry for her being married to him. He's a serial groper.'

'And there's me thinking I was special. But I reckon she's just as bad. You should have seen her with Alex at their dinner party. Talk about a rash, she was more like a full-on dose of shingles.' To be fair, Juliet knows that Alex was encouraging her, lapping it up and loving the attention. Afterwards, when she told him how unamused she was, he said he was doing it just to see what reaction he would get. He says he invents these little games to stop himself from getting bored. Juliet thinks he does it so that he can reinforce his belief that people aren't to be trusted. He likes to test people by targeting their vulnerabilities. He's like a honey trap, setting people up just so that they can fail. Alex views people either as enemies or allies. And even allies must prove themselves before they can be trusted. Jesus, what she wouldn't give to have the old Alex back.

'Well, I honestly wouldn't worry about it. She's not a patch on you. I'm afraid she's rather overdone the Botox and fillers, poor love.'

'God, I wouldn't mind a few fillers, but Alex would be furious.'

'If you went to someone really good he probably wouldn't notice. He'd just tell you how good you're looking. Not that you don't … Oh hell, you know what I mean. You honestly don't need them.'

'Ha. Kind but not true. Anyway, he says he likes to be able to read my face.'

'Does he, indeed? I wonder why that is … Ooh, look, it's starting … phones ready!'

There's something about watching small children perform the nativity that is both heart-warming and heart-wrenching. Juliet watches Ben standing in front of the three shepherds. One of them has a crook – it's Rupert Hunt – and he keeps poking Ben with it. Ben gets hold of the end and tries to tug it out of Rupert's hand, but Rupert grips it tightly. Miss O'Connor reads the story while Joseph shuffles from one foot to the other, looking embarrassed at having to stand so close to Mary, and the Three Kings arrive blushing with mortification in their remodelled ball gowns and Accessorize tiaras. Gold, frankincense and myrrh are proffered to a nose-picking Joseph, and the baby Jesus – a floppy-limbed, grubby but life-like doll is picked up from the manger and dangled by one dislocated leg by Mary. Then the Messiah is dropped on his head provoking laughter from the audience, and Ben gives one final tug on the shepherd's crook which sends Rupert toppling into the manger, which in turn falls on top of the concussed baby. Mary bursts into tears and runs towards the audience screaming 'Mummy' and Rowena whispers 'Oh shit,' and stands up and shouts 'Here, darling.'

Miss O'Connor rushes to rescue the baby and rights the manger and then announces that everyone will sing 'Away in a Manger', which provokes even more laughter from the audience. Some bright spark of a father stage-whispers loudly enough so that all can hear, 'Perhaps we should sing "Away from a Manger".'

Finally, the end of term is announced. Everyone is wished Happy Christmas, and the children wait impatiently to be reunited with their owners. As it was in the beginning, is now and ever shall be, world without end …

Then most of the parents say 'See you later' because more of the festive spirit will be dispensed from number 94 this evening. Juliet and Rowena go together to collect Ben and Cordelia. They're still dressed in their nativity costumes, such as they are. Ben's cotton wool balls are looking a little matted and grey, while Cordelia's gown seems to be coming apart down the back. 'You used staples!' Juliet laughs. 'Genius!'

'Maybe, but it's gonna be one hell of a job to get her out of it. I think I'll have to attack it with scissors. Come back for a bowl of soup and a gossip.'

Juliet glances up at the clock and thinks about all the things she should be doing at home. 'Love to,' she says. They shuffle out between the coats and bags and bodies both small and large, and as Rowena's house is just around the corner from the school, they walk.

'The nanny's supposed to be good at needlework, all that creative shit, but she arranged to be off last night, leaving it all to me. Hence the ghastly mess I've made of it. Poor Cordelia ... But honestly, it's all getting a bit too bloody competitive.'

'I wouldn't have minded the frock that Arabella was wearing for myself; must have cost a fortune.'

'Even you wouldn't have squeezed into it, darling.'

'Ha ha. Guess you're going to the do tonight?'

'Yep. The usual round. Same every year. You can set your calendar by it. Nicholsons' tonight, the Moores' tomorrow, nothing on Christmas Day, thank God, and then you on Boxing Day. It's exhausting, frankly. Rob thinks we should "do" something ourselves but so far I've managed to wriggle out of it.'

They arrive at Rowena's house. It's Georgian and five storeyed and very grand. They shoo the children in front of them and descend the stairs into the kitchen. The whole of the basement has been gutted and turned into a barn-sized area with a playroom/snug/cinema at one end. A television screen the size of which Juliet has never seen, sits on the wall, surrounded by a massive library of DVDs. Ben and Cordelia take themselves off to choose something to watch while Rowena removes a bottle of white wine from the fridge. Having poured out a couple of glasses, she finds a pack of crisps and extracts two bags. 'OK by you?'

'Sure, it's Christmas ... although I wouldn't normally.'

'You're so good, Juliet. I do all the wrong things when Jade's not around. I think it's my way of being subversive – you know, Mummy is the nicest because she gives me chocolate and crisps.'

'And I bet you let her stay up late?'

'Christ, I'm hopeless at putting her to bed. We do the story, then she wants another one, then she wants a drink, then she says she's hungry, then she wants a wee, and then ... finally ... I escape, go downstairs and the next thing is she's frightened, she can't sleep. Honestly, I shouldn't be confessing to this, but sometimes I come home from work late so I miss the whole bloody bedtime rigmarole. You see, I really am a shocking mother.'

'Yes. You are.' Juliet giggles and takes a couple of sips of wine. Rowena returns to the fridge and pulls out some Duchy of Cornwall ready-made chilled soup; typical Rowena to go for the most expensive. 'Mmmm, see you've been busy.'

'Ha! Well if you'd gone for a pee or something, I could have chucked the packaging and conned you that I made it myself.'

'You don't honestly feel that guilty do you? I cheat and I'm at home all day. At least you've got an excuse, seeing as you're so bloody successful and busy at work. I envy you, you know, having your own life, financial independence. I'm terrified that I'm becoming really boring. At supper parties I sit next to some man and I get the inevitable "What do you do?" and I say "Oh, you know, I look after my son, stay at home." I can't say the word housewife without vomiting, and then more often than not he'll turn the other way cos there'll be someone like you sitting on his other side. Honestly, what do I have to talk about? Ben. Ben and Ben. Or, at a push, curtains! Soft furnishings ... not exactly the most scintillating topic.'

'Well I envy *you*, so let's start a mutual envy society, shall we? But before you were married, and before you had Ben, what did you do then?'

'Before I met Alex I mucked about, did ski seasons, nightclub hostessing, the kind of work that was fairly nocturnal,' she laughs, 'I failed to get into art college, but I did a bit of painting, drawing, even a few dog portraits while we were in Germany. I got really quite adept at Labrador jowls. Funny, they're all different, you know. The problem is that when you're married to someone in the Army you can't have a career. Not unless you're something like a nurse, or a nursery teacher. I dunno, but if you want to move with your man and he's on a two-year posting somewhere, well you can't just dump your job and go that easily. You make a choice.'

'You call it a choice? It's a bloody sacrifice!'

'Yeah, I suppose it is. But then no one's forcing you to. The things you do for love, eh?'

'You never mentioned your painting before. Why not start again?'

'Hmm, I should.' Juliet had had every intention of starting again when they got to the new house. She had even chosen a room for her studio, and bought all new paints and a few canvases to work on. She had *even* started work on a project until ... Well, until that awful night.

Rowena's busy laying the table, so Juliet gives her a hand; she wants to shut the memories out before they begin to surface. She's learned that's the best way to deal with stuff like that. Squash it. Forget it.

'God, can't tell you how glad I am that you've moved here. I mean it's not that everyone isn't, you know, nice and all that; but it's tough finding kindred spirits.'

'You mean someone to sink a bottle of wine with you at lunchtime?'

'Yeah, well there is that. Oh, I don't know what I mean. Maybe it's something to do with living here, this area. Everyone's a certain type. It's all so bloody corporate. And the competition isn't just between our kids – it's our houses, our husbands, the cars, dinner parties, holidays. 'Oh you went to Sri Lanka to a *hotel* did you? – we're off to Mustique to stay in our villa. OK, I know I'm exaggerating but you jump on the carousel and it's spinning so fast you just can't get off it. Maybe that's why you're different, you two. I hadn't given it much thought before, but being an Army wife, all that moving around, and being without Alex when he was in some fucking awful war zone, must have been *really* hard for you.'

'Yep. At times.' Juliet stares into her wine glass and Rowena notices it's nearly empty, so she tops it up. 'Thanks. Being an Army wife is strange, I suppose. It's impossible to ever feel settled. Some people bought houses of their own so they could feel rooted somewhere. But I think that could make it even more difficult, because you were always longing to go home, really home; whereas we never had a proper home, until now.'

'Why here? I would have thought Alex would have wanted somewhere in the country – commuter land, some space around him. You could have grown your own vegetables and Ben could have had a little pony. I can just see it. You and your Aga and your floral pinny.'

'Oh, shush. Hmmm, maybe one day. Besides, it's really convenient for Alex's job. And we're close to his mother, so it works. For now.'

'I couldn't bear the thought of being cooped up with just Robert. I'd go stark staring bonkers. I think we might kill each other. *And* he doesn't like getting mud on his shoes. There's a lot to be said for being able to walk to Waitrose. Not that I ever do ...'

'It is a bit weird, if I'm honest, having Alex home all the time.' Juliet is now on to her second glass of wine and she knows she is in danger of saying more than she should. 'You run everything when they're away and then they come back and it's like you've got to pretend to be less capable than you are, somehow. Otherwise you end up making them feel superfluous –'

'Which they are ...'

'If there's one thing Alex can't stand, it's feeling superfluous. He's one of those old-fashioned types – you know, the man's in charge. I don't think he'd like me to get a job, seriously. He likes the idea of having me at home, bringing up our son ... Oh God, Rowena, please don't take that the wrong way.'

'Don't worry, I'm a lot more thick-skinned than that. We're all different. Just so long as you're happy doing that, my darling.'

'Oh yes,' Juliet says a little too eagerly. She meets Rowena's eyes, which have suddenly become serious.

'Look, sweetie pie, I don't want to pry, and tell me to shut the fuck up, but sometimes I worry about you. I mean, I like Alex, don't get me wrong. I do. But I've noticed when you two are together he sometimes doesn't seem very kind to you.'

Juliet straightens her back and stares down into her glass once more. She can feel her cheeks colour. 'Really? Oh, it's just his manner. Used to giving orders. I think he sometimes forgets that I'm his wife and not his corporal.'

'So you're OK? I mean, really OK?'

'Yes, of course. Don't be silly. We're fine.'

'I know you are. Yes. Forget what I said, please. But if you ever need to talk – a shoulder, whatever … I'm very discreet. Promise.'

'Thanks. You're a sweetheart. Now if I'm not mistaken that soup's about to burn, missus. Shall we pretend that we're not pissed and give these children something to eat?

'Oh, fuck it. You see … a domestic disaster, although I do admit I'm a bit of a goddess in other areas. Now, listen, I'm going to tell you something and you've got to promise not to explode.'

'OK …'

'It's about that little bugger Rupert Hunt and something he said to Cordelia … I think you should know …'

* * *

Juliet walks hand in hand with Ben back to where the car is parked. His feet scrape on the pavement and he dawdles, pulling her back. 'Ben, come on. What's the matter?'

'Cordelia said I looked stupid today. A stupid sheep. And she said I was a baby cos I was wearing a baby's hat.'

'Ben, for God's sake. It's what all the smart sheep are wearing, honestly. Take my word for it.' Ben looks at her doubtfully and climbs onto his booster seat in the rear of the car.

'And you know Rupert made baby Jesus fall out of his cot?'

'Yes, I saw. But don't worry, it's not really Jesus, it's a doll. Only pretend, Ben.'

'He's not very nice, Mummy, Rupert isn't. Mummy, is Father Christmas all right? He will come and see me, won't he?'

Juliet straps him in, silently sending up a prayer for patience. 'Yes, darling. Of course he will, as long as you're good. You know he only comes to see good boys and girls.'

She looks at Ben in the rear-view mirror, and he's staring out of the window looking pensive. He's tired after his eventful day so hopefully he should sleep well tonight. When they arrive home mid-afternoon the house has a chilly feel about it, and there's so little natural daylight filtering through the windows that Juliet switches on the lights. There's something a little depressing about artificial light in the middle of the day. Across the street she can see Christmas trees already dressed and lit in the windows. Juliet and Alex never do the tree until Christmas Eve because Alex is a traditionalist. She rubs her hands together to warm them and then says to Ben, 'Blow it, it's nearly Christmas. Let's put the heating on – and don't tell Daddy, OK?'

Ben switches the television on and Juliet pours him a glass of milk and cuts, quarters and cores an apple for him. She delivers both the glass and the apple to Ben on the sofa and, satisfied that he'll be content for ten minutes or so, she fires up her laptop. She types in her password, navigates to her favourite support group and scans through the new messages to see if there are any comments or threads she wants to contribute to. She'd started looking into the chat room culture as a way to fill in the long evenings when Alex was away, a sort of harmless curiosity to know what they were all about. She soon discovered that there was an enormous cocktail-style list of tastes and flavours, ranging from the straightforward bored girl looking for clean friendship, to hot woman wanting to meet scorching man for dirty playtimes. You could visit these rooms as a guest, like an anonymous voyeur just waiting and watching to see what went on. If you wanted to visit any of the interesting-sounding rooms, though, you had to sign in with a name. Juliet had bided her time before deciding to take the plunge, because once she did she had no way of knowing what kind of Pandora's box she might be opening up. But as long as she was careful not to give anything away about her real identity or where she lived, she could adopt any persona she wanted.

There are about four or five sites that she visits regularly, and then there are the other sites that she uses for research purposes. Google really is the most amazing search engine. She can type in any phrase, all the stuff that she can't ask anyone else, and there'll be answers, lots of them. She can type in Alex's behaviour, his character traits, her suspicions about what's actually wrong with him. God, the hours she's spent, sometimes all through the night, just scrolling through stuff and thinking she can't quite believe what she's reading. Like it's *so* Alex. These people are writing about *her* husband.

She's made connections with people who are going through similar things and some of them are even becoming friends, of sorts. And the funny thing is that she finds it a lot easier to be open with them, online, than she could ever be with 'real' people. She doesn't know their names. They all adopt aliases so that they can't be tracked down. Juliet has called herself Sparrowhawk because it's a bird that is small but nonetheless feisty and not to be messed with. People have asked her – people in the support groups, that is – why she doesn't just leave Alex, but it's not as simple as that, and she can't really tell them why. That would be too dangerous because you never *really* know who these people are. It's funny, but for all she knows the woman that she's confided in so openly recently could be a man, or some kind of pervert. She could be being groomed. She's read all about that too, people pretending to be someone they're not. Apparently they're called sock puppets. They can lurk in chat rooms and cause trouble by bullying people, or inventing stuff ... like they're suffering from a terminal illness; they're weird attention seekers. But she's no ingénue. She's not stupid, even if Alex thinks she is, which is sometimes no bad thing.

There have been lots of really interesting books suggested by the groups, and since she got herself a Kindle she's been able to surreptitiously read loads about men like Alex. *Inside the Minds of Controlling Men ... Why does He Do That ... How to Break the Cycle of Manipulation and Regain Control of Your Life ... Men Who Hate Women & the Women Who Love Them ... The Devil You Know ...* Most of them have given her *some* insight into the way Alex behaves. But with Alex there's such a municipal-dump-sized heap of problems festering and eating away at him that it's going to take more than a Kindle and a catalogue of self-help books to sort him out. On the good days she can convince herself that Alex really is the same man she married, and she can try and forget about all the bad stuff and be the glass half-full person and believe him when he says it will all be OK. But sometimes something will blow up – something not even of her doing – that will push his buttons and leave her feeling nothing but fear and despair. Those are the bad days, the dark days, and she doesn't like to dwell on those because what's the point? For Ben's sake they've got to make it work. She wants him to have a secure home; a *proper* upbringing with both a mother *and* a father in his life. She owes it to Ben.

When Alex is loving he can be wonderful: kind and *really* gentle. And she has this hope that knowing what he was like before means that he can be like that again if he'll only agree to get some help. Christ, if only. When he came back from Afghanistan the second time, when she realized there was something very wrong, that a new Alex had returned, she pleaded with him to talk to her about what had happened to him, but it was as though he'd locked his emotions into a lead-lined vault and no one – especially her – would ever get anywhere near them. It all seemed so bloody unfair. She'd always believed there was an unbreakable tie between them, based on a deep understanding of each other's insecurities and what had caused them. She'd persuaded herself that one of the major strengths of their relationship had been this recognition of their similarities. It meant that when the bad things happened they could work things through. She'd tried to convince herself that it was the major crises in their marriage that brought them closer together, as though somehow battling through the traumas and crawling out the other side – scarred, maybe, but still *together* – made their marriage stronger. Sometimes she wanted to scream at him, 'For fuck's sake, Alex, just think of what we've been through, what I've put up with … and OK, what *you've* put up with … but we're still bloody here. So if you can't sort yourself out now, what the hell has it all been for?' When she'd felt brave enough she'd tried to raise the possibility of his talking to somebody else, perhaps a professional, but he'd told her to lay off, to fuck off, to drop it or else … Christ, he'd even said he'd kill her if she raised it again. Sure, he was only saying that, like people do, but it was the way he said it, which convinced her he really meant it.

Juliet is finding lots of things hard at the moment, but she finds it particularly cruel when Alex accuses her of being the one who's at fault. He has the bloody nerve to tell her she has mood swings. She tells him that they're not mood swings, they're just normal reactions to his behaviour. That anyone 'normal' would react in the same way as she does. He tries to make out that she's bipolar or something, like a manic depressive, but she knows she isn't. It's his way of justifying his own behaviour. It's just the effect that he has on her. God, that's the basic script of so many of their rows.

She's like an apple in a bowl of water, quite happily bobbing around on the surface, and then Alex comes along and gets his teeth into her to try and drown her. But he can't. She just bobs up again. She thinks it annoys him the way she bounces back, because it shows that he can't really control her fully.

'Why can't you just do as I say?' he'll ask her. 'If only you could just do what I want then we wouldn't have all these bloody awful rows.'

And what if she did? He wouldn't respect her for it, would he? He'd just get worse until there was nothing left of her own will. It's exhausting living with Alex but she has ways of coping, and she tries to show him that if he does treat her badly she'll give just as good as she gets. Alex used to say that had always been their attraction to each other – opposites creating sparks of friction which ignite passion. But then he used to say a lot of things. If it wasn't for Ben, Juliet doesn't know what she might do. Anyone looking in from the outside would probably tell her to leave. It just seems such a bloody waste of all the years she's spent longing for this, for him finally to be out so that they can build something worthwhile together; now that she doesn't have to worry about him every bloody waking minute, wondering if he'll come back to her, and if he does what state he'll be in. All the years she's sacrificed to the bloody British Army ... Yes, *her* – not just Alex. Years of anguish and fear and now he's back. They've finally given him back to her.

Juliet has always been good at distraction techniques, almost – she was once told – to the point of dissociation. It's a coping mechanism which lets her escape from the bad things, and Ben is a marvellous distraction. She always uses the time Ben spends in the bath playing with his ducks and boats to give his room a tidy up. She moves around the bedroom quietly and efficiently, matching up a sock with its partner, picking up a pair of pants, screwing them into a ball together with the socks ready to throw into the dirty laundry basket. Next she replaces the earless rabbit on the shelf with a menagerie of other soft toys and makes a mental note to sew the ears back on. She straightens the spines of the books on the bookshelf, picks up some random pieces of Lego from the floor and stows them in a blue plastic box.

'Mummy ...' she hears Ben calling from the bathroom at the end of the landing.

'Just a minute ...' she calls back because she needs to finish her tidying before she gets him out of the bath.

Juliet feels such a deep passion for Ben that it almost overwhelms her. The nursery, as they still call it even though Ben is five, is probably her favourite room in the house. It isn't just showy-offy like the other rooms; it probably sounds silly but it's like a material manifestation of the relationship between mother and son. Every prop demonstrates the degree of devotion which she lavishes upon Ben. Every *thing* is a symbol of shared memory between Juliet and her son. The map of their lives together thus far. Each item has a special significance, its own little history, a little story of which Juliet is the keeper on Ben's behalf. It's quite a thought. She feels a responsibility towards preserving this mental corkboard of memories because she has barely any memory of her own early childhood. There is no point in asking her mother to fill in the blanks because she'd only construct a fantasy, shutting out out all the bad stuff, including Juliet. Juliet has learned that guilt can do funny things to people; it can make them demonize the victim and defend the perpetrator. No, getting her mother to face up to reality is never going to happen. Not now, after all these years.

Juliet is different. She is determined to make sure she can supplement Ben's childhood memories. Juliet thinks that by reinforcing the positives and blanking out the negatives she can determine whether Ben is a happy, outgoing child, or a neurotic, unhappy, introvert. Without any doubt it is all down to her, especially until Alex sorts himself out.

'Mummy ... COME heeeere ...' Ben whines from the bathroom.

'In a minute ... just WAIT!' She shouts back. Sometimes the weight of motherhood bears down on her so hard. And this is no rehearsal. If it all goes wrong it's always the mother that gets the blame. You spoilt him, gave in to him, gave him too much love; or you were cold, unapproachable, not cuddly enough, too strict. Juliet is his guide, his keeper, his protector, the *everything* of Ben and *for* Ben. Who else other than Juliet can catalogue and caretake the small, seemingly inconsequential details that define the little space that Ben occupies in the world? Just look around the room, where there are boxes filled with toys, drawers stacked with puzzles and games; on the mantelpiece the painted wooden letters that spell out BENJAMIN ... from his godfather James. Dear James. Juliet reaches out and traces her finger around the curves of the 'B', and shivers. There but for the grace of God. She blocks the feeling, refusing to allow the thoughts to spread. They're too painful; too close to home. She should have asked Heather, his widow, to spend Christmas with them. She's one of Juliet's closest, oldest friends, but Juliet was too cowardly and now she's feeling ashamed of herself. She supposes there's a fear of contagion from Heather's grief, and also a sense of guilt that Alex survived, that they still have this supposedly perfect little family while she has nothing, not even a child. Some clumsy person had apparently told Heather that not having children would make it easier for her to move on, to meet somebody else. People can be *really* stupid. But perhaps most of all Juliet feels that she and Alex are not grateful enough. She doesn't want Heather to see the cracks. Juliet is the lucky one. She got Alex back. To be anything less than perfectly happy – and grateful – would somehow be an insult to James's memory and Heather's loss. It's complicated, guilt. It can make you behave in peculiar ways.

Juliet pushes the feelings – and the guilt – aside and distracts herself by straightening the special set of tin soldiers which line up in front of the slate hearth. They're too fragile to be played with – a special gift from Alex's mother as 'she'd saved them all this time in the hope of a grandson.' They have sharp, rusted edges and more than likely lead paint, so even these lifeless little facsimiles of soldiers come with a health warning.

She stands up and finds herself looking at the picture over the mantelpiece. It's a pre-Raphaelite-style painting of a small boy in an old-fashioned white linen smock, blond curls tumbling around his shoulders, blue eyes shining above pillowy, cherubic cheeks, a chubby fist reaching out for something beyond the picture. It was a very un-Juliet choice, but it is fabulously kitsch, and it did look a lot like Ben had done at the same age. It slightly redeems itself by having a decent gilded frame which looks original. It is the sort of romanticized, iconic image of a perfect child that can never really exist in real life. Rose-tinted cheeks of that hue could only appear if the child was febrile, Juliet knows. She imagines that the boy in the painting would have had an old-fashioned, proper nanny in his idealized and sanitized life. A sensible, no-nonsense sort of woman in a dark blue dress under a starched white apron; the uniform of the nation's child protectors; nothing like a uniform, eh? One of those Mary Poppins-type coats with a velvet collar, and a hat for when she wheeled her charge into the park and competed with all the other nannies as to who had the smartest perambulator, the springiest coachwork, the shiniest spokes; the most spotless starched pinafores on their charges. Just the sort of nanny that Alex would have hired if they were into nannies.

There is really no point Alex interfering in Ben's upbringing, because he can never be relied on to help, and because she's always had to do everything, it seems perfectly reasonable that it has to be done her way. Alex has missed so many of Ben's big milestones – birth, learning to walk, first birthday, first day at school, pretty much everything that has mattered so far – it's only natural that she'd resent his interference when he came out. Being married to a soldier was like being a single mum a lot of the time.

But the best thing about Alex being out is the fact that they live here. The house is one of the larger houses in the road because it's been extended upwards and outwards. They have a loft conversion to accommodate a large master bedroom with en suite bathroom – one of Alex's many hated expressions – and a dressing room, which was really just a triple set of wardrobes along one wall. Many of the other identical houses in the street had used the smallest bedroom on the first floor as the nursery, but Alex and Juliet can afford to use the larger room, the room which would have been the spare, as the nursery. It isn't just Ben's room, it's her special place. She's chosen everything in it for Ben and it all looks just so.

The two sash windows facing the street have striped blinds edged with twists of primary colours, and swirly, circus-tent like knobs on the ends of the poles. She remembers agonizing over wallpaper sample books to choose the frieze which marches underneath the picture rail with its Noah's ark collection of animals, and the *Fantasia*-style hippopotamuses poised like cartoon ballerinas on circus plinths repeated over and over again across the wallpaper. The seagrass-covered floor is scattered with cheerful rag rugs positioned strategically to make it soft for little feet. She's even found a sort of toy version of a tiger-skin rug in Peter Jones which goes with the whole scheme just perfectly. Ben had been terrified of it at first, thinking it might eat him all up in the night, but after a week or so he'd calmed down.

Getting the house just right had been Juliet's major project. On a whim she had emailed a few photographs of the house to the *Perfect Property* magazine website, and by the time she got the phone call months later, she'd forgotten all about it. The photography crew arrived together with a journalist who oohed and aahed over every perfect period detail and suggested they feature it in the Christmas issue. Juliet had made sure it all took place while Alex was away on business because she could guess what he'd say, and once it was done – well there wouldn't be much he could do about it. She knew he'd object because he had this thing about strangers being in the house, seeing all their stuff, not knowing who they were. But she didn't see the harm in a few photographs featuring in a low-circulation magazine. It was September and the magazine crew arrived with a van full of Christmas, even down to crackers, seasonal foliage, walnuts and fairy lights for Juliet's box lollipop trees. They decorated the tree with all things edible; the sort of things full of poisonous E Numbers that Juliet would never let Ben near in a million years. They had shortbread iced stars, gingerbread men, and those clever little biscuits that had melted boiled sweets set into them so that they looked like they had mini coloured glass windows. They entwined an ivy wreath up the banisters, and the dining table was laid with festive runners and a ludicrous amount of silver tea lights. And they'd even brought a cooked turkey and stuffed bay leaves up its bottom and surrounded it with satsumas and plastic Brussels sprouts. When Ben came home from nursery school it took a lot of explaining, because *obviously* he then expected a visit from Father Christmas, not least because a giant Christmas stocking was hanging from the drawing-room mantelpiece. Juliet did fret about what kind of psychological effect the whole charade had on Ben. It had taken ages to settle him that night because despite what Juliet said, he was insistent that Santa would visit. In the end she'd got cross and told him that he had to behave better if Santa was to come. Yet another thing to feel guilty about. She'd told Ben not to tell Alex, but as soon as he walked through the door Ben had rushed to him, sobbing, saying that Santa had forgotten him. So then she'd had to explain the whole bloody thing and needless to say he'd been furious. He'd asked her what the hell she thought she was playing at, and so she'd said, 'What do you mean, playing at?' and he'd said, 'Not only traumatizing Ben, but this ghastly thing, this awful exposure of us … what were you thinking?' and Juliet had laughed. Whenever she felt threatened by Alex she always ended up laughing, probably some weird kind of defence mechanism. And so that had really wound him up. 'I don't know what on earth you think is funny about this, Juliet. Just how could you have been so unbelievably stupid!' She'd watched how he'd squeezed his hands into fists and she'd stuck her chin out and said, 'Well you weren't bloody here to discuss it with me, were you, and what do you want me to do all day – sit around and paint my bloody nails? I thought it might be good for the value of the property. I thought it was fun. Remember fun?' she'd said.

'And what about the security, did you think about that? The fact that all our things – paintings, silver, clocks – are all up for cataloguing by any common felon.'

'Common felon. Honestly Alex. If you mean a bloody burglar it's not as though our address is going to be printed anywhere. It won't even say which road we're in. If you're so worried about security why don't you just tear your fucking face off, and then we can all relax a bit.' She chose not to recall what happened next. There were things she shoved into a secret drawer so she didn't have to think about them.

When the edition of the magazine came out towards the end of November, Juliet couldn't believe that this was really the house in which she lived. Things had been moved in order to dress the set; for example the vase of spectacularly tall red amaryllis, circled by wired-in limes, appeared in every room, posing itself prominently in the drawing room, the dining room and grandly in the centre of the hall table. When Juliet realized what they'd done she worried, she actually worried, that people – and by people she obviously meant people she knew – would think that she hadn't the imagination to produce more than a repeat of *one* floral arrangement, and as everyone knew, fruit and flowers together were becoming so last year. OK, so it might seem shallow, but the way you show yourself to the world, and how the world sees you ... these things ... *matter*. And so many bloody tea lights. Alex detested tea lights. Of course when one had old family silver candlesticks which were the real deal, what was the point of silly cheap little things that were available in sets of fifty from IKEA. She knew that Alex thought it smacked of affectedness, artificiality, attention-seeking, the sort of naffness that he attached to people who invited *Hello!* into their homes to show off nothing so much as an immense lack of class.

Deep down, Juliet fears that she has gone through the wrong set of sliding doors, but having invested so much thus far, she has no alternative but to see it through. For the moment. For Ben's sake. But if someone were to ask her when she had last felt truly happy, she would find it a struggle to answer. No. The real truth of the matter is that she feels that her life has become a kind of grand pretence, a sort of theatrical production which she has to stage for the sake of Ben, and in order to cope with Alex, and that if she lets the mask slip, she just might be capable of going out and slitting someone's throat.

Boy, does she have some weird thoughts. The basic Will Ben go to sleep tonight without waking up and waking me up develops into What if he goes to sleep and doesn't wake up at all, which quickly becomes What if he dies in the night ... What if no one believes it was a natural death ... What if she is unable to prove that she hasn't smothered him ... What if she went to prison and then got attacked, murdered even, for being a child killer. And how awful would it be, losing a child, the terrible bereavement, and then of being falsely accused, of having to live with the horror of being labelled the killer of your own child. It happened to someone in real life, and hadn't she committed suicide even after that so-called expert evidence was proven to be flawed and the guilty verdict overturned. That was a truly terrible story. And Juliet has a collection of equally horrible, sad stories in her head that she's read about. The awful things that people do to each other. But why? Why is her head filled with all this shit when all she's doing is tidying Ben's bedroom before getting him out of the bath, into his pyjamas and reading him a story. Just like any other night. And somehow she's managed to get herself from the salubrious surroundings of south-west London to Wormwood Scrubs, or wherever it is they send women to. Ford, was it? Or was that reserved for MPs these days? Is this level, or these layers upon layers of worry, normal? How normal is it to imagine locking your child into the washing machine, accidentally? Or getting a hand stuck in a running Magimix? (That was a really revolting one.) Not putting it in there, or anything *Chainsaw-Massacre*-y like that, just 'What if ...'

She would never hurt Ben. He is her most perfect production. Her beautiful, beautiful boy. Sometimes she tries to imagine an older Ben. A Ben with a gravelly, breaking voice, but finds it impossible to imagine him in any way other than he is right now. Somehow it seems inconceivable that he will grow up – oh no … sorry, God, she didn't mean that *literally* … it just seems inconceivable that he will grow up and away from her. That he will shrug her off as easily as his outgrown clothes. She wants him to stay like *this* – small, vulnerable and dependent upon her for everything. She knows that she is biased, she knows that all mothers think the same, but he really is the most perfect child, sweet and kind and popular. Juliet will not hear anything negative said about her Ben, because he is her creation. Her very greatest achievement and he is the most precious thing she has ever had. Ever.

'MUMMMMMMY …' Ben screams.

'Coming …' She shakes her head as if to shake out all the weird thoughts, like dust from a blanket, and mutters *'For fuck's sake …'* under her breath.

'Where were you …? I've got soap in my eye, and it really stings.' Ben is crying, but Juliet suspects they're not real tears. She hands him a corner of the dry towel. 'Sorry, my darling. Here, wipe it with this.'

'Where were you? Why didn't you come when I called you? Mummy, you're naughty.'

'You're right, Benjamin Miller, and do you know what Mummy will do to make it up to you?'

Ben shakes his head. 'No. What?'

'I shall read you two stories. How's that, little man?' Ben's smile returns and Juliet holds out the fluffy white bath sheet and gathers up her five-year-old son and gives him an enormous cuddle.

Alex gets up from his seat and positions himself by the doors and waits for the train to glide to a stop by the platform. The doors shhh open and a load of commuters spew out, stampeding left towards the stairway. Heels drum against the rubber treads of the wide staircase and a bored ticket collector barely bothers to examine tickets, barely bothers to look at anyone's face. But Alex notices things. He notices all the sounds, and even the way people move, the way they hold their briefcases, their newspapers, the phones clamped to their ears. Alex walks past the BP garage with its neon-flashing coloured lights, the buckets full of ghastly carnations, all festived-up with red roses edged with glued-on gold glitter and sparkly twigs. Minute bunches of mistletoe for £5.99 a throw, and paltry little holly wreaths. Alex doesn't hate Christmas, he just hates the vulgarity of it. No one does Christmas as badly as the British. There wasn't much to miss about Germany, but Christmas there was really special. He liked the way nothing happened before the actual start of Advent. The eve of Advent reminded everyone what it was really all about – a Christian festival. Not that Alex is madly religious, although it was something he had had to think about probably more than most, at times, it was more the fact that the whole event was based on the proper length of the festival, and nothing appeared in the shops until then. How refreshing it was not to have every retail outlet filling its shelves with Christmas tat from the end of September. And then the never-ending canned Christmas music. No, in Germany Advent was when it all happened: the decorations, the lights, the trees, the stuff in the shops. It made it so much more of an event, a celebration, and he loved the way they didn't do coloured lights, only golden, and the way villages were transformed into magical forests with the advantage of having real snow, and the delicious stalls of fast food like you've never experienced. Instead here are thirsty-looking poinsettias, unnatural-coloured chrysanthemums displayed unappetizingly on a dirty forecourt alongside piles of yellow plastic sacks of smokeless coal. He catches the smell of petrol mingling with the cocktail of exhaust fumes, oil and dust, and the cooking spices seeping out from the pores of the new balti restaurant.

He walks up Sheen Lane, past the slick hairdresser's with enormous white hydrangea heads sprouting out of a regimented row of test-tube shaped vases; past the newsagent's with Santa and his sledge flashing red and green, on-off, on-off; and then the estate agent's with the increasingly silly prices tacked on to photographs of almost identical properties, and silver-mirrored stars dangling down the window front on different lengths of blue ribbon. He reaches the junction with the Upper Richmond Road, waits for the lights to change so that he can cross, and then turns left past Pizza Express which has, unsurprisingly, adopted the strange fashion for strings of cold, blue lights, and then he drops in at the Indian corner shop to get a Kinder egg for Ben, and then turns right into Richmond Park Avenue.

Truthfully, Alex loathes this kind of suburban living, which is neither one thing nor the other. Either go the whole hog and have an apartment right in central London, as he did in the old days, or live in the country. But this pseudo *sub*-urban environment depresses him, because it lacks integrity; it can never be the one thing it aspires to be, a fresh open space where one can breathe in untainted air, watch the trees change through the seasons, be aware of nature. No, this isn't anything close. Bird tables, net bags of nuts and bloody cats everywhere murdering everything feathered they can get their paws on. A postage stamp of a garden which can be cut with an electric mower and an extension lead. And can one ever really get used to living with the six-foot-high fences all around one's garden, where it's impossible not to overhear every conversation, where every marital tiff can be heard through thin walls or open windows? How would an anthropologist analyse this kind of living? Tribal, in that all these people are culturally similar, ambitious, they have a collective identity; and yet despite being connected in so many fundamentally important ways, they seek privacy and separation from each other. Minor conflicts break out over whose shrubs have overgrown whose boundary, and who should have the damned prunings. Arguments over barbecues lit without warning the people next door who had just hung out their washing; the man hoovering up the leaves with a bloody noisy gadget during your evening drinks party in the garden. OK, so Richmond Park is a five-minute walk up the road to Sheen Gate. And there are worse places to live. But walking, jogging, riding a bicycle, pushing a buggy up there is like joining the bloody crowds in Oxford Street. There is just no way to get away from everyone ... or anyone. And if you do manage to find some private little corner where you can lie down and look up at the sky, listen to the delicate song of the planes thundering overhead, chances are that you'll be falling over a pair of fellating gays or a couple of tree-shaggers. And the sky. God, Alex misses the sky. Probably that is the one thing that more significantly illustrated the presence – or lack of – civilization. The big skies of the world. The night skies which are impossible to describe to those who haven't seen them. No point trying to take a photograph; what use is a tiny frame when you are capturing a space the size of several galaxies?

No. He doesn't suppose he will ever be truly content here, in number 83 Richmond Park Avenue, even if it is a prime piece of south-west London real estate. But it was what Juliet wanted, so it's what they've got. And she can bloody well knuckle down and be grateful for all his sacrifices and realize that he's trying his best to give her the life she wants.

Alex looks up at Ben's window and sees that there is light bleeding through the blind. He puts his key in the lock and pushes the front door open. The hallway is long and narrow, but wide enough to have a semi-circular table upon which his pile of today's post is placed. He picks up the pile, quickly flicks through it, and then replaces it on the table unopened. He undoes his tie, hangs it over the bottom balustrade, and opens the top button of his shirt, the evening ritual which is the beginning of the transformation into free-thinking human being, rather than pre-programmed automaton. The next part of the ritual is to slip off his suit jacket and place it over the banister. Then he opens the dining-room door, puts on the light and crosses the room to the drinks tray and pours himself a couple of fingers of whisky from the decanter. Then light off, out of the dining room, ice decanted from the hole in the fridge, the reassuring chinking noise as he swirls the amber liquid, the brief moment of delicious anticipation, and then the merest sniff before he takes his first sip. Swirling it around his tongue, letting it wash over his teeth, feeling the tingle, the silkiness, he swallows and then lets out a long sigh of relief. He's home, at last. He leans against the island unit which is almost large enough for a game of ping-pong and lets his eyes wander the room, acclimatizing to this other side of his life. It won't take many seconds for Alex to spot something out of place, anything new or missing. He knows he is tidier, much better organized than Juliet, but she won't have it. It's not exactly an argument between them, but just one of those typical little interactions that he supposes all married couples have. All appears in order. The dishwasher is humming away quietly, the surfaces have all been wiped clean, smoothed with a dry cloth to get them smudge free. The stainless steel of the sink and draining board are glistening, but he wrinkles his nose at the screwed-up dishcloth sitting in the middle half sink, still with tell-tale marks of tomato sauce sloppage. His stomach jolts. It's just sauce, nothing more. He turns on the hot tap and lets it run for a few seconds and then rinses the dishcloth, squeezing and twisting. He turns off the tap, wipes the excess splashes of water from the shiny steel and folds the well-wrung-out dishcloth neatly in half over the tap so that it can dry out properly, instead of festering and stinking, Juliet-style. The red stains are not entirely removed. The whisky helps. He will give himself a couple more moments of isolation from his family, so that he can let his mind settle. Another sip, another attempt to wipe the bloody dishcloth out of his head, then he places his half-drunk glass of whisky in the fridge, picks up his jacket and tie and heads upstairs, knowing that he will be in time to kiss Ben goodnight.

Alex pokes his head around Ben's door. The bedside light is still on but Juliet is not in the room. He can hear the sound of the shower running upstairs. They are going out tonight. He hasn't forgotten. But there is no rush. They aren't due there for another forty-five minutes or so.

'Daddy.' Ben says happily but sleepily.

'Hello, big man. You been good today?' Alex walks over to the bed and sits down on the edge. Ben nods and rubs at his eye with a knuckle of his left hand. It's such a touching, vulnerable gesture that Alex finds it almost too painful to watch. Once there was a well inside of him which was full of feelings, but it ran dry long ago. Although lately he seems to find a lump of emotion pulsating in his throat, he suspects it is nothing more than a mirage. He strokes Ben's thick blond curls, and thinks he should have a haircut soon. Or else people will begin to think he looks like a girl. Something else he and Juliet will argue over. He leans forward and kisses Ben's forehead, then straightens the duvet, even though Juliet will have done so moments before. 'Only two sleeps 'til Father Christmas comes, so you'd better be a good boy.'

'I *am* a good boy. Daddy …?'

'Yes Ben?'

'Mummy says she's going to make fucking sure that that little shit Rupert Hunt gets to know the truth about Father Christmas. What did she mean?'

'I can't imagine. And you know you mustn't say those words. You're not allowed until you're grown up. And naughty Mummy shouldn't have said them in front of you. Anyway, when did she say that?'

'I heard her talking to Cordelia's mummy. She said she wanted to take the little shit on one side and ruin his Christmas by telling him the truth about Father Christmas.'

'The truth about him? What could that be, I wonder. Perhaps he doesn't like Brussels sprouts, like you!'

'No, Daddy, it's because Santa's been already. Remember? He didn't leave me presents because I wasn't good enough.'

Alex strokes Ben's forehead one more time. 'I promise you, young man, that Father Christmas will be coming to see you. All that stuff before, well that was just pretend, for the magazine pictures. You've been a very good boy, promise.'

'I hope so, Daddy. I love Father Christmas and I want him to come. Otherwise it won't *be* Christmas.'

'Well, yes, it would, actually Ben. Because we'd still have Jesus, and we mustn't forget that Father Christmas comes with presents because it's really Jesus's birthday.'

'But Jesus is dead. Miss Wood says that he can see us all the time and he hears what we say, but I've never seen him, and even when we say prayers at school he never says anything back.'

'Just because you can't see him doesn't mean he's not there. He just might be very good at hiding himself.'

'At least I've seen Father Christmas, so I'd be more sad if anything happened to him than anything. We saw him at 'fridges. I was a bit scared but he was nice. There was this elf, in a green dress and a green face. But no reindeers. Mummy said she expected they'd been parked on the roof of the NCP in Bond

Street. And he gave me present …'

'Yes, Ben, I think I remember. Which reminds me … I've got you a present. Alex reaches into his jacket pocket and pulls out the Kinder egg and puts it on Ben's bedside table. 'I was going to give this to you tomorrow at breakfast time so we could do the toy together, but you have to promise that you won't touch it 'til tomorrow. You can look forward to it, can't you, like Christmas?'

'Thanks, Daddy.'

Alex reaches out and gives Ben a big, warm hug and kisses his head. 'Night, son.'

Juliet has finished in the bathroom and is now getting herself dressed in the bedroom. He doesn't give her chance to speak before he launches into her. 'What the fuck do you think you're on, saying that stuff about Rupert Hunt and bloody Father Christmas in front of Ben? Don't you think you've fucked him up enough already with that bloody magazine fiasco?'

'Oh, hello darling, how are you? And what sort of a day have you had?'

'Yeah. Hello, darling, how are you? And what were you doing saying that stuff in front of Ben?'

'I didn't know he was listening. I thought he was watching television with Cordelia. He didn't tell me he'd heard. He was obviously saving it up for you.'

'I'm not surprised; hearing his mother using that foul language in front of him. What the fuck were you thinking about?' Juliet laughs.

'Listen to you. I'll tell you when I've got dressed. And I suggest you get showered, cos we're due out in thirty. And when you hear what the little darling did, you'll be tripping me up so that you can get to him first. Can you zip me up?' She lifts up her thick blonde hair and Alex pulls on the metal zip sealing the pink flesh inside black silk. 'Thanks. Do you think I need to talk to Ben?'

'No. I think he's settled.'

Juliet nods, then sits down at her dressing table and starts putting on her make-up, so Alex strips off his shirt and trousers, throws them on the bed, watches Juliet's frown from the mirror, and takes himself to the bathroom. It's still steamy and warm, and smells of Juliet's various feminine potions. The mirror is covered in condensation so he wipes his hand across it to reveal a small curl of reflected face. It looks tired and unhealthy. More greyish than pink. He needs to shave first so he takes the hand towel and wipes the mirror clear. He's an old-fashioned sort of shaver: block of lime soap from Trumper's, sable brush and cold steel blade. He contorts his face and goes through the ritual, flicking the foam and discarded whiskers into the basin of water. It's boring and repetitive, but it gives him time to think. It's calming – the mixture of concentration and practised, expert ritual. He grew a beard once. For a while it felt liberating not having to do the same old routine every morning and night, but then it felt hot, itchy and sweaty, and never really clean. He'd kept it for his homecoming. Juliet had been horrified, although she'd tried to hide it. He'd just wanted to see her reaction, to test whether her joy at having him home would overcome the revulsion to his beard. She'd always hated beards. Said she was allergic. That first night back they'd made love with the kind of passion that's fuelled by four months' separation, but she'd woken him in the morning with a mug of tea and her face pushed to his. 'Look … Look what that bloody beard's done to me.' She had a terrible rash. 'Look, Alex, I can't go out looking like this. You'll have to get rid of it.'

'Or I could just stop kissing you?'

'Only whores don't like being kissed.'

'You're my whore … Maid in the drawing room, chef in the kitchen …'

'And you're an idiot prick.' She'd slapped him lightly and then straddled him, lifted up the long T-shirty thing that she always pulled over herself before going down to make tea, and he was ready for her in a heartbeat. That was the way it used to be after a tour; they fucked like bunnies for the first few days, all loved up, almost tiptoeing around each other in order to be nice, and then all the tension of the separation would start to fizz out of the pent-up bottle. She would start moaning about all the problems she'd had to deal with by herself, things she said she didn't want to tell him on the phone, all the boring stuff, the little domestic dramas that seemed so important to her but so inconsequential to him: Ben's illnesses, bills, arguments over parking. Ben's teachers, his friends, her social life. And Alex would listen and try to be sympathetic, apologetic, supportive ... all the things he thought he should be, but without really feeling or meaning any of it. It didn't take much for him to start thinking things like 'And what do you think I didn't tell you on the phone? What did I do to try and stop you worrying?' Don't talk about it. Bury it. Leave it behind. There is there, and there is here. Two worlds, two men. One woman. Sometimes he would almost feel as if he'd left his body; as if he was watching this other Alex going through the motions of feeling, while the other one watched from above, detached, uninvolved. Bored, even. The only time he had felt normal was when he was out with the lads, where there was the unspoken acknowledgement that they *knew* each other, they understood who they were. They had respect for what they'd been through, understanding about the stuff they didn't talk about, because they didn't need to talk about it. They used the beer and the banter to swill it all away like shit into a sewer. But that's all gone now, and he feels very alone.

Juliet's already poured herself a glass of wine by the time Alex gets downstairs. She's put her hair up loosely, so that lots of stray bits escape; she looks sexy, messy, recently fucked. Not by him, though. Although he could have her right now. Pull that dress up, tip her over the cold granite worktop, slip her pants aside and slam right into her, get her where he wants her, begging for him, under his control if only while she's getting his cock inside her. He feels his erection growing but doesn't want to give her the satisfaction of noticing it, so he gets his remaining whisky out of the fridge and stands at the opposite side of the island, which is waist level. She sips on her glass, stares at him, but doesn't speak. So he just looks back. He thinks they're like a pair of flamenco dancers, enacting a sort of phony war, eyeing each other up, waiting for one of them to make a move, show a weakness. Who's gonna blink first? Actually, he's in no hurry to talk. The whole shower and change thing has calmed him down. He's mad at Juliet for saying what she said in Ben's hearing. But he's also slightly amused, though he might not tell her that. In the meantime only a few seconds have passed and so they're still eyeing each other up. Her hand rests on her throat, possibly defensively, as if she senses the hormonally charged threat in the air. Her neck is bare of jewellery as usual. That's Juliet's thing. Always understated, but nevertheless startling. She wears her make-up well. He doesn't think it has changed much since he first met her. She's barely changed – and he'd notice. When you're with someone every day, the glacially slow changes of the ageing process are barely discernible. But when you've been away for a few months, you notice these things more. Admittedly she sometimes looks tired, but even that seems to suit her. It makes her look a bit wasted, a bit fascinating. She uses lots of black around her eyes, a thin line across her top lids, and a further line inside her lower lids. She has ice-blue eyes. How do you describe ice-blue? Like the blue that you get in the Arctic, the blue trapped inside icebergs. A clear, translucent blue with shards of white if you looked *really* closely. Alex knows this, because he has seen icebergs. Juliet's eyes are an anathema, because they reveal nothing, but tell you a lot. They tell you that when she's looking at you it's as though she can see right into you and read your mind. But infuriatingly they reveal nothing about her. Like ice they absorb but do not reflect. Men, Alex knows, find her both interesting and a little bit intimidating.

'So do you wanna know about the little shit, or not?'

Alex nods once. 'But I don't like Ben hearing that sort of language.'

'Don't be so hypocritical. He hears you often enough. I said do you want to know, or not?'

'Sure.'

'He told Ben that his daddy had said that Ben's mummy is a bitch and that Ben's daddy has done bad things.'

Alex laughs. A hollow sort of laugh. He downs the last of the whisky. 'And why are you a bitch?'

'Because I screwed my heel into his foot when he *accidentally* stuck his hand up my skirt and ...' she stopped to laugh, ' ... and I said in a *really* loud voice "Marcus WILL YOU TAKE YOUR FUCKING HAND AWAY FROM MY FANNY" and he tried to make out that I was only joking. Freak. Anyway, Rupert pushed Ben over during the nativity play which upset the manger, and baby Jesus landed on his head causing tears and pandemonium, obviously ... And he also poured powder paint into the sandpit and blamed it on Ben. Ben said he was frightened of him. That he didn't want to be Rupert's friend. He was upset in case he did it again. So I spoke to the teacher about it.'

'And?'

'The teacher said that she thought it was, God ... six of one and half a dozen of the other. You know, all mealy-mouthed. Like she's got any idea what went on.'

'It could be ...'

'What, like Ben's called Rupert's father a bad man? And his mummy a bitch? Yeah ... reckon you could be right there.'

'Not Ben's style is it?'

'Well not unless he's changed dramatically into some completely different child in the last week. I don't think so ... Anyway, who cares if people think you're a bad man? You *are*, but I object to being called a bitch.'

'Juliet!'

'Seriously, Alex. We can't allow this bullying. And don't start telling me it's bloody well character-building, because it isn't. You of all people should know that.' The doorbell rings, announcing the arrival of the babysitter. Juliet throws on her dark mink jacket. 'The Hunts are going to be there tonight.'

'So we could have some fun, then.'

Juliet doesn't answer, but just shrugs, and lets in Louise, the sitter. She gives her the low-down on Ben, what's in the fridge, checks she's got mobile numbers, landline numbers of where they're going – actually it's only across the road – and then says sweetly to Alex: 'Come on, honey. Let's go and see the nice people at the lovely party.'

4

They walk up the road together, but apart. Juliet is huddled into her jacket with her head down, and Alex has been thinking. He is becoming angry. His son is not the kind of kid who's going to be intimidated by other people. And he is also very angry that any man could think he could help himself to what is his. 'Did he really ... Marcus ... stick his hand up your skirt?'

'Yeah. It's what men do ... pissed men. But they don't do it a second time ... not unless I ask them to. Anyway, Marcus gropes everyone, not just me. And don't forget what Caroline was like at that dinner – I thought she was going to have you for pudding. And you fucking well encouraged her. Though God knows why.'

Alex grabs her collar. Pulls her towards him and clamps his mouth onto hers.

When he releases her she says: 'God, Alex, you'll have ruined my bloody lip gloss – and it's all over *your* mouth, you twit.' Alex wipes his mouth with the back of his hand. It's sticky and smells of toffee. He grabs Juliet's hand and hangs on to it. Her stiletto heels with their metal tips clip-clip-clip on the paving stones, and then change timbre as they step onto the tarmac to cross the road, and he can hear the South Circular humming away in the background. The curtains at number 94 are open and a gaggle of people can be seen laughing and mouthing to each other, soundproofed by the double glazing.

'Look at the *size* of that fuck-off wreath,' Juliet says. 'Must have cost a fortune.'

'Ostentatious – and a waste of money. Only gets chucked away. Like bloody Christmas trees. They'll be a hundred quid soon, and they're in the house for what – two weeks?'

'You're so parsimonious. If you feel that strongly why don't we have an artificial one?'

They have the same discussion every Christmas.

'You know I'd never have an artificial tree in the house.'

They push the door open and immediately they can hear the tinny sound of a Christmas compilation providing background festive moodery. '*Do they know it's Christmas time ...*' An ear worm has been spinning the same track in his head all day; he just can't get away from the bloody thing. He sees that there is a man in a white jacket standing by a white table-clothed trestle table, pouring steaming red liquid into glasses, and his heart sinks even further. It was meant to be drunk when you were outside, frozen and numb-cheeked in some ski resort or other, when your taste buds were so bloody frozen that anything would taste good. Not for some chichi little drinks party in park-side East Sheen, with a thermostat that's probably set at around 25 degrees Celsius. There's a grainy film of something floating on the surface that hasn't quite dissolved, and the smell of cloves which reminds Alex of fillings and drills. What he could really use is a Scotch.

'Your favourite,' Juliet grins at him, and Alex thinks it might be the first time this evening he's seen a proper smile. Probably because she's amused by his misery.

'And yours.'

'I don't hate it as much as you. It's seasonal, festive – mulled wine, mince pies and sausage rolls'. She lowers her voice: 'Perhaps they'll have Twiglets and cheese balls ... oh and nibbles like cheese and pineapple and prawn vol-au-vents.' Alex is almost in awe of how many hated words Juliet can cram into one sentence.

He follows Juliet towards the room where all the guests are gathered. A wall of noise hits them as they step through the doorway. It's a familiar noise, a sort of phwar phwar phwarrring ... interspersed with a few hohohos and hahahahahas, and a few eeeehuws and high pitched REALLYS and OH NOS and ABSOLUTELYS. It's the tribal gathering sound of the professional southern middle-classes, where you'd struggle to find a regional accent, any residue of which would have been scrubbed from your tongue like a nasty dose of thrush, so that you could all be part of the same team. Being here meant you'd arrived. You'd made it. This was *it*. All one big club. There is something scarily similar about all the women – and the men, come to that. Perhaps it's because they frequent the same hairdresser – he or she of the moment, or they shop for their clothes in packs and cheer each other on to buy the same sorts of styles. Their nail varnish is even the same colour, the big chunky gold jewellery with a preference for turquoise, or thick swags of pearls. They have chains and hearts and keys from Tiffany's and jangly bracelets on slim, tanned wrists that were probably found in markets in Marrakesh or some other exotic location. Alex notices these things. Sometimes he just wishes his mind would flash up a computer-style warning saying: STOP – OUT OF MEMORY. The women are, mostly, pretty hot-looking. They put a lot of money and effort into keeping time at bay. Looking around the room there is a lot of black. A lot of that blonde-y, browny, streaky sort of hair, and teeth that have been whitened and straightened. There's no room for imperfection any more, which results in a universal blandness. They've all got great tits; tits are the new black. He knows this because Juliet got herself a brand new pair and started a trend. He hadn't been happy about it, but she'd insisted and now ... well ... actually he wasn't unhappy about them any more. Like his beard, she'd done it as a surprise for his homecoming. More interesting to play with than a tattoo. And it was true, they did stay upright when she was flat on her back, unlike the previous fried eggs he'd got so used to. There is something niggling him though, and he isn't sure yet what it is. That feeling of detachment is hovering around him. He is not a part of this – doesn't want to be, never expected to be – and feels a growing sense of suffocation as he glances around the room at the familiar faces of their 'friends'. These friends who know nothing about him, nothing about Juliet. It seems so fucking petty and pointless, but they've all got to play the game.

Juliet has melted into the fray and Alex knows what is expected of him. He must wear his social face; his approachable 'aren't I glad to be here' face.

'What are you smiling at?' Caroline Hunt is standing in front of him. A few too many whiskies and you had to watch your tongue around that one. Alex isn't smiling, his mouth just seems to lift and stretch at the corners when he's scowling. People often assume he's thinking the opposite of what he's thinking. It comes in useful. 'Oh, nothing. Just made myself laugh, that's all. Bad joke.' The lie trips off his tongue.

'Want to share?'

'It wouldn't be funny. The moment's passed. Nice dress.'

'Thanks. Good of you to notice. Marcus hasn't. Still, maybe that's a blessing. Saves having to go through one of those boring Is it new ... How much ... kind of conversations.'

'I bet he notices. He's just not saying. Keeping you on your toes.'

'Marcus? Come off it. He wouldn't have the imagination.'

'Then he's a very silly man. Should appreciate more what he's got.'

At this point Alex would expect a woman's eyebrows to lift, but Caroline's don't. She's got that tell-tale polished, stretched, cling-filmed kind of look that says Botox and fillers. Alex has forbidden Juliet to ever consider it. How could their husbands ever know what their wives were thinking – plotting, even – if they couldn't see their faces move, the truth within rather than the lies outside.

'My, aren't you the charmer?' She giggles in an unsubtle, coquettish way.

'Just stating the facts. Your glass – it's empty. Would you like me to get you …'

Caroline brings her head closer to Alex. 'Between you and me, I'd much prefer a glass of wine, red or white … This stuff just reminds me of mouthwash, lukewarm mouthwash.'

This time Alex's smile is genuine. 'Not only do you look good, but you're also a lady of taste.'

'Mr Miller, you want to be careful with that smooth tongue of yours, might just get you into a slippery situation.'

'Not sure that's entirely complimentary. Slippery … Let's see, pinstripes too wide, wrong aftershave, brown shoes in London? Or maybe you were thinking of something more intimate?'

Caroline looks confused. Alex sees her pupils dilate just a fraction, but enough to tell him all he needs to know. She laughs because, Alex believes, she's embarrassed at what he thinks – he knows – she's been thinking. 'You're mad. Do you think we could do a raid on the bar, surreptitiously?' She's trying to sound normal, to cover the fact that he's really got to her.

'Yep. After you.' Caroline brushes past him and her hips scrape against his, and she gives him a sideways glance. Alex rests his hand lightly in the small of her back, uses his finger to put the slightest pressure on the sensitive mid-point of her sacro-iliac. They are back in the hallway, standing side by side in front of the bar table. 'Hi, you're doing a great job there, and that mulled wine was really good.' The barman nods his thanks. 'But any chance of a glass of wine for the lady?'

He's got an Italian accent, probably brought in from the wine bar down the Upper Richmond Road. 'Red or white?' Alex turns to Caroline.

'White, thanks.'

'And red for me.' Alex says.

Once they've got their glasses Caroline starts heading back to the main body of the party. But Alex catches her elbow, gently but firmly. 'Hey,' he says.

She turns back to him. Once again, this would be the eyebrow-lift moment. It's a bit uncanny, this frozen facial expression thing. It makes Alex uncomfortable because it challenges his reading skills. 'Just a second. There's something I want to show you.' Alex knows there's a little study just before the kitchen. He opens the door and grins at Caroline. 'In here.'

She should be frowning. But she can't. Still, she takes the bait and walks into the dark room in front of him. Alex closes the door, takes the glass from her hand, sets both his own glass and hers down onto a desk. Then he pushes her up against the wall. He can feel the pace of her breathing quickening, her head going back, exposing her neck. He places one hand on her shoulder and stares into her eyes. There's enough light coming from the glazed panel over the door just to be able to see a flicker of something there. No resistance, just an open invitation. He starts tracing a delicate line with his fingertip from her neck down to her cleavage. He clutches and kneads her right breast. Her eyes widen and her lips part. He thinks she's expecting him to kiss her. Instead he speaks softly. 'So what was it you said? I'm mad … and I'm also bad … and so I must be dangerous.'

'That's quite a seductive combination,' she says.

Then he lets his hand drop down to her hip. He leaves it there long enough for her to feel the heat of it, and to imagine what's going to happen next. Then he starts gathering up her dress. She's got stockings on, hold-ups. Juliet would never wear hold-ups. He slips his fingers inside her flimsy silky knickers and then strokes her cunt with one finger. Mrs Hunt's cunt. She really is slippery. Wet and slippery. He stops abruptly, removes his hand. Then he says, 'Take them off'. She wriggles her knickers down over her hips, over her legs, and then steps out of them. He holds out his hand. 'Give them to me'. She hands them to him. Then he says, 'Pull your dress down.'

'I don't … I don't understand.' She shakes her head, but he just stares at her blankly. Then he lifts his mouth so that it gives the impression of a smile.

'This isn't the time ... or the place ... I just wanted to check you out, to see if you were willing.'

'And now you've got your answer? What do you intend to do about it?'

'I don't know. I haven't decided.' Poor Caroline. If only she hadn't Botoxed. She could be expressing all sorts of emotions right now. She straightens her dress.

'My knickers?'

'I'm keeping them.'

'I don't understand. Alex ... what the hell?' He doesn't answer, just picks up their glasses. Hands her the white, and keeps hold of the red. Her hand is trembling. Alex's commands are rarely countermanded.

He takes hold of her other hand and leads her back to the party. He searches the room, finds the face he's looking for, and keeps a firm hold on Caroline's hand as he heads for him.

Marcus Hunt turns to him. 'Alex, hi? How are you mate?' Even though she has the face of a plastic doll Alex can almost scent the fear in Caroline.

'I was looking for Juliet but found Caroline instead. You've got a hot little wife, Marcus ... really quite the bad girl ...'

'Oh, stop it, Alex. Don't listen to him, Marcus. He's only trying to wind you up. We've been discussing school, actually. Haven't we Alex? Hardly naughty ...'

'Was it school? I'd forgotten that. Yes I suppose it was about school, partly.'

'There you are, too dull to remember ...' Caroline giggles and takes a long sip of her white wine. Alex notes that her hands are still shaking. 'There's Juliet, over there, Alex. Didn't you say you were looking for her?'

Alex ignores her and puts his mouth close to Marcus's ear. At the same time he removes Caroline's scrunched up knickers from his pocket and gets hold of Marcus's hand and plants them into it. 'Just remember that if you ever try getting anywhere near my wife's knickers again, you'll have to deal with me, and I'm an old-fashioned sort of guy. Eye for an eye ...'

'I don't know what the hell you're talking about.' Marcus looks at the lacy black triangles of silk in his hand. Then he looks at his wife. His face is a picture of confusion. 'Caroline?'

'For God's sake, Marcus, he's just having a sick game with you. With both of us ...' she narrows her eyes at Alex and mouths '*Fuck you.*' Alex finds her comment vaguely amusing in the circumstances. He raises his glass to her, winks and says 'Thank you.' Then lowering his voice so that they both have to draw closer to hear him, he says: 'If I hear from my child again that his mother has been called a bitch, and that his daddy has done bad things, then you will be one more bad thing on the list. Understand?'

Marcus is beginning to get the message. He is beginning to look afraid. Which is good. Alex is back in his comfort zone. Marcus seems to have lost the power of speech. But he manages to nod. 'Sounds like you owe Ben and his classmates a new sandpit. And don't worry, I don't expect Rupert to apologize to Ben. It's not his fault he's got such shit parents.'

Alex leaves them to begin a marital 'discussion' which could run and run. He has no feelings of guilt because it is obviously a marriage already in its death throes. He just might have pushed it a few steps closer to its end. Besides, they were a dangerous pair, trying to assuage their own misery by playing with other people's partners. They'd be no loss to the local married circuit. He's actually done quite a service to everyone. Before returning to Juliet he nips into the downstairs loo to wash his hands. Back at the party just a few moments later he sees no sign of the Hunts, strangely enough.

Alex reckons they've been at the party now for about forty-five minutes. He checks his watch and is bang on. He can see Juliet at the far end of the knocked-through drawing room. She senses his eyes upon her and stares across the gap. She slow-blinks an acknowledgement without smiling and then turns back to Jonathan Roberts, their host. She's obviously said something funny, because Jonathan is laughing. There's a tiny nugget of jealousy but Alex squashes it almost before it has a name.

* * *

The front door closes behind them, cutting off the noise of the party and the cold December night makes Juliet shiver. Alex puts his arm around her shoulder and pulls her in close. The rhythm of her heels changes as she sidesteps into him. They're both a little tipsy.

Alex puts his key in the lock and lets Juliet go in front of him. He pictures what is ahead of them. Juliet heading straight upstairs while he pays off the babysitter. A brief chat with her about how everything was, to which she'll answer, fine. Really good, not a problem at all. She'll be struggling under a pile of school books which she will have been studying diligently. He will watch Louise cross the road and walk the few yards down to her own home, and then she will turn and wave to say she's got there safely. She's a good kid, and has been babysitting for most of the couples in the street since she was fifteen.

Juliet doesn't come downstairs until Louise is just about to leave. She is standing in the hallway with her school bag slung around her shoulders, clutching her mobile. She's turning into a very pretty girl, Alex notices. She's losing the puppy fat and her hair is blonde and thick, falling below her shoulders. She does that thing that girls do, pushing it back with her hand and then flicking her head to swish it.

'His temperature's up,' Juliet says, unable to hide a note of something accusatory in her voice. 'Did you check on him at all, Louise?'

'Yes. Definitely, I always do. It was about nine – an hour ago, I guess. And he was sleeping soundly. He seemed fine.'

'God!' Juliet snaps and marches back up the stairs.

Alex shuts the front door behind them. 'Sorry about that. She didn't mean to snap at you, it's just that she worries about Ben.'

'I'm so sorry. Honestly, I thought he was OK. He looked so settled.'

'He'll be fine. Thanks for tonight, and have a good Christmas.'

'Thanks, and you. Night, Mr Miller.'

'Night, Louise.'

Alex goes up the stairs two at a time. He enters Ben's room and Juliet gestures him to stay quiet. She places the back of her hand on Ben's brow and he stirs, but doesn't wake.

'He feels hot,' she says. 'I ought to give him some Calpol.'

'Be a shame to wake him up,' Alex walks over to his wife and stands beside her. 'He's sleeping peacefully.' He places his arms around her waist and gently nuzzles the back of her neck. She shivers as his breath hits the sensitive skin.

'Don't,' she murmurs, and she strokes the back of her neck as though she is brushing the feel of him away. Alex wants to make love to her. He wants to fuck all the mess out of his head.

'Come downstairs. Let's have a drink together. We can check him again in half an hour or so. I'm sure he's fine, probably just over-excited about Santa coming to see him.'

Juliet looks from Alex back to Ben. She's obviously reluctant to leave him. 'I don't know …'

'Come on.' Alex takes her arm and pulls her towards him. Juliet looks at her watch.

'All right, but I'll check him in half an hour, OK?'

She follows Alex downstairs and into the kitchen. He gets a couple of glasses from the cupboard and then takes a chilled bottle of white wine from the fridge. He pours a glass for Juliet and then disappears to get himself a whisky from the drinks tray in the dining room. When he returns to the kitchen Juliet is leaning against the sink, staring out into the semi-darkness of the garden. He walks over to her and kisses her bare shoulder. She shudders. 'Alex!'

'What? You looked beautiful tonight. Looked like you were having fun – not that I saw very much of you.'

'Nor I you. But I saw you speaking to the Hunts. Alex, Caroline came over to me and she said something really weird. I honestly think there's something wrong with that woman. She didn't say hello or anything, she just said, "Your husband is dangerous and you should keep him under control," and then she walked off. I mean, how bloody rude was that? So I followed her and I *accidentally* spilled my mulled wine down her back. I know it was childish, but after all that stuff with Ben I just lost it. But then afterwards I wondered if maybe you'd said something?'

'Christ, let's not talk about them now. They're not worth thinking about. Let's go and sit down.' He leads her by the hand into the sitting room. The curtains are drawn, the lamps are on and it feels good to be home, just the two of them, away from the braying crowd of people. All Alex wants to do right now is relax with his wife. Juliet puts her glass down on the coffee table and starts to plump the sofa cushions where Louise has squashed them out of shape. 'Leave them. Come on, sit next to me.'

'It looks messy.'

'Juliet, for God's sake, just sit down and relax.' He can hear the frustration in his voice and he senses Juliet tensing up. She sits beside him and he places his arm around her. He strokes the nape of her neck and then starts to gently massage her shoulder. Her skin is silky soft and yielding beneath his fingers. She leans into him and then tucks her legs beneath her. 'That's better,' he says. He kisses the top of her head. 'It feels good to be home with you, babe.'

'Does it? I'm glad. When you think back, all those Christmases when you were away. I used to dream of this ... one day ... and here we are. It's a shame you missed the nativity. I can't tell you how sweet it was. I nearly cried. But when baby Jesus fell out of his crib, it was terribly funny. I'll show you the photos tomorrow once I've uploaded them.'

'Well I don't think we'll have to worry about the Hunts anymore.'

'So you did say something? Alex, you'd better tell me, especially after what she said to me. Why did she say that?'

'You really want to know?'

'Yes, I do.'

'I took Caroline into a dark room. I pretended I wanted her, and Christ she was an easy target. I got her to take her knickers off – and then I handed them to Marcus. It's an Old Testament thing, an eye for an eye. That's what you get for sticking your hand up *my* wife's skirt. That'll make him think twice in the future. That's some kind of shit marriage they have.'

'Hang on,' Juliet says sharply, 'you did what? You took her into a darkened room? You seduced her into taking her knickers off? You are having me on. You *touched* her?'

'I just pinned her up against a wall – I *certainly* wasn't going to kiss the woman. Oh no, my darling, this was sweet revenge. And then I started lifting her skirt and I simply asked her to get 'em off. And she did.'

'Just like that? I don't believe you ... and even if I did it's just so bloody unthinkable that you'd do something like that. I mean, can't you see how that makes *me* feel? And what about Caroline? What's she going to tell everyone? And Marcus? Is that going to help us settle in here? God, Alex, I just don't understand you.' She's pulled away from him and she's just staring at him with a look of loathing on her face. 'I can't do this anymore, Alex. I try. God knows I try. But when you go and do something like that! Just tell me you didn't. Tell me this is all some kind of cruel joke. You didn't, did you?'

'Juliet, I don't know what you're making such a fuss about. I sorted it, all right?'

'No you didn't, Alex. You didn't sort anything. You fucked it.' She stands up and marches out of the room. Alex hears her going upstairs. No doubt she's going to see her precious Ben.

He gets himself another whisky and as he pours it his hand starts to tremble. Bitch! What's the point? Can't she understand what he's trying to do, to protect her from arseholes like Marcus Hunt? Christ, she complains about the fact that *he's* the one who's changed, but look at her and her insistence on acting like a bloody ice queen. No wonder he's on edge. She's the one who keeps telling him he needs help, but with a wife like her it's no bloody wonder. Why can't she be more supportive and sympathetic towards him; why can't she try and *really* understand him? Call herself a wife? He empties his glass and pours himself another. The trembling has subsided; focussing on Juliet and her behaviour is making him angry, and anger is good. Why can't she just let him love her for once instead of throwing it back in his face? Why else would he have taken it upon himself to sort out the business with the Hunts? Because he loves her, that's why. All he wants is just to be able to feel normal again, to try and get back to the person he was ... before. And you'd think that she'd understand that, that she'd be able to see how hard he's trying to be a good husband and father. If she could only let him sort everything out in his own way then maybe they could move forward, or go backwards to rediscover the people they used to be. He drains his glass. He'll have just one more.

An hour or so later, alone in their bedroom, he undoes the top button of his shirt and removes the bone collar stiffeners, then unhooks the cufflinks. He places them neatly in a small leather gentleman's stud box, which has his initials tooled onto the lid. Beside this he has a set of ivory-backed brushes, also engraved with his initials. He lines up the brushes so that they are an exact distance apart. Then he trains his ears and listens to the thick silence coming from Ben's room on the floor below. He throws his shirt into the dirty laundry, lines up the folds in his trousers and drapes them over the chair arm. Then he uses the bathroom quickly, cutting short the two minutes on the electric toothbrush. Basically he just can't be arsed. Instead of rinsing the evidence of spit from the basin, he leaves it there, and leaves the seat up on the lavatory. The little things that annoy Juliet. His anger is rising. He wants his wife. He deserves his wife. He could have had Caroline Hunt with a click of his fingers. But his wife ... She should be *grateful* that he hadn't taken advantage of the situation. She should appreciate him. He gets between the sheets and lies on his back, thinking, or rather trying to control his thoughts. There are tricks he's learned which help. Focus on the minutiae, remember ... think back to this morning. Getting up, going to the bathroom, the journey to the office. The day's business. What did you have for lunch, Alex? Focus ... What calls did you make? What meetings did you plan? Christmas – think about your mother's arrival. The tree you've promised to Ben tomorrow. The visit to the country's most expensive garden centre, the ritual of getting the box of decorations from the big oak coffer. The moment you discover whether the lights will light or not. Juliet saying: I told you we should have bought a new set. Focus. Focus on all these things and then you won't think. He turns onto his side and strains his ears for any sound of movement downstairs. Harder – he concentrates so hard that it seems the cavity in his ears is growing bigger, hollow caves sucking in every microscopic wave of sound, and he thinks he can hear tapping, almost rhythmical, like the sounds of rodent feet scurrying across floorboards. Then it stops. There's silence again. He thinks about Juliet, he thinks about Caroline's stockings. Marcus Hunt's frightened face. He thinks about Ben. And Ben's fear. And then he stops himself ... the tapping starts up again … the rodent dance. But it's not rodents, its fingers on a keyboard. Alex gets out of bed, pulls on his silk robe and goes down the stairs as quietly as he can, stealthily, just like a cat would stalk a mouse. There's a faint glow of light coming from Ben's door, which isn't quite closed. He pushes it open and sees Juliet look up. Her face is lit by the reflection from the laptop screen.

'Come to bed,' he tells her.

'No. I'm watching Ben. I'm going to stay here tonight.' She keeps her eyes fixed on her screen.

Alex feels his temper rising. This is not good. Things can get ugly. Instead of raising his voice, he lowers it. 'I said *come to bed*.' He walks over to her, takes the laptop from her hands and snaps the lid shut. Then he takes her hand, pulls her out of the chair and says, 'Good girl. Come on. Don't worry, Ben will be fine.'

Back in their bedroom, he says, 'Shall I unzip you?' She doesn't reply.

He slides the zip down to where it ends just above the cleavage between her buttocks. He pushes the shoulders of the dress down to her elbows so that the dress slips towards the floor. She steps out of it. She's wearing tights.

'What are these?' He asks.

'They're tights.'

'I hate tights.'

'I know that.'

'But you still wore them.'

'Yes, I still wore them. I'm not your fucking doll, Alex.'

'You are my doll, my little girl doll that I can do with whatever I please.'

'I am *not*!' She hisses.

'Take them off!'

She looks at him defiantly, and then with a sigh of defeat she pulls the tights down and steps out of them. Alex grabs her hand

and pulls her over to the bed, then pushes her onto her back. The bedside lights are still switched on so he can see her face quite clearly. That light in those iceberg eyes – it's fear, he knows that. But it's also arousal. He knows that she loves the edge, the riskiness, the never knowing what to expect. That's why she'll never get bored of him. She's still got her bra and pants on. 'I like seeing those new babies of yours shown off, like they're framed, presented for me,' he says, as his hands explore her, pushing her knickers down her legs and pulling them free. She closes her eyes. He kisses her lips lightly, then her cheek, then his mouth is next to her ear: 'I love you, Juliet Miller. Never forget that.'

Juliet opens her eyes and he smiles down at her, and then as he enters her he can feel her body start to tremble. He knows she wants him; she needs him. They *need* each other. And for a while, just a short while, while he fucks her as hard as he is capable, his mind escapes to a better world altogether. Afterwards he pulls her into him and wraps his arms around her. He nestles his head close to hers and then he whispers into her ear: 'You are mine, *all* mine, and I couldn't live without you.' Juliet doesn't respond, so after a few moments Alex says, 'You hear me?'

'Yes, Alex, I hear you,' Juliet sighs.

CHAPTER
5

Juliet is up and in the shower before Alex or Ben have stirred. Sometimes she loathes Alex so much she has to stop herself from getting a blunt instrument and smashing him over the head. She feels dizzy with it and has to breathe slowly to get herself under control. All the time Alex had been fucking her last night, all she could see was Caroline Hunt's face smirking at her. Fucking. That's what they do, she and Alex. Or rather that's what he does to her. She doesn't think he's really *with* her any more. She's not even sure if he remembers who she is – or even whether he's aware that she's actually there – when he's driving himself into her. One time she imagined that she was the enemy, and his prick was a bayonet, stabbing away at her insides, until finally when he came, it was as though *his* life was ending. His eyes, even when open, are unseeing, as if there's a film over them blocking his focus. He doesn't seem to notice that she is withdrawing deeper and deeper inside herself; that she is searching for somewhere to hide away – somewhere safe in her head, if not her body. He doesn't seem to realize that she no longer responds to him; that her limbs are flaccid and lifeless beneath him. He doesn't seem to realize that he could be fucking a dead body, for all the response he gets. She scratches the shampoo into her scalp, feeling the rake of her sharp nails. If she could just scrub the dirty feelings away. She rinses the soap out of her hair, and then takes the shower head from the clip and runs it all over her skin, imagining the hot jets washing away the contamination of her husband's body. Is it time to admit he's beyond help? That they are both beyond help? This house, everything she's been trying to salvage for the sake of Ben, for herself, for the salvation of Alex, is running away and she's unable to stop it, like the water pouring through her fingers. He's like one of those retired Army guard dogs that's too fierce to be turned into a pet and so the only thing for it is to put it down.

It seems that too much time has passed for talking – to her, that is. One night she heard him screaming, begging almost: 'I don't want to die ... please God ... don't let me die.' She thought her heart had fractured. All she wanted to do was to gather him into her arms, but she didn't dare risk it in case he attacked her. Sleeping beside Alex is a bit like sleeping in a minefield. If she kicks him or nudges him he is more than likely to explode into a full-on assault. How can you watch the man you love disintegrate like this? A man who's fought and survived the bloodiest of battles, a man with medals to show how damned good he is, but who's afraid to show his emotions just in case he might be considered weak. Weak. Now there's a word. A word that doesn't exist if you're a trained warrior. She has said to him so many times, 'Alex, it's OK not to be strong all the time, it's OK to be weak', and all she's got in return is his blank, unseeing stare of dismissal, as if she barely exists. Christ, what she's had to put up with. And now this.

Is she supposed to feel OK about Caroline Hunt? How many women would *really* feel OK with their husband removing another woman's knickers? And what will Caroline Hunt do about Alex? What would Juliet do if she were Caroline? Juliet – if she were Caroline – would spread the word that Alex had molested her. She'd have to do that in order to take the heat off herself, so that it didn't look like she'd encouraged Alex. But she had. Without question she'd given Alex every come-on signal in the book. But maybe Caroline would say that she feared Alex would be violent. That she had to take her knickers off in order to get away. Her knickers or her life. Yep, that's the way Juliet would spin it if she were Caroline. Question was, was Caroline manipulative enough, or clever enough to twist it in such a way that Juliet and Alex would be ostracised from the group's inner circle before they'd even set foot over the perimeter.

What a fuckwit he was, as usual. And those were just the sexual politics, aside from the pain of betrayal, the cheapness and the downright seediness of her husband's actions. She wonders how it is humanly possible to feel love for someone, to care about their suffering and their demons, to watch their disintegration with despair, and yet at the same time be able to feel so much hatred ... and fear. It can't be love that she feels for him. It has to be some kind of unhealthy emotional dependence. Traumatic bonding, maybe? She's read about that, obviously.

She finds Ben standing on a stool in front of the cereal cupboard. 'Ben, what on earth ... ? You'll fall.'

Ben turns and the stool wobbles. Juliet flies across the room and sweeps him safely onto the floor. 'Ben! For God's sake. How many times have I told you not to do that? You've got to wait until Mummy comes downstairs.'

'I was hungry.'

'Even so, you'll fall and hurt yourself. You know what day it is today?'

'Christmas Eve. Father Christmas Eve. He will come, won't he Mummy?'

As Juliet nuzzles her nose into Ben's hair, murmuring, 'Yes, of course, darling', she smells something acrid. 'Oh, Ben.'

'What?'

'You know what. You've wet the bloody bed again.'

'Don't swear, Mummy. It's rude to swear. Daddy says –'

'Ben, I don't care what Daddy says. It's what I say that counts. Now come on, let's get you upstairs and out of these pyjamas. I'll have to strip the bed. Honestly, Ben. You're five years old. You're not a baby any more.'

'Sorry, Mummy,' Ben mutters quietly. Juliet knows she

shouldn't be cross, that her son can't help it. But it's such a pain. She seems to spend much of her life stripping and changing beds these days.

'You need a bath. Go and take your pyjamas off and get into your dressing gown while I run it.'

Juliet goes into Ben's bathroom and turns on the taps. The cistern next to their bedroom on the floor above will be noisy and will probably wake Alex. He'll be angry. Not with Ben, but with her. She can write the script for the row. She'll say: 'I had to wash him, I couldn't leave him like that.' And he'll say: 'You could have waited until I got up.' And she'll say: 'But his skin will feel sore and sticky and he smells.' And Alex will say: 'You're so bloody prissy. He's a boy. Let him man up a bit.' And she'll say: 'Just because you're used to spending weeks up to your neck in your own waste down some bloody hole doesn't mean you have to put your five-year-old in training.' And finally Alex will say: 'For Christ's sake, couldn't you for once just do as you're bloody asked.'

She goes into the nursery and finds Ben shivering, only half into his dressing gown. 'Here, put your arm in the sleeve.' Then she ties the belt around his waist. He stands watching as Juliet deftly pulls the bottom sheet off the bed, revealing the plastic mattress protector which is stained yellow. Then she rips open the poppers on the bottom of his Spiderman duvet cover and drags the duvet out. She feels the duvet for dampness, and then she sniffs it. 'Eeeugh, Ben. It stinks of wee.'

Ben looks down at the floor. 'Sorry,' he mutters once more.

'It doesn't matter.' Juliet threads the duvet over the top of the radiator. She won't have time to wash and dry it today, of all days. It will just have to stay stinking. 'Come on, let's get you in the bath.'

She pours bubble bath under the hot tap and swirls the water to make it foam. Then she adjusts the temperature by adding more cold water. 'OK, ready now.' Ben's fingers pull at the knot in the dressing gown tie. 'Here,' she says impatiently. As she pulls at the knot, Ben almost loses his balance and his head rocks backwards and forwards as if a supporting screw in his neck has come loose. 'Stand up properly,' she orders.

'Sorry,' Ben says again.

'Ben, for God's sake stop saying sorry. It's all right, babe.' She gives him a hug and then slips the dressing gown off his body. His legs are getting long, he's getting thinner, stretching like elastic, although he still has a little childish pot belly. She holds his hand as he climbs into the bath, and then he plops down into the water, staring at his hands which are clasped together in his lap. 'Ben, it's OK. It doesn't matter.' She puts her hand under his chin and lifts it. His eyes are wet and there's snot escaping from his nose. 'Don't cry, darling, it's all right.' Deep down she suspects that the bedwetting is really their fault. Ben's neither deaf nor blind and she knows he's seen and heard things. She is so desperate not to fuck him up, but how can she protect him, with Alex the way he is?

'Father Christmas won't come and see me now cos I haven't been good. Do you think he'll know, about the bed ... like Jesus. He can see everything?'

'Oh Ben ...' Juliet suddenly feels that she's in danger of crying too. Her throat constricts so much that she feels if she takes a breath it will just erupt into a loud sob. And she doesn't want to cry in front of Ben. She tucks her head down and tells herself to get a grip. She can't give in to weakness.

'Of course he's going to come. You've been a very good boy, darling. I promise you. Now let's get you washed, because we're going to get the tree later and we've got to get all the decorations out. Shall we put chocolate on the tree, like last year? Do you remember?'

'One, two, three, four chocolates a day, Mummy.' Ben holds his fingers out as he counts. 'I like the red balls best, can we have lots of red balls and all the presents underneath?' Amazing how quickly he can change his mood.

'We're having gold this year darling, and you can help put them on.'

'We can decorate it when Granny comes this afternoon.'

'Granny smells funny.'

'Don't be silly, of course she doesn't.'

'She does. Like Daddy does when he's drinking whiskery. Eeeugh. Granny smells like that.'

'Granny doesn't drink whisky. Probably just something's she's eaten, darling.'

Juliet wonders if she's been a little unsubtle in the choice of goodies she's procured for Geraldine's stocking. The off-licence had been a great help – miniatures of vodka, four cans of ready-made gin and tonic, a pretty little bottle of sloe gin which Juliet couldn't pretend she'd made herself, but she had bought it at the Country Living market, which was the next best thing. She shouldn't really be encouraging her, facilitating her, but what the hell … it's Christmas. Geraldine drinks because it takes the sharp edges off her life. It helps her pretend that it's a lot better than it is, and was. She's what Juliet supposes is a functioning alcoholic. She doesn't ever appear to be blind, falling-over drunk. Alcohol is just the drug that her body has become dependent upon, and in order to function she just needs to keep her levels topped up. So actually Juliet is helping her. Perhaps she will give Geraldine her stocking in private, And then after she's opened it they will just exchange a quiet wink about it.

'Oh *Christmas*!' Juliet says aloud as she helps Ben out of the bath. The same – year in, year out. Pissed mother, desperate wife and fucked-up husband. And now, very possibly, *another* psychologically damaged son to carry on the family tradition.

With Ben breakfasted and finally settled in front of CBeebies, Juliet opens up her laptop and logs in to one of her chat rooms. There's a private message for her from FightbackGirl asking how she is. She's one of Juliet's regulars and so she types quickly, telling her about last night – well, some of it – and within seconds of her pressing send she sees that FightbackGirl is online and is typing her response. A question Juliet's not really got time to answer properly but she feels deserves a response, however brief.

> What was it like at the beginning? Passionate – once I got over my initial aversion to him. He was SO not my normal type. My mother loved him and that was just the kiss of death for me. He was perfect for her. Just SO bloody perfect it made me NOT want to go out with him.

Juliet pauses and takes a sip of her coffee. FightbackGirl is typing again. Juliet responds:

> We've got history, my mother and I. Not exactly what you'd call close. Sorry. I've got to go. A million things to do. I'll be online later if I get chance. I love 'chatting' to you. Keeps me sane. Ta for listening. Hope you're OK and you have a peaceful and happy day. Hugs X

She sits down with a blank piece of paper and pen, ready to start yet another of her endless lists, but instead of writing she finds herself daydreaming, thinking back to that first time and wondering how they got to this. Maybe if she hadn't gone to that wedding ... but then if she hadn't met Alex she wouldn't have had Ben. And she could never regret that, no matter how many regrets she has about everything else. He was standing in the doorway, directing people to their pews; the usual thing, groom on the right, bride on the left. Juliet had come by herself. Anna, the bride, was her cousin and so no 'plus one' had been issued to Juliet. The family would have been far too scared of who she might bring. He was dressed in a fancy uniform with lots of gold bling and red toothpaste stripes down the outside of his trouser legs. Anna was marrying an Army guy. Juliet had met him once or twice and he'd done nothing to make her reconsider her prejudice. This one looked typically self-satisfied, smug and over-confident. Just the type that Juliet loathed. He gave her one of those looks that lasted a bit too long, like he was studying a menu. 'Bride,' she said.

'Alex', he said, and put out his hand. 'Your hand is cold,' he said, giving it a second squeeze. She snatched it away from him.

'*Freezing* cold heart too.'

'Don't believe that. Bet I could warm it.'

'Christ!' she said. 'That's so bloody corny.'

'You started it,' he said.

'No, I didn't, you did.'

'And you just blasphemed in church.' He was grinning at her and she wanted to tell him to fuck off, but even Juliet had to draw the line somewhere.

'Guess I'll probably be struck down then. Ah well, perhaps we could hold the funeral at the same time, seeing as everyone's gathered here. Save money on the wake.'

'Be a shame though.'

'What, champagne at my wake? Be just how I'd want it.'

'I mean, as we've only just met.'

'Look, I don't know how to say this politely, but you're SO not my type, I wouldn't waste your time. Can't you hit on a nice bridesmaid instead?'

She gave him a tight-lipped impression of a smile and headed off to take her seat.

The reception was a sit-down affair: lots of round tables, and hand-written place cards with their names. When it came to take her place for dinner – surprise surprise – *he* was sitting next to her.

'You moved the cards,' she said. 'And I was probably going to get someone really nice.'

'Actually you were due to get a seventy-year-old.'

'I'm not ageist. There's some pretty hot seventy-year-olds

around. Anyway, I don't believe you. I expect it was someone Anna picked out as being just my type. That's the way it goes at weddings, isn't it? Your mates fix you up with suitable partners and then hey-ho in a year's time we can all get together for a rematch in someone else's marquee?'

'So you're looking for a husband?'

'A husband!' Juliet nearly choked on her champagne. 'Me? You must be bloody joking. That's the last thing I need.'

'So you're not disappointed, then, that I'm sitting here?'

'As long as you're not looking for a wife.' She barely managed to stifle a yawn, and picked up the menu card on the table and glanced at it quickly. Familiar fare: duck pâté with apricot blah blah ... rack of lamb ... and lemon tart or yukky pavlova. Food did nothing for Juliet. She fiddled with the card, keeping her eyes down, hoping that this guy would get the message.

'So what do you do?' he said.

'Don't you know it's terribly *de trop* to ask someone what they do?'

'It's pretty obvious what I do, so it's only fair that you tell me what you do, isn't it?'

'No. Anyway I've no idea what you do, apart from ponce around in a fancy uniform, and kill people occasionally.'

'Maybe you're a little rich girl, and Daddy keeps you and you don't do anything, and that's why you're so shy of the question.'

'Fuck off.'

'Ooo ... dear me, perhaps I've hit on a nerve. Well whatever Mummy and Daddy do, they certainly taught you a colourful way of conversing.'

'A colourful way of conversing ...' she mocked. 'Are you for real? I didn't know there were people who spoke like that. I bet I can guess where you went to school.'

'OK.'

'Eton or Harrow or possibly Winchester. And you've joined

Daddy's old regiment, and you probably didn't do university because you're a bit thick between the ears, and so the Army was the obvious place for you. And then after a few years shooting and shouting at people, you'll come out and get a cosy job in the city – possibly in Daddy's old stockbroking firm.'

'Very perceptive, aren't you?'

'So people say.'

'OK. My turn now. I bet you didn't want to go to normal school. You were far too special, far too arty-farty and ...' he made little quote marks in the air ' ... individual to go anywhere ordinary. Bedales would be the place. I'd put money on the fact that's where you went. And while you were there you got yourself into a nice little drugs culture, and picked up an eating disorder, too, by the look of your skinny little frame.'

'You're bloody rude!'

'Ah. So I guessed right, then.'

'You've been talking to my mother or some other helpful relative, haven't you? Been doing your homework?'

'Put it this way,' he said. 'When I come across something that interests me, I make it my business to get to know everything about it.'

'I'm not a fucking object, and you sound like some kind of weirdo, like a bloody stalker.'

'I find you fascinating, like a puzzle that needs solving. Complicated but ultimately satisfying. This front you put up, it's because you're scared of something. All feisty and strong on the outside but all of that's a cover-up. Something or someone hurt you. It's what people do, like animals, all aggression on the outside and fear on the inside.'

'You don't know me. You think you've found out a few things about me but actually you don't know anything about me. I think you're spooky – no, worse than that. I think you've got that inbred arrogance, that sense of entitlement, that posh boys like you imbibe at your mothers' breasts. And you sit there and think that your pathetic little nugget of armchair psychology is enough to define me. Jeeesus Christ ...' He caught hold of her arm and pulled her towards him and then he somehow managed to press his mouth onto hers. She struggled for a second or two and then there was something about his mouth, the warmth of it, the hard pressure of his lips against hers, the scent of his skin, that sparked not only anger, but something else, something sensual and scary. When he took his mouth from hers she was speechless. All she could do was return his stare, and for those few moments it seemed that there was no one else in the room but the two of them. Then she picked up her handbag and almost ran to the ladies' to splash some cold water on to her face and try and calm herself down as she redid her make-up. How dare he! Who the hell did he think he was? And what gave him the right to speak to her like that? She should never have come. These people – men like Alex – they were everything she despised. She took the little purse from her handbag and decanted a line of coke onto a tiny mirror and then used a rolled up note to inhale the precious white powder. Then she brushed the telltale traces of white from her nostrils. She could hear the music, a live band striking up, and as she stood in the shadows of the garden, waiting for the drug to take effect, she was pleased to realize they were actually quite good. She waited until the dance floor had filled up and then slid herself between the swaying bodies and let the music take over. If she closed her eyes she could imagine herself alone and sinking into the music, becoming a part of each instrument, the song of the guitar, the pulse of the drums, every lyric evoking a memory or an unfulfilled desire. She seemed no longer there in the mental sense; she was oblivious, removed from the bodies around her, there was just herself and the music. When she felt the firm hands on her waist and opened her eyes she expected it to be him. She didn't resist when he pulled her body so close that his pelvis clamped against hers, nor did she mind when they swayed together as one. She liked the strength, the muscular feel of him. And when he put his mouth on hers she relaxed her lips, letting his tongue slip inside her mouth, tentative and teasing at first and then deep and insistent. Later she couldn't remember which one of them had made the first move that would lead to the inevitable. But they ended up outside and nor could she remember if there had been much in the way of foreplay. But what she did remember was the intensity, the eroticism, the feel of him thrusting into her and then coming with him, his hand over her mouth stifling her screams. She remembered him slipping out of her and the slow return to reality and the realization of what she had just let happen. No regrets. No point in regrets, and a fuck was a fuck, nothing more. 'My knickers' she said.

'Uh-huh. Mine.'

'Are you some kind of pervert?'

'What do you think?'

'Yeah, that's what I think. A twisted, stalking pervert. Keep 'em if you want. Add them to your collection. Listen, what just happened … It was great, really. You're a good fuck. But honestly, you're not my type. So let's not go through that charade of taking my number, the "I'll call you" business. It ain't going to happen, and no hard feelings, OK?'

'Sure. What makes you think I was going to ask for your number, anyway?'

'I didn't assume … Oh, fuck it. Just let's get on with our lives, shall we?'

'Absolutely. Great meeting you.' And with that he disappeared into the trees and she didn't see him again. The next morning Juliet's mother cornered her over breakfast and told her how lucky she was that such a wonderful young man had shown interest in her. Juliet handed her mother a cup of coffee and then said: 'He's a complete weirdo, Mummy … but a great fuck.'

The thing about Christmas, Juliet believes, is you set out to make everything perfect, but all that seems to happen is that each one piles another layer of shit onto the festering compost heap of previous years. All her memories are coming out along with the decorations. Memories of the stupid things that went wrong when Alex *was* home flood back like they happened yesterday; the pointless rows caused by nothing but the tension of trying to make everything and everyone happy and OK, because the next Christmas he might not be here. Not just here as in *here*, but anywhere. Christ, it was like waiting for a terminal diagnosis. The saying goodbye, all that shit. Feeling that you should remember every little thing, just in case. And above all else you mustn't row, you mustn't complain, you mustn't spoil anything, because it's all got to be one hundred per cent fucking perfect.

And then the loneliness, the sheer bloody pain of missing him when he was away from them and the silent prayers even if you never set foot in a church: please, God, let it not be today. Juliet knows that there are people around them – friends – who can measure out their Christmases like Eliot's coffee spoons. All of them engraved by the predictable and the unremarkable, the familiarity of repetition, the importance of the minutiae of established family tradition, the sanctified festivity, the redemptive Christian flirtation with charity and forgiveness.

But for Juliet all the glitter is dulled and the baubles are tarnished. Her experience of Christmas is mostly of something to be borne, to be suffered, to be got through without breaking down and spoiling things for everyone else, regardless of whether Alex was home or not. And now that he's home for good and she doesn't have to worry any more, she still can't enjoy it because of what's happened. Once again she's going to have to pretend that everything is happy and wonderful, for Ben's sake. So that is why Juliet feels it wholly appropriate that a magazine came in and staged their Christmas, because Christmas has become no better than a staged magazine shoot, a parody, with everything on the surface arranged perfectly but bearing no relation at all to the real thing. Still, one must go through the motions, one must try and swim through the shit.

She's so tired of acting. But it's Christmas – ironically the *real* Christmas – and she still has to act. Alex has to act, Geraldine has to act, they all have to act for Ben's sake. Maybe next year he won't even believe in Father Christmas. Some little monster is bound to tell him. Or maybe he'll see Juliet planting the stocking at the foot of his bed. Alex is more than happy to leave it to her because he says her footstep is so much lighter and she's less likely to wake him up. He's happy to drink Santa's whisky – yes, whisky and not sherry – and stuff down the mince pie. He draws the line at Rudolph's carrot so Juliet will crunch her way through half of it and leave the rest on the hearth. Then she will make a footprint in the ashes with Alex's boot.

*   *   *

Juliet is standing with Ben in the hallway. Both of them are bundled up in coats. She looks at her watch accusingly. 'Alex, if we don't get a move on we won't be back before Geraldine arrives. In fact, why don't you ring her to tell her to come an hour later? The traffic's bound to be terrible. And as we've left it so late we might not even get a bloody tree.'

'Don't swear, Mummy.'

'There'll be loads. God, why do you always have to make a

drama out of things?'

'Alex, I'm not making a drama. It's just that it's lunchtime on Christmas Eve and the rest of the world and his friend has bought their tree two weeks ago. Just because you're so hung up on bloody tradition.'

'Could you just stop being negative?'

'I'm not being negative, I'm being realistic.' Ben skips ahead of them to the car, chanting, 'We're going to get a tree hee-hee … we're going to get a tree, with Mummy and Daddy and me …'

Alex pushes the key in the ignition and Adrian Edmondson's voice blares out. Alex turns the volume down. '*Cat in the Hat*, Daddy. Want *Cat in the Hat*.'

'Later, Ben. Let's just get going, shall we? How about some nice music?' Alex flicks the controls and AC/DC fills the car. In spite of his irritation, he smiles at Juliet. 'My little rock chick.'

Alex puts his hand on her knee and squeezes, then he rests it there. This feels good. At the moment it's all right; his wife and his child in the car doing normal things, the sort of things that normal families do. They sit at the junction of Sheen Lane waiting for the red lights to change. A motorbike comes up on the outside and sits unnervingly close to the door. The rider is covered from head to toe in black. Alex can feel his chest tightening. The visor is dark, making the face invisible. Alex focuses on the gloved hands, waiting for any movement. He flicks a look in the rear-view mirror. All Alex can see is a vast radiator grill of a large lorry which is almost grazing his tail. He's hemmed in. He clears his throat but it's hard because his mouth has gone dry. He tickles the accelerator and turns the music right down. He touches the gear stick, wipes his palm on his thigh, then rests it on the gear stick once more, brushes his foot over the accelerator, checks the rear-view mirror, the motorbike at the side of him, a cyclist on the inside, his wife and child in the car. He lets off the handbrake and moves forward.

'Alex, the lights are still red ...'

He edges forward, dodging a car coming in from the right. The car hoots and Alex hoots back, then he's free of the junction and he puts his foot down, overtaking the car in front. He almost hits the bollard in the middle of the road, but he manoeuvres past it. He can feel Juliet's tension beside him. 'Alex, what the fuck ...'

He is breathing heavily. His chest still feels tight. 'It's fine,' he says. He forces a smile and squeezes his hands on the steering wheel. The wheel feels oily and slippery from his sweat. He wipes his palms one by one on his thighs. Juliet can see what he is doing. She knows what's going on. He's showing weakness. He's showing he can't cope. But he can. He just knows more than most people what the threats are; he knows what to look out for, the dangers coming from every corner because you just never know. You've got to be watchful all the time, otherwise you're likely to be taken out, annihilated, turned into pink mist.

His body starts to shake. 'Alex, pull over. Let me drive. Sweetheart, look, you're in no fit state. It's OK. Come on ... please ... pull over.'

'I'm fine.' By clutching the steering wheel he can make it go away. If he takes some deep breaths. If he thinks about the tree, the decorations, the boxes they've got to unpack, the bloody fairy lights, his mother and how he's going to cover up his lack of patience with her. Will he be able to get through Christmas without snapping? Just a couple of days, that's all. Just a couple of days.

It's subsiding now. He's beginning to feel he's getting a grip. The tree lights, the fuses, the whereabouts of the screwdrivers. The need to buy lots of batteries. All of it a distraction; if he focuses upon it hard enough he will be OK.

When they get to Petersham the car park is bursting with vehicles. Juliet says she'll go on ahead, take Ben. 'Fine,' he says. 'I'll meet you inside.' He watches his wife and son, hand in hand, retreating from his view. Exhaust fumes from the car in front fog the air. Smoke, explosives, gunfire ... just an exhaust ... in greater London ... the suburbs. Nothing to be afraid of except finding the right change for the ticket machine. It's a shop, no need for a ticket. They just want you to spend lots of money. The tree – there'd better be a bloody tree after all this. And what else will she buy? He'd better hurry up and get in there so he can see what she's doing. Christmas, just one big bloody expense. The smoke in front of the car... it's spreading over the bonnet. He can taste the fumes, lead and diesel and petrol. Where's the cordite ...? He should be able to smell the cordite. But he's not there, he's here. 'Jesus Christ, help me,' he prays silently. He's not a religious man, but any port in a storm ... Christ, can't you get out of the bloody way and let me park. His anger is rising. He needs to hit something. In a moment he's just going to put his bloody foot down and ram that bloody bastard idiot in front of him and just get him out of the bloody way. He winds the window down. Thick smoke, lead, diesel and petrol filling his lungs. He screams: 'Get out of the fucking way before I fucking kill you ...' But his words are lost in the petrol-thick, frost-heavy air and the car in front moves slowly forward and Alex finds a parking space and then he turns off the car engine and leans his head upon his hands on the steering wheel and for just a few moments he sobs like a child.

*   *   *

'Got them working yet?' Alex is sitting on the floor with a red plastic light bulb tester patiently – seemingly – checking each tiny bulb. It's the same every year that Alex has been home. The times Juliet's been on 'put away' duty after Christmas she's either fixed them or chucked them, so that she doesn't have to go through this whole effing palaver on Christmas Eve. And the times Alex has been away she's got the tree a whole two weeks before Christmas.

So what if it was almost bare by the time Christmas came around; it was just the joy of doing something *her* way.

'I can't decorate the tree until we've got the lights on. We should have bought some more. They're so cheap these days. The time you're spending trying to fix them –'

'Juliet, could you do me one small favour …'

She raises her eyebrows, anticipating what he's about to say.

'Just shut the fuck up.'

'Language, Alex.' Geraldine has brought in a tray of tea.

'Thanks, Geraldine. You've just arrived in time for the light show – or lack of it …'

'Oh look, well done, darling …'

'Oh, well done, darling …' Juliet echoes.

'Well done, Daddy,' Ben comes jumping into the room and bounces onto the sofa. Can I put them on the tree, please?'

'Let Mummy put them on and then you can start putting the balls on.'

''K, Mummy.'

'I expect Granny would like to help, too.'

Geraldine is not a difficult guest. Juliet is fond of her because she feels an affinity, and an understanding. But she hates her weakness, even though she understands the source of it. Women were supposedly different in those days. Of course they weren't really different at all, they were just subjugated and brainwashed into being domestic slaves. At least that's what Juliet thinks. And here's Geraldine, a living example. Alex is much nicer to his mother than he is to Juliet. He would never, for instance, call her a 'fucking bitch' or variations on the same theme. He is able to control his outbursts in front of his mother, but then she is wealthy and they depended on her largesse. There she goes, being cynical again.

Alex's sister, Lucinda, lives mostly in Scotland, having married an impoverished Scottish earl on some godforsaken, impossible-to-get-to, midge-infested island, with her four obnoxious children, and so, not surprisingly, Geraldine wasn't that keen on travelling there alone. Alex's father had, much to everyone's relief, dropped dead of a stroke at the age of sixty-nine. Geraldine had been of independent wealth before she married, and so once her husband died it finally meant she could get her hands back on her own money. It was ironic that Geraldine was the one with means but was timid and retiring while Deborah, Juliet's mother, was the flamboyant socialite. She and SF (stepfather or Sad Fuck as Juliet called him) were spending their Christmas with 'friends' in Gstaad. A great opportunity for Deborah to parade around in her mink without getting cans of red paint thrown at her. Perhaps the difference boiled down to the fact that Deborah relied on a man, while Geraldine was perfectly self-sufficient and, once bitten, had no need of one.

How have they managed to accumulate so many decorations? It's slightly tricky because Geraldine keeps adding to the stocks: 'I thought you might like this, dear, I was having a clear out and look what I found ...' Juliet likes her tree to be organized and themed. She might change it each year – last year it was mostly red with a few touches of orange, and this year she's planning to go all gold. She's already earmarked the correct box of baubles, but, annoyingly, Alex is opening up the others and trying to act as though he's helping. Ben is always interested in what Daddy is doing, wanting to copy him, so naturally Ben is delving into Daddy's box. 'Darling, not that one,' Juliet says. It's all getting a bit out of hand because now Geraldine is starting on the red balls. 'Geraldine, I thought we'd go gold this year. They're all in the box just here. Benjamin, not that one.'

'It doesn't matter, they're just decorations. Why do you have to be so fussy? I think the tree looks better when it's got all sorts of different balls on it. We don't want it looking like something out of Selfridges' shop window, do we?' Alex says.

''Fridges is where I saw Father Christmas,' Ben adds.

'I'd be perfectly happy if it looked like Selfridges' window,' Juliet sighs heavily.

'Just think, they must have to do hundreds. I saw a programme on Liberty's and these poor women had to do about two hundred in one night. Just imagine. I didn't work it out but they must do them terribly quickly.'

'Really, Geraldine? If anyone wants to leave me to it, honestly, I'd be perfectly happy,' Juliet smiles through gritted teeth.

'No, no, we'll all muck in. So much nicer if we all do it, don't you think? And we must all share the work, Juliet. Otherwise it's not fair on you.'

After another ten minutes of subversive behaviour from her willing helpers, Juliet stands back to look at the damage. Yep, it looks truly awful. 'Wonderful,' she says. 'Well done everyone. Just *soooo* pretty.'

'There you are, dear. I told you it would be best if we all did it.'

'Thank you, Geraldine. Now, surely it must be time for a drink!'

* * *

Ben comes leaping onto their bed squeaking with excitement. Alex always had a shooting stocking as a child, and every year argues that is precisely what should suffice, but the contents of Ben's stocking require something larger. Geraldine is a particularly fine needlewoman and so Juliet commissioned her to make a special giant-sized stocking, a red background *appliquéd* with a large white 'B'. Ben is lugging his personal stocking. 'Look, Mummy … look, Daddy, Santa came to see me. I must have been a good boy. Look …'

'What did I tell you?' Juliet says.

''member when we got stuck in one of those big car parks, Mummy, and you used the F-word a lot, and then the man came and it was all right? I was thinking, what if Rudolph got stuck in the car park. Cos do you 'member, Mummy, that's where you said Santa parked it when we went to see him at 'fridges …?'

Juliet interrupts the monologue: 'Let's see what Santa brought you, darling.'

'Gloves. Look they've got little flaps that go over my fingers and a tiger … *roawrr* …' Ben delves further in and pulls out a pair of stripy socks which he throws onto the bed with barely a look. Next there's a torch with different colours which he flashes into Alex's eyes, and Alex says: 'For Christ's sake, Ben, do you want to blind me!' As he gets deeper in, he barely glances at each gift, before casting it onto the bed and reaching for the next item. There's a set of crayons, and pencils with Ben Miller written on them, and then near the bottom is a DVD. There's also a small book on knots and another on bird identification. Juliet wants him to notice the other book, the one that's personalized and has Ben himself going on all sorts of adventures, but he doesn't notice, he wants to get to the bottom. Finally he reaches the satsuma in the toe of the stocking.

'Goodness me, what a lovely stocking Santa has left for you. Shall we put it all back in now, and you can play with it later? And come here, darling …' Juliet pulls Benjamin in close and gives him a surreptitious sniff. 'Well done, sweetie. You managed not to wet the bed. Clever boy.'

'Probably because he hardly went to sleep, waiting for Santa to come.'

'You were very excited, weren't you? And we're going to have a lovely day with Daddy and Granny, and I'll tell you something else, young man. I won't even make you eat Granny's Brussels sprouts just this once.'

'Eeeugh. Sprouts are yukky.'

'You ought to eat them. They're good for you.'

'Oh shush, Alex, it's Christmas Day. Shall we get you dressed, young man, and then we can take Granny a cup of tea?'

'Going to see Granny and show her my stocking.'

'Knock first, and wait 'til she tells you to go in.'

''K Mummy.'

After Ben leaves the bedroom, Alex reaches for Juliet's hand. 'Come back to bed. Just a few more minutes before all hell breaks loose.'

She tries to pull her hand away but Alex's grip tightens. 'I've got loads to do. I've got to get up.' She tries to pull away once more. 'Alex, let me go.'

'Juliet, I said come back to bed.'

'Alex, I don't want to, OK?'

'Still sulking, are we?'

'Sulking? It doesn't exactly make me feel good to know what you did to Caroline Hunt. Don't you get it, Alex? It's just not normal behaviour. It's not what normal husbands do. I'm hurt and I'm angry with you.'

'But it didn't mean anything, you silly thing. I was teaching them both a lesson, don't you get it? He stuck his hand up your skirt, and I'm sorry, but I wasn't going to let him get away with it. They're a dangerous pair and I doubt they'll be quite so cavalier with everyone else's marriages in the future.'

'Alex, you're amazing the way you can twist something like that and make it like you're doing the world a great big favour. Don't you see what's going to happen? She'll probably say that you attacked her, that you were going to rape her. Hasn't that occurred to you? Don't you worry that we might end up with no friends here? You know this is all I wanted, all I've waited for. And I just think it's really vile of you to try and fuck it all up.'

'Hey … that's enough.' Alex's voice has got a tell-tale hard edge to it. His grip on Juliet's hand is so tight that it's hurting. 'Don't speak to me like that. She won't say any of those things because she'll feel too damned humiliated. Believe me, I don't think either of them will mention it, so don't worry on that score.

And I am *not* trying to fuck everything up. If anyone's doing that, it's you. Christ, have you any idea how cold and distant you've become? It's like trying to get close to a fucking iceberg. All you're interested in is Ben – Ben and your bloody computer. I come way, way down your list. Doesn't it occur to you that I've come here because it's what you wanted? Haven't you thought through the fact that I've taken on a job which I loathe in order to give you and Ben the life you want here? For fuck's sake, Juliet, you can be so damned selfish it's unbelievable. Why can't you just be a normal supportive wife for once and realize just how good life is for you, and what other people are doing for you?'

'That's so typical of you. Instead of admitting that the problem might perhaps lie with you, you throw it all back at me. Can't you take a little bit of responsibility for what's happening to us? Christ, Alex, you're unbelievable. Look, for Ben's sake let's try and give him a nice day, shall we?'

'There you go again. For Ben's sake … Ben this and Ben bloody that. He's all you care about.'

'He's my son, and your son too.'

'Is he?'

'Oh don't start that one again. *Please*.'

'Then shut up about Caroline Hunt.'

'One's real, one's imaginary, as you well know.'

'Then you can appreciate how very dull it is to be accused of something that has no justification.'

'Alex, you're impossible, the way you twist everything, and it's plain cruel to bring that up again. Just get a damned test.'

'I'm sorry. You're right. It was cruel and unkind of me. Of course he's mine. Come here …'

Juliet sinks onto the bed. All the fight has gone out of her. There's nothing she wants more than a hug but she's scared of being hurt even more. Alex places his arms around her and pulls her down onto the bed beside him. She wriggles against him, so that they are lying like spoons. She pulls her knees up into a foetal curl. She wants to cry but she doesn't want to show him that he's really upset her. She knows the pattern: cruelty, then love. The emotional wearing down until she is only capable of becoming a sobbing, pathetic heap. Then he can say 'There, there … I'll look after you … All you have to do is be a good girl …' So she lies curled up against him, and she thinks of the feel of the bed underneath her body, the touch of the sheets against her skin, the sound of her breathing contrasted against Alex's, and she settles her mind until she thinks, until she believes that she will be able to get through this without being destroyed.

7

Juliet and Geraldine are prepping lunch while Alex is once again tracking down a rogue fairy light. Ben comes into the kitchen wearing an Army camouflage assault vest and helmet. He's waving a toy AK-47 at them. 'Thank you, Granny. This is just what I wanted. It's brilliant. Fantastic. Yay ... gonna show Daddy.'

'Here, let me do it all up properly,' Juliet says. 'Don't you look the part. A proper little soldier. And you've got a proper gun. My, won't Daddy be proud of you.' She zips him up and hooks the chin strap in place. Then she takes the gun from him. 'What about the noises, darling? Geraldine, this looks terribly realistic. How clever of you.'

'Well, a certain someone gave me a little hint.'

Juliet winks at her. Then she pushes the power button and sets the volume control to 'loud'. 'Try it now – here, see, this button. If you press and hold it, it makes a good sound.'

'Thanks, Mummy.'

Juliet opens the kitchen door to let Ben into the sitting room. She hears Ben scream at Alex, 'Hands up, Daddy, I'm gonna kill you ...', and then the cracking sound of the little toy AK-47.

She is curious to know how Alex will react. She peers round the kitchen door, and at first doesn't see Alex. Then she spots him, curled up behind the sofa, his hands over his ears, shaking. She walks over and looks down at him, but his eyes are tightly closed. 'There, there ...' she whispers. He doesn't seem able to hear her. She puts her hand out to touch him, but then withdraws it. His body convulses every so often, as if an electric shock is pulsing through it. He is also whimpering. Juliet stares down at her husband and thinks that she should feel something, but a quick scan of her emotions confirms that she feels nothing, nothing at all. Ben is standing over him: 'Daddy, wake up. It's not real.'

'It's OK, Ben.' She hands him the new DVD which he got in his stocking. 'Let's leave Daddy for a moment. Why don't you put this on? Here.' As she retreats towards the kitchen she can hear the sound of explosions and gun fire. The DVD is something she picked up on Amazon. Some war thing or other, with a PG certificate on it, but Juliet has never been too fussed about that sort of petty censorship. Ben only had to catch sight of the six o'clock news to know what an ugly place the world is. She obviously doesn't recognize the weapons being used, but they're those repeat-fire, short, sharp bursts, a bit like Ben's toy, only much much louder. Geraldine is standing in the doorway. She hasn't noticed her son trembling on the floor. Juliet walks towards her and shoos her into the kitchen, closing the door behind her.

'Coffee?'

'I don't mind. Everything all right in there?' Geraldine asks.

'Absolutely fine. Ben adores his gun. Anything to do with fighting. Obviously gets it from his father.'

'Juliet, I know it's none of my business, but do you think it's a good idea to, you know, let Ben watch those sorts of films. I mean, they're quite violent from the sound of them.'

'He's fine. Honestly, he watches them all the time. Perfectly normal at his age.'

'I did wonder if it was appropriate, you know, getting him interested in guns at such a young age. People can be funny about it, can't they?'

'God, don't you hate all this politically correct nonsense? Just let boys be boys. If you don't give them guns they just make them out of something else – you know what children are like. He thinks he wants to be a soldier like Daddy, and maybe if we let him play with guns now he'll get it out of his system. Anyway, how's your garden, Geraldine? Not much happening, I expect, at this time of year, except for the sprouts. Thanks so much for bringing them, by the way. Lovely to have them on the stalk. They always keep their colour so much better, don't they? I was wondering about the brandy butter – salted or unsalted do you think, icing sugar or granulated? I know Alex always likes granulated, but I think it would be nice to have icing just this once. How are you getting on with the potatoes?'

'All done, just bringing them up to the boil.'

'I suppose we should have done them yesterday. Funny isn't it, no matter how organized one thinks one is –'

'Is Alex all right?'

'Why do you ask?'

'He just seems a little preoccupied, and I'm sure he's lost weight.'

'He's been on a diet but he doesn't want anyone to know. I think he's a bit self-conscious about the fact that he's not as fit as he once was.'

'I thought he was looking rather exhausted.'

'He's fine. I'll go and see if he's going to come and open some champagne for us. It's nearly midday, for God's sake, and it *is* Christmas Day.'

'What a lovely idea.'

'Thought you'd like that. Me too.' Juliet is all smiles and warmth as she steps through into the sitting room.

The DVD has been turned off. Ben is nowhere to be seen. Alex is seated in the chair, chalk-faced. He looks at her but says nothing. He has his arms crossed in front of his chest, and his knees are touching.

'You OK?' she says breezily.

'You bitch. You did that on purpose,' he says in a voice so quiet she can hardly hear him.

'Did what?'

'The uniform, the gun, and the bloody war DVD. What the

hell were you thinking about?'

'For your information, I didn't get them, your mother did, so don't blame me!'

'With a little hint from you, no doubt.'

'That's a horrid thing to say. Why would I do something like that? I'm the one trying to make you get better, so I'd hardly do something so awful, would I? God, Alex, what kind of cruel bitch do you think I am? Now pull yourself together and open some champagne. Your mother's gasping and I could use some myself. Why don't you pour yourself a whisky like you usually do, hey sweetheart?'

He is out of his chair so fast that she doesn't have a chance to take even one step backwards. He grabs her arms and his nose almost touches her forehead. She can feel his breath on her skin. 'You're hurting my arms,' she hisses, and she struggles, trying to break free, but his grip just tightens.

'Behave, Juliet. Or else –'

'Or else what? You don't scare me, Alex Miller.' But she is lying. He scares her a lot. She just knows that it's vital she doesn't show it. 'Perhaps you're the one that should behave – particularly with our neighbours' wives.'

'I know what this is all about. You think you're getting your own back.'

'That's a ridiculous thing to say. Now can you just for once act as if you aren't in the middle of a fucking war zone and open the champagne?'

He releases her and she steps backwards, rubbing at the red marks on her thin arms. She pulls the sleeves of her cashmere jumper up towards her elbows, so that the marks can be plainly seen. They're getting redder even as she looks at them. 'Where's Ben?'

Before she has time to answer, Ben reappears, pointing his new toy gun at his father. Alex just looks at him and then, very slowly, he raises his hands above his head and says: 'Don't shoot, Ben, I surrender.'

Ben presses the trigger and a tinny, high-pitched series of cracks issue from the toy.

'Now Ben, that's not very nice,' Juliet admonishes him. 'Daddy surrendered and you shot him. I think Daddy had better explain the Geneva Convention to you.' She looks directly at Alex but he has a look upon his face as though he has travelled a very long way away.

* * *

Ben has been tucked up in bed surrounded by his new presents, and is mesmerized by the little book that features himself. Alex is in the study. Juliet and Geraldine are relaxing on the sofa in front of the television. There's nothing much on that either of them wants to watch, so Juliet switches it off and refills both their glasses. 'Lovely day, darling,' Geraldine says. 'Thank you so much. I can't tell you how good it is for me to see you all settled now.'

'Well, thanks to you, Geraldine. We couldn't have moved here without your help.'

'No point in having all this money if I can't use it to lend a hand to my family.'

'Well, we really appreciate it.'

'And you are glad to be here, aren't you? Everything's all right between you? It's just that, to be honest, Alex doesn't seem as happy in himself. I'm not sure that he's really been the same since he left the Army. It's all been quite an adjustment for him, starting a new career at thirty-seven. Not easy for anyone.'

'Perhaps. But he couldn't stay in forever, and it was very tough on Ben and me, all that moving around.'

'Oh, I'm thrilled he's out. Obviously. All those years of worry – especially latterly. I still can't fathom what on earth we were doing there, and what good it's done. I know Alex would disagree, but personally I think as soon as we pull out, the Taliban will take over again and it will all be as if we had *never* been there. A waste of time, and all those lives lost for what? Not to mention the lost limbs. All so bloody awful.'

'Yes.' Juliet has heard it all a million times.

'We are all so proud of him.'

'Yes,' Juliet repeats, and sighs loudly. 'One of the elite, the chosen few.'

'I used to wonder if Alex only joined the Army because of his father. But that really didn't make sense, given his feelings towards him. But it suited him so well, didn't it?'

'You think? God, sometimes I wonder if they removed their hearts during training, along with their pain receptors.' Juliet is in danger of saying more than she should. As far as Geraldine is concerned, Alex is the epitome of perfection.

'He thinks the world of you and Ben. He always has.'

'I know, we're lucky.' Juliet feels she might choke on the words. She refills Geraldine's glass. 'You said: "Alex's feelings towards his father ..."' She knew what a bastard Alex's father had been towards Alex, but she was curious to learn more by drawing Geraldine out about George and his bullying, to see if there was maybe a pattern, some kind of genetic predisposition that was now showing itself in Alex.

'Alex was really a shy little boy, and his father was such a big character. I'm afraid he rather bullied him. It's amazing that he's turned out all right, considering.'

Juliet was tempted to laugh at Geraldine's perception that Alex had turned out 'all right', but she managed to control herself. 'Considering?'

'He was very old fashioned. Very hard on both of them. Seen and not heard. Spare the rod and spoil the child ... you know.

'I remember once when Alex used to have to say his times tables by rote every lunchtime. And when it came to nine ... I always thought that was the most difficult one, he got his 45s and 54s mixed up – he can't have been more than six, not much older than Ben – and George grabbed his arm, dragged him out of the room and kicked his bottom as hard as he could. You know, I'll never forget the scene, and poor Alex biting his lip, trying desperately not to cry because his father would have been even angrier with him. He was too harsh. Much too harsh.'

'Couldn't you stop him?'

'Oh, no. He was a force of nature. There was absolutely no stopping him when he got into one of his black dogs, as he called it.'

'And Alex, how do you think it affected him?'

'He was fifteen when his father died. I think – although he's never said – he felt a huge sense of relief. I *know* that he hated his father. I remember the funeral. The three of us – Lucinda, Alex and myself – people thought we were all so composed and stoical. There was not a tear shed between us. You see, we were free of George's tyranny. A huge weight was lifted from us. We could never admit it, but I think we were all relieved. He wasn't a nice man, Juliet.' She held her glass out for a refill.

'So he was violent towards *you*?'

'No point in thinking about it now, it's so far in the past.'

'But he was?'

Geraldine nods slowly. 'Yes. He was violent to me *and* to Alex. He spared Lucinda because she was a girl, a very pretty little girl, and she knew how to be very good. He was a vicious bully. An animal. There, I've said it.'

'God, poor you. I bet you feel better for it. Saying it out loud.'

'Oh my. You sound like one of those awful counsellor people. All that nonsense about talking. Not in our generation. We just got on with it. And marriage, well we really thought it was for life. Mainly because it was so damned difficult to get out of it. For most women they were shackled by the fact that they had no money of their own, whereas ironically I had pots of money.'

'You must have been quite a catch. But you didn't see through him? You didn't realize what he was really like underneath? I guess these men are clever like that, aren't they? They can be so charming when they choose to be, when there's something they want.'

'Oh yes, you're right. George could fill a room, if you know what I mean. He was very handsome and clever – just like Alex, and so much older than me. He was a great friend and contemporary of my father. They served together during the war. George made it back after D-Day, but sadly my father didn't. Can you imagine how awful it must have been for my mother? I'm not sure she ever really recovered emotionally. She was what you'd call "fragile". Strangely enough, George was also a posthumous baby – his father died in the First World War. I was named after my father, Gerald. I imagine it was a natural choice that George should be my godfather. I remember him when I was little, arriving for the weekend in his sports car and bringing laughter into the house for a change. I think there was talk that there was something between him and my mother, and I've no idea if there's any truth in it, but she never remarried. She died in a swimming accident when I was fifteen. I was away at school when it happened so I got called in to see the headmistress. I remember racking my brains as to what I'd done wrong, so being told my mother had drowned was quite a shock – not at all what I'd been expecting. At the time there was talk of it being suicide, but the currents were very unpredictable even though she was an experienced swimmer. She was the only family I had, but there was plenty of money, all tied up in a trust fund until I was twenty-five. The money came from mines, you know. In Staffordshire. Opencast mines. My grandfather was a coal millionaire. And after my mother died everything passed to me. So there I was, a very rich young girl, all alone in the world. But George would come and see me a lot and make sure I was all right; he was like an unofficial guardian, and when I was old enough I developed a terrible crush on him. Well, any girl would. Imagine, he used to whisk me off to the theatre and then give me splendid dinners in smart London restaurants. And the dancing, the nightclubs. Because he was my godfather no one saw the need for me to be chaperoned. Oh dear me, it doesn't bear thinking about. Looking back, he really was a rogue. Then he'd deliver me back to school and I was sworn to secrecy not to tell anyone what we'd been up to. And we seemed to have so much in common even though there was a twenty-four-year age gap. I suppose now you'd say I was looking for a father figure. While he was looking for an heiress,' Geraldine finishes, bitterly.

'And after you were married, what was it like?'

'Very happy at the beginning. Only after I had the children things changed. He was too old, too set in his ways to have the patience to deal with little ones. He became very domineering, treating me like a child. I think something happened to him in the war, you know. I think perhaps it brutalized him and it was only when I knew him intimately that it became clear. It's terrible what our men have to go through.'

'War changes them. Maybe some are a lot more susceptible than others, like George ... and Alex,' Juliet adds, quietly. 'And the money? He took control of everything?'

'Yes. I don't know how he managed to do that. It was sneaky. Surreptitious. Making me sign things, suggesting accounts, brokers, investments – and before I knew it, most things were registered in his name. So it probably sounds awful to say it, but his death was an enormous release both emotionally and financially. And thank God Alex turned out all right, considering what he went through as a child. He saw things, between his father and me, that he should never have seen. You know once he actually stepped between us. He was such a brave little boy. Can you imagine a child doing that?

He stepped between us to stop his father from hitting me. You don't forget things like that, and I was worried that he might not. And then he was so unhappy at school …' Something catches in Geraldine's throat. 'I wanted to bring him home but George wouldn't have it. "Character-building," he said. "Make him stand on his own two feet!" And if I'm honest I suppose I thought it was best that he was away from George, that he'd be safer. You just never know what to do for the best, do you?'

'No, I suppose not.' Juliet's head is spinning. There's so much she could say, and it's really tempting to open up to Geraldine, but something stops her. Maybe the fact that there's a risk anything she tells Geraldine might get back to Alex, and then he'd be angry with her for being disloyal to him, especially to his mother who truly believes he's her superhero. It would feel really good to tell her the truth, to unburden herself, but the relief would be temporary, and it would do nothing to alter her situation. Best that she says nothing, and just mulls over everything that Geraldine has told her – things that confirm how completely fucked up Alex is, and why – and she can nurture the small nub of comfort that Alex's problems are *not* her fault; that maybe he never really stood a chance of being anything other than he is. Christ, she actually feels profoundly sorry for him. Poor Alex.

8

Juliet starts to type a general message to the forum as soon as she logs into the support group.

> Hope you all had a good day ... Mine wasn't too bad. Kept everyone happy I think. But just had really uncomfortable conversation with OH's mother, telling me how well-adjusted he is, considering his awful childhood. Well, I'm sorry but that's b*****cks. He's so screwed up ... and dangerous. F**k it, I spend half the time wondering if I'm going to wake up alive. More than once I've been woken up by him lying on top of me, trying to strangle me!! And I've got a five year old here. I may have mentioned in previous posts that he's ex-Army. It's not normal, is it, to be going off to be shot at, year after year. If you're constantly seeing people around you being maimed or killed it's bound to screw you up a bit! If you're normal, that is. If you never know if your next footstep is going to either blow you to bits, or take your legs off, or your testicles. And when they return it's those left behind that have to pick up the pieces. He's not the same man I married. They build these men up into being something they should never be: machines, automatons, programmed to carry out their missions, no matter what. They push them to their breaking point, and then build them back up again. But you don't get the same person back. Does anyone else have a similar experience?
>
> *Posted by Sparrowhawk on 25-Dec-13 23.40 GMT*

Juliet waits for a few moments and unbelievably – given the time – she gets an answer:

> Hi there. I'm really sorry ur going through this shit. Am sending hugs. But what r u going to do? Sounds like he's really screwed up, as you say. Guess he's seen some bad things. Now having flashbacks. PTSD. He really needs help. Have you talked about that? Getting him some counselling. There's organizations out there, Combat Stress, the British Legion – you should talk to them. Better still, get him to talk to them.
>
> *Posted by FightbackGirl on 25-Dec-13 23.46 GMT*

> Hi again FightbackGirl, and thanks for responding. I've tried. Believe me. It was the first thing, after it started coming out. But it's like he doesn't want to admit there's anything wrong. He's too proud. I think he believes he can deal with it himself without anyone else noticing that it's happening. Maybe he thinks if it's only me that notices, then it's not really important. He can control me, or at least he thinks he can. He knows I'm really scared of him, even though I try really hard to hide it. Oh shit. I'm frightened. I can never let him know it, because that would make him worse. I have to pretend all the time that I'm strong and feisty, but inside I'm shit scared. Sometimes in his sleep he lashes out. He's actually beaten me up, I mean really laid into me. I don't want to be this victim-type of person who feels she has to walk on egg shells around her husband in case he thumps her. It's not fair. Oh never mind … sorry … I'm just ranting now …
>
> *Posted by Sparrowhawk on 26-Dec-13 00.02GMT*

> Feel free to rant away. That's what this site's for. Ranting and support.
>
> *Posted by FightbackGirl on 26-Dec-13 00.08 GMT*

Thanks for listening. It may sound stupid, but when we moved here to our new house, the house of our own after he left the Army, I thought everything would be OK, like we'd have this great new life, but he just wants to fuck it all up. Upsetting the neighbours – I can't even tell you what he did to one of the women. It's like he just wants to wreck everything I set up. You know sometimes I feel like I want to kill him. Is that bad? LOL

Posted by Sparrowhawk on 25-Dec-13 00.13 GMT

Normal. But I'd say: be careful. And I know it's hard, but you really do have to try and be a bit understanding. I know this. Believe me I do. My brother was in the Army, and he didn't talk to anybody. He didn't get any help at all.

Posted by FightbackGirl on 26-Dec-13 00.16 GMT

So what happened?

Posted by Sparrowhawk on 26-Dec-13 00.18 GMT

He took himself off into some woods and hanged himself. So you want to make sure your husband doesn't do the same.

Posted by FightbackGirl on 26-Dec-13 00.21 GMT

God. I'm so sorry ... Your poor family. I can see now where you are coming from. Forgive me if I haven't been understanding enough. I didn't realize ... I should have asked ... Another thing Alex accuses me of ... being self-centred, everything's all about me. So here I am, 'guilty' as charged.

Posted by Sparrowhawk on 26-Dec-13 00.24 GMT

No. Honestly ... It's OK. Don't worry. You weren't to know.

Posted by FightbackGirl on 26-Dec-13 00.21 GMT

I feel so sorry for you – I just keep thinking of what it must have been like, when he was found, and I want to cry for you.

Posted by Sparrowhawk on 26-Dec-13 00.24 GMT

It's OK ... Please don't cry ... Look I have to go now. I hope you get your life sorted. Good luck.

Posted by FightbackGirl on 26-Dec-13 00.26 GMT

These cyber conversations are Juliet's life line. Without them she doesn't know how she'd survive. She can tell the truth without fear because online it doesn't matter who you are or what you say. These faceless individuals make her feel safe, so she can say anything at all. In fact online interaction has been far more helpful to her than all the years of counselling, the psychiatric in-patient sessions, the detox clinics, all the psychobabble that she's had to listen to in the past. All she'd learned was that more often than not people chose not to believe her. The truth seemed just too uncomfortable for them. They made out she was a fantasist who invented everything – a view encouraged by her mother, obviously. When she told the counsellors that the Sad Fuck referred to her as his little nymphet and also threw in other allusions to Humbert Humbert's narrative, she wondered if they took a certain prurient fascination in the scenes and the experiences she described, a real life Lolita sitting in front of them. Not that the actual story wasn't dramatic enough. Christ, a 54-year-old man and an eleven-year-old girl – isn't that drama enough for anyone? Clearly so dramatic that it was unbelievable. It just confirmed to an adolescent Juliet that there was much in life that made no sense at all; the people who were supposed to protect you didn't protect you, so all you could do was try and protect yourself, walk away. And if you couldn't walk away all you could do was try and fucking ignore them. Detach. Crush your feelings. Disguise and protect yourself by assuming pretend feelings in order to act like the person you needed to be, a person who didn't care, who couldn't be hurt. But if you hide your feelings for too long you run the risk of never being able to find them again.

The funny thing was, Alex had been one of the few people in her life who'd been able to break through her barriers. Perhaps he recognized something in her that mirrored himself. They say that opposites attract, but in their case while they appeared on the outside to be polar opposites, internally they were identical, and so it was perhaps inevitable that their two damaged souls would seek refuge in each other.

After they'd met at the wedding, he'd been clever, like a true stalker, leaving it just long enough to make her think she wouldn't hear from him. She didn't want to hear from him, she'd told herself. Yet the longer she didn't hear from him the more she realized that she was irritated by the fact that she didn't. It was one thing for her to call the shots, to be the cool one, for her to be the one using *him*, but this wasn't good. He wasn't playing her game. The more time passed the more time, maddeningly, she found herself wondering about him, and thinking back to the amazing sex, and the way the world had stood still when he kissed her. It was exactly six weeks and three days since the wedding that her doorbell rang. A Tuesday evening. She wasn't expecting anyone. She didn't recognize the male voice on the end of the entryphone. But as soon as he said his name she felt her stomach lurch. She didn't know what else to say other than: 'Come on up.'

She stood aside to let him in, conscious of her messy hair, her loose vest T-shirt and her torn jeans, her bare feet with the chipped nail varnish on her toes. He was carrying a large wicker picnic basket and a carrier bag swinging from his right wrist. 'Give me a hand,' he said.

He looked different out of uniform; older, leaner and taller but still wearing impossibly short hair. She took one side of the basket. It was heavy and stamped with Fortnum & Mason on the top.

'Christ, what have you got?'

'I take it you do eat sometimes?'

'Sometimes. And what are you doing here?'

'What does it look like?'

She laughed. 'I honestly haven't a clue. For all I know you might have a pet snake stashed in there. Or a week's worth of dirty laundry.'

Her flat, he later told her, was what he would call bohemian, and basically showed that she was completely deranged. But he said it was 'in a nice way', as if deranged could ever be considered 'nice'. She'd been going through her Indian phase, and the walls were draped with candy-coloured, gossamer-thin sari fabric, printed and edged with gold. In the corner was a life-sized stuffed bear dressed in a pink ballet tutu, which she'd rescued from some junk shop and somehow managed to get up the stairs. It didn't fit the theme, but it was whacky enough to warrant a large space. There were candles everywhere because she didn't much like stark lighting, and joss sticks scenting the air with patchouli, which Alex said he loathed. There was also a large sofa draped with leopard skins, and on the wall behind a gilt-framed mirror with more candles held in dainty little sconces. There were lots of books everywhere – in piles in bookcases at either side of the chimney breast – and giant damson-coloured velvet cushions spread around the floor. Juliet watched him taking it all in, and guessed that by the very nature of her flat, this visual extension of her character, this man would recognize that their worlds were a million miles apart.

'Got any champagne glasses?'

She fetched a couple of Moroccan tea glasses from the pine dresser. 'Only these.'

'Camden market, or Marrakech?' he asked.

'The latter, of course.'

'Bet you went on a dope-fest with your junky mates, didn't you?'

'Why are you here?'

'Because you fascinate me.'

'I don't like Army officers, you know. I find them boring.'

'Then I'll just have to re-educate you. Next weekend, what are you doing?'

'Drugs, of course. What else would you expect?'

'Want to come away with me?'

'Not remotely.'

'It's a house party, in Northumberland. Smart. Shooting and partying. I'll drive you up. You'll need warm clothes and a pair of wellington boots. I suppose you have a pair?'

'No. Of course I don't.'

'What size are your feet?'

'Four.'

'God, that's almost a child size. Perhaps your eating disorder stunted then.'

'I didn't ... Oh what the fuck. How do you *know* I had an eating disorder? Oh yeah, I remember, my mother. You did your research, didn't you?'

'Not nearly well enough. You can tell me all about yourself over supper.' He opened up the Fortnum's basket. 'Do you eat foie gras? I suppose I should say, do you eat at all?' She was tempted to say no, just to spite him, but the truth was she loved it, so she nodded. 'And smoked duck breasts?'

'OK.'

'And Scottish raspberries?'

'Maybe ...'

'Well that's a start. But I don't really suppose the way to your heart is through food.'

'Has anyone told you just how rude you are?'

'I'm not rude, I'm direct.'

They ate their way through the contents of the hamper – well, Alex ate his way through most of it. Juliet rather gave up after the pots of chocolate mousse and the pistachio macaroons. But she had happily accepted a glass or two of pudding wine. She sat, cross-legged, on one of the velvet cushions and rolled up a Rizla paper and some loose tobacco into a cigarette. Alex stuck with his Marlboros. It was probably mostly the alcohol, but possibly the fact that she was warming towards Alex, ever so slightly, that made Juliet open up to him. Yes, she had suffered from anorexia, but then so did everyone, pretty much.

'The psychologist at the Priory said it was a way of avoiding growing up, a fear of being mature, of sex and all that. You know, wanting to stay a little girl, cos that way you're probably going to be more protected. But I said that was a laugh. I told him he was a prat to think that little girls were more protected. He only had to listen to my story.'

'Your story? There's more?'

'I mean … no. There isn't any more. That's what I meant.' Stupid of her to say so much. Alex tried to draw her out, but she just sat with her knees up under her chin, wishing she could take it back. Alex knelt down on the floor in front of her, and put his face reasonably close, but not too close, to hers.

'Sorry. Please don't think I was prying, because I wasn't. Now, I'm going to pack up the hamper, and then I shall come and pick you up at 3 p.m. on Friday. That OK?'

Juliet surprised herself by nodding.

'Excellent. Bring something slinky for Saturday night. Otherwise jeans and warm jerseys.'

*   *   *

The following morning Juliet awoke with an almighty hangover and, initially, no recollection of Alex's weekend proposal. When she *did* remember, her first instinct was to telephone him and tell him it was all a mistake and she had no intention of going. But then she realized he had cleverly not given her his telephone number. So she was left over the next few days in an agony of wondering what she should do, but the nearer Friday came, the fuller her suitcase grew, just in case she decided to go.

Why she found herself with her bag packed and nails freshly painted at 3 o'clock on Friday afternoon was a question she would spend much of the rest of her life trying to answer but, up until then, she'd lived mostly thinking any new experience was a good experience, no matter how weird.

Cars didn't impress Juliet, but Alex's BMW convertible was at least comfortable, and the sound system wasn't too shoddy either. She imagined that he would have dodgy taste in music, but it was pretty decent. The Who, AC/DC, U2, a bit of Springsteen for the retro feel, Simple Minds and the Stones. But his clothes, for fuck's sake. Here was a 29-year-old guy dressed like a 60-year-old. On the way there he told her about himself, about his mother and sister, about his father who died when he was fifteen, about his Army career and about his ambitions, while she listened and gave little of herself away.

When they arrived at Alex's chum's stately pile in Northumberland she was whisked off, with her suitcase carried by their host, up two staircases, along three corridors and into a twin-bedded room with a fridge-like temperature. Someone had kindly left the window open so that any heat coming from the rusting radiator was seen off. The lighting was inadequate, the furniture dark and imposing, and when she tested the bed, it had a mattress the depth of a fingernail covered by a worn linen sheet, scratchy to the touch, a blanket and a dust-scented eiderdown. The bathroom was a two-hundred-yard hike – or so it seemed – along two more corridors where there was a loo with a pull chain which needed at least ten tugs, and a huge enamel bath covered in brown stains and telephone taps coughing and spluttering with emphysema.

Having unpacked her bags and put a brush through her hair,

she got lost countless times before following the sound of a load of braying hoorays into the library. At least there was a blazing fire in the grate, which she headed for. Alex was at her side straight away, pressing a glass of champagne into her hand. 'OK? Everything all right?'

'Just as I imagined it would be,' she said.

She was offered around the room like an unappetizing canapé, and all that she could think to herself was, What the fuck am I doing here? Juliet hoped she was actually, deep down, a well-mannered girl and she wasn't an unkind person, at least not then. Life hadn't always been exactly normal. She'd chosen to spend much of it with the sort of people her mother would never approve of – junkies, nutters, thieves – and she liked to think she was capable of mixing with anyone, no matter what their background. The fact that these were the very type of people her mother would have killed for her to mix with could have brought out the very worst in her, but there was something that stopped her from getting out her Rizlas and rolling a joint, something that stopped her from going up to Leo Millington-Parkes and reminding him that he still owed her for a line of coke. Or from contradicting Melanie Wellings when she said they'd never met before, when Juliet had been there in the club on the night that Melanie performed a simulated blowjob on the dance floor, and then threw up on the pavement before begging Juliet for some money for a taxi, seeing as she'd had her handbag nicked because she was so off her face. Oh, the stories she could tell. But she didn't. For some reason she behaved. The expected night foray by Alex failed to materialize – which she found mildly disappointing – and she made it down to breakfast on time and even donned the new Wellington boots that Alex had bought for her and borrowed a tweed coat from the house and watched while the guns laid waste to the wildlife.

Alex couldn't have been more attentive, despite the fact he

hadn't found his way into her bed. On the way home he told her how much he'd loved having her with him. He even apologized for the fact that he guessed the company wasn't entirely to her liking, to which of course she demurred. And some of it had been quite fun. Not that playing sardines would have been her game of choice after dinner. She was treated rather like some exotic specimen, viewed with curiosity by the men and suspicion by the girls, especially when she suggested that instead of playing brag for money they should play for their clothes. Oddly enough it was Alex who'd said no.

OK, so she did *quite* like him. He seemed kind, and he was charming and attentive. But she was surprised that there had been no tongue wrestling, no groping, no slimy insinuations – especially after that incident at the wedding. And she'd stopped herself from demanding her knickers back. And she did want to see him again. But as for his life, his friends, the things that made Alex Alex, it was a bit like visiting the Natural History Museum – educationally diverting but of no relevance to her own life. There couldn't possibly be any future in it.

He played her like a fish, reeling her in a little, and then letting her run. So many days had gone by after their weekend away without hearing from him that she began to assume that was it. She'd told herself it was probably just as well; the best thing about him had been the sex, and if that wasn't on offer then it was all a bit of a waste of time. She was working as a so-called hostess at a nightclub on the King's Road. Hostessing meant getting the right people in, making sure the best people got the best tables and ensuring that they poured enough expensive champagne down their necks to float the City of London. It didn't mean lap dancing, pole dancing or letting anyone get anywhere near her hidden parts – no matter how much money was offered. When Alex pitched up with a crowd of mates it was impossible to know whether he just 'happened' to be there, or whether it was a set-up. Juliet behaved with both professionalism and distance. As did Alex. He introduced her politely to his companions as 'a good friend' and then he offered her a drink, which she declined, and with that she carried on with her hostessing duties. When it got to around three a.m. Alex's party departed with a wave and a hailing of taxis. So that was that, she told herself. Weird, definitely, but she'd had so many weird experiences that this was relatively minor on the Juliet scale. But still there was that little niggling feeling of disappointment and confusion.

He called the next day. 'Sorry, I'd forgotten that was your club. I didn't want to inflict their company on you. These Army chaps – you know what they can be like. A bit over-excited at hitting the bright city lights. Listen, I don't suppose you'd have dinner with me tonight, would you?'

'Sorry, busy tonight.'

'Tomorrow?'

'Can't do tomorrow either.'

'OK, when can you do?'

'The day after?'

'I'll pick you up at 8.'

They made it through the main course in the quiet little brasserie not far from Juliet's flat, but by pudding the only thing either of them wanted was each other. A quick dash back to Juliet's, a thorough ripping off of clothes and a tempestuous fuck followed by a few long slow and equally satisfying screws, and after that they just slipped into being an item.

Alex would call her every morning, just as soon as she was awake, and ask her what she was doing with her day, and then he'd call her again in the evening and they'd chat for an hour about nothing in particular, just enjoying the bliss of hearing each other's voices. As soon as Alex had any time off work he would whizz up to London and see her. Sometimes she'd cook for him, which nearly always made him laugh. So then she started taking her cooking more seriously, following recipes and finding that she actually cared whether her food tasted all right. Yes – she, Juliet, who had never been remotely interested in food.

She told him some bits, but not all, about her childhood, and then school. And the rather liberal culture. She told him that she'd wanted to go to art school, that she'd been told she was good enough, but then her anorexia and the drugs had got in the way. She just didn't make the grades. Stupidly she'd thought that she could get away with just being Juliet. That she could waltz into St Martin's having presented her portfolio – which they would swoon over – and she'd be given a scholarship at the very least. Princess Juliet who thought she was a gift to the world. Ha! What a fucking joke.

And he listened. He sympathized. He would take her hand and hold it while he gazed into her eyes as if he understood every shredded piece of her, and she began to think that he might be the person who could put her back together again. Strong, brave and protective. Gradually she started to believe that no harm could ever come to her while she was with Alex. For the first time in her life there would be someone to look after her.

What she didn't realize at the time was that they were the same; two bad halves of an imperfect whole. When they were on honeymoon, sitting on a beach in the West Indies, watching the sun go down, they finally shared their secrets. They explored together the damage that made them who they were, and for a long time after it seemed the confession of their wounds and their weaknesses forged them together. Later those same wounds and weaknesses would be forged into weapons. It's a funny thing, how the mind can shut off the uncomfortable things, the frightening things that are just too difficult to deal with. She can understand Alex's reticence at admitting there's something very wrong with himself, because to do so will be facing up to the fact that he is weak when he has lived his life trying to prove how very strong he is. That little boy who got bullied by his father and who knew that in order to survive he had to stay strong, to rely on himself, determined to prove to himself that he was *not* the person his father saw – the pathetic, useless, good-for-nothing son, the boy who was unable to protect his own mother. So if he now has to face himself and admit that he's lost control – that everything he thinks he knows about himself is false – how could he face the shame and the humiliation of having to admit that he's fallible and weak?

For Juliet, too, it's the shame that keeps her tied to her inner gaoler. Like Alex she can't admit to anyone that she's fucked up, that she's a helpless victim, that the perfect life that she has built to show the world just how successful she is – she and Alex and Ben, the perfect family unit – is just a sham. If anyone had told her that she could become this person, she would have laughed in their face. Me? Never! I'd never be some sad, battered wife, oh no, if my husband laid a finger on me I'd pack my bags, you wouldn't see me for dust. But she knows now that this is how it works. Because she is still here, pretending, just like Alex.

But the problem is that you can't really pretend forever. You can't do it because all the stuff, all the crap, all the memories, all the trauma is still there, superglued to your mind. When the busyness stops, when the jobs are finished, and you get to spend time alone with yourself, it's all you think about.

Alex closes the lid on his laptop. He's afraid he's losing his grip on everything now. His wife, his child, his work, his entire life is becoming something over there, something he's completely detached from, and unable to either influence or control. He hasn't talked to Juliet – what would be the point? – but his position at work is tenuous at best. He's been pulled up for having too short a fuse; for being overbearing – rude, even – with clients. His absences – the time he needs to take himself off somewhere quiet just to try and claw back some control – have been noticed. Yes, it's true, he's certainly demotivated, but then he was never interested in the first place. It's all for her. Everything he's done, he's done for Juliet. And he's done it because he loves her. Maybe it was inevitable that he'd end up in some security role in a company with Middle Eastern interests. Security Advisor to an oil company who found his fluency in Arabic indispensable, his M.Phil. in Asian and Middle Eastern Studies impressive. Inevitable but intolerable. He doesn't know how much longer he can go on with it. He feels that he is sinking under an unbearable weight of loss. Juliet is intent on being at war with him; instead of providing solace, support and understanding, she seems to relish tormenting him. He's simply lost the ability to reach her, to make her see how hard he is trying to hold everything together, for *them*. He knows that she uses Ben in her games. The gun and the uniform are just a couple of the many little ruses she's come up with to push him a little closer to the edge. Loud bangs from DVDs, a sudden interest in recording any programme to do with Afghanistan and it 'happening' to be on when he got in from work, the leaving of spilled ketchup on dish cloths, pork joints left sitting on a plate, fireworks for Ben's birthday. OK, so he's done things he shouldn't have done, things which he's ashamed of and which he chooses not to think about, but Christ, if she'd seen what he'd seen, lived through the unending days and nights of hell, perhaps she might understand – or even if she can't understand, show a little bit of sympathy, instead of making his miserable existence completely unbearable. It was scary the way she could be so emotionally withdrawn, even with Ben. He thinks, actually he knows, that she has a major problem with empathy. She doesn't seem to realize the effects her behaviour, her volatility, will have on Ben in the long term. Alex thinks Ben's becoming introverted, and sometimes he has noticed that Ben seems afraid of Juliet. A child needs to feel safe and secure, otherwise the foundation is laid for all sorts of shit in the future. Alex can't afford to lose control, for everyone's sake. It's vital that he holds on to himself, that he stays one jump ahead of Juliet, that he watches what she's up to so that he can protect Ben.

His hand starts to shake like an alcoholic in withdrawal. He stares at it, as if by doing so he might force it to stop by sheer power of will. It refuses. Then his knee starts, slowly at first, and then faster, more frantically, as if he's doing some weird seat dance at a silent rock concert. The chair legs beneath him begin to vibrate and so he slaps his hand onto his leg and presses it down into the seat as hard as he can. The muscles feel hard and unyielding, yet still his leg trembles, so he punches it and at last it settles, but only for a moment before starting up again. He feels like crying. Alex, a hardened soldier, reduced to fighting back the tears because he can't control his own body any more. He squeezes his fist so hard that his short nails dig into the cushion of his palm, but his pain receptors are so numbed that he can barely feel them. He can't go to bed like this. He's got to settle himself down. He closes his eyes and tries to shut out the pictures, the replays that refuse to leave him alone. He knows they're called flashbacks. He knows they're a symptom of something he doesn't want to put a name to. He's stronger than that. He can deal with it himself. He is strong. Not weak. A whisky. He gets up and feels dizzy, short of breath, so he has to stand still for a moment, hand resting on the back of the chair for support. He knows it will pass. But the images will stay. He makes it to the drinks table and splashes whisky both into the glass and onto the polished wooden surface. Never mind. His hand is still shaking so much that it's a struggle to get it to his mouth. It's jerking, as if someone else is operating it. He drinks the whisky neat and it burns his throat, but it's a good feeling. Two more swigs and it's finished. Inside he feels the warmth, while outside he feels clammy and shivery.

He doesn't want Juliet to see him like this. Maybe she'd take some kind of perverse enjoyment from it, seeing him suffer. But as long as he watches what she's up to he knows he can handle her. If she thinks she can wear him down with her stupid ruses, then she's a fool. Does she really think she can win against him? Someone who's studied tactics, studied everything to do with soldiering? When he came out he was recognized as one of the best, the elite. He's been involved in things that are never going to appear on any records. Off the radar, and off the map. He knows about the military: weapons, intelligence-gathering equipment, the latest military technology that very few people know exist. He has contacts – not friends, but people who can be useful in all sorts of non-conventional ways. People who operate on the periphery of society. Support people who are discreet and *almost* invisible. God help anyone who'd want to take on Alex. Not with his expertise and back-up. If he can stand it, it is almost tempting to let Juliet get on with her supposedly covert psy-ops just for the hell of it, for a bit of fun, to see where and how far she takes it. Except he isn't finding it fun. His mind is becoming a giant screen with a film programmed on repeat. There is no off switch.

Sleep is an elusive luxury. At least the sort of sleep that isn't filled with nightmarish replays of scenes Alex yearns to forget. He fantasizes about cutting out the bits in his head that hold the memories. If there was some kind of electronic zapper, a laser, that could be targeted on those cells that serve for nothing except mental torment. What the Taliban were capable of was beyond human. If they caught you they'd likely skin you alive, maybe cut off your balls and stuff them in your mouth, and then string you into a tree to leave you to die. Another favourite of theirs was hanging body parts from the branches of trees, body parts of guys you served alongside, ate alongside, pissed and shat alongside. Yeah, they were barely fucking human. And the way they didn't give a toss about the women and children. The way they used them. Boys aged not much more than Ben bribed to be dickers, watching from the roadsides, reporting ISAF movements to the bastards with their fingers on the triggers and the initiation switches. Mostly, the children didn't die at ISAF hands, but through the sadistic ploys of the Taliban. Perhaps they salved their consciences – if they had any – through thinking these children would be sent off to some better place. It wouldn't be hard to imagine a better place than these godforsaken mounds of rubble, the ruins of thriving villages and towns, now nothing more than bullet- and bomb-raddled targets surrounded by opium crops nurtured to bring more misery and death. What a headfuck of a country. And yet the people – the real people, not the fucking insurgents – were proud, generous-spirited. Sometimes even hospitable. But exhausted. Young men turned old by the age of twenty-five, their faces riddled with lines etched by anguish. How many years of war had they lived through? And as for the women – scuttling around in whatever shadows they could find, keeping out of sight, covered in black from head to foot – all that marked them as female were the screams, shrill and bone-piercing. Something else to fill the nightmares. And sometimes the Taliban made the women carry the RPGs to hide them or deliver them.

They did that because they believed the Western forces had sensibilities about blowing up women. Collateral damage; there was a cover-all phrase for you.

The explosions, the blood, the shredded flesh, the severed limbs and the hopelessness of trying to hold a comrade's body together while the remnants of life pump out of him. That desperation in the eyes that shows the realization that this is it, the last moment. The pleading, the terror, the acceptance and then the dull emptiness. One minute, one second ago there was life and then nothing but nothing.

Yet not nothing. They left a lifelong legacy of their last moments. Fuck the forever in our hearts nonsense. More like forever in our heads. What a contradiction: soldiers – strong, muscular, bodies honed into warriors. But warrior flesh was no match for metal, and warrior minds no match for memories.

At some point you turn into an adrenalin-addicted zombie. You fear action and yet you yearn for it. Every sound, every movement becomes a threat, you spend every conscious moment in a state of hyper-awareness, hyper-vigilance, and then even through the nights, in sleep, there is no respite as the mind replays and revisits the horrors and the fear and the excitement ... Yes, the raw, bloody, vengeful excitement of destroying those bastards, of unleashing the dogs of war upon them. The satisfaction of watching the bloody fountain of a dying man several hundred yards away, the screams carried on the wind and then the brief silence as the black puff of smoke – like a djinn rising – twists up into the cloudless sky. Smoke and dust and heat and screams and sweat. And unassuageable fear. And then the fear subsides, as though the acceptance of grim inevitability settles upon you; the inevitability of not if, but when. They say when this happens that there is something in the eyes that shows you have crossed over from a state of man to a state of machine. You are unofficially dehumanized. The eyes seem to void themselves of emotion and to look into them is to see nothing but an empty stare. The window to the soul is shut, because the soul has already left the building. And then you know it will be a long road back to reach the human you once were but who is no bloody use to you here in this hell on earth.

*   *   *

Juliet lies awake next to Alex. He is on his back, his throat vibrating with every intake of breath. It's unusual to listen to him sleeping so deeply. She can see the faint orange glow of the street lamp filtering through the curtains, projecting the window square onto the ceiling. The only sound she can hear, apart from Alex's snoring, is the distant yowling of cats. Tonight of all nights is the quietest of the year; no one getting up to go to work. Not even the street cleaners, although it would be too early for them even if it wasn't Boxing Day. While the house sleeps, Juliet's been lying here awake, beside her husband, for maybe half an hour, just listening and thinking. Downstairs Ben will be sprawled like a starfish in his little bed, his duvet half off, while Geraldine will be rendered unconscious by the amount of alcohol she's poured down her throat.

She's been thinking back to FightbackGirl's message about her brother killing himself. Juliet wonders if Alex ever considers it, and what she and Ben would do if he carried it out. She's read on the internet that soldiers under constant attack, losing men every day, imagine what it will be like to die – not if, but when; instead of hoping they will live, they transfer that hope to *how* they will die, how they will live their last minutes, what kind of a death they will have. If you put a human into that situation, contemplating their death every waking minute, what kind of a person comes out at the other end? Juliet knows the answer: a person like Alex. That almost makes her laugh because it is such a ludicrous statement. Alex didn't come home; Alex is dead. The person she knew as Alex does not exist any more. Like a 1960s horror movie, everything about him, externally, convinces you that you are getting back the person that you knew and loved, but as time goes on you realize that the exterior is just that – a shell, a piece of window dressing to confuse you – because inside that person, that thing, is actually an alien. All the emotion, the love, the feeling, the empathy, has been stripped out, because as a killing machine, a picker-up of shreds of their comrades, a seer of things never meant for human tolerance, how can you expect a human to survive?

But how would she feel, without him, if he did choose to end it all? Would she be like Geraldine, feeling both relieved and free? She tries to picture herself dressed in black, with Ben at her side in a tiny black jacket and matching short trousers. Would she be wearing Alex's medals pinned onto her coat, or would that be inappropriate under the circumstances? Is she crying or dry-eyed in the picture? Does she feel regret as the curtain swishes closed on the silent runners removing Alex forever? She searches as deeply inside of herself as she is able to go, but she can't find any feelings. She can see herself so clearly, but she can't actually inhabit herself, or attach any emotional currency to the scene. And because she can't *actually* feel, she tries to imagine the feelings. Would she feel shame because of what he has done – a war hero taking the coward's way out; a man unable to stand and fight any more? Would the shame reflect upon her? Would people blame her, somehow, for not being able to save Alex's tormented soul? What about poor James, who didn't have the choice to come home, and all the others who had no choice? Instead of getting the support due to a supposedly grieving widow, would she get rejection and derision? She hears Alex's breathing beside her, steady and strong. It's so weird trying to comprehend whether or not she would be upset, because so much of her married life has been lived in fear of losing him. Lying here, just thinking like this, she feels an almost irresistible urge to snuggle into him. It's illogical and foolish, but she yearns to have his arms wrapped around her to make her feel safe, like he used to be able to do, if only for a brief moment, just to try and recover the love. She supposes that she can't blame Alex entirely. She's not that stupid or even that vindictive. But she can blame him for the fact that he was the one person who seemed able to save her; Alex made her come alive again, and to take that away from her was something she couldn't forgive.

It started off as just verbal abuse, though even 'just' verbal abuse can be pretty tough to cope with. Barely noticeable. 'Oh fucking hell' and 'For Christ's sake' muttered under his breath when she said anything; it was so subtle that she didn't even know if she was meant to hear it. But it progressed to 'Just leave me alone and stop asking your fucking questions' and 'God, can't you stop your bloody nagging?' when she asked him something simple, such as 'What time would you like your supper?' But there was nothing physical, not then. She really did try to be understanding. It was something she and the other Army wives talked about. 'They've got to release their bottled-up aggression somehow' and 'You mustn't take it personally.' It just went with the job and she had a duty to put up with it. Well, fine. Fine if he could have balanced it with a bit of loving. What was really hard was the fact that she lost having Alex to talk to. She had never known, or imagined, the sort of loneliness that she could feel while inside a marriage. And it was nothing to do with the long absences on tour. She didn't get the same sort of miserable, gut-wringing loneliness, because she looked forward to him coming home and spent most of her energy worrying about whether he *would* come home. Well, maybe it was gut-wringing, but not in the same way. In many ways it was even worse when Alex was home, because it seemed as if the solution to her suffering was there, but he refused to provide it. He wouldn't, couldn't talk about what he'd been doing. He refused to open up about how he was feeling. He couldn't seem to settle into any sort of domesticity at all. The only time he seemed relaxed was when he was with the 'boys'. And it would have taken a bigger fool than Juliet not to realize that he was desperate to get back into theatre. And all the time she could feel herself shrivelling and dying inside. But she soldiered on, regardless of the fact that Alex didn't seem to place any value on the fact that it was hard for her, and for Ben, waiting and worrying. All the time that he was away she, like the other wives, children and parents, waited anxiously. If she was lucky she might get a phone call from him. More often than not he could never say when he would be returning. Information was scarce and often incorrect. Lots of wives had stopped watching or listening to the news, because it just intensified their agony. The awful waiting for the statement: 'The family has been informed ...', the sigh of relief, but so much more than relief. The sense that life is carrying on unchanged for a little while longer. But at the same time the guilty realization that the relief given to one family carries the heaviest cost to another. War is brutal, and the casualties are random. But in 2009 Alex's battalion came under the fiercest fighting since the conflict began. The news was full of the daily losses, but there were other stories filtering through via the squaddies who weren't on tour, but who had heard from their mates who were – that the men were vomiting up their breakfast as they left the compound, knowing that at least one of them was unlikely to be returning. The pressure they were constantly under, the fear they endured was incomprehensible to anyone not going through it. And that was the problem. Surviving intact was not the same as surviving unscathed. There were physical scars, and there were mental scars.

Juliet has read on the internet that post-traumatic stress disorder is caused by the brain's inability to process the memory of a life-threatening, or extremely traumatic life incident. Apparently at the time of the incident, the brain puts you into a sort of autonomic mode so that you can deal with the situation, because you have to act instantly and there's literally no time for thinking. The thinking and processing to memory part comes later.

Only when it fails to file itself into memory, then it becomes a disorder. It stays in the conscious part of the mind, replaying itself over and over ... and the more you try to stop it, the worse it will be, because it has to be replayed in order to be processed.

You need to get it sorted in your mind. So if you don't have a chance to do that, and you're in a war zone, where you're being traumatized over and over and over again, and the mind never ever gets a chance to assimilate it and file it, then hey presto, you end up being a headcase like Alex.

There was a time when Juliet felt sympathetic. There was a time when she tried to understand. God knows, she'd heard stories from other wives who were going through similar trials. It was no fun for any of them being left at home. She'd lived through the bereavements, the marches, the tributes.

She'd seen the headlights arriving on the patch late at night, the slowing of the engine. She'd felt the indescribable fear as you will yourself to get out of bed and make your way to the window, to see where the car will come to a halt. Will it be you this time? And you watch from the window as the casualty notification officer, immaculate in his khaki service dress, often accompanied by the padre, pulls up outside someone *else's* house. And then you hear that inhuman wail – no, inhuman is the wrong word, because it is probably the rawest, the truest expression of what it is to be human that you will ever hear. Primeval. Not a sound anyone would ever wish to hear twice. And yet on the camp, with all the neat little houses so close together, it was a sound one heard over and over. The sight of a window opening, a head poking through, the screaming repetition: 'No ... no ... go away ... NOOOOOO ...' Just thinking about it now, Juliet feels the hairs on her forearms stand up. She remembers the first time she heard it. Remembers rushing to the bathroom and throwing up. And then the nightmares. Night after night after night.

Then he came home.

Alex has no recollections of anything before, and barely any during. Is it the flailing arms, the legs kicking at him, the scratch of sharp fingernails on his forearms? Maybe it's something more subtle. Perhaps her scent, or the feel of her skin, the slimness of her neck against his hands. And the noise, the animal-like grunts that woke him. Because if Alex knows anything at all, he knows for sure that he was asleep when it happened.

He releases his grip and she slips from the bed to the floor, coughing and choking and gasping for breath. He flicks on the light and tries to make sense of the scene. Juliet's fingers are clutching at the red marks on her throat. There's an angry blue mark on the side of her head, and bleeding from her scalp where it appears that some of her hair has been pulled out. And there is a look in her eyes of absolute, concentrated hatred and raw fear.

'You fucking bastard!' she hisses, when she has gathered enough breath to speak. Her voice rasps from her bruised throat

'What did you do?' he asks quietly, getting hold of her arms and pulling her to her feet.

'Do? You ask *me* what *I* did?' She is sobbing quietly, rubbing at her throat.

'Yes Juliet. I'm asking you what *you* did.'

'You nearly fucking killed me. I don't think this is about what I did, do you?' Her voice is hoarse.

'You must have jumped me while I was asleep.'

'Oh yeah? You think I've got a death wish? When we all know what could happen. Right, Alex. That's really likely.'

Alex pushes her gently down onto the bed. Then he walks into the bathroom and gets hold of a towel. He runs the cold tap and holds a corner of the towel under it. Then he takes it to Juliet and starts dabbing at the blood on her head. The purple mark is getting darker and the blood from her scalp is running into her hair line and down into her hair. The white towel has bright scarlet stains seeping into it.

'You tried to kill me!' she repeats. 'You should be locked up, Alex Miller. You're a fucking lunatic!'

'You know the rules, Juliet.'

'Sure, I know the rules. I didn't touch you. Look at me, for Christ's sake ...' She gets up from the bed and collapses down onto it again. She puts her fingertips to her head and feels the sticky wet warmth. Then she looks at the red patches on her fingertips. 'You aren't going to be able to explain this away.' And there's a look of something unexpected in her eyes which Alex reads as triumph.

'What do you want, Juliet?'

'My life back. I want to feel safe when I go to sleep. I don't want to spend my life walking on eggshells wondering when I might be attacked by you. I don't want to have to worry every time I leave Ben alone with you that you'll harm him. God, just think what you've already done to me, Alex. Do you think this is what I wanted? What I planned for? What do you think I fucking want? I want a life. I want out. With Ben.'

Alex knows it's the adrenalin talking. That's what's making her brave; and no one knows more about adrenalin than him. Fight or flight, and she's pumped up and ready to fight. But there's no way she can win. Not against him.

'You can go, but you're not taking Ben.'

'I'm going to prove you unfit. I'm going to let the world see what you've done to me, and then no one will ever allow you to have Ben. You're violent. Dangerous. You need help, Alex.'

'And that's what you've been trying to do, isn't it – "help" me?'

'What do you mean?'

'All your little games. Your DVDs, Ben's gun. All your petty little ruses that you think will wind me up. Clearly you don't think they're working because otherwise you wouldn't want to up the stakes like this, would you?'

'Stakes? Games? I don't know what you're talking about.' She manages to get to her feet and then she walks past him into the bathroom and stands in front of the mirror, inspecting the damage. Alex looks at his watch. It's still dark outside, but it's almost seven o'clock. He pulls on his boxer shorts, and then jeans and a T-shirt. The heating must be just about to kick in, as the house is still hanging on to the cold of the night. He pulls a jersey off the chair. It's his Christmas jersey which was bought to entertain Ben. Ludicrously inappropriate in the circumstances, but sod it, it's to hand.

He goes and stands in the bathroom doorway, and notices that Juliet isn't doing anything to reduce the swelling, like holding a wet towel over the bruising, like mopping up the blood from her hair. Watching her, it's more like she's checking her make-up to make sure everything is in place.

'I'll make your excuses for the party. I'll say you've got flu ... or maybe food poisoning from your cooking.'

'Fuck off, you'll do no such thing. I want everyone to see this.'

Sometimes Juliet really can be her own worst enemy.

* * *

Juliet doesn't know how much time has passed since Alex did this unspeakable thing to her. She wasn't expecting it. She was far too busy thinking how he would have to grovel and apologize and be ashamed in front of their friends. How could she not have thought it through properly, crowing about the fact that she would show everyone? If she'd just kept quiet would he still have done this?

Alex: always the one to be in control. It was weirdly interesting – stepping outside of herself – watching him coldly and efficiently binding her up. First of all he came up behind her while she was examining her face in the bathroom mirror. He raised his hands to her hair and she thought he was going to be gentle, that he was perhaps going to stroke the place where her hair had come out. In fact, she flinched, waiting for his touch, afraid that it would hurt. But somehow, so quickly, he seemed to have got hold of her wrist, and then the other, and suddenly they were both tied behind her with a dressing gown cord. She turned around to face him, too surprised to speak, and then he picked her up and carried her into the bedroom and dropped her onto the bed. He took his tie from the chair and got hold of her legs. She struggled and tried to kick him but the next thing she knew he was lying across her legs so that she couldn't move at all, and like a magician had her ankles bound together before she could struggle once more. She wanted to scream, but her throat was too sore, her voice too hoarse. 'Alex … you fucking untie me right now …' That was when he picked up his cast off sock and shoved it in her mouth. Her tights were lying on the bedside chair so he used those as a gag over the top of the sock. She was crying but quickly realized her nose would get blocked and then she wouldn't be able to breathe at all. She could only plead with her eyes but she noticed that Alex avoided looking at her all the time he was about his work. His face was set into an expressionless mask. Next he went to her drawers and rummaged around until he brought out a bundle of silk scarves. He used these to retie her, presumably so that she wouldn't get marks on her wrists and ankles. Typical Alex – methodical and thorough.

They had held their Boxing Day drinks party for the first time the previous year and invited all the suitable neighbours and a few other London friends to join them. Today Juliet is expecting they will get around forty people. She wonders if some won't turn up because of the Caroline Hunt episode. Perhaps they will be boycotted, a no-show from everyone. She also wonders what Geraldine and Alex will do about the canapés, and sorting out the glasses and generally doing all the things that she would do if she was there.

Funny what the mind can do. Here she is, with a gag in her mouth and her hands and feet bound, and she's wondering about the bloody drinks party and whether her guests will be all right. She feels as though she could be floating above her own life. Instead of lying here bound up, she could be lying here dead. When Alex had his hands around her neck she really thought she was dying. White spots were swimming in front of her eyes and she was actually thinking, this is it. This is how it ends. And 'poor Ben'. Ben not remembering her. Would he remember her, only aged five? Alex would presumably do all he could to erase her existence from Ben's life. And she also thought, 'How stupid.' She must have somehow lashed out in her sleep. Perhaps a muscular spasm, the sort you have when you dream you're falling off a building and the sudden jolt that wakes you. But she doesn't remember the sudden jolt, she only remembers the hands around her neck and the lights swimming in her eyes, and the feeling that she was about to die. This isn't the first time that she's been afraid he will kill her. Each episode was so much more violent than the one before that she couldn't really imagine how it could get worse. But every time she would be left thinking, how was it possible to survive *this* one? What it came down to was just a slip of the hand, a moment's pressure, a kick too many or in the wrong place. A bang on the head to a weak point. The difference between life and death might be just the tiniest hair's breadth. Like the smallest pressure on a trigger.

And Alex would probably still be holding the drinks party if she were dead, pretending that she was unwell upstairs so that he could dispose of her body later on. But she's not dead. Not yet, anyway. OK, so all deaths are only a matter of time, but hers could be along in quite a short time. God, is she going mad?

She supposes that Alex will easily explain away her absence. Food poisoning will be the most obvious excuse. But he can't keep her up here forever – alive or dead – because even Geraldine will notice it's a bit strange that she's not putting in an appearance. And she might pop upstairs to see if Juliet is all right.

But until he comes back, there's nothing she can do other than lie still and think about how she will get him back for this, if she survives.

When you've lived with someone for several years you learn the little things that can really piss the other person off. The really silly, infinitesimally inconsequential things like the fact that Alex can't stand it when Juliet squeezes the toothpaste tube from the top. He uses a toothbrush handle to squash the contents up the tube, so when Juliet's *really* annoyed with him she just puts a great fat thumb print into the thick lump at the top of the tube and sends it back down. He can't stand things being moved. If you so much as touch the brushes on his chest of drawers he goes completely mental. Totally OCD. He won't rinse the basin after he's spat his toothpaste into it, or he'll leave a ring of shaved whiskers stuck to it. All petty, normal, domestic stuff. But if Juliet should leave a sock, or a bra – or, God forbid – a pair of pants lying around on the floor, then she gets the Alex 'not amused' treatment. And the kitchen? The fridge? Anyone would think he'd done a fucking degree in food health and safety. It's maybe the fact of his fastidiousness, the way he always likes things around him to be just so, the controlling, OCD part of his nature, that has led Juliet to believe that whatever little things he does that he knows annoy her, are done on purpose. Maybe if she hadn't said, a million times, 'D'you know what, Alex, when you've emptied the ice dispenser it would be *really* nice if you could refill the water,' he would have done it. The crumbs in the honey pot. The butter crud in the Marmite. Never being arsed to take the bottles to the bottle bank. Putting things into the recycling bin dirty, so that she has to take them out again and wash them up. There are so many other things that really irritate Juliet. Like the glass he uses for his whisky. Does he, for instance, choose the one that goes in the dishwasher, or does he choose the one that has to be washed by hand because it won't fit? And is *he* the one who's likely to wash it up? And, God ... when he's poured the whisky and dribbled it onto the polished table, does he wipe it up? You would think, wouldn't you, that Alex, who's so bloody meticulous, wouldn't want to ruin one of their prettiest antique tables?

And why the fuck can't he take Ben up to the swings and slides at Palewell Park just once in his life? Because he thinks it doesn't look macho enough? He's your son. She is inwardly hissing at him behind the prison of her gag, winding herself up into a frenzy of malice and vengeance. Oh, calm breathing ... calm ... in ... out ... in ... out ...

He did actually return to the bedroom once before the party. To remove his Christmas jersey. Juliet thought, naturally, that he was coming to let her go. So sure was she that he was coming to untie her that she was busy rehearsing the torrent of verbal abuse that she would pour on him. But once again he acted as though she wasn't even in the room, like she was part of the furniture, a lump on the bed. Pretending that he couldn't hear her squeaking as hard as she could behind his hideous sock, even though she now knew that too much squeaking would only result in pushing the sock further towards the back of her throat. The best way to deal with the torture was to lie as quietly as possible and almost reach a state of calmness, a meditative state. Which was a good state in which to plot. But when he closed the door once again, Juliet's anger went way up into the danger zone. Her whole body shook, not with the cold, but because her emotions were so tautly stretched the tension was just too much. How could he do this to her? And what else could he do to her? It was the way he became so detached and bereft of any emotion. Like Alex had left the building. There she goes again, expecting her husband to be Alex.

How many more times does she have to tell herself that Alex, the man she married, the one she fell in love with, doesn't exist any more. The man who tied her up is the man who came back. The man who has been slipping into such a dehumanized state that he is incapable of compassion is her husband.

So how will the conversation go then? 'Oh yes, the party. So sorry I wasn't there. No, no, I didn't actually have food poisoning, I was *actually* tied up by Alex. Yep. That's right. Tied up – oh, and gagged too. Yes. I did say *gagged*. So I couldn't move, couldn't shout out. What's that you say? Kinky? Sex game? No, darling. Not a game, but abuse.'

The thing about violence in a marriage – the term everyone uses is domestic abuse, apparently, Juliet's read all about this – is that the victims don't want to tell anyone. It's shameful. Really. Juliet knows this. It goes against everything you've ever thought you'd do, or whatever you've previously thought that other people 'should' do. Leave him. Just get out. Don't be a pathetic victim. What's your problem?

Juliet thinks that part of it is the admission that you are a victim. And that's not nice. And then the other part is that you *love* this person. After the event, the abuse, it all gets so confusing, because the person who hurt you turns into the person who comforts you and it's almost like the more you're hurt, the more vulnerable you become and the more desperate you are to be loved and safe. They call it the honeymoon period after the beating. The time when he's apologetic and can't seem to do enough for you. The time when he tells you he'll never hurt you again, he'll never leave you. He hates himself. God, he can hardly live with himself. He loves you more than life itself … blah blah blah … and it's what you want to hear, for Christ's sake. And what's the option? You say, Well actually, mate, I'm off. I'm taking the child/children and I'm leaving you. OK? Never see you again. Right. See you. Bye.

'They' say that the most dangerous time is when you leave

him. That's when you're most likely to be murdered. The statistics – Juliet can quote loads, by the way – are that three, yes three women die at the hands of their husbands or partners every week. Every bloody week.

And he's told her he'll kill her. Look at her, here, right now. Tied up with a fucking gag in her mouth. This is a man who is not just issuing a meaningless threat. She knows he means it. He's crazy enough to do it.

11

Alex barely thinks about Juliet upstairs. He has honed the ability to shut out unpleasant things in order to function efficiently. Shit happens, and you just deal with it. Move on. Moreover, he does not give a moment's thought to how he will deal with her later on. He and Geraldine have been doing the best they can getting ready for this bloody party. There's a load of Waitrose frozen stuff that Juliet's obviously bought especially for it, and between them they can probably follow the instructions which basically run along the lines of remove packaging and shove in oven. When he announced that Juliet had been sick all night, possibly with food poisoning, and wanted to be left alone to sleep, Geraldine started to run through, course by course, exactly what they'd eaten yesterday, what Juliet could have had which the others hadn't, and how long these things took to work through the system. She'd come to the conclusion that it must have been a dangerous bit of pork meat in the stuffing. Alex agreed, and the conversation then moved on to the dangers of stuffing a bird, and how it was terribly difficult to get everything cooked through, and so Geraldine always cooked hers separately. In future, she decided, Juliet must be persuaded to follow suit. 'But I know how difficult it is for a mother-in-law to tell her daughter-in-law how to cook,' she said.

'It's bloody impossible to tell her how to do anything,' Alex said under his breath. But they didn't make a bad show of putting everything together, as Geraldine said. 'Don't know what all the fuss is about, frankly,' Alex snapped.

'Well you know Juliet, she's probably got plans for the

flowers, the scented candles, all the little details she's so good at.'

'Yes. I know Juliet.'

Ben has been kept occupied with suitable DVDs and Alex has searched out his toy gun and stashed it on top of a wardrobe. Being left alone downstairs has given him a chance to have a bit of a tidy-up, including chucking out all the rotting food at the back of the fridge. Bloody useless woman. She's just so fucking infuriating. God, it was a close thing this morning. Waking up to his hands around her throat, squeezing. Just the vague thought of it now was giving him a hard-on. He knows he could choose to be sympathetic towards her and see how it must be from her point of view. But she's just been so fucking cold. He can't reach her any more. Not that he seems capable of reaching anyone. But she's his wife, for Christ's sake. Can't she just behave, keep her mouth shut and stop playing her stupid bloody games? Can't she just see what he's dealing with? Christ, no one makes him quite as angry as she does. Later. He'll deal with her later so that she never pulls a stunt like that ever again.

In the meantime there are people arriving and Alex puts on his social face. There's bloody mistletoe hanging from the ceiling above the hallway, so he has to go through the whole kissing thing and the squeaks repeated every time he lets someone new in, 'Oh, look ... mistletoe ... mwah ... mwah ...'

Coats are discarded and children are ushered into the playroom to join Ben and his DVDs. Bowls of crisps and bottles of coke and lemonade are already out on a table, and so the kids can fill up on junk food and E numbers and give their parents a hell of a hard time this afternoon. Juliet would have put out raw carrots and grapes, and little bits of cheese, no doubt, because she believes in proper food. Alex had had to go down to the corner shop to stock up on all the evil stuff, because Juliet wouldn't allow it in the house. Ben had been circling earlier, demanding glasses of coke, and Alex had to smile to himself at the fact that there was a guaranteed bedwetting session tonight to annoy the hell out of Juliet. Alex has no idea who she's invited, nor how many, so he's put out loads of glasses and opened half a dozen red and chilled a further half dozen white. There's also jugs of elderflower cordial with sprigs of mint added by Geraldine, and some fresh orange juice. There is no effing mulled wine, though he has put a bottle of whisky and some Stone's Ginger Wine out for those who might like a whisky mac. Alex has already had a couple before anyone arrived. His hands are reasonably steady and he's feeling pretty OK, considering.

Obviously there's no sign of the Hunts and their little shit of a child. Hard to think it's barely forty-eight hours since he had his hand up Caroline's skirt. Maybe he should have guessed that Juliet would be angry, but hell, it was a spur of the moment thing, and it did the trick. Marcus might be a bit more circumspect in the future before he starts trying to finger other men's women.

By one o'clock there's about twenty people milling around, chatting about their Christmases, moaning about their relatives, or the weather, or both. His mother's been in her element, pushing canapés at people, keeping on the move so that she doesn't have to get too involved. The fact that she's busy means she has less time to hit the wine. The thought has struck Alex that Juliet might somehow escape from her bonds, but if anyone knows a good knot it's him. But say she did, it would cause quite a stir if she walked in with her bruises and gashes. Coupled with Caroline Hunt's knickers it would be the topic of local gossip for years to come, and he would be persona non grata. No more invitations, no more chats outside the front door on a weekend morning. And how would Juliet deal with it? Given that all she wants is to settle, to bring Ben up in the sort of middle-class environment she's always yearned for, she wouldn't go through with her threat. Even though she said this morning that that was her plan, it doesn't make sense to Alex. Unless she really does want to go public about leaving him. Maybe he just hasn't made it clear enough how he feels. He knows that it's not what she really wants. He knows better than she does how she really feels. He knows what's best for her, for Ben and for himself. She just needs to be reminded of that. OK, so he's perhaps gone a bit over the top when he's lost it with her. But every time she's asked for it. He wouldn't have touched her if she hadn't wound him up. Just because he's a soldier doesn't mean he's a violent person. She knows that. But she needs to understand what he is trying to cope with. She's no fucking idea what he went through, and the adjustments he had to make. If she had any bloody imagination … But she's always been selfish, Juliet. Whatever she's said about her mother and stepfather and the way things were, she always got what she wanted pretty much in life. They're living here, for Christ's sake, aren't they? She should realize just how lucky she is. She's lucky he took her on, bloody screwball that she was back then. Who was it who got her clean, eventually? Who was it who dealt with her relapses when they were posted to Germany. If she could just stop to think about what he'd done for her. Coming back to quarters finding her wasted, but denying she'd taken anything. Then he found a bit of silver paper, smoke-blackened on one side, with the remnants of her gear. So what did he do? Locked her in the bedroom. Fed her, kept her clean, literally, even though she begged him to let her out. And she was bloody grateful. Not straight away because she was angry at him for banging her up. But when she realized what he'd done for her, she was just so thankful that he'd stopped her before it got serious. Alex tracked down the guy who supplied her and beat him to a pulp. He wouldn't be supplying Captain Miller's wife again if he valued his life.

Someone taps him on the shoulder and Alex spins round. That's the thing about being hyper-vigilant. The slightest touch puts you on high alert, battle ready. He can tell by the look in

Rowena Wood's eyes that his own eyes give him away. There's a hint of surprise, of regret, of fear ... 'I'm sorry,' she said, 'I didn't mean to make you jump.'

'It's OK.' Rowena is a real looker. More natural than a lot of them, but maybe she just goes to a better clinic. It's impossible to tell. But what he likes most about her is that she's always direct. Alex remembers Juliet telling him that she's got some high-powered job. So she's used to dealing with people and giving them instructions, and she seems to have that honesty that comes with not needing to be liked. She doesn't do the platitude stuff, 'How was your Christmas? How many did you have? Goose or turkey? House is looking lovely ...' the conversation by rote. 'Is Juliet OK? I mean, are you both OK? You caused quite a stir the other night. I've only just heard, but apparently Caroline Hunt is saying you assaulted her ...'

Alex's hand holding his glass remains steady. He's amused to hear this. 'She came on to me, I rejected her advances. She's obviously feeling sore.'

'Really?' Rowena doesn't sound convinced. 'Is Juliet really OK? Should I go and see her?'

'No. I mean, yes, she's OK, but she's sleeping. She didn't get much last night – you know what it's like – and so she just needs to rest.'

'Poor love. Lucky you didn't get it if it's food poisoning. Maybe it's a bug.'

'Yeah, then we can all look forward to it.' Alex is uncomfortable with her questioning. There's something that makes him feel edgy. Rowena somehow manoeuvres him into a corner of the kitchen.

'I thought I should warn you about Caroline – it's not the sort of thing you want going around, is it? I was concerned that might be why Juliet isn't here.'

'On the contrary,' Alex says, his face now serious. 'She's got food poisoning. Perhaps the supposedly injured party ought to have a word with me before she goes around trashing my reputation. If you happen to speak to her or Marcus, you might mention that. I don't know what their game is, or their motive. Maybe because their boy has been bullying Ben they're trying to get the upper hand. Weird way of going about it.'

'Look, I don't know if this is the time to tell you, but I know that you and Juliet were really cross about Rupert Hunt and the powder paint in the sandpit, him blaming Ben for it. Well it *was* Ben, not Rupert. And he thumped Cordelia during the nativity play. She teased him about his funny hat so he socked her one. He gave her quite a bruise.'

'Who's word is that? Rupert's? Cordelia's?'

'Spoken like a proper parent, Alex. It's tough when we discover our little darlings aren't quite the angels we think they are.' She puts her hand on his arm and looks him straight in the eye. 'Just be careful, Alex. I know it must be difficult for you sometimes. I picture you as some kind of wild animal cooped up in a zoo, restrained and restless, and looking for a fight. You can pick it with me if you like. I just hope you're not picking it with Juliet.'

'As if it's any of your business.'

'You're right, it's not my business. But when I see a friend sporting a black eye I'm not the type of woman to stand back and say nothing. Let's hope Ben isn't copying his father.'

'What's Juliet been saying?' Alex is unable to hide his anger. He grabs hold of Rowena's arm and squeezes it, hard.

'You're hurting me,' she hisses.

'I asked what Juliet has been saying.'

'Nothing. She hasn't said anything to me. I've got eyes in my head, OK?'

Rowena gives him a long, unblinking look, and then nods her head. He expects her to say something, but she doesn't. She just continues to watch him, a look of examination, as if she's attempting to see inside him. Many people have tried, none have succeeded.

'I think it's time you left. I don't like your insinuations. In fact it's bloody insulting.'

'You're right. If I'm wrong then you're absolutely right. But if I'm right, then just be aware that I'm watching you, Alex.'

And then she smiles and winks – yes, winks. Jeeesus, Alex thinks. However much you think you know people, people in general that is, there's always room for surprise. As he watches her whisper in Robert's ear, and Robert turns towards him mouthing thanks and goodbye, Alex squeezes his hands together so hard that his fingers hurt. His body flushes all over with a hot, red energy so intense that he needs to hit something in order to release it. Fucking woman. Who the hell does she think she is, coming into *his* house and warning *him*? He's going to teach Juliet a lesson she'll never forget. *Never.*

* * *

Juliet needs to pee. Not wants, but *needs*. If only she could see her watch. Her limbs are cramped and painful and the ache in her arms is unbearable. She wants to cry but forces herself not to. But she doesn't think she can control her bladder much longer. It's so full that it's creating a sharp pain in her lower abdomen, and her pelvic floor muscles are giving up the battle. Underneath her is the thick feather duvet and a smart cotton cover from the White Company. She imagines that when she lets go there will be a lake of urine. At first it will feel warm, and then it will get cold, and make her feel chilled. Her wet pyjama bottoms will cling to her legs and the urine will sting her skin. It will stink. She will stink, just like Ben. She squashes her lips together as hard as she can, as if by doing so she can also seal up her urethra. She squeezes her eyes tight shut and tries to escape the pain. Please, she begs silently – Alex, come and let me go. The fight's left her now. She wants to say to him: 'I promise I'll be good. I promise I'll do what you say from now on.' She'll say anything to avoid him doing this to her again. And when he does come, and he sees what she's done, that she's wet the bed, she'll feel ashamed and dirty.

*　*　*

Alex closes the front door behind the last of the guests. Geraldine is already clearing up empty glasses and loading the dishwasher. He stops himself from saying, Don't …

'Do you think Juliet would like anything to eat? Should I make her a cup of tea, perhaps?' his mother asks.

'I'll go and check. Would you keep an eye on Ben? He might like a sandwich – that's if he hasn't filled himself up with crisps and coke.'

'Of course. Off you go. Tell her I hope she's feeling better.'

Alex climbs the two flights of stairs to their bedroom and gets the key to the door out of his pocket. He slips it into the lock, turns it and pushes the door open. Then he closes it, and locks it once more from the inside. He takes the key out of the lock and pockets it. Juliet is facing him, lying pretty much where he left her, watching him. He can see that there is a big circle of dampness underneath her where she has emptied her bladder. 'Oh dear, dear, just look at you,' he says. 'Got yourself into a bit of a mess, haven't you? What a dirty girl you are! A dirty, stinking girl. What are you? Oh, you can't speak can you? Maybe I should leave you like that. Be nice not to have you bitching on at me. Amazing how smoothly getting ready for the party went without you there. Been having fun up here?'

There's a groan from behind the gag 'Sorry? Can't understand you. So I expect you'd like me to untie you? Yes?' Juliet nods her head furiously.

'If I do, you'd better promise me that you're going to be a very good girl. Understand?' Her eyes narrow, and she nods her head once more. 'No more talk about you leaving. Because I honestly don't know what I'd be driven to do. I don't like disobedience, Juliet. It really fucks me off when you don't do what I tell you. Do you understand that, Juliet?' He keeps his voice low and menacing.

Then he goes into the bathroom and picks up a pair of nail scissors. He returns and sits down on the bed, level with Juliet's head. He brushes the points of the blades against her windpipe and exerts the tiniest pressure. He can see the raw fear in her eyes. 'You know what happens to bad girls, don't you Juliet ...? Bad things happen to bad girls.'

She nods for the third time.

Then, roughly, he pulls her head forward and unties the knot behind her head and pulls the sock out of her mouth. She draws on huge gulps of air and coughs, a dry, rasping sound. 'Thirsty?'

'Yes,' she croaks. Then he grabs her ankles and unties the scarves. She stretches her legs out and groans with pain. Alex knows her muscles will be cramping and spasming after being in the same position for so long. But she'll get over it. Then he shoves her onto her stomach and releases her wrists. She pulls her hands in front of her and starts rubbing at her skin. 'Don't tell me I hurt you? I wouldn't want to do that, would I?'

She doesn't answer.

'I said "Would I?"'

She shakes her head.

'Cat got your tongue?'

'No, Alex.' Her voice is rough and dry and she coughs again.

'Don't move!' he orders. He goes into the bathroom and flushes some water into a tooth mug and then returns with it. 'Drink slowly,' he says. She tries to hold the mug, but her hand is trembling so much that she spills it. She holds it in both hands to steady it and then takes a sip, then a bigger mouthful, then more until she finishes it. She wriggles away from the dampness underneath her. 'Stay there,' he tells her.

He goes into the bathroom and puts the plug in the bath tub, then turns on the tap. He scans her bottles of scents and then, not finding what he wants, he opens the cupboard underneath the basin and squirts in some lavatory cleaner. The water turns a delicate, swimming-pool blue with the same cleansing smell of bleach. He returns to the bedroom where Juliet is now sitting up. There are tears spilling down her cheeks. 'Stand up,' he orders. She wriggles to the edge of the bed, and then gingerly tips her legs over the edge and rests her feet on the floor. She tries to lever herself up but her legs are wobbly. 'I said stand up.'

'I'm trying ...' she snaps weakly.

Alex slaps her across the face. 'Don't answer back. Just do as you're told. Do you understand?'

'Yes, Alex.' She whispers.

'I can't hear you,' he says.

'YES Alex.' Her voice cracks, and she stands up, watching him, rubbing at the new mark on her cheek, eyes filled with the wariness of a cornered animal.

'Take off your clothes.'

She's only wearing her thin pyjama bottoms and a T-shirt. He watches her face grimace with pain as she tries to raise her arms over her head. Then she strips off her damp bottom half and stands facing him, her hands resting in front of her pubes. 'Put your arms by your sides,' he commands.

She does so. She's shivering. She looks so vulnerable and lost, he almost feels sorry for her. But almost is a long way from actually. This lesson is long overdue.

'Into the bathroom.'

He follows her. She stands with her shoulders hunched, looking down at the rising water. Alex bends forward and swishes the water around. It's barely warm, just the way he wants it. 'Get in,' he orders.

She puts first one foot in, then the other. 'It's cold,' she says.

'It's perfect. Sit down.'

She grimaces, and lowers herself down, keeping her knees up, and her arms wrapped around them. Her shivering is becoming more violent. Alex splashes water onto her back and she recoils. Then he takes the other tooth mug and throws water over her hair.

'Please, Alex, put some hot in,' she begs. Her teeth are chattering. Alex reaches for the cold tap and turns it on. Juliet squeezes her eyes shut and bites her lip. 'More complaints mean more cold. Now lie back,' he says.

She just looks at him, and then she slides back, very slowly, flinching as her flesh touches the cold water. Alex puts his hand to her neck and pushes her head under so that her hair is submerged. He splashes water over the dried blood in her hairline. Then he pulls her up and reaches for the shampoo. 'Wash it.'

She scrubs hard, her hands working through her hair furiously, in order to try and get this over with as quickly as possible.

'Harder. I can still see blood. Get it all out.'

She squeezes more shampoo into her hand and spreads it into her hair and starts rubbing and squeezing again. Then she lies back and rinses it away. Alex gets the soap and lathers it in his hand. 'On your knees,' he orders.

She gets hold of the sides and kneels. 'Open your legs.'

She stretches her knees apart, leaning forward slightly so that she can keep her balance. Alex reaches between her legs and rubs his hand hard. 'Ouch!' she cries. 'Christ, Alex, what are you trying to do?'

He gets the soap and shoves it into her mouth. 'I said,' he growls, 'don't speak.'

She spits, crying out. 'Please … just stop … I'm sorry. Please

...'

He starts soaping her back and her arms, and he lets his nails rake into her skin as his hands slide over her body. Somewhere inside him, buried almost too deep to acknowledge, is the feeling that this level of brutality is not just dehumanizing Juliet, but him too. But then he is not trying to like himself, nor even to rationalize his actions. He's just trying to get his life sorted out, and if this is the only way to do it effectively, to control his wife and keep his son safe and with him, then the use of moderate force must be justifiable. Besides all that, he hasn't felt as alive as this, nor so connected to himself since he was in Afghan.

He uses the shower attachment to give her a cold rinsing off, and then lifts the plug.

'Stand up.' He sees her eyes flick towards the white fluffy towel hanging from the heated towel rail. He gets hold of her arm and helps her step out of the bath, but he doesn't get the towel for her. She is shivering uncontrollably and her teeth are chattering. Alex knows what it's like to be cold, really cold. For your clothes to be soaked through and to have no way of warming up. To spend a whole night with your teeth clacking together so hard you think your jaw will disintegrate. She knows nothing.

'Please, Alex – the towel.'

He shakes his head. 'You'll soon dry. He pushes her hair back and examines the marks that his hands have left around her neck. They're red, with just the faintest hint of blue. She can wear a polo neck or a scarf. Then he looks at her head. The blood has all gone and there's a red gash, but it looks clean enough. Her hair will cover that. His hand has left an angry red stain on her cheek, but that will fade. At least there are no black eyes or broken bones. He'll have to keep his eye on her until the bruises fade. Get her phone, make sure she doesn't take any pictures – but he could say those were faked, that she used make-up. His mind easily switches into strategic mode, looking for threats, evaluating the danger, taking the necessary action. Juliet has no idea just how good this is for him; you might even call it therapeutic. While she shivers in front of him, he muses on what he will do with her next. He's had an erection ever since he put her in the bath. Her skin is milky white. Faint blue veins snake below the smooth skin of her breasts. Beneath them her ribs are visible, and then her flat belly framed by sharp hip bones curves down to where her legs meet in a triangle of dark hair. Long, slender legs, and frivolous splashes of red on her toe nails.

He pulls the soiled duvet off the bed and dumps it on the floor. Then he unzips his trousers and lets them fall to his ankles before stepping out of them. Juliet's eyes have widened. She raises her hand to her mouth and she retches. 'What's the matter, babe? Don't like what you see?'

. 'Alex, don't. You can't treat me like this. Look at me properly, Alex. Remember who I am … Come back to me, Alex!'

'I'm right here, my love. Now get on the bed, on your tummy.'

'Alex, no. I beg you.'

'Beg me, would you? Yes, I like the sound of that. You can beg me. Go on, say it – Please, Alex, I beg you to do what you want with me.'

She's sobbing now, her body shivering, and great wracking sobs convulsing through her. Coughing and sobbing and begging.

'Say it, bitch.' He brings his hand down on her backside as hard as he can. She shrieks in pain. 'I said, say it.'

'Please …' her voice is barely a whisper, ' … please do what you want with me.'

'That's better.' Alex spits on his hand and rubs it over the end of his cock, then he spits on his hand once more and rubs the saliva over Juliet's arse, and then he pulls her hips up towards him, positioning her against him. First he puts his finger inside her, and then he takes it out before ramming his cock into her. Juliet's screams are guttural, choking, she's sobbing and screaming for him to stop, her fingers raking against the sheet, struggling to climb up the mattress, to get away from him, but Alex holds her firm, shutting out her moans, and he fucks all his anger, his tension, his fear and his hurt into the body on the bed.

12

Juliet lies on the bed, sobbing into the pillow. Alex has thrown the duvet over her and left the bedroom. He hasn't locked the door this time. Perhaps he's assuming, correctly, that there's no way she'll be venturing downstairs. She feels violated. It was rape; no other word for it. Her husband has raped her. She sobs harder, not only from the emotional trauma and the humiliation, but from the shooting pains in her rectum. Alex stuffed a tissue between her buttocks and she checked it to confirm that she was bleeding. The obvious thing to do is to call the police, to have him arrested, but that would mean her being examined. The shame of having to tell a stranger – or worse, that people she knows should know – that she has been anally raped by her own husband. She can already feel the fingers pointing. 'Oh, she's the one … the victim …' Or worse: 'She probably asked for it … wound him up … easily done after what he went through … poor fucking Alex.'

But apart from all that, and most important, was the fear of what would happen if they didn't arrest him, or if they did and then they let him go. Wasn't that what normally happened? Wouldn't he be let out on bail? Knowing Alex, with his smooth tongue and his experience in security and God knows what, he'd be able to talk himself out of it, he'd probably know the right people who could 'look after him'. Maybe he'd know the right people who could look after her. He'd seek some sort of revenge. It's what he's always said in the past, that he'd come after her; that he'd hunt her down. And it wouldn't take a huge leap of the imagination to suppose that he'd recruit someone to do it for him, if he couldn't do it himself. So dare she pick up the phone? If she did, there'd be no going back. Even if she backed down and decided not to press charges, the police could go ahead without her consent, provided they felt they had enough proof to stick a decent prosecution together. And if they saw her like this – the mark on her head, the bruises round her neck, the faint, but discernible marks around her wrists and ankles, not to mention her internal bruising ... Oh yeah, they'd probably find that enough evidence to stick a charge on him. So why doesn't she just pick up the phone? She takes a deep breath, and then another to try and calm herself. There's a huge knot of fear in her stomach. She thinks about Ben and her responsibility towards him, about the future, or lack of it, that they will have with Alex. She summons all her courage and picks up the telephone and presses the dial button. It's dead. She presses it again. Nothing. She replaces it on the base unit and realizes there are no lights active. She switches on the bedside lamp, but that isn't working either. Alex must have turned off the fuse supplying the plug sockets. Her mobile. Where did she leave it? In the bloody kitchen where she left it last night, where she always leaves it, on charge. So she has no choice. There's always tomorrow, and the next day. As long as she's still alive by then. But the first thing she must do is bathe herself properly. There is nothing she wants more than to feel the soothing heat of a hot bath on her battered body. And then she must begin to plot their escape.

* * *

Later, much later, Juliet has cried herself to exhaustion and has been dozing fitfully, trying to escape from the pain gnawing through her body. Despite the hot bath, she shivers with an untouchable coldness. She hears the sound of Alex's footsteps thudding on the stairs, and then the opening of the door. She pulls the duvet around her and curls up tighter, all her muscles tensed, and hopes he might leave her alone if he thinks she's asleep. The room is pitch black, but when he flicks on the light she can feel it glaring through her screwed up eyelids. She hears the sound of something sliding on a tray. Perhaps he's got some new mode of torture for her.

'Juliet,' he says, softly. 'Come on, baby. I've got something for you.' She flicks open her eyes and blinks unseeingly for a moment until they adjust to the light, then she sees a mug and a plate of something which Alex is carrying on the tray.

'Hey,' he says. 'I thought you might be feeling hungry. And I've brought you a cup of tea – and one of Mum's mince pies. You like those.' The softness in his voice, such a contrast to how he was when he left her, makes her cry again. She doesn't want to cry. She doesn't want to show Alex any sign that he's broken her, but she can't help it. She is in so much pain. Her back passage feels as though it has had a red hot poker shoved up it, and every time she moves her legs a stab of pain shoots inside her. Her head aches and her neck and windpipe are severely bruised. What she wouldn't give for some painkillers right now. She thought she had some in the bathroom cabinet, but they seem to have been moved. Perhaps Alex thought she might be tempted to end it all. She's confused by the thought, because surely it would solve everything for him if she wasn't around any more. He could have Ben all to himself, without the hassle.

'Thank you,' she says. Weird how manners can kick in at the strangest times.

'That'll make you feel better,' he says, smiling at her with a soppy look which could almost be mistaken for sympathy. What she really wants is him on his fucking knees, begging forgiveness.

'You hurt me, Alex. You hurt me so very badly.' And he thinks a cup of tea and his mother's mince pie is going to make her feel better?

'Shhh, I know … I know,' he says. So now she's getting the soft soap. The loving, almost contrite Alex. It's a familiar pattern, and she knows that it can't be taken at face value. Every muscle in her body is tensed, wondering what he will do next. He is despicable. She despises him utterly. He hands her the mug and reflexively she wraps her hands around it. She looks at the mince pie on the plate and her stomach spasms with hunger pains, but she doesn't want to eat, she doesn't want to give in to her body. She doesn't want to accept anything from Alex, but her body is begging for it, betraying her. She takes the mince pie from the plate and eats it in two mouthfuls and then feels overcome with guilt at her weakness.

'That's better.' He's looking at her, but there's something weird about his eyes. Like he's looking *at* her, but at the same time looking straight through her. They've gone sort of blank. 'Juliet – you know I love you, don't you? You know that I love Ben and you more than anything in the world, and that I would do anything to protect you both, to look after you?'

She doesn't answer but just thinks: like beating the shit out of me and treating me like an animal … worse than an animal. Like something dead. Yeah, like a slab of meat. That's how I felt. Ever felt like that …? is what she really wants to say.

Eventually she says, 'You need help, Alex.'

'Juliet … Juliet … shhh … it's quite simple. If you just can learn to do what I tell you then everything will be fine. But if you ever talk to your friends about us again I will kill you. Now get a good night's sleep and tomorrow we'll get you looking presentable and ready to face Mum and Ben. OK?'

She doesn't know what he means. She hasn't talked to anyone, apart from her online friends, and she's been too careful with her passwords, and deleting her browsing history. He couldn't possibly have had access to that. She's exhausted; bruised and battered both physically and emotionally. She leans back against the pillows and shuts her eyes. She hears his footsteps retreating, and the sound of the bedroom door closing. He will kill her, eventually – of that she has no doubt.

* * *

Alex sits on Ben's bed and starts to read Ben's new favourite: Ben goes to the zoo and helps the zookeeper feed all the animals. It involves both Alex and Ben having to make lots of animal noises. Ben curls his little body around Alex and tucks his fists under his chin. Alex sees that he's struggling to keep his eyes open. He's got a crescent of thick, chestnut-coloured eyelashes weighing down his eyelids, and his skin is downy and plumped with the remnants of babyhood. Alex feels such a fierce desire to protect his only son and he simply cannot understand why Juliet can think for a single moment that he would allow her to deprive him of Ben. No. It will not happen. What Juliet has to realize is that he will always be one step ahead of her. He knows the way her mind works; he knows her strengths and her weaknesses. He knows that if he wants to he can get her back on smack with a click of his fingers and a few days of making her feel low enough. All that is required is for the temptation to be put in front of her and her own weakness of character will do the rest. The thing about Juliet is that when she touches rock-bottom she self-destructs. Eating disorders, drug addiction, fucking up her education, maybe even marrying him ... there's a distinct pattern to Juliet's behaviour over the years and Alex isn't sure that being mother to Ben is enough to alter it. He could be wrong; and if he is, well he's got a plan B, just in case.

Alex is halfway through the story and Ben shifts onto his back and draws his knees up to his tummy. 'Daddy, want Mummy. Got a tummy ache.'

'Mummy's not well, Ben. She's in bed.'

'Want Mummy. Tummy hurts. Da-deeee ...' Ben's voice increases in volume and shrillness. 'Pleeeeeeese, Da-deeeeeee.'

'Ben, shhh. I'm here. What would you like? A glass of water?

Shall I rub your tummy?' Alex pulls back the duvet and places his hand on Ben's abdomen and starts to rub lightly.

'Get off, Daddy. It hurts. Want Mummy.' Alex places the back of his hand on Ben's forehead. It's warm, but not overly so.

'Ben, it's OK. You've probably had too many crisps and Cokes. Too much excitement. Would you like me to get Granny?'

'Noooo. Granny smells.'

'No she doesn't.'

'She does, Daddy. She smells like you do after you've drunk that brown wizzy stuff. Want Mummy. Please ...' Ben starts to cry.

'Ben, you can't have Mummy. What did I tell you? She's not well. Understand?'

He throws his head back onto the pillow and sobs convulsively as if his heart is about to break. 'Ben, for goodness sake. There's nothing wrong with you. Just *stop* it now. Do you want Daddy to smack you?'

'Noooo,' Ben cries shrilly. 'Don't, Daddy. You're not to smack me. You're naughty to smack.' Ben lifts his hand out from under the duvet and smacks Alex. Alex catches hold of his wrist and squeezes a fraction too hard. 'Owwww,' Ben shrieks. 'You hurt me, Daddy.'

The door pushes open and Alex looks up to see Juliet standing in the opening. 'Alex? What's going on? What's wrong with Ben?'

'Mummy ... Daddy said he's going to smack me. Don't want Daddy – I want you, Mummy.'

'Daddy's not going to smack you. *Are* you Alex?' Juliet walks gingerly over to Ben's bed and sits down. She winces as the bed makes contact with her bruised body. She doesn't look at Alex but takes hold of Ben's hand. 'It's OK, Ben. Mummy's here. Now what's the matter? Aren't you feeling well?'

'Too much junk food and over-excitement.'

'And whose fault is that, I wonder?' Juliet feels Ben's forehead. 'He's fine. He hasn't got a temperature.'

'And you'd know?'

Alex sighs heavily and squeezes his hands into fists and then releases his fingers and stretches them out. 'Mummy, what's happened to your head?' Ben asks. He reaches out and puts his little fingers on the newly formed scab. 'Ouch, Mummy.'

Juliet stares at Alex as she answers. 'Clumsy Mummy knocked her head on the cupboard door.'

'Silly Mummy.'

'You can leave us now.' Juliet's voice is low but authoritative. It's not a request. It should be Juliet who wears the defeat from this battle, but Alex senses it is him. He just feels empty. He knows this feeling. It's the post-adrenalin come down. He bends over Ben and kisses the top of his head. 'OK, big man. Sleep well. Don't forget we're going to see your cousins in Scotland. We'd better have you feeling OK for that.'

Juliet looks at Alex as if he has completely taken leave of his senses. She turns to Ben: 'I'm just going to get some medicine for you, darling. You just lie there quietly and I'll be back in a moment.'

Once outside Ben's bedroom door she hisses at Alex: 'You really are something else. You seriously think going to Scotland is an option? After what you've done? Look at me, Alex. Look at my face. Is this what you want your sister to see? I'm not going. And neither is Ben.'

'You'll do as you're told.'

'You can't break me. No matter what you do to me. You can't break me, Alex Miller.'

'We'll see,' he says, and then he walks away. She waits until he has gone down the stairs, and listens for the sound of doors opening and closing, of the muffled conversations between mother and son and the general clicks and bangs of people moving around. Then she goes back up the stairs to the bedroom to find something for Ben.

13

Alex finishes off restacking the dishwasher, sighing at his mother's inability to arrange everything in its correct place. 'I'm beginning to wonder if it wasn't the stuffing after all.' Geraldine says, placing a cup of coffee in front of Alex. Instant. He can't drink it. The only reason they keep a jar is for the daily. He pours it down the sink when Geraldine isn't looking and makes himself an espresso.

'Sorry?'

'Well it's probably a bug if Ben's gone down with it too. I hope we don't get it. Be awful not to be able to go to Lucinda's, but we wouldn't want to give it to them. Not with such a young baby in the house.'

'It'll be fine.' Alex is surprised that Ben's gone down with a dose of diarrhoea. When he went to check on him last night, his bed was empty so he went upstairs to find he'd gone to bed with Juliet. And so Alex had spent most of the night in his study and then eventually tried to get some sleep in Ben's small single bed. This morning he'd taken Juliet a cup of tea and a piece of toast and marmalade, and a boiled egg and soldiers for Ben. Breakfast in bed as a treat for them both. But Ben was sitting on the loo whining and still complaining of bad tummy pains.

'He's been ill all night,' Juliet said. 'I'm really worried about him. If he doesn't get any better he'll have to see a doctor.' Her voice was still rasping, as if she was going down with a bad sore throat.

'If he needs to go, I'll take him,' Alex said, and placed the breakfast tray on the bed beside Juliet. She ignored it.

'You're worried a doctor might wonder how I got this?' She

pointed to the bruise on her cheek and the gash on her head. Alex walked over to her and took a large lock of her hair in his hand. Then he twisted it so that she had to lean her head towards him.

'I said I'll take him. Understand?'

'Yes, Alex.'

Alex once again felt the surge of something almost comfortingly familiar. 'Eat your toast, you barely had anything yesterday. And I've brought Ben an egg. Anything else I can get you?'

'Ben shouldn't eat anything and I'm not hungry.'

And so he'd come down to report on the absence of his wife and son at breakfast. 'Ben's still feeling ill, and Juliet had a really nasty fall in the bathroom. She slipped on the wet tiles. They're lethal. I'm thinking of getting them changed. She's feeling a bit fragile – battered and bruised – but she's going to join us for lunch.'

'Oh, goodness me. Poor darling. Is she all right?'

'She'll be fine, just a bit knocked about.'

'Do you think I might go upstairs and just see if there's anything I can do?' Geraldine asks.

'No thanks, Mum. They're both resting. I said I'd give them a couple of hours and check on them after that.'

'I just feel there should be something I can do to help. Perhaps the ironing …'

'Sure. That would be great.' Alex is preoccupied with his own thoughts, as usual. In the past he's relied on the fact that Juliet's been too embarrassed to show off her bruises. She's used concealer make-up and the right clothes. But after yesterday he's worried that she'll go public. And if she does, it could ruin him. He's got to watch her very carefully to make sure he knows what her plans are. The thing about modern technology is that you can connect with the outside world in secret. Passwords, secure IDs and private browsing, search histories and all of that stuff which, if you don't know what you're doing, might be vulnerable to interception by someone. And you've also got to be really sure of who you're speaking to. Juliet's on the computer so much these days and Alex wonders if she really understands just how vulnerable she is. Anybody, really, could find out what she's talking about if they really wanted. Modern technology. Bloody dangerous.

'... Alex?'

'Sorry, Mum. Miles away. What did you say?'

'Would you like me to turn some of the leftovers into a soup? I don't suppose Juliet and Ben are hungry at the moment, but they might want something later on. And you and I will want some lunch. There's the turkey to deal with. Lots of meat left. Do you want to strip it? I could perhaps make a curry? You always used to love a turkey curry after Christmas, remember? Mind you, I do prefer goose, but it's no good for big numbers. I'm surprised Juliet didn't get a goose this year as there's only four of us. We could have had a pheasant. Forman's do those boned three- or four-bird roasts ...'

'Yes, Mum. Why don't you make a soup. And a curry ... whatever you think.'

'I think if I made a curry, we could take it up to Scotland with us, but then they might be sick of it. Do you suppose they will have had turkey? I must remember to ask Lucinda next time I speak to her. Will you be speaking to her, darling? You'll want to let her know about Juliet and Ben, won't you?'

Alex finishes his third espresso. His hands are shaking, but then so are his mother's, so it's quite funny, really, the passing of the cups. Rattle, rattle ... Of course both of them pretend not to notice. Geraldine would probably pass it off as possible Parkinson's. Not that she's ever been a hypochondriac. If anything, quite the reverse. No, she's not physically fragile, but the old whisky bottle hasn't done her any favours. Nor the gin bottle, or the vodka bottle, or the sherry bottle ... His mother has largely shown a preference for spirits, but then she is 'old school'. As she has often told him in a post-rationalization sort of way, they didn't really drink wine 'in their day' unless it was a very special occasion – and always with food. 'No,' Geraldine says, 'we didn't have wine. We had a whisky, or a gin and tonic, not like you young who always seem to have a bottle of wine on the go.'

Juliet usually has a bottle of wine on the go. But he doesn't think she hits the bottle during the day. Not when she's looking after Ben. She's an after-he's-gone-to-bed-treat sort of drinker. Alex is more like his mother. And he supposes that if she really is an alcoholic, in that old school sort of way, then he has the genetic propensity to join her. Yes, he's drinking heavily. But what the hell? He could be on some bloody awful, mind-numbing antidepressants. And who wouldn't need a fucking drink with a wife like Juliet? Part of the problem, Alex thinks, is that she got used to having too much control when he was posted away. She had control of the money, she paid the bills, looked after their quarters if anything went wrong. So, yeah, she was a single parent making all the decisions. But that was when he was away. When he came back it was only natural that he should take charge again. And he was the one earning the money, the breadwinner, so why would she have a problem with that? She had an allowance for her clothes and stuff – and Ben's – and if there was anything special she wanted she only had to ask him. He *liked* to dress her. She was lucky – most women would kill for a man who'd shop with them. It gave him a kick to get her in the changing room with a whole load of stuff that he'd picked out for her and just sit down in a comfortable chair and watch the floor show. He liked to see her in stuff that showed off her figure – tight, stretchy, well cut. She'd always had a great body, and pregnancies hadn't ruined it, thank God. She was lucky. She didn't know how lucky. They'd sort this out. He'd buy her something nice to cheer her up, and the Scottish break would do her good. A bit of clever make-up and the usual excuses and all would be fine, especially if his mother would just shut the fuck up and stop getting on his bloody nerves about the frigging turkey. 'Yeah, Mum. Make a curry. If there's anything you need you can always pop down to the Indian corner shop, can't you?'

'It's a shame about little Ben. I was hoping to be able to take him up to the park. Let's hope they're both feeling a bit better. But Alex, there's something I've been meaning to ask you, darling.'

'Oh?'

'Yes. This house, the job ... You are happy here, aren't you? Everything is OK between you and Juliet? I know it's none of my business, but you know how mothers worry, and of course I do feel a bit responsible having helped out financially, but do you think you would have been happier in the country? I suppose the good thing is that it's a very sound investment. Even if you stay here for two to three years you're bound to make money. And then you could move out and buy something very nice. Be healthy for Ben wouldn't it, to be in the country when he's a bit older?'

'Perhaps.' Alex does not want to have this conversation. He's got enough on his mind without having to discuss their life plan for the next five years.

'I know that Juliet's set her heart on St Paul's, and that he's down for Colet Court if he's clever enough. I worry you know, about this hot-housing sort of stuff. Choosing schools for children before you know what they're going to be like. That's precisely the mistake your father and I made with you. Not that I had much say in it.'

'Perhaps it's not so much the school, but the people in it. Anyway, Mum, I've got things to be getting on with. So if you don't mind I'll just disappear for an hour or so. Feel free to iron, won't you?'

Before he goes into his study, Alex picks up Juliet's laptop and charger and takes it upstairs. She's dressed and her hair looks tidy, but she hasn't put any make-up on so the bruises are obvious.

She's lying on the bed beside Ben. Ben is curled up under the cover, looking pale. 'Daddy,' he says. 'Got a tummy ache. Mummy says it's your fault for letting me have all that Coca-Cola and crisps yesterday. Naughty Daddy.'

'How's it feeling now, big man?' Alex sits down on the bed next to Ben and strokes his hair. 'You'll learn that in life everything good comes with a consequence, doesn't it, Mummy?' he says to Juliet.

'If you say so,' she says coldly.

'I've brought you your laptop,' Alex says.

She looks surprised. That's because it's a way of contacting the outside world, of letting people know what he's done to her. She would have expected him to deprive her of it if he was going to keep her prisoner. But Alex has a way of playing his game – good cop, bad cop. That way it's much more unsettling to the victim because they never know what they're going to get, which means they can't predict and plan. Basic stuff.

'I think we need to get Ben to a doctor, Alex.'

'It's a bank holiday. The surgery'll be shut.'

'Well then I should take him to casualty.'

'No. He'll be fine. Now put some make-up on, you look awful. Mum's making some soup for lunch. You can come down for it.'

'I don't want to.'

'Yes, you do.'

'Well, if it's an order, Alex,' she says, weakly.

'Juliet …' Alex says softly. 'I don't give orders, silly girl. I just suggest what's best for you. You know that.' He watches her, reading her, wanting affirmation that she will do as he says.

'Whatever you want.'

'That's the ticket.'

There was a time when he used to experience shame and disgust at himself, a deep self-loathing at what he was capable of doing to her. Maybe that was when he still had feelings. Feelings,

Alex had learned, only led to weakness; let feelings get in the way and you were finished. They had to be squashed, obliterated, so that he could function effectively. They were an unnecessary encumbrance which only served to get in the way of getting the job done. What feelings could you afford to have if you were blowing up a Taliban stronghold and you couldn't know for sure whether they would be using a human shield of women and children? What feelings could you afford to have when you saw the aftermath of what you'd just done? The shredded lifeless mess of bits that were once people. No. Feelings were an indulgence and once you rid yourself of them you could finally be in control – not only of yourself, but of those around you. What use was guilt? You couldn't go back and change the things that you'd done, so why carry regret and shame? You were doing your job, following orders, using your training, acting like a true professional. Feelings … fucking waste of time. Not that he didn't feel love. That was different. He did love Juliet. He wouldn't treat her the way that he did if he didn't love her. Because then he wouldn't care and there would be no point in trying to get her to change, to behave in the way that he wished. He just wanted her to understand him. Not to wind him up, or challenge him. And if she thought she stood the smallest chance of duping him, or beating him, she was a very foolish and reckless woman.

* * *

Juliet is surprised that Alex has brought her laptop upstairs, but she's desperate to get online because she needs advice urgently. Apart from Ben's comforting little half snuffles and half snores, the house is silent.

I am almost too ashamed to tell you what happened to me. It just makes me want to throw up. I feel so violated … so powerless ... so traumatized ... My husband tried to strangle me. I thought I was going to die. He tied me up and gagged me. He left me in the bedroom for hours and when he came back he raped me ... anally. I feel lucky to be alive. I don't know how to get away. I've never been so terrified in my life. I don't know what to do. Please help, anyone!

Posted by Sparrowhawk on 27-Dec-13 11.40 GMT

Please, you must run away. Get out of there. Call the police. Dial 999 now. Or else just grab your son and get out. You can get your stuff later – with a police escort. Your life is in danger. Just get out.

Posted by StopitNow 27-Dec-13 11:55 GMT

I can't ... He's watching me. He says he'll kill me if I leave. And he'll kill me if I get the police involved. I'll have to be clever. Somehow go when he's feeling off guard. I don't have any money of my own, and he'll make out I'm sick. That my son's at risk with me. I know what he's like. He's got friends in the right places. Dangerous friends. Oh God help me, I'm so bloody scared. I thought I could handle him. That maybe we could work it out. But after what's happened I don't think I can ever face him ... you know ... as a wife again. What was so terrifying was the fact that he didn't see me as even human. I need somewhere to run to and I don't know where.

Posted by Sparrowhawk on 27-Dec-13 12:04 GMT

You really must do as StopitNow says. Just call the forum helpline. They can tell you where to go. They'll help you. It might seem impossible and terrifying, but it's not. Think about yourself, and your little boy – before it's too late.

Posted by Pink Petal on 27-Dec-13 12:09 GMT

Be careful … If he's as dangerous as you think he is, will he follow you? Don't do anything rash. Just be careful you know exactly what to do and where to go so that he can't follow you. You should make a plan, and start collecting all your important documents together in case you need them.

Posted by Lil' Miss Happy on 27-Dec-13 12:20 GMT

Thank you for the support. Don't know what I'd do without you all. I just feel too vulnerable walking out with nothing. I think if I could plan a bit … maybe lull him into a false sense of security … then it might be safer to make a planned getaway. I need money. I need to find somewhere safe to stay. Maybe that's the time to get the police involved, when I actually walk out. I'm terrified that they might turn up and just give him a caution and then what would I do?

Posted by Sparrowhawk on 27-Dec-13 12:29 GMT

Listen my lovely … Do you have bruises? If he did all of that to you, there must be medical evidence. You need to be seen by a police surgeon as soon as possible so that it can all be recorded against him. Call the police and just don't hang around. Do it while you've still got chance … while you are still alive. I don't mean to be harsh, but you won't be any good to your son if you're dead, will you? I'm not being dramatic. Just look at the DV death rates.

Hugs and praying for you

Posted by StopitNow on 27-Dec-13 12:38 GMT

I completely understand that you feel reticent about going to the police. I went to them and they made me feel like shit. It's not a nice feeling – just being a kind of forensic object. And if he won't let you out of the house it sounds as if it might be impossible for you, anyway. If you like you could let me have your email address and and I'll do what I can to help. Just let the moderator know that you'd be happy to let me have it. I might be able to help you find somewhere safe for you and your little boy to stay. I just really want to help you if I can.

Posted by Lil' Miss Happy 27-Dec-13 12:49 GMT

I don't agree with you, Lil' Miss Happy. Ring the police. Or get the moderator to do it for you. That's the only way you'll be safe. They'll arrest him and protect you.

Posted by StopitNow on 27-Dec-13 13:03

OK then ... I'll tell you. My husband stripped me naked, took me out to his car, and then bent me over the bonnet before shoving a beer bottle up my p***y, just to show me he's the bloody boss. And other times he invited his mates round and watched while two of them raped me in turn. Men are animals. And the policemen didn't believe me. Do you know what they wrote on their reports? That I was a fantasist. They only started to believe me after he posted photographs on websites of me naked and spreadeagled on the living room floor. He also made me do phone sex to earn him some extra money. He'd listen in while the johns jerked off. The only way I could get through it was to tranquillize my brains out. Life wasn't worth living. I prayed to die it was so bad. I couldn't see any way out of it and the only way I did get out of it was to run away without letting anyone – and I mean anyone – know where I was going. He'd have had me sectioned – would have convinced everyone that I was mad. It was only after I'd gone, and I got a proper solicitor involved, that the police finally confiscated his computer and found all the sick images – not just of me, but of every other kind of filth you could imagine.

Posted by Lil' Miss Happy on 27-Dec-13 13.26

Leabharlanna Poibli Chathair Baile Átha Cliath

163 Dublin City Public Libraries

Oh My God ... You are amazing Lil' Miss Happy that you got away – and that you're strong enough to speak out. That you've still got fight inside you. These men are bastards. Animals. I can't believe how evil they can be. Now I understand why you don't have any faith in the police. To say you were unlucky sounds like the understatement of the century. I pray you are safe and OK now, and that you are happy as your 'name' suggests.

Love and hugs.

Posted by Sparrowhawk on 27-Dec-13 13:46

Juliet snaps the lid shut on her laptop, feeling nauseous. These stories are too much to take in, too much to stomach. How on earth do these women ever survive emotionally – even if the physical scars heal? Could Alex's violence really escalate to that level? But hell, what's she on about, what level of violence does it take to actually kill someone? A blow to the head in the right place could be *just one blow*. She knows she has no choice now. It's just a question of when, how and where. She will think over the offer from Lil' Miss Happy about the accommodation she might know about. It's risky, giving an email address out – but given what that woman went through, she's hardly likely to shit on a fellow victim of DV.

Ben wakes up with the sound of the lid closing. His cheeks are flushed. Juliet feels his forehead. It's hot and dry. His eyes have that feverish, glassy look. 'How's your tummy, darling?'

'It really hurts, Mummy.'

'Do you want to go to the loo again?'

'No.'

He's floppy and lethargic. 'Have a drink of water, darling.'

Ben shakes his head and whimpers quietly. He's shivering, so she pulls the duvet cover up around his chin. She's given him some Calpol so hopefully that should get his temperature down. But if it doesn't, somehow she'll have to make Alex realize he needs to be seen by a doctor. Reluctantly she decides to leave Ben and go downstairs to see what's going on between Geraldine and Alex. She wants Geraldine to see what Alex has done to her, even though she knows she will be devastated. Geraldine has to realise what her son's really like. She's already dressed in jeans and a warm sweater. She leaves the bedroom door slightly ajar and walks gingerly down the first flight of stairs. There's an overwhelming smell of curry drifting upwards. She pauses on the landing at the head of the flight of stairs to the ground floor and listens. She can't hear any voices. She pads on quietly down the stairs and sees that Alex's study door is half open. He isn't behind his desk. Then she turns towards the kitchen door which is closed. She doesn't hear anyone until her hand is already on the knob, twisting. It's a sort of half-grunt from Alex. She pushes the door open and both her husband and her mother-in-law look up. Geraldine has the newspaper folded on the crossword section, while Alex is reading what looks like a manual of some sort.

'Juliet …' Geraldine's eyes widen, and whatever she was about to say is choked off.

'Geraldine.' Juliet says.

'Oh my goodness. I …' Geraldine seems to be struggling with her words. Juliet turns to Alex. He is scowling at her. That's because she's ignored his instruction to cover up her bruises. Her left cheek is a livid red colour with blue edges, while her right cheek is a cool ivory. She has pulled her hair back into a pony tail, so that the gash on her head is clearly visible. Geraldine doesn't know where to look. 'Would you like some soup, dear?'

'Please.' Juliet walks to the fridge, takes out a stoppered bottle of white wine from the door, and gets a couple of glasses from the cupboard. 'Join me?' she says to Geraldine.

'I don't mind … if you are … How's Ben?'

'His tummy's still bad. Actually, I'm really worried about him.

He's got a temperature. I'd really like him to see a doctor, but Alex is in charge.' Juliet lets her fingers slip to her throat. She's wearing a V-necked sweater and so the marks on her neck are clearly visible. She watches Geraldine's eyes follow her fingers and then widen as she sees the evidence of her son's violence. She hands an overfull glass of wine to Geraldine and then raises her own glass. 'Good health, as they say,' she says, smiling.

Geraldine smiles back, hesitantly, and takes a large sip from her glass. Juliet notices her hands are shaking. 'You've been busy, Geraldine. Curry. Alex loves your turkey curry, don't you, Alex?' There is nothing that Alex hates more than turkey curry. He says it reminds him of the filthy, reconstituted ration packs they lived on in Afghan for weeks on end.

'Eat your soup, Juliet. It'll soothe your sore throat,' he says.

'These Christmas bugs. Always something going round,' Geraldine says awkwardly. 'Have some chilli sherry, dear, that'll help.' Juliet notices that she's already halfway through the glass of wine. Poor Geraldine. Juliet can't help but feel sorry for her. She doesn't know how to handle this.

'I hope you don't mind, dear, but I did the ironing. I thought it might help.'

'That's really sweet of you, Geraldine. But you shouldn't have. You are on holiday, after all. You're supposed to be having a break, not doing my housework.'

'I don't mind ...' There she goes again, Juliet thinks. Of course she doesn't bloody mind. She's had every shred of minding knocked out of her. That's what happens. You stop fucking minding any more. One step away from I don't care any more. Juliet takes a couple of slow, deep breaths as she feels her anger rising. She looks at the table, at the Christmas candle and the holly woven around it, and the coloured baubles that she attached so carefully with flower wire. She looks at the special Christmas napkins and the nativity scene in the window. She wants to smash it all. She wants to sweep every little bit of festive shit onto the floor and stamp all over it. She wants to screw the candle into Alex's mouth and shove it down his throat so he can know ... just a little ... what it feels like to be so powerless and helpless. To understand that from now on all she can do is hate and plot. The plate of soup sits untouched in front of her. She gets hold of the bottle of chilli sherry – made by Geraldine, naturally – and splashes it onto the soup. Then she picks up her spoon and stirs it, roughly, into the beige-coloured slop. She takes a spoonful and feels a weirdly appropriate satisfaction as it burns her mouth, and then her throat. She coughs as it hits her gullet and her eyes fill with tears. She looks at Alex through her tears, and then at Geraldine, then she picks up her wine glass and downs the whole thing before setting it back on the table so hard that the glass snaps off from its stem. Then she shoves her chair back from the table, letting the legs scrape over the floorboards, and walks out of the room.

* * *

Ben has been sick on Juliet's pillow, and it's got into his hair. She takes a tissue and gently wipes his curls. His eyes remain closed. 'Ben,' she murmurs. 'Ben, are you OK, darling? How are you feeling?' His eyelashes flutter like moth's wings and then open. He doesn't seem to be focussing on her.

'How's your tummy, darling?'

Ben groans, and then whines, 'Ooooouuw, Mummy.'

She doesn't hear Alex come in, but suddenly she is aware of him standing there, at the foot of the bed looking at them both. He moves to the side of the bed so that he can get closer to Ben. He grabs hold of Ben's hand and feels for his pulse. Juliet watches, wondering what the hell *he* knows. Then Alex lifts up Ben's eyelids. He feels his forehead.

'Juliet, he's burning up.'

'I know. I told you he had a temperature.'

'Start sponging him off. We need to get his temperature down. Where's it hurt, Ben?' Ben points to his lower abdomen, and to his right hip. 'It might be his appendix.' Alex punches numbers into his phone. 'Ambulance,' he snaps into the receiver, and then gives out their address, Ben's age, symptoms, Alex's relationship to patient. Oh, good for bloody Alex, Juliet thinks, like suddenly he's the perfect fucking father.

'Can you get him some clean pyjamas? A couple of teddies and books that he likes in case he's got to stay in hospital? And write down what medicine you've given him. Oh, and don't forget his toothbrush, toothpaste, hairbrush. Slippers, dressing gown. In a bag. Quick as you can.'

'Always so good at giving orders, aren't you?'

'Yes. Now hurry up.'

Juliet puts everything together in a holdall, and then goes back upstairs to the bedroom where Alex is still watching Ben. She starts throwing things into her handbag. Hairbrush, lipstick, iPad. Scent. Then she opens up the wardrobe and takes out a jacket.

'What are you doing?'

'Getting my stuff together, why?'

'You aren't coming with us.'

'Of course I am. He's *my* son. Alex, please ... be reasonable.'

'You will stay here with my mother. And *that* is an order.' He lowers his voice to a warning growl: 'And if you want me to force you, then I will. Understand?' For a moment she stands her ground, raising her chin defiantly, but the feral look on Alex's face reminds her too much of yesterday, of what he did to her, of what he is capable of. She drops her handbag.

'Fine. Have it your way.'

He nods. 'I'll call you and let you know what happens.' He bundles Ben up in a blanket and carries him gently downstairs.

Juliet follows with the bag of Ben's things. By the time they get to the bottom of the stairs, Geraldine – unable to hide her confusion – is opening the door to a pair of men in high-vis jackets. She stands aside as Alex pushes past her.

'Oh my goodness, what's going on. Alex? Juliet?' Juliet watches as the rear doors of the ambulance are opened up, and Ben is handed in. She expects Alex to climb in after him, but he doesn't. Then the doors are closed and the ambulance speeds off with its lights flashing. 'Why aren't you going with him?' she calls out to Alex. 'He's going to be petrified in there. What the hell are you doing?'

'I'm taking my car, and he's in good hands. Now go back inside before you make a spectacle of yourself!'

'Christ almighty,' Juliet swears aloud. 'Alex Miller. The perfect fucking father.' She watches his car drive away, following the screech of the ambulance's siren, and her fear for her son makes her feel sick.

Feeling defeated and both physically and mentally broken, Juliet closes the front door. She answers Geraldine's questions woodenly, shrugging her shoulders and spreading her hands out in a gesture of helplessness. 'Alex thinks it could be his appendix, though what the hell he knows about it...'

'He had to do a lot of medical training, didn't he? Poor, darling Ben. I thought it was food poisoning, or a bug. But appendicitis? Oh dear me. Poor lamb. Shouldn't you have gone too?' Juliet sits down at the kitchen table. She feels like bursting into tears and so she swallows hard. The fact that she hasn't gone with Ben cuts through her like a knife.

'Yes, I should. But Alex wouldn't let me.'

'Oh. A cup of tea?' Funny how people think a bloody cup of tea will put things right, Juliet thinks. She just shakes her head, ringing her hands together, taking deep breaths and trying to stop herself from crying.

'Look Juliet, I know it's none of my business. Actually it is my business. You are my family – you, Ben and Alex. It's obvious that something serious is going on – I mean apart from Ben. Otherwise you'd be with him. And those bruises, for heaven's sake tell me what's happened.'

Juliet's eyes well up. 'Honestly, Geraldine, right now the only think I can think about is Ben. I should be with him. He'll be so afraid if I'm not there. How could Alex be so cruel? Christ, he didn't even go with Ben in the ambulance.'

'I'm sure he only thinks he's doing what's best.' Geraldine says weakly.

'What's best? That's almost funny, Alex doing what's best. He beat me up, Geraldine. First he tried to strangle me, and then he beat me up, if you really want to know.' Juliet isn't ready to tell her mother-in-law about the other stuff. A sob escapes. 'I guess he's just like his father, isn't he?' she chokes on the words.

'But Alex ... I can't believe it ... he's not violent ... he can't be ... please don't tell me he is ... I have to ask this. Did you ... in any way ... provoke him?'

'You mean did I ask for it? For Christ's sake, Geraldine.' The shock on Geraldine's face serves only to encourage Juliet to continue. It's like she can lash out at her instead of Alex. 'You told me that Alex's father was violent towards you. Did *you* ask for it? You told me that Alex even tried to intervene.'

Geraldine is crying now. She tears off a piece of kitchen roll and blows her nose. 'It must be the Army. I can't believe ... I mean the fact that he was away at school, I believed he was safe there.'

'Geraldine, you know what happened to Alex at school, *don't you*?' Juliet asks gently.

Geraldine is shaking her head, turning away from Juliet to concentrate on the kettle and tea bags and two china mugs.

'He got buggered senseless by the headmaster.'

'NO!' Geraldine chokes on the word. 'That's not true, Juliet!'

'It *is* true, Geraldine. He used to be called in to see the headmaster. He would ask him to take down his trousers. And then he would ask him to take down his pants. And then do you know what happened next? He would go behind Alex and start stroking his buttocks. And then he would take hold of Alex ... he would take hold of Alex and then he would bugger him. And Alex had no one to tell. NO ONE.'

'I don't believe you.'

'It's true. And you do believe me. You know it.' Geraldine is sobbing. Juliet is sorry for her. She goes over to her and stands behind her and places her hands on Geraldine's shoulders. 'It's OK. I understand. It wasn't your fault. It was the fault of circumstances. I dare say he wasn't the only boy in the school. Your son is a tortured soul. A dying soul. He has had all the humanity stripped out of him.'

'What are you going to do?'

'Oh, I don't know. I'm certain that he's suffering from post-traumatic stress disorder – combat stress. I've read that if you've had some kind of trauma in your childhood then you're much more susceptible to it. Something to do with the wiring in your brain going wrong. But he won't get help because to do so would be to admit that he's weak, that he needs somebody else's help. And maybe he's just too terrified of what might come out if he was made to go to counselling; everything that he's locked away for all these years. I think that's a lot of his problem. It was all right while he was so busy fighting other people, and it's sort of OK while he's got me to fight, but without that the only one left to fight is himself.

'The reason he didn't want me to go to hospital is because people would see my bruises. Honestly, Geraldine, the pain of being separated from Ben like this is worse than being physically beaten. But if I go there, if I defy him, I'm scared of what he'll do. I am desperate. I just feel so alone and frightened.' She is crying and barely able to speak any more. 'I've got to go upstairs ...' she says between sobs. 'Sorry ...' She runs upstairs to the privacy of her bedroom where at last she allows her tears to fall.

Juliet has tried to call Alex's mobile but it went straight to voicemail. Another way to torture her. Really, there's nothing to stop her getting into her car and going straight to the hospital. Nothing at all, except being scared of what Alex might do to punish her. In the meantime she must make use of the time that he's out of the house to try and do something positive, to start making plans. She sends a direct message to the forum moderator, asking her to pass on Juliet's private email address to Lil' Miss Happy. She brushes away the thought that she could be a nutter. But what alternative does she have? She could go on to the internet and look for properties to rent but that would mean getting references – bank references and so forth – all of which would be time consuming and could lead Alex to track her down. She needs money. Maybe she could pawn some jewellery – sell it, even. Not that she had much of any value. Alex had some hideously ostentatious diamond cufflinks that had been given to him by some grateful and wealthy Arab, so those could go. He wouldn't even miss them. And she could flog the car – except it's registered in Alex's name, so she probably can't. Maybe she's stuck with the car because even if she buys another – some old heap of a thing – she'll still have to get insurance and that all means that she's traceable. Basically, if you stay legal, you can't disappear. And if she goes down the illegal route, she risks being arrested and having Ben taken away from her. So she doesn't have any choice. If she gets somewhere remote and safe, she needs a car – she needs *the* car. So the main thing, then, is money and transport. Oh, and somewhere she and Ben can live.

Documents, isn't that what Lil' Miss Happy said? Make sure you've got all your important documents with you. Things like her and Ben's birth certificates, passports, her national insurance number – NHS numbers – God, what else had certificates and numbers? She has to make sure that whatever she does, there is no trail left for Alex to follow. Maybe that's why women went to the special refuges, because they were the only places where you could be guaranteed complete safety.

What Juliet must keep reminding herself of is the fact that she hasn't done anything wrong. She is the innocent party here. She just needs to convince other people that she needs protection from her own husband.

The telephone rings. 'Alex?' she says straight away.

'Yeah. The doctor thinks it could be his appendix. They're doing blood tests, and it'll be a while before they get the results. So I'll just have to wait here.'

'How's he feeling?' Juliet feels that she's being eaten up inside; poor little Ben, her baby.

'He's very poorly.'

'Is he asking for me?' She listens to the moment's hesitation, the silence on the line between them. 'He is, isn't he? I want to come, Alex. I promise I'll put some make-up on – you know what I mean.'

'Wait there. I'll call you when I know more.'

'But I …' the line goes dead. Juliet growls into the mouthpiece: 'Fuck you!'

She Googles appendicitis in childhood and a list of sites appears. Juliet is good at speed-reading through stuff, scrolling down to pull out what's relevant. She learns that fever, vomiting and stomach ache around the navel and perhaps spreading to the right are common signs of appendicitis. She learns that the appendix is a hollow, finger-shaped appendage in the bowel, and that it can become infected. In severe cases the infection can become so bad that it bursts. She learns that there are ways of removing the appendix which are either keyhole, using two or three holes, or a conventional surgical cut. She learns that a burst appendix is potentially life threatening as it explodes its poison into the abdominal cavity. She also learns that one must not administer medicine for constipation, because it increases the likeliness of the appendix bursting.

So she may have put Ben's life in danger by giving him the laxative. *Oh my God*. But how the hell was she to know? It was supposed to be gentle, vegetable-based, natural – and should have done him no harm. OK, she might have given him a teeny bit more than the recommended dose, but that was just to make it look as though he had a touch of the squits, so that she could reinforce the idea of the Christmas bug and wriggle out of the trip to Scotland. But she couldn't possibly have guessed that she'd be threatening her beloved Ben with a burst appendix. Poor darling, and all the time his little tummy was getting more and more sore, and he was really quite seriously ill. Because she feels in need of a 'group hug' she sends a message to the forum:

My little boy has had to go into hospital, an emergency, because he's got a suspected burst appendix. I'm so worried I'm beside myself. And in case you're wondering why I'm not there at his bedside, that's because my OH told me I wasn't allowed to go. Why? – because the medical staff might wonder how I got so many bruises. I've been told I can visit tomorrow if I put my extra-special make-up party face on. I expect lots of you know what I mean by that. Heavy-duty concealer, out with the BB cream again. The funny thing is he's usually so careful not to hit me on the face – must be losing his touch. Sorry about the black humour, but sometimes it's the only way to keep myself from crying. I wonder how I ever got into this life and I can't see any way out of it. I keep thinking about the other people out there – the normal people – and I guess they just don't realize how lucky they are. Hugs and hope you're all having a better day than me.

Posted by Sparrowhawk 27-Dec-13 15.45

*   *   *

The afternoon is dragging its feet and she doesn't feel like going downstairs and facing Geraldine, partly because she is now beginning to feel guilty about upsetting her. It's not her fault that Alex is the way he is. She sees herself in Geraldine – the fear, the inability to escape, the powerlessness to control her life. And now Geraldine has her freedom and her money, and her family to enjoy in her old age. A son she should feel able to be proud of and grateful for, and her precious grandchildren that she can watch blossom and grow, and presumably feel content that the next generation is secure. And Juliet has ruined her happiness, such as it was, she has shattered her belief that everything was all right, and that history was *not* repeating itself through her son. So will Ben turn out like Alex, Juliet wonders, in the same way that Alex has turned into his father? Is it flawed parenting that does the damage, or is it flawed genes? If Geraldine had escaped from her abuser, would Alex have been different? Juliet has to believe that it would have saved him, otherwise how can she change Ben's destiny? She has no alternative but to get him away from Alex, to break the cycle and save Ben from his father's malign influence.

She lies on the bed and thinks of all the things she needs to do until eventually the light seeps from the sky and the street lights herald the arrival of evening. Juliet's limbs are stiffening up as the bruising begins to show, and so she stretches carefully and painfully before getting up and heading downstairs where she finds Geraldine dozing in the armchair beside a dying fire. Her mouth is wide open and there's a thin line of dribble escaping down her chin. She looks small and vulnerable, and once again Juliet feels guilty at causing her more hurt and worry when she's already had half a lifetime's worth. Juliet chucks a couple of small logs onto the fire and Geraldine stirs and opens her eyes. She seems disorientated, and when she focuses on Juliet she thinks she sees a brief look of something akin to fear. 'I must have dozed off. I hope you don't mind, I lit the fire. It was getting rather chilly.'

'Good idea.' Juliet moves around the room, switching on the lamps, looking out of the window and seeing everyone's twinkly Christmas tree lights in their windows before she draws the curtains, thinking about the time they are all having in their perfect families. 'I'll make us a cup of tea,' Juliet says, and then returns a few minutes later with tea and a slice of Christmas cake for each of them.

'Any news?' Geraldine asks.

'Alex called. He said they were waiting for blood tests. It just seems incredible to think of Ben there, in hospital, scared and in pain and I can't be with him.'

'Alex said you'd had a fall. Couldn't you say that, if anyone asks?'

'I'm used to telling those sorts of lies. I expect you were pretty good at it too. The cupboard door, a fall – people must think I'm really clumsy.'

'I can't tell you how painful it is for me to see you like this; to know that Alex is capable of doing this to you. He's my son and I love him, of course, but to know now … that he's like his father … that you have to go through what I went through.' Geraldine's shoulders lift and sink as she takes a sigh that seems likely to burst into a sob at any moment. She shakes her head and puts her hand to her mouth as if she is fighting the urge to vomit. 'It's almost too much to take in. I thought he was all right … different, you know. I was so proud of him; but to know that he could do this …'

Juliet feels so badly for Geraldine that she can hear the words forming inside her mind: 'It's not that bad ... I provoked him ... he's not normally like this ... he'll never do it again ...' All of which would be lies. She sits down on the chair nearest to Geraldine and speaks gently.

'His experiences on tour, the things he saw, the things he had to deal with ... Something's broken. He's just not Alex any more.'

Geraldine is nodding. 'So what are you going to do?'

'I don't know – leave, I guess. I don't think I can do anything else. I'm afraid – and please don't think I'm being melodramatic, because I'm not – but I'm afraid if I stay he might kill me. I'm also afraid that if I leave he'll be so angry that he'll kill me anyway. Christ, Geraldine, I don't know what to do. It's as if he barely recognizes me any more. In his mind I seem to have become dehumanized, like this is a war and I'm the enemy.'

She has a momentary flashback to after he'd raped her, to when she'd pleaded with him to come back to her, to look at her, to realize who she was, but he had that dead-eyed stare that showed he wasn't seeing her at all. Perhaps in his ravaged mind he was getting his own back on that headmaster all those years ago. Another of his wars. Who knows?

'So I have to get away. And I don't have any money, and I don't have anywhere to go.'

'If there was something I could do to help ... to make things better for you all ...'

'I believe I'd be an unfit mother if I let Ben grow up with Alex's influence, like this. I can't allow Ben to turn into Alex, in the same way that Alex has turned into his father. I want Ben to grow up happy and unafraid. I don't want him to have to stand between Alex and me. I don't want him to have to witness ... God forbid, Alex murdering his mother. I can't think what else to do. Staying here, letting things go on as they are isn't an option. I mean, just look at me, Geraldine.'

Geraldine coughs, and then Juliet realizes it isn't a cough at all, but a big, choking sob. 'Oh my God. What have I done? What have I created? It's all my fault. I should have done something. I should have left. I thought I was doing the right thing, keeping the family together –'

'But you were scared. It was too difficult ... and you didn't have access to any money, so you were trapped, like a prisoner ... like me.'

Juliet lets her words sink in. She needs to give Geraldine time to think, to feel the guilt and the responsibility. Juliet *needs* Geraldine to come up with the solution all by herself, so that she doesn't feel that Juliet has coerced her into it; and Geraldine needs to feel that by helping Juliet she is somehow assuaging her own conscience, making amends for all the things that she didn't do as a mother but that she can now do as a grandmother. Not for Juliet, but for Ben. As the silence lengthens between them, Juliet prays that Alex doesn't choose to telephone now. Everything hangs on what Geraldine is thinking, and what she chooses to do.

'You really think that's the only solution – to leave him?'

'I can't think of anything else to do. And it's not safe to do nothing.' Juliet thinks that this would be the moment to cry. She needs Geraldine's sympathy and support. She needs to appear as vulnerable and desperate on the outside as she feels on the inside. She lets her eyes fill and then, as the tears begin to overflow onto her cheeks, she sits on the floor in front of Geraldine's chair. 'Will you help us, Geraldine? *All* of us. Will you help save your son and your grandson?'

'Of course I will. Although – God help me – I feel I'm betraying Alex ...'

'You mustn't think that. You're not. You're helping him, Geraldine. It's like this is his last chance. And you're doing it for Ben. You're breaking the cycle. It's up to us, Geraldine, it's up to us women to make it better, to make them better. It will be the kindest thing you've ever done for him.'

'What do you need?'

'I need somewhere to stay with Ben, while Alex gets himself sorted out. Somewhere he can't find us until he's had treatment, when I can be sure he's better … and safe.'

'How much money do you need?'

'Ten thousand pounds.'

'That much?'

'I'll need to place a deposit on a rental property. I'll need money for a lawyer, to set up the legal process to protect us … And then there'll be bills to pay. Maybe ten thousand won't be enough, I don't know. But just remember that we're doing this not just for Alex, but for Ben too.'

'I'll sort it for you. I just hope you know what you're doing, Juliet. That this really is the right thing to do. In spite of everything, he's still my son.'

'I know,' Juliet says soothingly. 'And my husband. We both love him, and we're doing the right thing. We're going to ensure that he gets help.' She takes hold of Geraldine's hand and gives it a reassuring squeeze. 'We need to try and get the real Alex back. Trust me, Geraldine. It'll all be OK. Promise.'

* * *

Alex sits in the waiting room, elbows resting on his knees, fists clenched together, the muscles in his forearms stiff with tension. There are other people in the room, but Alex is so deeply buried in his own head that he is unaware of them. At first he was able to do a few essential bits and pieces on his iPhone, but the longer Ben is in surgery, the harder it becomes to focus on anything other than him. His son. Helpless, frail, so young and so small and so vulnerable. He feels empty; so empty it's as if his innards have been scraped out of him. It is extraordinary how much pain the body can suffer despite the fact that there is no visible, physical injury. But the injury inside – the emotional injury – stays with you always. OK, sometimes it might lie dormant and manageable for a while, and you might even begin to believe that it's *safely* filed away with no pain memory, like physical pain. But it's not. It never will be completely healed because it can flare up again without warning, and when it does, it devours you. Alex thinks it's possible he might have moaned aloud, but when he opens his eyes and looks at the strangers across the room, still wrapped up in themselves, it is clear that his despair remains invisible to the outside world, still locked inside himself. He checks the time. Ben has been in surgery for forty-five minutes. Alex knows something isn't right. It's too long … But just as he stands up, not really knowing what he's going to do, but needing to do something, even if it's only to pace up and down the corridor, a young woman registrar comes towards him. 'Mr Miller?'

'Yes. How is he? Is he all right?' Alex is reading her face intently. Is she about to give him the worst news of his life? He's expecting it. His worst nightmare, every sinew in his body is tensed, waiting to hear what she's going to tell him.

'He's fine. He's in recovery. And he's sleeping. We're happy with his progress. Would you like to come and see him?'

Alex stands over the bed. There are tubes and monitors everywhere and Ben looks so very small and defenceless. His blond curls are sticking to his head, but his skin colour looks healthy – far healthier than it did earlier. Alex bends over him and places a light kiss on his forehead. Ben smells of antiseptic and starched linen, and vaguely of vomit. His chest lifts and settles reassuringly; there's a heart beating soundly, blood flowing through his veins, oxygen feeding his cells. He is alive. Christ! He's alive!

And yet Alex's head is feeling all wrong; sick, faint, unfocussed. Ill. He has to get out. 'Sorry … I have to go …' he murmurs to the duty nurse as he strides past her. He rushes for the exit, and has to wait while security opens the door for him. Outside it is raining, pissing it down. Alex is wearing just a thin shirt and jeans but he doesn't feel the biting wind, or the icy temperature. He's numb. Numb is good. Alex climbs into his car. He fires up the engine and noses onto the road. He drives towards home, but he doesn't want to go home. He needs somewhere else to go … somewhere where he can breathe … where he can be alone … somewhere quiet. Christ, somewhere he can have some fucking peace. Some rest. Some respite from himself. But he has to take himself with him. He puts his foot down, racing towards the M4, not caring about speed traps or traffic police, not caring about anything other than wanting to get the fuck away from the voices in his head. His father's voice: 'You miserable little specimen, you stupid little excuse for a boy.' Naughty. Bad. Stupid. Useless. Ashamed … yes, that's it … his father was ashamed of him. Why? Because Alex pleaded with him not to be sent back to school. Aged eleven, Alex actually begged. 'Please, Daddy, don't send me back. I hate it …' And his father telling him: 'Be a man, face up to it and don't be a little coward.' And then when his mother intervened, his father telling him: 'It's good for him, character-building. Knock some spine into the snivelling little idiot.'

And sir. Oh yes, sir. 'Come in here, Miller. I hear you've been inattentive in class, Miller. I see your test results are not up to scratch. Not good enough, Miller! Know what I'm going to do to you Miller?'

Alex tightens his grip on the wheel and speeds faster, the needle hitting 105 mph. The road is almost clear, with vast gaps between himself and the next pair of lights in the rear-view mirror. He should feel like the king of the road, but instead he feels like he's imprisoned. He thinks he will never, ever escape, and the sense of helplessness is so utterly overwhelming that he can't think clearly … just 'Please, sir, please sir … no … sir, it hurts … please … STOP, sir … please …' And then afterwards the filthy old bastard would sit Alex on his knee and try and calm his sobs. 'There, there … it wasn't so bad, was it? Our little secret. Don't you ever tell or I'll kill you, understand?'

'Kill you. Kill you. Kill you …' over and over and over in his head as he glides down the motorway. What if? What if he just twisted the steering wheel the slightest degree to the right, what if the car crashed into the central reservation at 110 miles an hour? He sees it hitting the barrier, he hears the explosion of metal against concrete, the car flying into the air, somersaulting over and over and then coming to rest. The car smashed, his body inside smashed. But what if he survived? Injured, helpless … no, not the way to do it. It would need to be controlled.

At the next exit he leaves the westbound lane and turns around to head back to London. Slower, now. The tears are beginning to flow. The adrenalin is fading, he reckons. He hates himself; no, hate is not strong enough. He despises himself so much that he doesn't know how he can live with himself. His head is now filled with Juliet and what he did to her. The tears flow faster and heavier so that he has to wipe them away. His nose is running. Weak. Look at him, a snivelling, weak little coward. He doesn't want to think about what he did to her. It wasn't him. He was somebody else. Sir, his father, anyone – please let it be anyone other than himself. He couldn't do something like that. But he *did*. He *did* do it and there's no taking it back. Another moment of madness in his life to add to all the others. She will go, he realizes that. And she'll take Ben. And then he will be left with nothing but himself. He laughs to himself – through his tears – as he thinks of the phrase, the cliché, a fate worse than death. Yes, it fits – a fate worse than death.

Juliet has checked her emails at least half a dozen times but still nothing from Lil' Miss Happy. And she's also tried to call Alex several times. Eventually she calls the children's ward at the hospital and asks if they've had a Benjamin Miller admitted. At first the nurse on the other end is cagey, no doubt wondering why a mother wouldn't know where her own son is. Juliet explains that it was all a bit of an emergency, that she's returned home from a visit and her husband couldn't get hold of her, and now she can't contact her husband on his mobile. She gives Ben's date of birth, the name of his GP, his symptoms and eventually the nurse confirms that yes, Ben is there. 'He's had an emergency appendectomy and he's back on the ward, but he's still drowsy from the anaesthetic. Yes, his father was there, but now she doesn't know where he is.

Much as Juliet is desperate to go to the hospital, she's too scared of Alex and what he might do to her. He might tie her up again, or even keep her locked in their room so that she'd be completely at his mercy. He's just so bloody unpredictable. She has no alternative, even though it breaks her heart, but to wait at home until he deigns to speak to her. All night long she lies awake, fully dressed on top of the bed, in case he should call, and so that she's ready to leave at a moment's notice. And she tries to stop herself from wondering how Ben is feeling, scared and in pain in a strange place, without his mother by his side to comfort him.

It's seven a.m. when her phone finally rings.

'Alex! Why the hell didn't you call me?'

'The battery on my phone was dead.'

'I just wish I was there. I just want to hold him,' Juliet's voice catches. 'I should be there. How is he?'

'The surgeon said everything was fine.'

'And how long will he have to stay in hospital?'

'I'm not sure – three or four days. I expect he's going to be feeling quite sore.

'Where the hell have you been? I hope you stayed with him ... You did, didn't you? You didn't leave him all alone in there?"

She hears Alex sigh. 'Look I'll be home soon, OK? I've got to go.'

Juliet puts the phone down and leans against the bedroom wall for a moment. Her legs feel weak and shaky. She's not sure how much more emotional and physical turmoil she can deal with. She can't bear the thought of Alex returning home without Ben. Her son has had an operation and she wasn't even there. She should have been at his side. Alex could have called her. He could have asked to use a telephone to let her know what was going on. This was just one more way that he could torment and punish her.

* * *

Colours don't have language barriers. Instructions, descriptions, conversations, these all need interpreters, but anything visual is universal. That's why the directions to the various hospital departments are colour coded, with corresponding arrows and lines marking the route out like underfoot rainbows. Colours have associations and identities that everyone can relate to. It doesn't matter if you don't speak the language because everyone knows the language of colour. Blood. There is nothing that crosses the boundaries of race and creed like blood. Skin, hair, eyes, language, culture, religion, education and class divide us, but blood is the thing that unites us. Alex has seen so much blood; enough to know that even blood has its own variation in colour. Nothing so red as rich arterial blood, nor as black as the baked-on dried stuff on a two-day-old corpse, nor as scarlet as the blood from a fresh flesh wound. The feel and scent of it, viscous and sour. He tries to block the thoughts. A sudden image of a man beside him – one minute functioning, swearing, alive, and the next in pieces. Alex splattered with flesh and blood but unable to assimilate it, because he has a job to do. He has to keep on firing, keep focussed; what's left of his comrade must be ignored for the moment. Yet one more body bag to be half-filled with what's left.

The stink of the hospital, of the disinfectant, the waxed floors, the overheated air thick in his nostrils, makes him feel ill. Juliet walks beside him with her head down. She has made herself up and styled her hair in a way that covers the gash on her head. Alex is satisfied that she won't raise any eyebrows or invite difficult questions. They continue following the blue lines to the children's ward. They have to press a buzzer, disinfect their hands and then have their identity confirmed before they are allowed to pass into the ward. Alex is aware of Juliet putting her hand to her mouth when she sees Ben in the bed at the far end. There is a drip stand at the side of his bed, and a tube going into his nostril. His face is white and his eyes are glazed. Alex knows it is a look of pain; not the sort of extreme agony he has witnessed many times, but the more bearable, gnawing discomfort that puts a mask of strain over the face. He sees it in the way Ben's mouth is tight at the corners and the tension across his forehead. Juliet bends to kiss him. 'Poor darling,' she says. 'How are you feeling?'

'Sore, Mummy.' His voice is barely more than a hoarse whisper. 'I want to come home.'

'Soon, sweetie. But you have to get a bit stronger. Just another day or two.'

There is a cannula on the back of his hand where the drip connects, and Juliet picks up his hand and says, 'There, there, baby. Is this hurting you?'

'A bit. I hate this thing in my nose. Make them take it out, Mummy.'

Alex is standing at the side of the bed, looking at the picture of his broken family. Inside he feels himself hurting so much it's as if there is some kind of giant parasite gnawing at his guts. He needs to make everything better and yet he feels powerless to do so. They could have lost Ben. Juliet is doing her best to be cheerful.

'Darling, look, we've brought you a drawing book, and some chocolate but we'll have to ask the nurse if you're allowed to have it. That's one of the nice things about being in hospital, you get lovely treats. And Mummy's going to stay here with you now, darling, so you won't be lonely, OK?'

'Please, Mummy. Please stay.'

She leans over and kisses his forehead. 'Everything's going to be all right, my darling. You'll soon be better, and no more nasty tummy aches now that naughty appendix has been taken away.'

'I'm sleepy, Mummy.' Ben's eyes close and his breathing deepens. Then a nurse arrives and checks the drip.

'Everything OK?' she asks cheerily.

'I don't know, you tell us,' Alex says bluntly.

'Oh young Master Miller is doing very well. We'll take the drip down tomorrow and then he can go onto oral antibiotics. It was lucky they were able to do keyhole surgery, so he'll be on the mend a bit quicker. The ward's quiet because we're not doing any routine stuff over Christmas. No children want to be in hospital when Father Christmas comes. So at least he won't get too disturbed.'

'Is it all right if I stay here with him?' Juliet asks.

'Oh yes. We find that nearly all parents stay in with their little ones. You could have been here last night ...'

Juliet looks at Alex accusingly and then responds: 'I wanted to be, I really did, but my husband *insisted* I wait at home.'

'There didn't seem much point in both of us being here, and he wouldn't have known if you were here or not, after the anaesthetic. He was deeply asleep when I left him.'

Alex senses the nurse is picking up on the tension between them. She looks at each of them in turn and says diplomatically, 'Quite right. He had a peaceful night, apparently, and he managed some breakfast. We'll be getting him mobile tomorrow. But if you want to stay we can arrange a comfy chair or a camp bed. I'm afraid it's not the most comfortable hotel in the world. And there's also a little kitchen you can use, with a microwave and fridge, so if you want you can bring in some food. There's tea and coffee, biscuits and stuff, so help yourselves.'

'Thanks, that's very kind.'

Alex picks up a chair from a nearby bedside and places it on the opposite side of the bed to Juliet. Her antipathy towards him is tangible in the way she doesn't want to look at him; her eyes drift everywhere around the ward, at Ben, at the medical paraphernalia, but every time her eyes risk settling upon him, she quickly glances away.

'Juliet, we need to discuss Scotland.'

'Do we? What's to discuss?'

'Whether we go or not.'

'Don't be ridiculous. Ben can't possibly travel. We're talking about three days' time. He may not be out of hospital.'

'Yes, I know. But my mother would be very disappointed. I know how much she looks forward to it.'

'So what are you suggesting?'

'That perhaps I take her. You can stay with Ben and I'll only be gone for two nights.'

'Yes, I suppose that does make sense. If you're happy about that.'

'I'm not happy about leaving you both. Naturally.'

'No, but as you say, Geraldine will be terribly disappointed. I think it's a good idea.'

'Fine, then.' For the first time she looks at him directly and Alex can see the relief in her eyes. It hurts him to see it, but he's helpless to change it. Who can blame her? If he was truly honest with himself he'd admit that the violent episodes were getting worse. He didn't mean to hurt her. He just wanted her to understand him, to really understand who he was and what he really wanted for them as a family. If she didn't have such a bloody-minded, stubborn will of her own things could be so different between them. What was that expression 'If you really love something let it go … and see if it comes back to you?' or some rubbish like that. He knows he's taking a risk, leaving her home alone with Ben, but sometimes one has to set the hare running in order to capture it. He never wanted to have to view Juliet as the enemy, but he knows she can't be trusted, and that she has an agenda of her own which goes against all of Alex's best interests, and so she leaves him no choice. Well, he just might have to let her go in order to make her see that she would be making the biggest mistake of her life, that she would experience only regret and unhappiness. He'd make sure of that.

CHAPTER

16

Alex has gone home, leaving her alone with Ben. Juliet has found out from the nurse that there is an internet café and is desperate to hear from Lil' Miss Happy about the possible refuge and so when Ben drifts off to sleep she tiptoes away from his bedside and sets off with her iPad.

Hi there Sparrowhawk or can I call you Juliet? Thanks for letting the mod have your email address and hope you're feeling a bit better than you were last time you were online in the forum. How's your little boy? Was it appendicitis? He's quite young, isn't he? You must be going out of your mind with worry. I am really sorry for what you are going through right now and I'll try and help you in any way I can. Are you really sure that you can't stay and work it out with your OH? I guess it depends on just how bad it's got for you, but sometimes it can make things worse – harder to sort things out if that's what you ultimately want. You mentioned he'd been in the forces so maybe it's a post-traumatic thing? None of my business, but I can't help thinking they deserve a bit more sympathy cos of what they've been through, rather than some bad-arse mean bastard who just beats up women for the fun of it. Anyway, just my opinion fwiw. Only you know what's best for you so good luck with whatever you decide. I don't know if this will be of any help to you, but my brother has got a cottage in Herefordshire near Brecon. It's rural but not too cut off and he doesn't want very much money for it and it's available now. Let me know if you're interested and

I'll put you in touch with him. Oh, and cos he's my brother he knows all about the sort of things you'll be going through. He's used to listening to me rant about my ex, so feel free to rant away to him. Let me know how you get on, obviously, and just email me if you want to 'talk'.

He's called Mark Price and his email is
markprice263@gmail.com.

Hugs and take care

Lil' Miss Happy aka Claire Price

Juliet responds straight away:

Hi Claire and I just can't thank you enough for helping me out. I'll get in touch with your brother straight away cos I really am getting to the stage where I can't stay put any longer. It's ironic cos the Brecon Beacons used to be one of my OH's and my special places. Where he proposed!!!!!!!

Yes, my little boy has just had his appendix removed and he's quite poorly in hospital – I'm with him now – drips and stuff and it's all really upsetting for him. He's such a little chap … awful isn't it and you just wish you could suffer for them. I hate it, I really do. Anyway, hopefully he won't be in hospital for very long and then as soon as I get him home I can start making proper plans to get away. I don't think my OH suspects what I'm planning. Like I said in one of my messages, if he knew I think he'd probably try and kill me. Least that's what he's threatened and I believe him. God I'm so scared. I'd better go now and see my little boy, but I'll be in touch and let you know how I get on with Mark. I just can't tell you how grateful I am to you and I don't know what I'd have done if I hadn't had the support of the group.

Hugs and love

Juliet XX

Juliet can't believe how everything seems to be falling into place. So many problems that have seemed insurmountable are now being overcome. The money is in place – Geraldine has texted Juliet to say that she's been to the bank and everything is OK. Alex is happy to go to Scotland without her and Ben, so he can't watch her every move or hold her prisoner. And now there's the possibility of a safe house. God, it almost seems too good to be true. All she now needs is for Ben to get better.

'Juliet! Wait …' Someone is calling her name. She is nearly back at the children's ward, cup of coffee and a giant chocolate cookie for Ben in her hand. It's Rowena, looking flushed, her hair in its loose 'not-at-work' messy style. She's carrying a bag and half jogging to catch up. 'I called your house and your mother-in-law told me about Ben, so I thought I'd pop up and see how he was, and see if you were OK, if there's anything I can do.'

'You are such a sweetheart. How very thoughtful.' They kiss their hellos and Juliet thinks that she sees a flicker of surprise as Rowena closes up on Juliet's cheek. Juliet has to stop herself from wincing as Rowena's lips hover over her bruised cheek.

Rowena is frowning, and she takes a moment longer to check out Juliet's face. 'Honey, what happened?'

'Oh, silly me, I hit it on the wardrobe door knob … you know … kneeling on the floor and then I got up and just … you know … hit it. Stupid. Bloody sore, too. Does it look really bad?'

Rowena tugs on Juliet's arm and pulls her over to the side of the corridor. She lowers her voice. 'Juliet, I'm not an idiot. You don't have to tell me, but I'd put good money on the fact that it wasn't a door knob. And this isn't the first time. Christ, what's the matter with him? You poor love, just look at you.'

'I thought I'd done a good job in covering it.'

'Maybe from ten yards. Oh, Juliet. You've got to do something. Now's not the time, obviously, but whatever I can do to help, you know I'm here for you. Just promise me you won't let him do this to you again.'

'I ...' Juliet is fighting back the tears. 'I can't talk about it. He'll go mad if he thinks I've been telling you. Promise me you won't say anything to him! You've got to promise.'

'I'd like to punch his fucking lights out. But I promise.'

'Do you mind if we don't talk about it ...? Please ...'

'Sure, whatever you want. How's Ben?' Rowena sounds completely off-balance and embarrassed and she's obviously trying to cover it up for Juliet's sake. 'Is it OK if I come in and say hello? I've brought him a couple of things.'

Rowena clucks around Ben's bed, pulling out a picture book and an old-fashioned kaleidoscope which Ben, in spite of his tubes and discomfort, has already put to his eye and is twisting the cylinder to see the different patterns. 'I remember having one of those as a child,' Juliet says. 'Clever you – you are kind.'

'I've brought something for you too, sweetie.' Rowena hands Juliet a copy of the latest issue of *Vogue* and a tissue-wrapped bottle of Jo Malone hand lotion. 'I thought you might need some TLC yourself.'

Juliet suddenly finds her eyes welling up and her chin starting to tremble. She reaches into her pocket and pulls out a scrunched-up tissue before a great big sob escapes. Rowena closes the gap between them and puts her arm around Juliet's shoulders. 'Hey, honey, don't cry. Come on ...' She gives her a big hug, and Juliet sniffs loudly, nodding and taking deep breaths and stammering 'Sorr – ry ...' between them.

'Poor darling.'

But Juliet shakes her head and struggles to control herself. Her internal voice is screaming at her: 'Hold it ... just hold it together ... just a bit longer ...' She takes a couple of deep breaths and the tears stop. 'It's just seeing Ben in that bed, with all the tubes and everything. I can't bear to watch him suffering. Poor little mite. Sorry. You're such a good friend to bring all of this.'

'Looks like I should have bought a hip flask with some whisky in it, my darling. It'll be OK. He's in the best hands.'

'I know. I know. He'll be fine.'

* * *

Mark Price's response to Juliet's email is both businesslike and informative. Juliet has given him no indication of her personal situation and is obviously unaware of whether Claire alias Lil' Miss Happy has done so.

Dear Juliet,

Thanks for getting in touch about the cottage. I travel a lot and so when I'm away it's just good to know there's someone there looking after things. It's an old place. What they call 'characterful', I guess. But it's cosy and warm. Obviously it's furnished with my stuff but you can bring your own linen and I'm not much of a cook so you might want to bring whatever kitchen stuff you want. You won't find food processors or cake cooking tins. I just about run to a couple of saucepans and a roasting tray. There's one double room and one reasonable-sized single, plus a tiny room which I use as my office. There's wi-fi – I couldn't survive without it – and a bit of a garden. I'm only looking for nominal rent and obviously all bills paid. That's oil, water, electricity, wood for the fire. Oh yeah, there's central heating and a Rayburn which is pretty crap but it does heat the radiators and water, and I've got an ancient electric freestanding cooker which is a bit dodgy cos the door's prone to falling off. There's a shed in the garden for bikes and stuff. I don't need you to sign a lease or anything. You can have it for three months … maybe a bit longer depending on what my plans are. But I've got mates around that I can shack up with, so no worries really. Just give me a few days' notice and I'll get it ready for you. I've

attached a couple of photographs for your info.
Best
Mark

So, her safe haven will be Brecon. How bloody ironic is that? But this trip will be a *little* different to the last one.

Alex had been due to go on a training exercise to Jordan for a month, and so before he left he'd booked them into a B & B in the Beacons. It was to be a romantic weekend, a farewell to each other. They woke to thick fog on the first morning, and Juliet remembered thinking that they would be able to have a lie-in, maybe sit in front of the fire and read cosily, find a nice pub for lunch. But Alex insisted they get kitted up in their outdoor gear. They set off, barely being able to see two yards in front of them. Juliet wasn't nearly as sure-footed as Alex and she was *not* an outdoor kind of girl. The ground was wet and slippery and she kept losing her footing. All she could tell was that they were climbing. Alex kept up a pace which was too fast for her and sometimes she completely lost sight of him in the swirls of fog. She would call him, and her voice just seemed to get soaked up in the thick, damp air. At one point, she just stopped, feeling close to tears because she had no idea where she was, and Alex seemed to have abandoned her. But from out of nowhere he appeared. 'Alex!' she shouted. 'You bloody idiot. Don't leave me behind. I'm scared.'

'Trust me. You'll be fine. Your life is safe in my hands,' he laughed.

Then he took her by the hand, and after what seemed like at least an hour of stumbling and slipping, the mist began to clear, and she had to admit that the views were astonishing. There was nothing but acres and acres of rolling green, mauve and brown hills with a scattering of dishevelled-looking sheep.

'Aren't we there?' she asked, wherever 'there' was.

'Nope, come on.' She was knackered, cold and wet, but he was already ahead of her and she didn't want to get left behind again, even though she could now see him. Maybe another half-hour passed. She'd got beyond measuring the distance in time, focusing instead on her exhaustion. She called out to Alex: 'Enough. You're so much fitter than me!'

'Come on. You're capable of more than you think!'

'Alex I'm not one of your bloody squaddies on some God-awful fitness test. Seriously, I've had enough.'

'They're not squaddies, they're guardsmen', was all he'd said, and then increased his pace so that when he rounded a corner she was alone, again. She remembered the feelings of disquiet, a sense that there was something more to Alex's route march. Some kind of test of her stamina and her strength of character. So what if she failed the test? What if he left her here? She remembered feeling just a tiny bit unsure of him. Was this actually a kind thing to do? For the second time she felt like bursting into tears. But when she rounded the spur that hid Alex, she found him sitting there with a bottle of champagne and two glasses, laying out some smoked salmon sandwiches. He had spread a white linen napkin over a boulder and flourished a rose at her. 'Your table awaits, milady', he said.

'Alex, you bloody idiot. It's wonderful!' She was so relieved that all the effort was for this, for her. She felt an overwhelming sense of gratitude towards him. Of course later she could rationalize her feelings and realize that her relief sprang from the fact that her ordeal was over, the fear she'd felt had melted away. Adrenalin. That was where the buzz came from, and she'd mistaken it for love.

'Reckon you've earned your lunch?'

'Oh, God. Give me a drink. But I'd better have some water first, otherwise I could down the whole bottle.'

After he gave her a glass of the champagne, he produced a small, perfectly water-proofed bag of kindling and some larger chunks of dry wood from his rucksack. 'Wood? You brought wood all the way up here?'

'Yeah? Of course. My gas stove wouldn't exactly be romantic, would it?'

'It must have been heavy.'

'Not as heavy as I'm used to carrying. You're hot after the climb, but soon you'll start to feel a bit chilled. This'll help dry you out and warm you up.'

He set to lighting a little fire, while Juliet had a chance to really take in her surroundings. It was indeed a gloriously perfect day and it seemed as if they had the entire landscape to themselves. Miles and miles and miles of nothing but rocky hills and scrubby grassland. If she stood up, she could almost see for 360 degrees, the hills falling away and then rising again in the distance. There was no cultivation, no hedges or fences, but here and there a track or a stream relieving the contours.

'Do you still love it up here, even after all the time on those horrible, cold exercises? I'd have thought you wouldn't want to be reminded of them.'

'Not me. Nothing better. Testing oneself and coming out a stronger person at the other end. Surprising yourself. Finding hidden resources – you know, when you think you're finished and then you go on and on, like you never thought you could. Imagine, Juliet, how that feels. It's the best feeling you can ever experience. Pushing and pushing. Like you did. Go on, tell me that you don't feel a little bit proud of yourself. Remember, when you said you couldn't go any further, and you did? Doesn't that make you feel good?'

'I suppose. But most of all I'm relieved that we've stopped, and fucking dreading the downward trip. Alex, my muscles are screaming. They feel like lead, solid and painful. And my bloody feet. These boots, they're new. Look at yours, worn in and loads of miles on the sole. D'you know what? I know you love this, and it's all beautiful. I can see that. But … honestly … I'd be a lot happier if I didn't hurt so much.'

'Don't whinge.'

'I'm not bloody whingeing. But this is what you love, what you do. I'd have been happy curled up in front of a nice log fire with a good book and a supply of decent coffee.'

'But look around you. When are you ever going to get a view like this?'

'You're right. I'm glad I'm here. Got any plasters in that bag thingy of yours?

'Get your boots off and I'll sort your feet out.' And maybe it was the way he looked at her blisters, the way he carefully drained them with a sterilised needle and then applied blister plasters, that she thought, 'Aaaah, he's so sweet and caring.'

While Juliet was just grateful to be resting, trying to push aside the thought of the descent, enjoying the warmth of the fire and stuffing a smoked salmon sandwich in her mouth, Alex suddenly dropped down onto one knee and took hold of her hand. 'Juliet, would you do me the honour of becoming my wife?'

She spat out her champagne and laughed. Oh, God. Imagine. It was such a terrible thing to do. It was just the way he said, 'Would you do me the honour ...' Not 'Will you marry me.' it was so Alex. His face was a picture. First of all surprise that she was laughing, and then a bit hurt that she wasn't taking him seriously, and then he too smiled. 'You are such a one-off, Alex Miller,' Juliet said, stroking his cheek. 'Of course, I would be honoured to accept your proposal.'

'So that's a definite yes.'

'Yes. A definite and absolute yes.'

They made love, obviously, to seal the deal, and Juliet remembers it not just because it was exceptionally romantic, but also because it was fucking uncomfortable

*   *   *

Because Ben has to recover from his operation it's not feasible to escape while Alex is in Scotland. He's sore and finding it difficult to move around which, for a five-year-old, is ultimately frustrating. Five-year-olds don't generally do 'sedentary'. Well, only if it's between bouts of furious energy. Ben, though, is happy to curl up on the sofa with a selection of games and DVDs. Juliet finds it calming to settle down beside him and watch hours of mindless cartoons. Rowena popped round with a basket full of food. That woman, she's just an angel. There was homemade soup, a comforting casserole – chicken, so that Ben wouldn't complain – and a chocolate cake. All made by the nanny, but who cares. It was a lovely thought, and Juliet almost feels guilty now for not opening up to this lovely, generous-minded woman.

'You are sure you're OK?' Rowena had said, screwing her eyes up at Juliet's still-livid bruise.

Juliet had nodded, the lump in her throat making it difficult to talk without bursting into tears – again.

So, here they are, she and Ben, with just themselves for company. And this is how it will be, she realizes. Just the two of them, leaving the lovely big house behind. Leaving her firm base, everything that she's yearned for most of her married life, and she is voluntarily chucking it all in. Will it be forever? Is there a chance that they might be able to patch it all up? What's that cliché? Never say 'never'. Fucking Alex. Fucking Army. Fucking life. It doesn't *have* to be like this, does it? And how will Ben react? OK, so he'll miss Daddy, but blimey, it's not as though Alex has been a huge part of his life so far, is it? Ben and Mummy is the norm. 'So,' Juliet tells herself, 'remember this is OK. This is nothing new. Alone, on your own, single parenthood, is just normal. She's got to block these feelings of fear because they only serve to paralyse her into inaction. And what is fear but an abstract concept? It's relative, it's controllable and mostly ... ordinarily ... it's really not necessary.

All she has to do now is bide her time, prepare thoroughly, and wait for the right moment. Sometimes, Juliet reasons, it's almost as if the major decisions in life are being made for you; it's not a question of sitting and thinking, 'Right, this is what I'm going to do, and this is when I'm going to do it', it's a slow, evolving process which includes pondering various forks in the road. Like having the bruises to show Geraldine helped persuade her to get the money for Juliet. Fifteen thousand pounds now sitting inside a shoe box at the bottom of Juliet's wardrobe. Ben's appendicitis was horrid, but it meant that Alex was out of the house for two nights and three whole days. The lovely Claire alias Lil' Miss Happy providing a hideaway. Far from feeling sick with anxiety – her normal state these days – she is beginning to feel a sense of lightness as the anxiety subsides. She can see a way out with Ben. Really, she thinks, what the fuck, she's a civilian, yes – Army term, right – but she's a civilian living in London amongst normal people going about their normal day-to-day lives, and she's trying to join in, but she's *actually* living in a war zone. She might just as well be in Helmand fighting the bloody Taliban. Alex is jumpy as hell. She's jumpy too. But, and she knows this from her psychotherapy sessions, if your adrenalin level is constantly being pumped up to enable you to deal with a threatening situation, it takes fewer and fewer stimuli over time to get that adrenalin surge, the fight-or-flight high-alert state of mind which can induce attack or defensive strategies, the required level of anger or fear. You don't have a gradual progression from la la … isn't life lovely and relaxed to hmmm, maybe this situation's a bit different, just give me a bit of time to assimilate it … to take it in … to judge how I should react to it … oh dear … looks like I'd better react cos I just might get killed. Oh no. The adrenalin, stress, PTSD junky is more like: 'What did you just say … right, I'll fucking kill you …'

That's why, Juliet reckons, the prison population is so full of ex-soldiers. That's why garrison towns have a dread of weekend nights and the inevitable skirmishes at chucking-out time. The Army turns normal human beings into killing machines, and then when it's finished with them, it spews them back into society and … well … what's the deal? They aren't killing machines any more? Oh yeah? Well how exactly does that work?

But the *good* thing is, Juliet is going to leave her killing machine. Weirdly, there is a part of her, despite all that's happened to her – the bruises, the broken ribs, the black eyes, the cuts, the scars on her skin that can only be seen when she's naked – that still loves Alex. Oh yeah, she's tried to convince herself that she doesn't. Well, who wouldn't? What kind of a weirdo do you have to be to still love someone who has hurt you mentally – not just physically, who has *hurt* you in every possible way – to admit to yourself, let alone anyone else, that you still love that person? That's masochism. So when she talks to herself about Alex she tries to convince herself that she doesn't love him at all. But honestly there's a bit of her that does. Or is it something other than love? Something akin to love – a love impostor, mimicking the feelings of attachment, reliance, dependence, addiction, need. Yes, that's it, the unhealthiness of love. The loss of self, the merging into the other, the subsuming of the weaker into the stronger. Not just subsumed, but consumed. Alex has devoured her *almost* totally. But this little shred of Juliet that's been left is the shred that she now needs to nurture back into a whole person, whoever that might be. Like Ben, she's almost a person under construction, only with Ben he's a new build while Juliet is a restoration. Without Alex she's not even sure she will know who she is because there hasn't been any room inside herself *for* herself for so long. Perhaps, she wonders, if there has ever been much room inside herself for the real Juliet to thrive.

* * *

Alex calls home. Although he's fairly confident Juliet won't have left, he still feels a surge of relief when she picks up the home landline. It's a fairly cursory conversation along the lines of 'How's Ben …' even 'Happy New Year …' and his brief description of what he calls the tortuous reeling party, the freezing house and his ill-disciplined nephews and nieces. He hears that Juliet saw in the New Year with only Jules Holland on the box for company. He learns that Ben is getting stronger and beginning to get more physically active and generally being more Ben-like. He suspects that Ben's recovery will bring their departure another step nearer.

Alex knows that his mother has been very withdrawn during their trip; in fact on the flight north, she barely spoke a word to him, unless it was to voice her concern about Ben. He's not a fool. He can guess why she's so reticent towards him. But he chooses not to acknowledge her upset, because then he might have to revisit what he'd done; and that, in turn, would cause him shame. His mother's always been proud of him and it's only natural that her loss of respect for him is deeply painful. She saw Juliet's bruises. She now knows the truth about him. But what it boils down to, at the end of the day – God, he hates that expression – is just one single issue. He loves his mother. He feels protective towards her. He would hate to hurt her in any way. But his main struggle with her is the issue of respect. The thing is, there's always been the residual feeling, buried inside him, that she could have done more to make things different. If she'd been a bit more assertive with his father, if she'd been more assertive over his schooling, then maybe Alex's life could have been a hell of a lot easier and perhaps he wouldn't be the person he is now. Alex doesn't particularly like himself, but again that's not something that requires any self-indulgent navel-gazing. He is who he is. Like everyone else. If you asked anyone to say, honestly, whether they *really* liked themselves, what answer would you get?

His mother is weak. A reactionary, passive creature who has

been pretty much used and abused for most of her life. An heiress unable to control her own fortune, married to an abusive man, with a son who had no choice other than to shut down emotionally and therefore distance himself from her. Oh yes, there were things that happened between them; things that neither of them have discussed and which Alex would never raise. You don't as a general rule say over your gin and tonic, Oh, by the way, Mummy, do you remember that night when Dad was holding a knife to your throat? When I came in and got between you? Oh hell, what a funny old time we had. What it all boils down to is the suppression, the blocking of unpleasantness, of things that are just too vile to think about. It's unfortunate because in many ways it could have brought them closer, but actually it's become, to Alex at least, more of a hideous example of powerlessness. It is the beginning of a pattern of powerlessness which eventually transforms itself into anger and aggression, either turned inwards upon himself or outwards against others. Funny old life, the way patterns just keep on repeating and repeating.

But not this time. Alex will never ever again be without power or control.

PART
2

RETREAT

Juliet checks Ben in the rear-view mirror. He is crying. She reaches into her handbag, which is open on the passenger seat beside her and finds what she's looking for, a packet of cereal bars. She hands one to Ben who is strapped into his seat in the back. 'K'you, Mummy.'

He's quiet for a few moments, and then he asks: 'Where are we going, Mummy?'

'To the country, darling. It's an adventure. I promise, you're going to love it.'

'Why isn't Daddy coming, Mummy?'

'Because Daddy's too busy.'

'I want Daddy to come. Why's he too busy?'

'Just because, Ben. Now be quiet, there's a good boy, I'm trying to concentrate on driving.'

'Want Daddy. Can we phone Daddy? Can we ask him to come?'

'No, Ben. Now shut up, OK?'

'But I want Daddy ...'

Juliet sighs. She has to stop herself from shouting at him, 'Well you can't have bloody Daddy ...' Instead she ignores him. Her headache is killing her and they've still got a long drive in front of them. Every few seconds she glances in the rear-view mirror to check that the van is still within sight. She doesn't quite trust them. They came out of the small ads. Man with van. And it's only a small van, because Mark's house is furnished. He and his partner arrived at Richmond Park Avenue at ten o'clock this morning. She sensed they'd seen it all before. When it was time to collect Ben from school they had almost finished the loading. Over the past couple of weeks she had been preparing, bagging things up, putting the bags into the backs of wardrobes, any space she could find where Alex wouldn't notice. Ben's toys were the challenge. Not because Alex would notice, but because Ben had a solid inventory in his head of just about every little thing he possessed. Then there were Juliet's clothes – just winter ones for now – and a few items which she was really attached to, and some essential kitchen equipment which she guessed Mark wouldn't have.

They have travelled beyond the motorway lights and can't see the van so easily now, so she slips into the inside lane and waits for it to catch up.

'I need a wee ...'

'No you don't, Ben.' She sighs again.

'I do, Mummy. Otherwise I'm going to wet my pants.'

'Oh for God's sake ...'

'I need a wee NOW!'

'We can't stop, Ben. If we do we'll lose the van with all our things.'

'Why has the van got all our things?'

'Because we're going to a new house.'

'Will Daddy be there?'

'No. Daddy won't be there.'

'Why won't Daddy be there? I want Daddy ...'

'BEN, WILL YOU PLEASE JUST SHUT UP!'

'I want to go home ...'

'We are going home. To a new house. You'll like it. There'll be lots of lovely places to play. A new bedroom. It's going to be exciting. I promise.'

'I don't want to go to a new house. I want our old house. I want MY bed, Mummy. And I want a wee.'

Juliet picks up the half-full water bottle held in the cup-holder. She unscrews the cap and then opens the window. She empties the water from the bottle into the slipstream, and the draft of air almost pulls it out of her hand. The sudden jet of cold hits her in the face and Ben cries, 'No, Mummy, that's cold.'

She closes the window. She hands him the bottle. 'Ben, darling. Can you wee into this?'

'Wee into a bottle?'

'Yes. Mummy can't stop, so you can do that? Can you be a clever boy and do that?'

Ben giggles. 'Eeeeuw, Mummy, that's 'sgusting. Wee-wee in a bottle.'

'It's an emergency, Ben. You'll be a really clever boy if you can do that. Like you've done at the doctor's, remember?'

She hears the dull squirt of fluid flushing into the plastic bottle and tries not to think of it spilling over Ben, or the car seat. The sound stops. 'Finished,' he says. 'Mummy I've finished. I've done it.'

'Well done, darling. Now pass it … carefully … to Mummy.'

Juliet reaches behind her and Ben feeds the bottle into her hand. It has wet patches on the outside, and it feels warm. She can smell the uric acid. She tries to put the cap back on one-handed but it slips and splashes onto her jeans. 'Fuck!' she says, too loudly.

'Naughty Mummy,' Ben says. 'You said the F-word. Smack naughty Mummy.'

Juliet manages to get the cap on, screws it tightly closed and then places it on the floor of the passenger foot well. Her hands are damp with Ben's urine and as it dries they feel sticky. She puts her hand up to her nose and smells the urine. She needs to wash her hands. She thinks about the contents of her handbag, mentally sifting through it to find a tissue or a packet of wet wipes. But she knows there aren't any. Can she wait another couple of hours before washing her hands? Christ! If it wasn't for the bloody van she would get off at the next service station. She feels in need of a cigarette, although she hasn't smoked for three years, and a strong cup of coffee would be welcome. But she can't because of the bloody van. She checks the rear-view mirror once more and she can't see it. A lorry has slotted in between them. She indicates, waits, and then pulls into the middle lane and slows, letting the lorry pass her on the inside. She sees the van. It has slipped right back, so that there must be four or five cars separating them now. What the hell are they playing at? She slows down to sixty-five and can sense the agitation of the driver directly behind her. Two headlights grow brighter as the car closes in on the rear window. Then it overtakes, as does the car behind, and the car behind that. She is closing the ground between herself and the van. Then she sees that there is an exit coming up. They have passed the 300-yard mark. She thinks she should get behind the van, just in case they decide to turn off. She has a bad feeling about this and she needs to be following rather than leading. She brakes and slows even more and the car behind her flashes. Tough, she thinks. Now she is almost level with the van as the 200-yard mark comes up. She looks up at the driver – Lewis – and smiles and waves. His mouth twitches and he holds out his wrist, stabbing a forefinger at his watch. 'Sorry...' she mouths. She falls backwards again, and slips into the inside lane, behind the van now. If they go off the motorway she can follow them. The left-hand indicator on the back of the van flashes, So she was right to trust her instincts. She flicks on her own indicator and follows them. They go past the main car park and head to the petrol station. They pull up by the pumps. Juliet parks behind, opens the car door and steps out.

'OK?' She says to Lewis.

'Yeah. Just need to fill up.'

Ben's eyelids are drooping. 'Won't be a minute,' she whispers, as she climbs out of the car. She locks the car and then heads for the shop and follows the 'toilets' sign. She dives inside and washes her hands beneath the tap which warns: beware hot water. She dries them in the hand drier. She comes out, back into the shop and checks to see that the van is there. Lewis is just replacing the nozzle in the pump. He says something to Dean, the other guy. Then he walks towards the shop. Juliet collects a fresh bottle of water and a bar of Galaxy and a bag of crisps. She glances at the coffee machine but worries that it might take too long and she wants to be ready to go when the van is. Then she sees Lewis make his way to the coffee machine. She jumps in front of him.

'Do you mind ? Only I don't like leaving Ben on his own.'

'Sure. Look – we didn't realize it was going to be so far.'

'I did tell you.'

'Yeah... but... we're going to need more money for fuel. The thing is... Dean was all for heading back to London -'

'With all my stuff.'

'A hundred quid. Extra, otherwise there might be a problem.'

Juliet sighs, puts the cap on her cup of coffee and heads for the checkout. She pays, heads back outside and gets the cash from the locked glove box, and then approaches Dean in the van's passenger seat. He's leaning back, his woollen beanie pulled low over his forehead, almost covering his eyebrows. He looks surly. His eyes seem to watch her impassively, as if she's not really human at all. He waits to open the window until she is standing right against it. He barely looks at her; focussed instead on the wedge of cash in her hand.

'Here,' she says. 'One hundred pounds extra to finish the job, OK?'

He takes the money and counts it deliberately. Then he nods and closes the window. She feels as though she's just done something illegal, as though she's dealing drugs. She feels so guilty that she finds herself looking around them, glancing up at the CCTV cameras recording her every move.

She can imagine a man in a tiny, windowless room somewhere, crouching over a desk, scrutinising this grainy transaction recorded on camera, wondering what can be going on between the incumbents of the battered old van, and the expensive-looking woman in her brown leather jacket and skinny designer jeans, and her year-old BMW coupé. Alex would make a lot of mileage out of it, if he saw it. There is something unsettling and vaguely threatening about the men in the van. Deep down she isn't really sure that she wants them to know where her new house will be. But that is yet another worry that perhaps isn't warranted. It is going to be a long night.

The click of the car door closing springs Ben's eyes open. He stretches and looks at her, and then out of the window. It is clear he is disorientated, blinking at the bright lights of the petrol station. He looks as if he might cry again. She puts the polystyrene coffee cup into the cup-holder and slides into the driving seat. She clicks on the seat belt, and then puts the key in the ignition, all the time keeping her eyes glued to the van. She tears at the chocolate wrapper, breaks a row of chocolate from the bar, and then splits it into two. She gives half to Ben. 'Don't make a mess,' she warns.

Then she stamps her foot onto the clutch, turns the ignition and fires the engine. They are on the move again. Once on the motorway, she overtakes and pulls in front of them.

She checks the satnav – two hours to their destination. The steering wheel feels sticky.

* * *

Alex sits on Ben's bed. The duvet and pillows have gone. All the soft toys have gone except for one small, earless rabbit which he finds underneath the bed, obviously forgotten. He picks it up and lifts it to his nose and tries to identify something that will remind him of his child. Still clutching the toy, he opens Ben's wardrobe doors knowing that he will find it empty. Next he examines the drawers.

He goes into the bedroom that he shares with Juliet and repeats the same process. The bathroom looks oddly tidy and hotel-like. Juliet's various bottles and female paraphernalia have all been removed apart from a disposable razor with a rusting blade on the window sill.

Alex swallows hard. He tries to clear the lump in his throat but it refuses to go away. He turns all the lights off before going back down the stairs and returning to the kitchen. The letter, now open, draws his eye once more. The telephone rings. Alex looks at it, checks the number on caller display. He doesn't recognize it. After six rings it stops. He stands in the kitchen still holding the slip of folded white paper in his hand. In the other hand he clasps a large whisky diluted by just a splash of water and a cube of ice. Her note states: '*Do not try to find me. I will contact you. Ben is safe with me.*' As he rereads the final sentence he senses something, a feeling, something dark filling up the empty space inside him. The whisky tastes bitter but he gulps it back. Then he picks up the telephone. There is the interrupted dialling tone, telling him there is a message. He dials 1571, presses 1, and listens. Rowena saying her nanny is taking her daughter swimming in the morning and would like Ben to go with them. Alex deletes the message, disconnects and then reconnects to get a dialling tone.

This is it. It's happening. After all the waiting, it's time to deploy.

* * *

Juliet relies on the satnav instructions for the last leg of their journey because it is not an area she knows. The van sits on her tail, and Ben sleeps in his seat. She thinks about what she will do when they arrive. Mark will be there to welcome them, to show them around. Juliet doesn't feel like being sociable but maybe he'll be sensitive and keep it short. She can always just be straight with him and say they're exhausted, they just need to get in and get to bed. There's always tomorrow. Yes, that's what she'll do. Tell him to go through the basics tomorrow. Her priority is to get Ben comfortable so that he can sleep, so that she can get on with things without him bothering her. She has his duvet and pillow in the boot of the car, along with a suitcase containing all the essential things they will need both for tonight and tomorrow.

The satnav orders her to turn right off the A road which bypasses the nearby town. They negotiate a large and complicated roundabout, and she worries once more about the van. But it stays with her. After another two miles she is told to turn left into a narrow lane. The hedges have been trimmed, and there are deep ruts at the edge of the road where cars have pulled over to avoid oncoming vehicles. Random trees make arches above them and the lane starts to climb upwards. The trees become sparser, and the moon breaks through the clouds so that she can see the outline of the hedges around the fields. In the distance there is a ridge of high hills, with just a few dotted lights scattered far apart; more isolated hill farms.

The instrument panel shows her that the temperature has fallen by two degrees since they left the motorway. A sheen of condensation marks the windscreen and she has to switch on the wipers. She is warned that they will reach their destination on the right in five hundred yards. She feels apprehensive, but also strangely exhilarated.

CHAPTER 18

Mark helps her in with the stuff from the car, while the removers empty the van. Juliet senses that Mark is a little taken aback with the amount of boxes and bin bags, but hell, leaving home was bad enough; she needs to have at least *some* of her things around her. Though, having seen the cottage, she will find it a challenge to fit them in. She's put Ben to bed, and then when she goes back downstairs Mark has poured her a glass of wine. He's opened a bottle and put it on the kitchen table, and she notices there is just the one glass. He obviously doesn't intend to join her – for which she is grateful. He has also, very thoughtfully, put basic stuff in the fridge, and has bought a supermarket cottage pie and some frozen peas, in case they are hungry. His kindness makes Juliet want to hug him, but she holds back in case he gets the wrong impression. He's probably around forty, she reckons, stockily built, short hair and the thick neck of a rugby player He looks fit and not unattractive in a rugged kind of way. He speaks to her softly, as if he understands that she is feeling vulnerable, but he hasn't asked any questions beyond 'Are you OK? … Is there anything I can do …?' And having shown her around quickly and telling her how things work, he leaves her in peace promising to return tomorrow.

The cottage is a little outside the village, and the village is really more of a hamlet with a scattering of buildings. She'd been expecting a close-knit, old-fashioned village, with terraces of houses and pavements and the comfort of people in close proximity. But when she steps outside to get a sense of where they are, she realizes that she can't see any neighbouring properties. The silence is deeply unsettling compared to the constant flow of arterial activity through London. Real silence doesn't exist there. Here the silence is so profound that you can hear the blood pulsing inside your own ears. But as she looks up at the clear night sky, free of any light pollution, she begins to realize that the night isn't silent at all. She can hear the wind sighing through the long grass at the perimeter of the garden. Then she hears a dry cough not many yards away. Almost paralyzed with fear she manages to train her torch in the direction of the noise and finds a sheep, its yellow eyes reflecting back through the blackness. An owl hoots, and then is answered by another. They are alien sounds, reminding her that she is in an alien environment, and yet it is supposed to be a place of safety. She cannot afford to let fear of the dark and fear of the silence intrude upon her real fears. Whatever fantastical creatures lurk in her leftover childish subconscious, nothing can be as frightening as reality.

She has to convince herself that she is safe here, that there is no way Alex can find them, otherwise she won't be able to function. She has been so careful with her planning. Even down to throwing away her mobile sim card and using a new, pay-as-you-go phone, just in case. She has laid false trails on her laptop, filling up her search histories with innocuous-sounding sites. She'd even opened up a new Amazon account so that Alex wouldn't find out what books she'd been reading. Living with a man who was trained to spy, who saw it as a bit of an art form, was hardly going to make things easy. But she has used her time well, and has used the expertise of people in the support groups online to advise her on how to do things to keep them safe.

*   *   *

The phone rings at 8.00 a.m. Alex is already pacing the kitchen, trying to marshal his thoughts into a coherent strategy, but the sound startles him. He jumps on it and barks 'Hello.'

It's Rowena. She sounds a little nervous and hesitant having picked up on his tone. 'I'm really sorry to call so early, but I left a message about swimming. It would be great if Ben could go with Cordelia. Would he like to?'

'He's not here. Juliet's not here either. She's gone. Taken Ben with her ...' There's a crack in his voice, and he doesn't go on but listens to the brief, shocked silence at the other end, the response he is anticipating. 'I just ... Jesus ... I feel like ... I don't know ... like my life's been ripped apart. I mean, why? She never said a word to me.'

Another pause. 'God. Really? And you've no idea where?'

'No. No idea. I'm really worried about them both, especially in her state. I'm worried ...' his voice cracks again as he leaves the sentence hanging.

'Poor Juliet. I ... Alex ... there must be a reason why she's gone, a reason why she'd want to leave?'

Whatever Rowena knows, Alex needs to know. He needs to know everything so that he can stay in control, always a step ahead. He doesn't mess about, but comes straight to the point. 'You think? I mean, you're her friend, maybe you'd have more idea than me. Look, can I come over and talk to you?'

He can hear Rowena sigh. It's obviously the last thing she wants, but it's hard for her to say no. 'Sure. If you like. Come tonight, around seven?'

'Thank you. I appreciate it.'

Alex is feeling wired, as though every nerve is pulled taut, every muscle tensed, waiting. Waiting and watching.

* * *

'I don't like this house, Mummy. I want my old house.'

'Ben, for God's sake, you're giving me another headache! Can you please just go and play quietly, for five minutes?'

'When can we go home?'

'Look …' Juliet picks him up, propping her knee against his backside and resting her arms underneath his on the wide window sill. He's getting much too heavy to hold. 'See the sheep in the field over there?'

'Sheep?'

'Mm hmm. Real sheep. Like we used to see at Granny's house, remember? And what noise do they make?'

'Baa, of course, silly Mummy. Do they bite?'

'No. They don't bite, darling.'

'What do they eat?'

'What do you think they eat?'

'Would they eat me?'

'No, silly. You know what they eat. They eat grass.'

'I'd hate to eat grass. It's got slugs and worms in it. Mummy, can I have pizza?'

'Tell you what, if you're very good this morning and start putting your toys into the cupboard, I'll make you one for lunch, OK?'

Ben nods and slides onto the floor. He drags his feet and stamps his way upstairs. Juliet is still finding her way around Mark's cottage. The sitting room is small but it's cosy. A nice smell of wood smoke permeates the air and there's a comforting stack of neat logs in a basket. He's obviously bookish because the shelves at the side of the chimney breast are stuffed full of them. Juliet hasn't had chance to examine the titles, but she can see a few autobiographies and crime novels. A couple of tooled leather floor cushions, and some rather fine rugs cover a tired-looking carpet. The curtains are typically male – plain, dark green velvet attached to wooden poles. There are just one or two pictures, but the walls are intersected with beams. The squares and triangles between the beams have been painted a warm terracotta colour. It's not to her taste, but it's kind of nice. One large sofa is of the type you can almost disappear into. She tries to imagine Mark curling up with one of his books, but it doesn't quite fit with the image of the burly rugby player she met last night. The kitchen is fairly blokeish, simple and basic. There's an electric free-standing oven with old-fashioned rings. No dishwasher and no fridge with water dispenser and ice machine. No special thermostatic wine cooler. There is only a complicated and expensive-looking coffee machine. You were spoilt, she tells herself. This is fine. It will be good for you. There's not much storage space. An old pine dresser and a couple of battered kitchen units. But, like the sitting room, it has a certain bucolic charm. Juliet thinks that if it reflects the personality of its owner, then Mark must be OK. There's not much basic stuff in the cupboards, but that's easily rectified. Once they've had time to settle a bit, she'll hit the local supermarket and do a decent shop. But first things first … Her bedroom has a large double bed, and Mark has emptied his things out of the wardrobe and drawers. There are two smaller bedrooms – pretty miniscule but large enough for Ben and for a study. She's already checked out the wi-fi connection and password set-up, and so will go online shortly. She wants to thank Claire – Lil' Miss Happy – for sorting all of this out.

There's a creak of rusty hinges and the slam of metal outside and then she sees Mark passing the window. She goes to the door and opens it. 'Everything OK?' he asks.

'Perfect, thanks.'

'Did you manage to get a good night's sleep? Hope you were warm enough. It was bloody cold last night.'

'Your house is really cosy. I think we'll be just fine here. Thanks for everything. I …' Her throat catches, 'I don't know what I'd have done if I hadn't … if Claire hadn't been so kind. Where are you staying?'

'I've got a mate down the road who's away at the moment.' Mark smiles. 'It's a bit like musical houses.'

'Coffee?'

'Sure, if I'm not disturbing you.'

'You can show me how the machine works. I notice that you haven't got much in the way of kitchen equipment, but you've got a state-of-the-art coffee machine. Got your priorities straight.'

'Yeah. And a corkscrew, and a freezer for the vodka and ice. There's a woman, Denise Long, who comes in to clean every so often. She had a good go through yesterday, so if you wanted her to come in for you, I'm sure she would like the money.'

'Maybe. Though I might have so much time on my hands I can do it myself. There seems to be a lot to get sorted, like school for Ben. Any young kids in the village?'

'Yeah. A few. I'll introduce you. I'll be around for a few weeks so anything you want just shout.'

'Thanks. You're really kind.'

'Listen, I know it's none of my business, but my sister ... Claire ... she went through hell so I kind of understand how frightening it is, and how difficult. And your husband, he doesn't know where you are?'

'No. Definitely not. Nobody knows. Not even friends. You and Claire are the only people. If he found us ... oh, sorry, it's not the sort of conversation we should be having on first meeting. Otherwise you'll end up wondering what kind of nutcase you've got living here. I promise I'm quite normal. More normal now I've got out. Though I expect my husband will do his best to persuade everyone otherwise.'

Mark hands her a cup of coffee. 'Sugar?'

'No, thanks.'

'Wi-fi working OK?'

'Yes.' She laughs. 'My lifeline, as you can imagine.'

'You've found my office. Feel free to use it. It's a good signal in there. These walls are so thick that it doesn't work so well downstairs.'

'You travel?'

'Yeah. When I can. But I'm around for a while.'

'I just … kind of thought … that you'd be away, which is why the house would be free.'

'I was going, and then it was cancelled. I often have to go at short notice …' Mark looks as though he's feeling a bit uncomfortable.

'Sorry. I don't mean to be nosy.'

'You're not. It's just the weird kind of life I lead.'

'No time for a girlfriend then? Oh there I go again, being nosy. Sorry.'

'I can't afford ties at the moment. I was married, but it didn't work out.'

'Ah.' Juliet doesn't feel she should ask any more personal questions.

'Listen, I'd better get going. But you've got my mobile number, so whatever you need just call. I'm around.'

'Thanks. I mean, really. Thanks.'

After she's closed the door behind him, Juliet can't help wondering why someone would move out of their house in order to shack up with a mate down the road for such a minimal amount of rent. But maybe, as he said, he likes the house to be occupied and he could hardly find a tenant for three months at short notice. She washes up the coffee cups and starts to reorganize the kitchen. If Mark doesn't like it, he can always rearrange it back when she's gone. Whenever that might be. She has no plans for the future. Up until yesterday her future started and ended right here. She's got a strange mixture of feelings. On the one hand there's the amazing sense of achievement, of having actually done it, and of being somewhere safe and free from fear; yet on the other there's a scary sense of detachment. She doesn't know anyone. She has no idea what she will do from hour to hour, let alone what she will do tomorrow. But she's trained to set up in new places. Being a stranger in a new place is almost her modus operandi. And like on the internet, she can reinvent herself once again and be whoever she wants to be. 'Ben?' she calls up the stairs. 'Come on, sweetie. Let's make pizza.'

'Mummy, I'm bored. When can we go home? I want to play with Cordelia.'

'There's no such thing as bored. Have you finished sorting out your toys?'

'That's boring.'

'Honestly, Ben, you're beginning to get on my nerves.'

'You always say that. I want Daddy.'

'Ben! You can't have Daddy. Daddy wasn't nice to us and so we've had to come here, OK? Aw, Ben. That's a long face. Come on. Do you want to help me make that pizza?'

She takes out a pizza base from the fridge and a jar of passata, things that she brought with them in a cool box, and sets them on the kitchen surface. There's a high stool which is rather fragile-looking, but perfect for Ben to watch over what she's doing, so she picks him up and sits him on it. She turns away and there's the sound of wood snapping, Ben squeals and then there is the sickening thud of his head hitting the hard flagstone floor. There's a breath-long moment of silence and then a high-pitched scream.

'Oh God! Ben ...'

'Ow, Mummy ...' he screams. 'You pushed me ...'

'I didn't push you. The stool broke.' His screech is high-pitched, searing into her eardrums. 'Ben ... Ben ... it's OK. Stop screaming.'

Ben is trembling, so she scoops him up in her arms and takes him through to the sitting room. She sits down and cradles him on her lap. His tears wet her face and she can feel the sliminess of his snot on her cheek. She wipes it with her sleeve. 'Come on, Ben. It's OK. It's just a bump.' His screams have reduced to a whining squeak, like a puppy shut the wrong side of a door. 'Shhh ...' she breathes into his hair. 'It's OK ...' she repeats. She feels the back of his head and finds a large bump. She looks at her fingers and the tips are covered in blood. She doesn't want Ben to see, because she knows it will frighten him. She scrunches her fingers into a ball and wipes her fingers across the heel of her hand. Perhaps she should take him to casualty. 'Ben, are you feeling dizzy? Or sick?'

'My head hurts.'

'I know. Look at me, darling. Can you see me properly?'

'You're a bit blurry.'

She holds up one hand in front of his face. 'Can you see my fingers?'

'Hmmm.'

'How many, Ben?'

'Two.'

'Are you sure?'

'Three. Stop it Mummy, my head hurts.'

She slides him off her lap and onto the sofa, placing a cushion behind his neck to keep the blood off the covers. Then she fetches a towel from the downstairs loo and puts it to the back of his head.

'Ben. We're going to casualty, just to make sure that your head's all right, OK?'

'I don't want to go.'

'It's for the best, darling. Just to make sure.'

'I hate hospitals. The smell makes me sick.'

'I know, sweetheart. And you've really only just come out of one. I'm sorry, but we do have to go. Perhaps it will have a nice smell, and some nice toys to play with.'

Ben sucks his thumb. He's stopped crying now that he's got something else to be upset about. She collects her phone, handbag, car keys, iPad, a book for Ben and their coats, and then locks the door behind them. This is not the way she had planned to spend their first day of freedom. She's just clicked the key fob to unlock the car when she sees Mark across the road.

'OK?' he calls.

'No. Ben's hurt his head. Where's the nearest casualty?'

'Abergavenny.'

'How do I get there?'

Mark crosses the road. 'Turn around, back down this road for a mile, then turn left, another couple of miles and there's a T-junction, turn right ...'

Juliet's eyes are glazing over. His directions are a jumble. Maybe she can just set the satnav. She gets her phone out. 'What's the hospital called?'

'I don't know.'

'Oh, Christ. I need to type in the name, get the postcode. Shit.' Ben's whimpering but his face is white as a sheet.

'Look, would it help if I came with you? I'm not doing anything and it'll be much quicker if I show you.'

'You're an angel. Really? You don't mind?'

'No. Be glad to help. Shall I drive, then you can hold Ben?'

'Please.'

All the way to the hospital Ben's head just keeps on bleeding. Juliet knows about heads. It's not really the bleeding that concerns her, but the fact that he's so listless. When they arrive Mark drops them at the entrance. She finds a wheelchair and puts Ben into it. The familiar smell hits her as she walks along the wax-squeaky corridor. It's painted spotless cream, with a dado rail made of purple rubber sliding along the walls; a bumper barrier for gurney beds. Juliet is reassured to see how modern and clean it appears to be. They push through the final pair of swing doors into A & E, and Juliet parks Ben by the row of chairs while she goes to the receptionist. She's sitting behind a window, presumably to protect her from drunks and lunatics. Juliet explains that they're new to the area, that no, they haven't registered with a doctor yet. She gives an address for their doctor in London, but misses off a vital piece of the address, because she doesn't want Alex to be able to track them through this. When she sees the doctor she will explain the situation, but there's no point in spilling her personal tragedy to the receptionist. It's all just a formality, anyway. The main thing is to get Ben seen by someone as soon as possible.

There's a digital sign in the waiting room: approximate wait one hour and ten minutes. At least Ben seems to be more alert. 'Hate hospitals.'

'I know, darling, it seems no time since your appendix. But your poor head needs checking and I don't think we'll be very long. Does it hurt?'

'A bit. I'm hungry.'

'That's a good sign. Maybe we'll make that pizza when we get home.'

He kicks his foot against the seat and wriggles.

'Do we have to stay, Mummy? Can't we go home? Can we telephone Daddy, now?'

'Later. Shall we look at a book together? Or shall we find a game on the iPad?'

'Please.'

Mark appears. 'Sorry, took ages to find a space. What's happening?'

'Just waiting to see someone.'

'I'll go and find us a cup of coffee. Something for Ben?'

'Better not, just in case.'

'But I'm hungry, Mummy.'

'I know darling, but you've got to wait and see the doctor first.'

Ben is getting sleepy and he's climbed onto Juliet's lap. She checks to make sure that he isn't leaving blood on her cashmere sweater. Then a young woman with a small girl in a buggy comes and sits in the chairs near them. Juliet smiles at her, and she smiles back. The child's nose is snotty, a band of cream slime glistening like Evo-Stik between her nose and upper lip. Why doesn't her mother wipe it, Juliet wonders. Her mother has taken a phone out of her handbag and is busy texting while the girl stares expressionlessly at Ben. She has long dark eyelashes and purple bruises below her eyes.

'Ben Miller,' a nurse calls out. Juliet gently pushes Ben off her knee and stands up. She takes his hand and walks over to her. 'That's us,' she says.

'Hello. Follow me.'

They walk through another pair of swing doors behind which is a row of curtained cubicles. They are ushered into one. It looks the same as any other; narrow, high bed against the wall, oxygen tank, bin for sharps, roll of paper, selection of instruments. Juliet sits down on one of the small metal chairs and puts Ben on her lap once more. They go through the form-filling: name, date of birth, allergies, address, name of doctor.

'We haven't registered yet,' Juliet explains. 'We only moved here yesterday, from London. Ben fell off a stool and hit his head. I'm worried he might be concussed.'

'Let's have a look at you Ben …'

'Isn't the doctor coming?'

'I'm going to have a little look first.'

She holds up three fingers and asks Ben how many.

'Three,' he answers.

She uses her torch to check his pupils, and then asks him to follow the light.

'OK,' she says. 'Now tell me, Ben, are you feeling sick?'

Ben shakes his head.

'He said he was feeling sick five minutes ago,' Juliet says.

Ben speaks. 'But I wasn't sick, Mummy.'

'Yes, darling, but you were *feeling* sick.'

'Are you feeling sleepy, Ben?' the nurse asks.

Ben nods. 'And hungry.'

'He just went all floppy afterwards. That's why I was so worried. And he was bleeding, look here …'

'Heads do bleed a lot. But it doesn't necessarily mean there's anything frightening going on. His pupil response is fine, I can't see that there's anything to worry about. 'So, Ben. Bangs on the head are a bit scary, but I think you're going to be fine. Just keep an eye on him, and if he gets any sleepier, or is sick, then bring him back, or see your doctor.'

'We haven't registered with a doctor yet. Shouldn't you keep him under observation, at least?' Juliet is petrified that if there's anything seriously wrong with Ben, when the grand showdown with Alex finally happens, this little episode might seriously count against her. Ben *has* to be looked after properly. She has to be *seen* to be looking after him properly.

'I think he'd be much better off at home than in some noisy ward.'

Juliet takes a big breath. 'I'd like him to see a doctor.'

'It really isn't necessary. Believe me, I know what a serious head injury looks like, and Ben is going to be fine. Please don't worry.'

Juliet squares her shoulders: 'I would like to see a doctor.'

It is now the nurse's turn to sigh. 'They're all tied up.'

Juliet stands up, and grabs Ben's hand. 'Honestly ...' she says as she pushes open the curtain. 'Bye, Ben,' the nurse says.

'Bye-bye,' Ben answers.

Mark is in the waiting room fiddling with his phone. He looks up, and Juliet is touched by the look of concern. He holds out a cup of coffee. 'Bit cold by now, sorry.'

'Thanks. It'll be fine.'

'How are you, Ben?'

'My head hurts a bit. I hate hospitals. Mummy likes hospitals,' Ben says.

Juliet frowns at Ben. 'Don't be silly, Ben. Of course Mummy doesn't like hospitals. Nobody likes hospitals, because they're full of hurt people, sick people. They're not places that people like to be at all.'

'We left Daddy behind in London to come to a new house. But I don't want a new house, I want my old one. I want Daddy.'

'You'll have fun in your new house. And I think you might find some nice new friends to play with.'

'I don't want new friends. I want Daddy,' Ben says. 'I hate Mummy. Mummy's scary. I want Daddy ...'

Alex takes a bottle with him; whisky not wine. He knows it's going to be a hard night and he needs to make sure that his drink is his drink of choice, not some cheap bloody Argentinian piss. For once it's OK not to smile. It's OK to be himself, the man he knows himself to be on the inside. For once there doesn't have to be the small talk, the inane conversation that clogs these south-west London kitchens like Polyfilla sealing up the brain cells against anything sensible leaking out. He's feeling hyper-alert to everything, and it's a good place to be.

Rowena's wearing a white shirt, tight at the waist that shows off her washboard stomach. There's a Goth cross and a few gold chains strung around her neck which gives him a jolt. Juliet never wears necklaces, but he mustn't think about that, he must concentrate on now – on Rowena. She's got a nice arse. Long legs and high buttocks poured into ripped jeans. Normally she'd have given him a hug, but he notices that tonight she doesn't. Just the merest graze of cheek against cheek. He smells her shampoo; it's tropical, coconut. Her scent is floral. Too floral. Doesn't go with the image. Robert takes the whisky. 'You'd like?'

'Thanks.'

They move through to the sitting room from the kitchen. Alex glances around and then places himself in a corner of one sofa, Robert on the other. Rowena sits on the same sofa as Alex, leaving space in the middle. She pats the cushion, then leans forward to pass him an olive. He shakes his head. For a moment there's an awkward silence. 'So ...' Robert says.

'You had no idea?' Rowena asks.

He shakes his head. 'No. No idea at all.'

'Awful shock, mate.' Robert says. Mate. Doesn't sit well on Robert's lips. It's phoney, this mateyness: I understand. I share. But of course he doesn't.

Alex takes a slug of whisky and the ice cubes clink against his mouth. He can feel it warm his gullet, sending a good, burning sensation over his tongue. He takes another. Then he gets straight in. 'You're sure she didn't say anything to you?'

He watches Rowena's reaction. Is there a slight hesitation? The way she looks at her glass, takes a sip before raising her eyes to meet his? Is she hiding something?

'No, Alex. She never said.' There's an edge to Rowena. It's the bruises. She must have seen Juliet's bruises.

'I just feel … so … bad that I didn't take any action, that I didn't sort out what was going on. The usual thing. Busy at work.' Another slug and a pause for emphasis. 'I got back last night and all Ben's toys had gone. That was the most painful thing. You don't realize just what it is that makes a house home, you know, until all those important things that go to make up who you are aren't there any more. I'm so bloody worried about him.'

'But Ben'll be all right with her.'

'I've been worried about her drinking. I don't know if anyone noticed, but it's been creeping up. She'd started to hide it.'

'Hide it? What do you mean?'

'Christ, I feel disloyal. But now … I suppose it's all got to come out in the open. I hate it. Like our private lives are going to be sifted through. But I started to find bottles in the bin. Vodka.

'I thought it was back under control. The trouble is, when she's drinking she gets really short-tempered. Irrational. When I think back to some of the arguments. Crazy stuff.'

'Like?' Alex knows human nature, knows its vulnerabilities, its extremes. Sympathy or prurience; it doesn't really matter.

'Ben sometimes wets his bed. He's only five, so I guess it's pretty normal. But one night he woke up crying and she got up to go to him. And I heard her screaming at him, like really shouting at the poor little bugger. "Don't you dare do that again, Benjamin Miller. You're dirty and disgusting and Mummy will have to throw you away with the rest of the dirty and disgusting rubbish." Ben was barely awake, but he was crying. So I got up to see what was going on. I was obviously worried about her being so over the top. She had Ben by the arm, dragging him to the loo. Ben was screaming, "No, Mummy, please ... no ... Mummy you're hurting me ... " She stood over him, saying "Pee, you little sod. Go on, pee now. Not in your bed so that Mummy has to get up in the night and make it. Mummy's tired and doesn't want to wake up. And if you do I shall make sure that Mummy makes all of your toys sleep in your wet little bed so that they all smell like you, so that they'll stink of piss just like you do."

'Ben was beside himself by the time she'd finished having a go at him. So I told her to go to bed and I calmed him down. Changed the sheets, settled him. And do you know what he said to me? He said "Daddy, I'm scared of Mummy. Please don't leave me alone with Mummy." And so that's why I'm worried. I think she's seriously unstable and I don't think she should be somewhere I can't find her, when she's got a child with her who's scared of her.'

'I can't believe it ...' Rowena leans towards Alex, and Alex wants to believe she's being drawn to his side.

'And then on Christmas Day ... Remember she wasn't at the drinks party on Boxing Day? The stomach bug thing? She was so drunk that she fell over, crashed into a chest of drawers. She was a mess. Bruises on her face, a gash on her head. I mean, a real mess. I thought I'd have to take her to hospital but she refused. That's why she wasn't there. And then, when Ben was rushed into hospital with his appendix, she was too drunk to go with him. That's why she didn't see him until the next morning. She could barely walk. So you see I'm really worried about her ... and Ben.

About what she's capable of, given that she's become so unstable ... so bloody volatile.'

'Christ,' Robert says.

'I saw the bruise. I thought ... oh, never mind what I thought,' Rowena says awkwardly.

'So if she gets in touch, Rowena, if she gives you any inkling where she is ...'

'Of course, I'll let you know. Honestly, whatever I can do to help. Poor little Ben. No wonder he was having problems.'

'Problems?'

'Well, yeah, everyone knows that Ben's been going through a difficult time. I told you about the sandpit incident, didn't I? How he blamed Rupert Hunt? But he's been hitting the other kids, especially the girls. I'm sure Juliet knew about it, but she never mentioned it?'

Alex puts his head in his hands. 'No, she didn't. Christ, I had no idea. Little bugger. Why didn't she tell me?'

'I dunno, Alex. Maybe she was scared to.' Rowena looks at him over the rim of her glass and he senses that he's got a way to go before she's completely onside. She's playing a game tonight, much the same as he is. She's definitely no pushover. Bright. He's beginning to find her rather interesting. A bit of a challenge. And there's nothing Alex likes more than a challenge.

* * *

Juliet has cooked – well, really more thrown together – supper for Mark. He's lit the wood-burner and found all the candles, explained the idiosyncrasies of the ancient oven, and overseen the preparation of Juliet's fallback favourite, spaghetti puttanesca, or tart's spaghetti, as Delia calls it. Mark's brought some salad from the local village shop, a loaf of bread and provided the wine, and despite the trauma of the day Juliet's feeling mildly happy. Mark's put music on, Maroon 5, and is keeping her glass topped up. He doesn't drink any more but has brushed aside Juliet's embarrassment at drinking alone. 'It just didn't suit me,' he told her, 'so what's the point?'

Ben is settled and asleep. After returning from hospital he perked up and ate the whole pizza, and then spent the afternoon playing games on Juliet's iPad before venturing outside to inspect the large but neglected garden. There are sheds to hide in, and sheep to watch, and Juliet dares to hope that he might even adjust to country living. The least she could do was to offer supper to Mark to thank him for everything that he's done. She's emailed Claire to say how lucky she is to have a brother like Mark, and how she will be eternally grateful to her for helping her to find this sanctuary. She has asked Claire for her address because she wants to send some flowers to say thank you, but so far she hasn't heard back.

'I just don't know how to thank you and Claire. I honestly feel like you've saved my life.'

'Come on. All she's done is put you in touch with someone who wants a reliable house-sitter. It's a bit of a no-brainer.'

'But what she went through. The abuse she suffered. When I read about it on the support site I honestly found it hard to believe what men are capable of. Like she was treated worse than an animal ...'

Mark is looking down at his plate, and when he looks up, Juliet senses he's feeling embarrassed. 'Sorry, it must be really painful for you ... as her brother. I'm being really insensitive bringing it up, and reminding you.'

'Yeah. I suppose I like to think it's behind her now. She's all right. Recovering slowly.'

They're sitting at the little scrubbed pine table in the sitting room. The fire is blazing, the curtains are drawn. There are lots of candles, and the light from a couple of table lamps makes the room feel secure and cosy.

'It feels really safe here. I feel safe … for the first time in ages. I had this constant knot in my stomach and it's gone. I never thought I'd get out alive. Being here is like a dream. I want to pinch myself to check I'm not going to wake up.'

'It's not a dream. Here, can't have you with an empty glass,' he pours red wine for her and Juliet notices that more than half of the bottle has gone already.

'I'd better slow down. Remember I've got Ben upstairs. Wouldn't Alex have a field day if he could see me now, getting tipsy with a strange man?'

'Not that strange, I hope. Coffee?'

'No thanks. Keeps me awake. But help yourself – it's your machine, after all.'

'I will, back in a sec.' Mark clears the plates from the table and disappears into the kitchen. Juliet listens to the peaceful silence and then she tiptoes upstairs and pokes her head around Ben's bedroom door. The light from the landing illuminates his face and she can see that he is sleeping soundly, his breathing slow and rhythmical.

She goes back downstairs and curls up in the corner of the large sofa. She checks the cover where she and Ben were sitting this morning, just in case there are any blood stains, but it looks fine. Only this morning, but it seems days ago. So much has happened in the last thirty-six hours. She feels pleasantly sleepy and could easily drift off but Mark returns with his coffee. Once again he refills her glass. 'I shouldn't …'

'Don't worry, I won't let you do anything untoward. Remember I'm stone cold sober.'

'I should be too. You'll be thinking I'm an unfit mother.'

'Sure I will – especially after seeing you with Ben today.'

'Yeah, poor Ben. Alex would make something out of that too. Probably say it was my fault. I kept running through stuff like what if Ben was seriously injured – would I have to call Alex to let him know? Honestly, I was terrified. I can't tell you how relieved I am he's OK. There I go again, talking about being terrified. I fantasize that one day it will be a word I don't use any more. Happy ... secure ... safe ... protected ... free ... hmm, those are all lovely words.' Juliet closes her eyes and smiles. Then she opens them and looks at Mark. 'I'm not a nutter, honestly.'

'If you keep on I'll start believing you are.' He laughs. 'So this bloke of yours, Alex, what happened? How d'you end up with him?'

'A question I have asked myself over and over. I should have sensed there was something wrong with him before we were married. He was really controlling. Wanted to know what I was doing all the time, you know, who I was seeing. But I was so stupid, I thought it was flattering. I thought it meant love.'

'So you got married.'

'Much to my mother's delight. Alex was the son-in-law of her dreams. I don't know why I'm telling you this, but I wanted to really hurt her by marrying the most unsuitable man possible. A punk rocker, or a penniless artist. The sort of man who would loathe her and everything that she represented.'

'Represented?'

'Oh you know. Her world was a stupid fantasy. Shallow. Ridiculous values. Like you could only be acceptable if you came from the right family, went to the right school, had the right job. It's because she had none of those things. She came from nothing – her word, not mine – and because she was pretty and flirtatious she landed herself a smart husband. But he got bored with her after five years and fucked off with his secretary. I hardly saw him because he moved with his new wife to the States. And then ... oh well ... I don't really think about "and then". But she got a job on a magazine writing all the society stuff, going to all the right parties, knowing who was who. A walking social encyclopaedia. She was out all the time. I never really saw much of her.'

'Then who looked after you?'

'My stepfather. He was happy to stay at home with me while she went out at night to earn money and party.'

'You don't sound as though you like her very much.'

'Like her?' Juliet laughs harshly. 'No. I don't *like* her very much.'

Mark puts more logs on to the wood-burner, more wine in Juliet's glass and then leaves the room. She snuggles deeper into the cushions and watches the flames lick around the wood. It all feels so good, being here, being able to talk freely. Talking to Mark is a bit like talking to the faceless people on the web, because he's a stranger. He doesn't know her so she can be anyone she wants to be, if she chooses.

'OK?' Mark says as he sits down at the opposite end of the sofa.

'Oh yes. Very OK. Just don't let me bore you with all my awful stuff. It's just been so long since I had someone to talk to ... someone that wouldn't judge me, or go and talk to other people. It's hard to trust people. That's why the internet's been so good for me. I like the anonymity, the invisibility. And the fact that you meet people exactly like yourself. And I wouldn't be here without it.'

Mark has placed a packet of Rizla papers on the large trunk which serves as a coffee table. Then he places a packet of Virginia tobacco beside them. 'Do you mind?' he asks.

'God, no. I used to smoke. I still love the smell. Especially of rollies. Takes me back.'

He chuckles and gets out a small brown nub of dope.

Juliet looks at Mark, raises her eyebrows and then she can't help grinning. 'I haven't seen anyone roll a joint for years. Suddenly I feel twenty again. I must remember Ben's upstairs. That I must be responsible.'

'Yes, you must.'

'Oh, sod it. I'm fed up with being responsible. Besides, who's going to know?'

'Is that a bit of the old Juliet coming through?'

'Maybe.' There's something soothing about watching Mark deftly make a filter, place it on the paper, and then mix the tobacco and dope together, before rolling it. He makes a very neat job of it. Finally he seals it by twisting the loose paper tightly, then he runs his fingers down the length, satisfied with his work. He strikes a match, and lights it. The end flares up, burns, and then a flake of burned paper floats down onto the table. He takes a drag, holds the smoke in his lungs, and then exhales. The smell is unmistakeable. Fragrant and herbal and evocative. Mark hands the joint to Juliet and she doesn't hesitate. She takes two drags, holding the smoke as long as she can. She coughs. It's been so long since she's had smoke in her lungs that she feels immediately light-headed and a bit nauseous. Lights dance in front of her eyes and she screws them shut for a moment.

'OK?' he asks.

She coughs again and her eyes water. 'Yes. Fine. It's been a long time. I'm out of practice.'

'So you used to indulge, then?'

'Everyone did. It was part of the culture. Especially with the people I hung out with. Only, to be honest, it got a bit out of hand. I liked it too much.'

Mark hands the joint back to Juliet. She takes another toke on it. And it feels good. Too good. 'So what happened?'

'Happened? I got led astray. I moved on to coke. You know … I was a part of the club culture, it was what everyone did. But then someone kindly introduced me to smack. I never injected, just smoked. But it was still a problem. I have what they call an addictive personality. I blame my mother, naturally.'

'Everyone blames their mothers.'

'Do you believe in nature or nurture?' Juliet asks. It's a

pertinent question on all sorts of levels. Alex, his father; Juliet, her mother ... the other stuff ... and Ben with all his problems at school, repeating the same old patterns.

'Both. I think there's a map we're born with. Genes that we can't change. And then there's upbringing, the lottery of whether you get decent parents or not. Perhaps if you've got good genes you can cope regardless. You still turn out OK. Not every kid who's been beaten turns into a batterer. I don't suppose every homicidal nutter begets another homicidal nutter. Free will means we can choose how we deal with our lives. People get over some really bad stuff. Look at you.'

'Me? Fucked up. Damaged. Maybe you're right, maybe we can turn out OK regardless. But the things that happened to me, it was like I couldn't leave them behind. I used drugs to escape, to send my mind to a different place. They were like my best friends, numbing everything for the first time in my life. They were a fuck sight better than therapy. But I got off them. You know, I shouldn't be doing this.'

'It's just one night, one night which might help you ... Maybe this will help you realize that you *are* in control, Juliet. That you're recovered.'

'You're bad,' she laughs. 'But I like you. I haven't had a night like this, since ... God ... since way before I was married. It's like everything's clear for once. I don't have to be a victim, do I? I'm so bloody angry with Alex though, for what he did. I have flashbacks about that, but I never tell anyone.'

'You *never* talk about it?'

'Only to a therapist. But what's the point, anyway? You get sick of hearing yourself speak and it didn't help, otherwise I wouldn't still be thinking about it, would I?'

'Bury it. Let it go.'

'Bury it. That's funny. You've no idea how funny that is ...' It's not funny at all, it's just the effect of the wine and the dope. She starts to giggle, and then her laughter bubbles up like poisonous sulphur, choking her and making her gasp for air. She takes a drink from her wine glass and her hands are shaking so much she spills red wine on her jeans. It doesn't matter. Nothing matters. 'When Alex came back from Afghan the last time I knew something was wrong. I met him off the plane at Brize Norton and he wasn't the same man. There was a hardness in his face. There was almost a cruelty there, especially in his eyes. I asked him what had happened but he just said, "Don't you dare ever ask me again." So I didn't. I tiptoed around him trying to please him. But everything I did was wrong. My food was shit – my hair, my clothes, just everything. Ben was just over a year-old and he was really short tempered with him, too. And what made it even harder was the fact that I was seven months pregnant. You'd think, wouldn't you, that he'd have been happy about that? The timing wasn't ideal, the fact that the babies would be so close together, but it's just the way it happened. It wasn't *entirely* my fault.

'At the time I thought I could cope with the bickering, the complaints, the nasty personal attacks, because it was all part of readjusting to civilian life. And everyone knew that they'd all gone through something terrible. Honestly, I tried so hard to be supportive to him.'

Mark offers her the joint. She shakes her head. She feels a tear spill from her eye and quickly wipes it away. She's still shaking. She hasn't talked about this for such a long, long time. 'Then one night he came home late, drunk. I was nearly asleep. He put the light on and shook me and said: "Hey bitch, are you awake?"

'I opened my eyes. I said "Alex, don't speak to me like that. You're drunk. Go and sleep in the spare room."

'He pulled the duvet off me. I remember curling up and beginning to feel really scared. I didn't know what he would do. "You're just a fucking whore," he said. "I know what you've been doing. You lying bitch."

'I screamed at him: "Alex what are you talking about?"

'"The baby isn't mine. You've been fucking Mike Herberts, don't you try and pretend ... don't you lie to me ... "

'It was crazy talk. Mike Herberts was one of the guys in his regiment. He was happily married. It was such a ridiculous thing to say. I told him: "No. It's not true. Alex, don't be stupid. Listen to me ... "

'"I'm going to teach you a lesson," he said. Then he unzipped his trousers and let them drop. He stepped out of them. All the time he was looking at me, with this dead-eyed stare. Like it wasn't really me he was looking at. Like he really had gone crazy ...'

'You sure you want to tell me all this?' Mark said.

'Yeah. I've locked it away for so long I feel like I'm going to burst if I don't.'

Mark nodded. He was staring at her like he was hypnotized, fascinated.

'I shouted: "Alex, for God's sake, stop it. Listen to me!" He leaned over me and then he punched me so hard in the stomach. I tried to put my hands over ... God ... I really tried to protect my baby but he pushed them away and then he punched me again, with all his strength. I was screaming, hysterical. Please, please ... my baby ... don't hurt my baby ... and he said: "I'll fucking kill you both."

'Then he turned me on my side and told me to keep still, to do what I was told or he would punch me again. He entered me from behind. It hurt. He raped me ... Then he said: "That'll fucking teach you to play around," and he got dressed and left.

'It was terrible. Truly, unbelievably terrifying. I've tried to block it out, like it didn't happen to me; someone else, but not me. But it did. That's my husband. Thank God little Ben slept through it all.'

'So what happened to you ... and the baby ...?' Mark's voice cracks and Juliet wonders if he might be about to cry.

'I started to bleed almost straight away. The pain was so bad I knew it was labour. I was so scared for my baby because I had another two months to go. I didn't know where Alex was. I called a neighbour to come and get Ben, and then I called an ambulance. As soon as I got to the hospital, into the ward, the baby came. She was dead, poor little thing. The placenta had ruptured. He killed my baby, our baby. He killed his own daughter – a beautiful baby girl, so tiny that she fitted into the palm of my hand, so perfectly formed. My little girl.'

'So she *was* his?'

'Of course she was his. I think some idiot made a stupid remark in the bar, like "Your missus got well looked after while you were away …" It was just a stupid, thoughtless remark to wind him up. A sick joke. This other guy wasn't even around when the baby was conceived. It was all just unbelievably stupid, so desperately unnecessary.'

Mark just looks at her. 'Why didn't you leave him then?' he asks quietly.

'I honestly don't know. There was Ben to think about. And afterwards … This might sound really weird but it was as if I'd got Alex back. He was devastated by what he'd done. He said he wanted to kill himself. I was in such a terrible, dark place that I also wanted to kill myself. It was, I suppose, the fact that he and I were the only ones who could really understand what we were going through and share the depth of our grief. We had each other to lean on. He said he loved me and I needed more than anything to be loved. He was so gentle and kind to me. And don't forget, I loved him. You can't just switch it off, unfortunately. The only way I could deal with it was to block it. Nobody knew what really happened. I didn't tell the hospital because I thought they'd probably tell the police, and he'd get charged with murder. I had all these thoughts of him being locked up; the fear of the newspapers, of all the publicity. I didn't want to be married to a murderer and I wanted to protect Ben. I suppose I began to make excuses for him; to tell myself that perhaps it was all connected to what he'd been through. I could almost relate to the damage he'd suffered, because I know what it can do to people. I thought that together we'd be able to work through it. I wanted to help him. I loved him. I've always wanted to help him, but the only person who can help him now is Alex.

'What an absolute cunt to do something like that to you. Christ, you must have really loved him to stick with him after that.'

'I did.' Juliet nods, staring into the fire. 'I really, really did. And we still had our beautiful boy.'

'Do you still love him?'

She shrugs. 'Ask me tomorrow when I'm sober. Right now it's all like some bloody awful nightmare. Like I said, it's as though it's all happened to someone else. I feel sorry for him because, you know what? I don't think it's his fault. I think his childhood, the Army, whatever it was that he went through, has all just broken him. And I can't put him back together again.' She sobs, and then hides her face behind her hands for a few seconds, breathing deeply. She parts her fingers and looks at Mark: 'Oh God, if I start to cry I just might never stop.' She tries to give him a smile. 'Best to forget I've ever told you all this. Maybe tomorrow we should both pretend that I haven't.'

Mark offers to refill her glass, but she waves her hand over the top of it. 'I've had enough, thanks. Look at me, pissed and stoned. How good a mother does that make me? God only knows what I'll feel like tomorrow. I must go to the loo.' Juliet stands up and wobbles. Her legs won't perform. Her feet seem glued to the floor. She feels dizzy and nauseous and falls back on to the sofa. The room is spinning and then the next thing she knows she's being shaken by someone. She opens her eyes and sees Ben, his face wet with tears. 'Mummy, you wouldn't wake up … I was scared, Mummy.' She's disorientated. She's lying on the sofa, with a blanket covering her, and the curtains are drawn back to reveal the daylight outside. She blinks hard to clear the drowsiness, and then looks at her watch. It's almost eleven o'clock. 'Ben … I'm sorry darling. You must be starving.'

'I had some bread.'

'How did you cut it, sweetheart?'

'With the knife, Mummy.'

'Oh my God, Ben, you know you're not allowed to use knives.'

'I didn't cut myself, though. I'm a big boy now.'

'How's your head?' Hopefully a lot better than her own, Juliet thinks.

'A bit hurting, but OK.'

'That's good. Mummy's going to get you some proper breakfast in a minute.'

'But why wouldn't you wake up, Mummy?'

'Because I was very, very tired, darling.'

'You scared me, Mummy.'

*   *   *

Someone's knocking on the front door. Alex shuts the computer screen down, curses, and opens it to find Rowena on the other side.

'Sorry, are you in the middle of something?'

'No, just a bit of boring stuff for the office. Come in.'

Alex steps aside and Rowena walks through into the kitchen ahead of him. He sees her look around, no doubt taking in the lack of toys, the atmosphere of emptiness post Juliet and Ben's departure. Then she focuses on him. 'Christ, Alex. You look terrible.'

'Thanks.' He's barely had any sleep, and he hasn't got around to shaving or showering. He's still wearing yesterday's shirt, and guesses he probably doesn't smell too sweet, either. Last night when he wasn't on the computer, he just dozed on top of the bed.

'I just wondered if you'd heard anything from Juliet? I can't help feeling so upset for you all. And is there anything I can do?'

'Thanks. Very thoughtful of you. No, I haven't heard from her. It's been thirty-six hours, just about.'

'Have you been to the police?'

'Not yet.'

'Don't you think you ought to? Just in case something's happened to them?'

'If something had, then I'd know. She'll have her credit cards, the car. All of that's traceable if necessary.'

'But what if she's got rid of the car? And say she's using cash?'

'Look, I'll worry about that in a few days' time.' He can hear the snappiness and the impatience in his voice. Bloody woman. But he's got to hold it together. 'She obviously hasn't been in touch with you?'

'I'd have told you.' Would she? She could be lying. One of his basic rules: never take someone at face value, never place trust in someone until it's been earned. People have their own agendas, and they're not always transparent or even logical. 'I tried her mobile, but it's dead. I tried her email too but so far nothing. I keep asking myself, why would she just up and go like that?' Alex knows she's fishing. He can guess what's behind it. She needs to reassure herself that he was telling her the truth last night. She's worried that Alex is lying. Well, she's a bright girl. It's understandable.

'She was worried that I might take Ben away from her. After Christmas I told her that things couldn't go on like this. She didn't like to hear it, but I told her she had a problem. She's got an addictive personality. There's something else you don't know about her …' Alex pauses for effect. 'She used to be a heroin addict.'

'What? Juliet? Oh come on, Alex, you're not serious.'

'In her early twenties, before we met. She'd been in and out of rehab. That girl was so screwed up but I took her on. I loved her. I think it was the wildness in her that attracted me. I thought I could be the one to tame her. Apparently not, though. She had a couple of relapses when we were first married. She didn't appreciate me locking her in a room, making her go cold turkey. Yeah, I was hard on her, but for her own good. I think she came to recognize that. And me being away a lot of the time didn't help. I hoped that being a mother would calm her down. But it seems not.'

Alex needs more coffee. He pours one both for himself and for Rowena. 'Thanks.' He senses that she is not about to leave now that she is getting a proper story out of him. Prurience and curiosity – like fishing with a spinner – never fails to catch the prey.

'So,' she says, confirming she is well and truly hooked, 'that must have been *awful*. Tough on you, as well as her.' She obviously doesn't know which way to swing just yet, so she is walking the middle line.

'Yeah, but you know, when you love someone you do your best, don't you? Until it gets too hard to handle.'

'So what happened at Christmas – you mentioned the row?'

He laughs drily. 'Which one? There were several. But the worst one was the night she picked up all the bruises. Christ, she was drunk. She said she'd tell people that I'd beaten her up, that I was violent and that she'd make sure I was denied access to Ben. But for all that, I still love her because I know she's so incredibly vulnerable – and volatile. I'm worried that if I make a clumsy attempt at going after her, if she feels cornered, with police turning up and all that entails, then she could be pushed over the edge. You know what I'm saying?'

Rowena is looking a little paler than she did when she arrived. She nods, and her mouth is attempting to frame words but no sound is coming out. She has a couple of sips of coffee. Finally she says: 'I don't know ... God, this is ridiculous. I just don't know what to say.'

'Yeah. It's pretty terrifying. But I know what I'm doing. There's other ways of tracking people.'

'And knowing you, you've got the right contacts.'

'What would make you think that?'

'Oh come on, Alex, your Army career, the fact that you're so secretive ... We can only guess ...'

'I'm sorry, but I'm not half the romantic figure you make me out to be.'

'No, just bloody inscrutable. But one thing still bothers me.' Alex lifts his eyebrows, guessing what's coming. 'Caroline Hunt. What you did to her. Part of me wonders if you could do that, then you might be capable of coming up with all sorts of stories about Juliet.' She watches Alex's features. He rocks his head backwards, in feigned shock.

'What?'

'I'm only saying what people might think, especially after Caroline.'

'OK, if you *really* want to know the truth, I was heading for the loo, and I didn't know she was behind me. She pinched my arse. Seriously! I was a bit taken aback. So I turned around because I really wasn't sure who it was, and she just grinned. Then she pulled me into a room and started making out – feeling me, stroking me, making suggestions. I was stupid because I just got angry. I knew about their reputation for playing around, and I just wanted to teach her a lesson. Sorry, but I didn't particularly appreciate being treated like a piece of meat. She took her knickers off and gave them to me, so I merely passed them on to her husband. I didn't want to tell you at the drinks party because ... well, to be honest, I felt a bit of a dick being set up like that.'

'They do have a reputation, those two. I know I shouldn't say this, but part of me thinks, good for you. Time they were humiliated into acting decently.' Rowena looks at her watch.

'God, sorry, got to get back. Look, Alex, I'm really sorry about everything ... what you've been through, both of you. None of us really knows what goes on behind closed doors. You never really know people, even if you think you do. I'm sorry about Juliet and just hope to God that both she and Ben are all right. Honestly, if you think of anything I can do, then let me know.'

She looks at him for a moment, as if deciding what to do, and then she steps forward and puts her arms around his shoulders and gives him a big hug. 'Take care, won't you?'

He gives her a brief hug in return. 'Thanks, Rowena. It's been good to have someone to talk to.'

Once he's closed the door behind her Alex goes back to his computer and refreshes the page. He needs to watch something one more time.

CHAPTER
20

Juliet has spent a very quiet day with Ben. They've played board games, done puzzles, built Lego, watched a couple of movies, caught up on CBeebies, all of which has kept Ben happy, and given Juliet the opportunity to recover from her almighty hangover. What the hell did she think she was doing? Imagining that she was *actually* back in her early twenties, with no responsibilities, no care for the consequences, no acknowledgement of the fact that she had a small child upstairs dependent upon her? Christ, she had no idea what happened after she passed out. Whether Mark had left last night or this morning was a mystery to her. She couldn't really remember what they'd talked about, but had a vague recollection that it all got rather heavy and the uncomfortable sensation that she may have given away far more than was wise. The only thing she had to be grateful for was the fact that Mark was a seasoned hand at dealing with emotionally and physically traumatized women like herself and Claire. Poor bloke.

Ben is much cuddlier today and she thinks … hopes … that he will settle down. He's always had this thing about Alex, about wanting Daddy, because it's like his fallback way of getting at her when he doesn't get what he wants. Funny how even children as young as Ben can be so incredibly manipulative. They know what buttons to push to achieve maximum damage. The Daddy card, as she silently calls it, because Daddy was hardly ever around. He could scream and scream until he was blue in the face about wanting bloody Daddy. 'Mummy, you're naughty … Mummy, I'm scared of you … Mummy, don't want you … don't like you … hate you … bad Mummy.' Just how Daddy wanted it.

She doesn't think she has a real reason to feel anxious about last night, but she certainly feels embarrassed. The aftermath said a lot more than words ever could. The bottles on the coffee table, the stub of the joint in the ashtray, and then poor Ben having to deal with an unconscious mother. Not exactly the best example of responsible parenting, but luckily she doesn't have to worry about Mark contacting social services seeing as he's the one who provided the drugs. She likes him, but she wouldn't want him to get the wrong idea about their relationship, and neither does she want to be lured back into any kind of drug culture. That would *really* please Alex. God, what would he make of her behaviour? He'd have a bloody field day. Alcohol, drugs, irresponsible parenting; letting a stranger into her and Ben's life; giving away her most terrible, darkest secrets. Not just her secrets – Alex's secrets. Maybe she *shouldn't* have been quite so open with him, but it really did feel very good, like chucking out something that's been festering for a long time. Last night was a definite one-off and from now on she needs to make sure that whoever she is spending time with can be trusted, not only for her sake, but for Ben's too. She knows from bitter experience just what can go wrong when you let someone come into your child's life. They charm, they groom, they dupe and then they abuse. No, she must be careful. Maybe Mark's not going to be an ideal influence in their lives. But it's tricky because they're living in his house and she doesn't know anyone else to turn to apart from her internet support groups. She'll start looking for somewhere a bit more permanent, and think about going to a solicitor to see if she can get some legal protection put in place. She's read about non-molestation orders and might try to get one of those, but she hates the idea of having to face Alex in court, and of having to return to London for potential hearings, and she knows that it will only serve to make him even more angry and unpredictable. She also knows that he'll be doing his damndest now to blacken her name, and so perhaps she should call Rowena and let her know the truth about why she's left, in case Alex tries to poison her mind. So much to think about, and so much of it hinges on distrust, and subterfuge and games. But it's time to start trusting people again and to believe that there are really good people out there, people like Claire and Mark.

Hi Claire

I know I've said it before, but thanks for everything. Your brother is so kind. The house ... everything ... It's so perfect for Ben and me. Ben – God, can't believe I've had yet another crisis – fell off a kitchen stool and gashed his head. So ended up having to take him to casualty. Your lovely brother came with us and was just brilliant. Ben's fine but it was really scary. Can you imagine if my OH knew about it? He'd no doubt blame it on me, say I was being irresponsible; one more reason for him to take Ben away from me. And OMG!!! Last night!!! I cooked supper for Mark – well I threw some sauce onto spaghetti, and we had a bit of a session. I think he must think I'm a complete and utter nutcase cos I ended up pissed and pouring my heart out. Christ! So much stuff that I've never told anyone else. He's a good listener, isn't he? You're really lucky to have a brother like that. I'm just glad I didn't make a complete fool of myself by throwing myself at him, ha ha. Though I could easily have done.

I feel so much better now that I'm away from London. I don't know what I want in the future. I do still love Alex, believe it or not. I think I'm addicted to him. Did I ever mention my addictive personality? But I can't go back, it's much too dangerous. I haven't had time to miss him yet, but I guess I will. Funny, but I can't think about the future at the moment, it's all I can do just to get through each day. Yeah, it's a bit lonely, but I'll make new friends. I shall also have to think about getting some kind of job. I'm OK for money for the moment, but I need to do something, more to keep me sane than anything else. I don't have any qualifications and I dabble a bit with painting, but that's not going to pay the bills and put a roof over our heads, long term. I really wanted to go to art college but I – excuse the language – fucked it up when I could have gone, after school. There were other problems in my life. God, looking back I can't really remember a time when my life wasn't full of problems. But I've just got to try and stay positive, otherwise I think I might just crack up.

Maybe now … dunno … if Ben and I moved somewhere near a college – Bristol or Bath perhaps. Just thinking aloud. Probably cos I haven't had anyone to talk to for so long. And knowing what you went through, well all of this seems minor in comparison. I really hope you're OK now. Give me your address cos I want to send you something. Maybe you'll come and visit soon. Am sooooo looking forward to meeting you.

Love and hugs

Juliet XX

Juliet's just pressed send when she hears a tapping noise on the kitchen window. She looks up and sees Mark there. He's got a beanie hat pulled low over his forehead, making him look rather dodgy, especially coupled with the dark beard growth on his chin. She waves and shouts 'Come in'. He wipes his walking boots on the doormat and shrugs off his jacket. The cold draught from the miserable day hits Juliet. 'Come in, close the door,' she says. He pulls off the hat. And then there's a few seconds' awkwardness between them, before they say in unison, 'About last night …' which makes them both laugh.

'Bloody hell, Mark. You look just about as bad as I feel. What did you do to me?'

'Nothing you weren't willing to participate in, missus.'

Juliet shakes her head. 'I am a complete and utter disgrace. But you did actually lead me astray. And God only knows what I said to you. Do me a favour, eh? Just forget everything. Wipe it from your mind ... please?'

'Already have. Can't remember a thing.'

'Yeah ... right. But thanks, anyway.'

'Ben OK?'

'Watching DVDs. But he put the fear of God in me this morning. I was fast asleep and so he helped himself to some bread – unsliced bread. I had visions of us ending up in Casualty again. They'd probably have arrested me, brought in social services ... and then maybe they'd have done a drugs test ... Oh Lord, listen to me, my mind on overdrive, worrying about the things that haven't happened when I've got enough to think about with the things that *have* happened.'

Mark's shaking his head. Juliet is expecting him to smile, but he doesn't. There's definitely something different about him today. 'Do you mind if I go upstairs and check on something?'

'No, be my guest. It's your house.'

Juliet sticks the kettle on, and she can hear Mark's footsteps moving around. Her bedroom is directly over the kitchen and she wonders what he might be doing in there. Then she hears him walking along the landing, into the bathroom. The sound of the loo flushing. He's gone for a good few minutes.

When he returns, she asks: 'Everything OK?'

'Yeah. Fine. The guttering's not great, and some of the roof tiles are a bit loose, so I just wanted to check – after all the rain we've had – that no damp was getting in. It's all right. You know what it's like with houses like these. Always a bloody problem somewhere.'

'You OK? You sound a bit ... well, low.'

'Still recovering. Didn't sleep that well.'

'Sorry to hear that. Cup of tea? Coffee?'

'No, thanks. Just had one. Just wanted to check that you – and the house – are OK.'

'You really are a nice man,' Juliet says. 'A rare find, these days.'

'I'm not. I really am not.' He sighs heavily, and then looks down at his hands. He twists the woollen beanie in his fingers.

'Modest, too,' Juliet laughs. 'Well whatever you think, I *know* you're nice.'

He grabs his coat. 'Gotta go.' And without dallying even to put his coat on, he's gone.

'Blimey,' Juliet thinks to herself. 'Did he think she meant it as a come on? Her and her big mouth. She'd never seen anyone scarper quite so fast.

But later he calls her. 'Just checking you're OK,' he says.

'I'm fine. Ben's asleep. I'm just watching some mindless telly, vegging out.'

'Heating OK? You've got everything you need?'

'Yep, everything's perfect. Please don't worry. You've done so much to help me.'

'Forget it. It's fine. You're doing me a favour. I might have to go away soon. I get called at short notice. Just as long as you know how everything works … that you'll be all right here.'

'Thanks. By the way, is Claire OK? I haven't heard back from her and I just really want to thank her.'

'Yeah, she's fine. I think she said she was going away for a few days. Maybe having a break from the internet.'

'Lucky her. I'm addicted to it, umbilically attached.'

'Listen, I was wondering if you'd like me to take Ben off your hands for a couple of hours tomorrow. Give you a break? I thought I'd take him to the park, kick a ball around?'

'Oh Mark, I really don't know … I'm not sure, what with the

bump on his head and everything. I guess I'm just feeling a bit over-protective. I'm sure you understand ...'

'Oh, come on. Be good for him to have some "man" time. And I bet he'd like some fresh air and a change of scenery. Up the road, maybe just for an hour?'

Juliet feels churlish saying no to Mark when he's been so kind to them both, even though she's vaguely uncomfortable about letting Ben out of her sight.

'I'm sure he'd love it, if you're sure.'

'I'll be there around 10.'

* * *

Even though Alex is supposed to be the puppet master he still gets the feeling that things are spinning out of control. He can direct the operations but he can't direct his emotions. Juliet leaving, taking Ben, even though he'd been expecting it, everything that's happened is stirring him up inside and making him lose his focus. Thoughts and memories are getting muddled and tangled so there are moments when he really does think he might be losing his mind. And he can't stop the tears. But at least with Juliet gone he can cry. That's one good thing. And with Ben gone he doesn't need to think about the fact that he's a fucking child murderer. He doesn't have to keep looking at Ben and remembering what he's capable of. No, he doesn't *have* to think about it, but he's still fucking thinking about it. The only thing that helps now is the alcohol. His tolerance is building up, so it takes just that little bit more to numb the pain. She wanted him to get help? Jesus Christ ... didn't anyone realize that there was no help for people like him? If you believed in God – and there had been occasions when Alex had erred on the side of religion, particularly when under extreme fire – then this was Eternal Damnation, the revisiting, the reliving, the nightmares running like a DVD on permanent repeat.

The only thing left inside his soul is torment. Help? What a bloody joke. Alex knows that the only time the memories and the guilt will stop for him is when the lights are switched off for the very last time. And what future is there for Ben? With two fucked-up parents what does he have to look forward to? But for now he mustn't lose focus. He's got to prepare, and do his kit checks. He needs to be ready. He can hear the planes overhead, their engines screaming as they come in to land. The sky is never silent; it's just like some bloody aerial motorway up there. It would be good to be able to turn the sound off, but he can't. Outside his quarters people are talking loudly. He wants to scream at them to tell them to bloody well shut the fuck up, he's busy in here, he needs to think and settle himself before he goes into action. He always knows there's a good chance he won't come back, but this time he's pretty sure of it. He's all packed up. He's just got to load the vehicle and make a phone call, then he'll hit the road. He'll feel better when he's behind the wheel and at least in control of *something*.

CHAPTER
21

Juliet's made sure that Ben has eaten a good breakfast: porridge, a boiled egg – maybe they'll get some hens of their own – and some soldiers. Ben loves to eat soldiers because he pretends he's eating Daddy's arms and legs, which he seems to find hysterically funny. He's in a good mood because he knows that Mark is going to collect him and take him to a playground where there are swings and slides – just like Palewell Park back at home – or 'not' home, and he can kick a ball around like big boys do.

Juliet offers Mark the use of his own coffee machine. 'Nah, thanks. Had one down the road.'

'Ben, wrap up warm. Keep your hat on, OK, otherwise you'll get ear ache. And remember about your operation. If you go on the swings you've got to do it very slowly. Maybe I shouldn't be letting him go with you,' she says to Mark. 'Do you think kicking a ball will be OK?'

'Tell you what, why don't we go and see what's on at the movies – maybe a pizza afterwards – something a little less energetic?'

'Well … that might mean you'll be out for a bit longer. I was imagining you'd only be gone for an hour or so, and you can't go buying him lunch.'

'Course I can. How about I take you for a pizza? And I bet you like milkshake?'

'Chocolate, with ice cream. Like when you can't get it up the straw cos it's so thick. And pizza – yeah – better than Mummy's.'

'I don't know …' Juliet is both worried and nervous. It was one thing to let Ben go out for an hour to the local playground, but ... She realizes that Mark is sensing her hesitation and that makes her feel embarrassed. She's just being neurotic and overprotective. 'That's incredibly kind of you. Let me give you some money ...' She reaches for her purse but Mark holds up both his hands, palms out towards her. 'No. My treat. Get your hat and coat, big man, and let's get out of Mummy's hair. Go and have a nap or something. A relaxing soak in the bath, whatever it is you women like to do to relax. Don't worry about us. Let's go.'

As Juliet watches them disappear from view, she shudders again. Mark using the same expression as Alex. Big man. Perhaps she'll tell him not to, or maybe she'll just make herself be less sensitive. Stop worrying, she tells herself. Enjoy the peace. She's got to admit it will be nice to have a little bit of time to herself, to get sorted out.

She goes upstairs and tidies Ben's bedroom. So far he hasn't wet the bed since they arrived. She's put a plastic cover over the mattress just in case, but she takes it as a sign that he doesn't seem to be too disturbed by what's going on. She moves quickly and efficiently around the room, straightening the bedding, plumping the pillows and opening the window to let in some of that fresh country air. From Ben's bedroom she can see a couple of houses about half a mile away, but apart from that they're surrounded by farmland. The sun is out, there's barely a cloud in the sky and the scent of the air is intoxicatingly pure. They'll be fine. They will be fine, won't they? She goes into her own room, repeats what she's done in Ben's room and then sits on the bed feeling a wash of loneliness. She knows she's in danger of crying if she lets herself think too much so she wonders what she can do to distract herself. Maybe she will have that bath. Maybe she'll do what she calls some body gardening. It's been ages since she's actually devoted any time to herself, and Juliet knows that it might well make her feel a bit better. 'Standards, darling.' Her mother's voice pops, unbidden, into her head. Juliet has never been able to completely obliterate her from her life, much as she'd like to. You can't ever really escape, because there is no bar to memories or thoughts, but she shakes her head and silently tells her mother to leave her alone.

* * *

Alex watches Juliet undress. Even though the phone screen is small the images are surprisingly clear, and he recognizes the way she moves, the routine of it. First she removes her socks. He can't help grinning as she topples slightly, catching herself on the bed. She sits on the bed and then lies back with her foot waving in the air like an upended beetle and bends her knee to catch at her toes and snatches the other sock free. She rolls forward so that she's sitting rather than lying and pulls the jersey over her head. She's wearing one of her silk thermal vests underneath. It's black and edged with lace, and so despite its utilitarian function, it's not unattractive. Then she undoes the top button of her jeans and slides the zip down before easing them over her backside. He watches her shiver now that she is standing in her bra and pants. She collects her towelling robe from the back of the door and shrugs herself into it. Alex frowns at the screen, wondering what she has planned for this time of the morning. She leaves the room and so he flicks on to another camera – waiting a few seconds for her to appear. The sound seems to have failed; he's got to get on to Mark to get it sorted. If she makes any phone calls he'd like to know what she's talking about. Bloody Mark. He was squeamish about installing a camera that included a full view of the bog. 'For fuck's sake, she's my wife – you think I haven't seen her take a piss before?'

'Yeah? Sorry, mate, but I just don't think there's too much she's going to get up to when she's taking a dump. You can see the rest of the bathroom, that's good enough.' And so over the last three days he has watched Ben's bathtime, Juliet's perfunctory ablutions, her brief dip last night when she was in and out of the tub within five minutes. But here she was, back again, turning on the taps, putting the plug in, testing the hot water. She is holding a bottle of something he recognizes as being the sort of smelly stuff that so recently graced their bathroom shelf – bath oil or bubbles or some such concoction that she liked. It was weird, this, watching his wife on screen. Her movements seem jerky, but they are clear enough for him to know what she's doing. She removes her robe and underwear. He tries to see if she's still got any visible marks on her body, but from where he's sitting she looks in pretty good shape. She feels the temperature of the water and then turns off the taps before stepping in. She sinks down slowly so that her back is turned towards him and all he can see is the top half of her head above the parapet of the bath. She's twisted her hair up into a knot on top of her head. He can imagine the rest of her because he's seen her naked so many times before. She lies still for a while and then she lifts her left leg out of the water and begins to soap the area between her knee and her ankle. Then she takes something in her hand. Alex can't see exactly what it is, but he knows it's a razor. She starts to run the blade along the length of her lower leg. She holds her leg in the air, free of the water, so that he can see the shape of her calf and the arch in her instep as she points her toe, unconsciously no doubt, and it reminds him of how gracefully she moves. He props his chin on to his hand, which is in turn supported by his elbow upon the car window sill, and he watches his wife continue with her toilette, feeling wistful, nostalgic and unimaginably sad.

*　*　*

Juliet rubs herself dry and then wraps the towel around her and twists the end so that it holds in place. She wipes the condensation from the mirror but it's too smeary to see her reflection. Probably just as well. She's in need of a haircut and her skin is sallow through the stress, lack of sleep and dehydration, and her eyes feel puffy and sore. The well-groomed, manicured and outwardly sophisticated 'London' Juliet has disappeared. Her mother would be seriously ashamed of her. Oh Christ, here she is again, determined to be heard. Her voice rings out loud and clear. 'Juliet, you have a duty to yourself to always make the best of yourself; it doesn't matter if you're seeing no one, the postman or the prime minister. You must always take pride in your appearance.'

'To what end, Mother?' Juliet says aloud. 'To be a sexual object to titillate men? Is that it? Is that what you want?'

She needs to get her out of her head. Thinking about her mother right now, and all the baggage attached, is *not* helpful. She pulls a clean pair of jeans out of the drawer and pairs them with a white cotton shirt and a cashmere, drapey cardigan. She has brushed her hair and curled it back into the casual top knot. She sits before the mirror, with her make-up bag open in front of her.

But when she looks in the mirror she sees another reflection – her mother's – and Juliet is carried way back in time, a little seven-year-old perhaps, or maybe eight at the most. There's a lit cigarette lying in a silver ashtray, the smoke rising in a dead straight line. There's something mesmerizing about that plume of smoke, a vertical stream wending upwards before diffusing into a little cloud of fairy gossamer floating above the top of the mirror – or looking glass, as her mother calls it. Calling things by their proper names is important, because it marks Mummy out as being *proper*. She picks up the cigarette and taps the ash from the tip before raising it to her lips. Scarlet meets scarlet. Her fingernails are so glamorous twirling the gold lipstick case. Juliet feels her own lips stretching as she watches her mother. Then her mother blots her lips together, opens her mouth to see if there are lipstick marks on her teeth, and all the while she watches her reflection at a tilted, sideways angle. She checks her earrings – big, shiny gold knots – and straightens the string of pearls around her long slender neck.

Everything about her mother is long and slender: her nails, her fingers, arms, legs. But one of the things Juliet loves best about her mother is her smell. She doesn't know it, but sometimes, when she goes out, Juliet sneaks into her bedroom and turns the scent bottle upside down once, like her mother does, and she takes out the stopper and dabs it onto her arm. Later, when Juliet is trying to get to sleep, she'll inhale the scent and feel comforted and safe. Juliet does this a lot, because her mother is *always* out.

Juliet is drowning in memories. She tries to stop them but they won't go away. The pictures are so vivid, so real, taking her back there, to that place, to *him*. She sees her own reflection in the mirror. She's painting her face to mask who she really is. He is standing behind her, encouraging her, talking to her in a soft, gentle voice. 'More, Juliet, darling. Look how beautiful you are.' Juliet's cheeks are too pink, her lips too red, the powder on her eyelids too blue. She looks like one of her own dolls. Juliet's eyelashes are very long, and so when she spits on the little brush, and rubs it over the black block of mascara, and brushes it onto her lashes, she looks even more doll-like. He leans over her, too close now, so that she can catch the scent of his suit. It carries the smell of the city, of his office, his tobacco, his sweat, his power. Juliet blots her lips together, opens her mouth to check her teeth for lipstick marks. She upturns her mother's scent bottle and then touches the stopper to just below her ears, the nape of her neck, her pulse points. He always makes her wear one of her mother's necklaces, but that is all. He likes her to be naked apart from the necklace, and the scent and the paint on her face. When he is satisfied that her *maquillage* – as he tells her it is called – is complete, he takes her hand and pulls her from the dressing table stool. Then he leads her into her own bedroom. He will push the teddy bears aside and then sit down. He will pull her on to his knee so that her back is nestled against his stomach. She can feel the warm wool of his suit material below her naked thighs. First he starts with his knees closed together but then he will manipulate Juliet's legs so that they are outside his, then he will open his legs, forcing Juliet's legs wide apart, and then he will put his hand in his mouth and wet it before touching Juliet between her legs and even though she knows it is wrong, and in spite of the fact that she knows what he is doing to her cannot be what grown men are meant to do to little girls, he makes her feel things that she doesn't want to feel. Then she will feel the stiff lump in his trousers, pressing up behind her bottom and he will shift her aside – it's not difficult, because she is so slight – and he will unzip himself and let that thing out before putting Juliet back in place and she will feel him hard and naked and warm between her legs. He will then manoeuvre her legs so that they are inside his, so it is now her knees that are tight together and then he will hold her by the hips, pushing her backwards and forwards, up and down, rubbing against her over and over and over until he cries out words that Juliet has never heard before, and he spurts out this stuff which feels sticky on her skin and it's a bit like wee because it comes from the same hole except it's not wee. Then he will kiss her back, and her shoulders and stroke her stomach and the places where she will one day have breasts. And he will tell her how much he loves her and how she must never, ever tell because this is their little secret and no one must ever know because if they did they would say that she was an evil, dirty little girl and no one would ever want anything to do with her, and her mother would throw her onto the streets. And then he will bath her, making sure that every streak of make-up is scrubbed from her face. And all the time he will talk to her about how much he loves her.

Most nights when he was looking after her while her mother went out they would have a similar routine. Juliet would plead with her mother not to go. She tried to stay with school friends, anyone who would have her, apart from *him*, so that she could be protected from him. But her mother refused to stay at home. She told her not to be so silly and so clingy, and that she should be a good girl. And she couldn't stay with friends all the time. As the months went on, he made her do more things. He made her use her mouth and her hands to please him. But he wasn't happy with the sex play, the masturbation. He raped her after her eleventh birthday. Juliet thought she was going to be split in two. She just couldn't understand how something so big could fit inside her, but God help her, her body allowed it. In spite of the revulsion and the guilt and the fear, her body betrayed her. A whore, that's what she was, nothing better than a dirty little whore.

She's back in the present. She looks at herself in the mirror and hates what she sees, but she dutifully finishes her make-up and even checks her teeth for lipstick stains. Then she dabs some scent onto her pulse points, behind her ears, the nape of her neck. When she stands up her knees feel unstable and so she sits down on the bed. Then the tears start, and the shaking, and the sobs, and she lies down and curls up like a baby, crying for the love and protection she has never had, because she's a dirty little girl and she doesn't deserve it.

*　*　*

Alex watches her, and first of all isn't sure why she has climbed onto the bed, and then he sees her body shake, and her hands tear at her hair, her mouth open and her lips drawn back. Without sound it's not obvious at first what she's doing, and then in an odd kind of way, watching her sob, in silence, makes it all the more upsetting. He finds himself wanting nothing more than to reach out to her, to gather her up in his arms and to hug her close to him. He wants to comfort her, to make her feel better. To make her happy again. But it's too late now, much too late.

*　*　*

When there are no more tears left to shed, Juliet goes to the bathroom, splashes cold water on her face and puts some of her expensive face and eye cream on her distorted, puffy features. She doesn't want Mark to see her like this. It's been a long time since she's had one of her flashbacks, but when they come they are as vivid as ever. She and Alex are so alike, so irretrievably damaged, and yet they can do nothing to help each other. He's still alive, the stepfather, or Sad Fuck as she thinks of him. He's still trailing around after her mother. Her mother has given up saying to Juliet, 'I wish you'd call me ...' Her mother knows, because the thing is, Juliet told her. When she started to make herself sick afterwards, after what he'd done, when she scrubbed herself so hard that she bled. When she realized just how dirty and defiled she was, how her childhood had been stolen, how her thoughts were not and should not be those of a twelve-year-old. She told her mother, but her mother refused, yes *refused* to believe her, and so Juliet's punishment was to be sent away to school to learn some manners and to get herself sorted out. But all Juliet learned was how not to eat, because she reasoned that if she didn't eat, she might stay a child and then she would never, ever have to do any of the things *he* made her do ever again.

How many thousands of pounds must have been spent on her counselling over the years, and to what good effect? So there you have it, two completely fucked-up people. Alex and Juliet – what kind of twisted joke was it that they should have ended up together? But maybe that's what happens in life. You recognize the damage in the other person, and you understand. You know them, and you know that they know you. Really know you. They're like a reflection of yourself; all the bad stuff is there in front of you and you can either choose to try and provide comfort, to help heal and make that person whole again, or you can use it to erode them even further, with nasty little needles that can be inserted over and over into the very source of the wound to keep it open and raw.

People do some very bad things in the name of love.

But where's Ben? He should be back. It's now three o'clock. She doesn't want to feel worried, but she does. She's tried Mark's mobile but it's gone straight to voicemail. Surely they've had enough time to have their bloody pizza by now. She tries to crush the bad thoughts, all the possibilities, the dangerous scenarios, and she can't. Juliet paces. She paces the kitchen, the hallway and finally the sitting room. She picks up a cushion from the sofa and plumps it, and then chucks it down again. She looks through the window, she opens the front door and goes to the gate, then she returns to the house and paces once more. Who the hell *is* Mark? What does she know about him? And why has Claire gone so quiet? And why doesn't she have her address? She begins to search through Mark's bookshelves to see if she can find something, anything that might reveal something about him. She barely knows him – Christ, he could be some kind of bloody paedophile, grooming them both. How could she have been so bloody negligent …? The unthinkable reality … the terrifying possibilities are filling her mind almost to the point where she doesn't know how to function. She needs to search for clues. She notices some photograph albums on the bottom shelf. She kneels down and pulls out the top one. It's so dusty that it makes her sneeze. Her fingers have left marks in the dust, so Mark will be able to see that someone – Juliet – has been nosy. But she couldn't give a toss. There's loads of photographs of mountains, huge, jagged, snow-covered peaks disappearing into the sky. Then groups of gnarly old women with extraordinary faces, dressed in glorious colours and framed by the snow-capped mountains. Bustling city scenes and railway stations, bicycles, cars, more mountains, a Labrador … and then something chills her. It's a photograph of a military headstone, and then another and another. She flicks more pages and she sees a photograph of Mark in Army greens, and on his head is a cap bearing a badge that she recognizes. She'd have to be some kind of a fool to believe in coincidence.

Her head feels as though it's going to explode as she tries to take it all in. Mark is Alex's man? So Alex knows where she is? And Mark's got Ben? He's taking him to Alex! She knows it. The lying, conniving bastard. And he had the barefaced audacity to pretend he was helping her. So he had a motive for getting her drunk, giving her drugs, making her talk – because all the time he was Alex's man. And Ben ... What will Alex do? He might take him away from her forever. Was that his plan, to prove her unfit? The fear is tearing at her insides, a pain so terrible that she can hardly endure it. The thought of losing Ben ... the thought that she *has* lost him. Frantically she calls Mark's mobile but it goes straight to voice mail. She leaves a breathless message: 'You bastard! How could you do that to me! Bring him back *now*!' Then she calls Alex. Again it goes straight to voice mail. 'If you do anything to harm my son I swear I will kill you, Alex Miller.'

* * *

Alex reaches the lay-by first. He knows where the nearest houses are, what the speed limit is, accident statistics, other uses apart from 'laying by'. He knows that there aren't any burger vans or tea stalls and therefore it's not the sort of lay-by likely to have people hanging around. It's not the sort of lay-by where people have time to take in the scenery and notice the other drivers and their cars. He gets out of the car and stretches. The air is damp but it's not raining. The visibility is only about sixty per cent, but it's not foggy. The temperature is six degrees, so not too bad.

A lorry pulls up behind him. He hears the expulsion of air from the hydraulic brakes and the squeak of heavy metal forced to a halt. The driver climbs down, goes to the hedge side and takes a piss. Alex doesn't waste any mental energy on him. He needs to keep everything focussed on Ben.

ELIZABETH FORBES

Mark's Audi A3 draws in beside Alex's Quattro. They're all welded to their Audis. Fast and reliable. Alex gets a warm feeling deep inside, because he's longing to see his son. Mark gets out of the car and walks around it. 'Good work, mate,' Alex says, shaking Mark's hand. 'Where is he?'

'Asleep. Let's talk for a minute.' He's got a ready-rolled cigarette, which he sticks between his lips and lights. Alex doesn't like smoking because it demonstrates a weakness of character, but in Mark's case there's no weakness of character. Alex knows this better than anyone.

'What are your plans?'

'Having a little holiday with my boy. Getting him away from Juliet is the most important thing, to make sure he's safe.'

'Look, I know it's none of my business ... except it is my business because she's staying in my house ... But Juliet – she's all right, you know. And she's pretty attentive towards Ben. Listen mate, he's a great kid. He loves you both. You could have it all ...'

'It's a bit late for that. Too much water, you know the old saying. It's a new war zone.' Alex can feel his chest tighten, his breathing shifting from diaphragmatic to clavicular so that it comes in short gasps, making it hard to speak. In: one, two, three; out: one, two, three; in: one, two, three; out: one, two, three ... better. He can get his words out without sounding panicky, maybe. 'And the head injury?'

Mark shrugs, wriggles his hands in his pockets and rocks backwards and forwards on and off the balls of his feet. 'An accident. They happen.' There's a defiant note in his voice.

'And the drugs? Don't forget I was watching it all, listening to you both ... like I was in the bloody room with you. Call that a fit mother? She's just one step away from becoming a junky ... again. Oh yeah, she can be very charming. So she charmed you? Come on, you're too bright to be fooled.' Alex knows he sounds derisive. But Mark is on *his* side. He has made all of this possible. It has all,

267

so far, gone just as Alex wants it to, largely through Mark's assistance, and he wants to *keep* him on side.

'That story about the miscarriage. You heard her telling me all about that? Not very comfortable listening, was it?'

'You believe her? Christ, you weren't taken in by that, were you? Yeah, made a good story, didn't it? A story, nothing more. It was all a pack of lies. But it worked, didn't it? Got you on her side. I told you to be careful, that she was manipulative. But I thought you could handle it. You honestly think I'd have done something like that? Thanks, mate.'

Mark flicks his cigarette butt into the hedge and exhales the smoke which forms a thick cloud in the damp air. 'I got the impression that she still loves you. And I also got the impression that she wasn't a bad mother. I've been doing a lot of thinking – not just since you got in touch with me a few months back, but since I lost everything. Zoe. Too late now. She's got a new bloke. A civvy – a fucking plumber, can you believe it? Still, at least he can look after her pipes properly, eh? I fucked up. I was an idiot. The drinking, the abuse – oh yeah, verbal and physical. I'm ashamed of what I did. But I didn't realize ... I couldn't admit it was me, my fault, that it was all going wrong. Oh no, I couldn't admit it was me, because I thought I was a fucking superhero.'

'Finished?' Alex just looks at Mark coldly. He doesn't want to listen to his self-indulgent whining. It's excruciating, ridiculous. He feels ashamed of him. He can't see the old Mark in there. He's on the verge of telling Mark what a mistake he's made in revisiting their 'friendship', in asking for his help; in following up on a fucking stupid bloody band of brothers vow made in a fucking desert, where they knew they would and could, very possibly, die for each other. And now here is the sad little git acting like some bloody nancy boy, going all touchy-feely. But he mustn't. He's got to keep Mark onside, because he needs him to keep in contact with Juliet so that Alex knows what she's up to. And Mark has specialist knowledge of spy equipment and surveillance.

'Listen, mate, I'm not saying that I'm any better than you are. I *know* who you are, Alex, because I *was* you. I love you, mate. I just don't want you to fuck everything up the way I did.' Alex feels his voice crack. It sounds like emotion, but it's not, it's suppressed rage. 'You're right.' He stares at the ground, at their feet facing each other like weapons. 'She's OK. I should maybe take some responsibility.' He can't believe he's saying this. 'I should maybe have listened to her.' Mark looks at Alex, the concern carved into his brow.

Alex goes over to Mark's car and opens the door. Ben is just waking up. When he sees Alex he grins. 'Daddy, where have you been? We went to a new house and I wanted you to be there. Are we going back to our old house now? Will we get Mummy?'

'Shhh, Ben. Let me get you in the car first, OK?' He turns to Mark. 'I'll be in touch.' He shakes his hand. Alex is shocked to see something moist in Mark's eye. Too much. Wanker, he thinks to himself. Fucking wanker.

'Come on, let's get you in the car.' He closes the rear door and turns back to Mark who is watching him intently. 'Thanks, mate, for everything. I appreciate it.' Mark nods.

Alex fires up the engine, checks on Ben, and then pulls out of the lay-by without looking back at Mark.

* * *

Juliet's phone pings with a new email alert: 'I've got Ben. Alex.' 'Oh Christ …' she sobs aloud. 'What the hell have I done? Ben … oh God … my poor darling Ben.' She can't breathe, she feels dizzy and nauseous. Her legs won't hold her up. But all the while she is making her inner voice speak to her. 'You've been through so much, don't give in now. Think what you've survived … you can't let him beat you now. What was it all for? Be strong! Hold it together. You have to be strong for Ben's sake.' She slows down her breathing, in: one, two, three; out: one, two, three ... she wipes the excess saliva from the edges of her mouth. She pulls herself up from the floor, using a chair to steady herself.

Think. She must think. She must go through the options minutely, she must make sure she doesn't do anything stupid, anything predictable. Her next moves will have been anticipated and planned for. Like a chess player, she feels already in check but if she manoeuvres carefully she might just be able to stay in the game. Don't do the expected, she tells herself. Neither trust nor rely on anyone other than yourself. Alex is the warrior, but she's a mother, and everyone knows how fiercely a mother can fight to protect her young.

Think, Juliet, she commands herself. The implications of discovering that Mark is Alex's man are only just beginning to sink in. She'd been introduced to him through Claire, his sister – the person who called herself Lil' Miss Happy online, the person who Juliet had been exchanging messages with in the forum for months ... She was just one of those sock puppets – a person who was pretending to be someone else. It had to be Alex. And if it was Alex, then it meant that he knew everything she'd been doing, her thoughts, her plans. When she bared her soul, supposedly in the sanctity of the forum, he was there, lurking, watching her. Oh God, it's all too much to take in. Fears for Ben and what she can do to get him back are all mixed up with trying to recollect the things that she said to Lil' Miss Happy, trying to recollect the stuff she's told *her*. What about the gang rapes? Wasn't it Lil' Miss Happy who said 'no point in reporting stuff' to the police? No bloody wonder. Well it's damned well time to go to the police now.

Ben will be safe, she tells herself. There is no reason why he shouldn't be. There is no point in Alex harming Ben. He will be fine. She must believe that Alex will look after him. She cannot allow herself to think beyond that.

Then her phone pings with a text from Mark. It doesn't make any sense. 'Don't do anything. Just keep your phone near you.' Don't do anything? Who was *he* to tell *her* what to do? And how brain dead must he be to imagine she *wouldn't* keep her phone near her at a time like this? What's he want to do, call for a cosy chat?

* * *

At the police station in Brecon Juliet hops from one foot to the other waiting to talk to the man behind the glass. There are just two plastic chairs in the foyer and they are both occupied by burly men in cheap leather jackets, unshaven and looking very much the worse for wear. The woman in front of her has been involved in a domestic, as she puts it, the night before. Juliet can't help but overhear. Her partner has been arrested. She wants to make it clear that she doesn't want to press charges, that she has no injuries. Juliet sees her pale face, the deep dark circles underneath her eyes, and she wants to give her a hug. But all she can do is give her a vague, impersonal smile as she takes her place at the front of the queue.

'I left my husband a few days ago because he became violent towards me. We have a five-year-old son. He was with me, and now he's been kidnapped. I believe he's with my husband. I'm very frightened for his safety.'

'Take a seat, madam, and someone will be with you shortly.' Juliet looks behind her. There are no seats to be taken. She hovers by the noticeboard, reading about women's refuges, drugs helplines, childlines – like it was a pinboard designed just for her. She waits ages ... well it seems like it. The minutes drag. Being here makes her feel even more helpless. Almost like some kind of criminal. She shifts her handbag onto her other shoulder, shifts the weight from her left foot to her right. She fiddles with the knot of hair on top of her head. She sighs. She wishes she smoked so that she'd have a reason to step outside. Eventually a woman PC arrives and invites her to follow into the inner sanctum. She is ushered into a room. The woman holds an A4 notepad and a couple of pens. Juliet can see this is going to take a very long time. Once again she explains the situation. Then the questions begin. 'Did you report the violence …?'; 'When was the last occasion …?'; Was your husband ever violent towards your son, to your knowledge …?' Juliet answers truthfully, mostly. She mentions bruises on Ben that were suspicious. She mentions Ben's nightmares. She mentions Alex's PTSD symptoms, his unpredictability. She says she fears that her husband has suffered from suicidal thoughts. And the more she speaks the greater the fear spreads inside her. 'Please,' she starts to cry. 'You must do something. You have to find them. Can you search for his car? His number plate? Don't you have cameras everywhere?'

'We have nothing on file against your husband. He has no criminal record, no official warnings. I'm afraid there's nothing we can do without any hard evidence against him.'

'Nothing you can do until it's too late …' Juliet is trying to hold back the sobs. She grabs hold of the woman's hand. 'Please …'

'I really am sorry. As you can imagine, this is not an unusual situation, unfortunately. The only thing I can advise is that you go to a solicitor on Monday and try and get the wheels in motion. Perhaps you could apply for a non-molestation order. I'm sorry, it's not my department. I advise that you go home and wait. If your husband has been violent towards you in the past, then it would be best to stay away from him until this is all sorted. I'm sure he won't do anything to harm your son.'

Juliet gets up, nods. It's hopeless. She's on her own.

She returns to Mark's cottage, goes upstairs and selects a bag, throws in some bare essentials. She has money, she can buy what she needs. She pulls out some old trainers which she used as running shoes a long time ago. She searches through the drawers in Ben's room, pulling out warm clothing for him, just in case. Then she searches around any cupboards and drawers in the house to see if Mark has left anything she might find useful, like a weapon of some sort, but he is far too careful. She grabs the photograph album and stuffs it into the top of the bag. Then she sits down on the sofa, because she doesn't know where she's supposed to go. All she seems able to do is sit and watch her phone.

* * *

The road has barely changed since Alex drove along it with Juliet all those years ago. It's getting dark and the sun is low, almost grazing the horizon ahead of them. There's a beautiful sky slashed with red and orange, and deep grey shading the edges of the thickening cumulus clouds. Alex turns the heater up as the temperature drops quickly now, hovering around two degrees. He's brought a two-man tent and a couple of Arctic sleeping bags. He's got a stove, kettle, ration packs ... Alex and Ben will pretend they're on exercise together or maybe on operations. Alex has even brought his cam-cream. He's excited about watching Ben's face when he sees what Daddy has brought for him. A little mini-Alex uniform, complete with boots. And Alex has even got Ben's guns so that he can play with them in a proper combat environment. He can see what it's like to be a real soldier. Ben must be taught to endure the cold. It will give him chance to man up, to learn that if you've got the right equipment you can survive anything. Well, nearly anything. Ben's fallen asleep now the DVD has finished. Alex has been watching him constantly via the rear-view mirror. In sleep he looks perfect; innocent, vulnerable, unsullied, un-screwed up, unlike his parents. But Alex knows how much looks can deceive. Alex doesn't wake him. Funny, Alex has been looking forward to this first camping trip with his son since ... well since possibly the day he was born. He hasn't been old enough, Juliet has insisted. But now, well it's not up to Juliet any more. The boys together. He's got beers, he's got whisky and he's got a gun. Alex might even let Ben have a go.

When they pull over to the side of the track it's hovering around freezing. Alex turns off the engine and kills the lights and waits for his eyes to adjust to the darkness. There is a moon three-quarters full spilling silvery light over the barren moorland. Ben's eyes are open but he is yawning. It's half-past six, and past his teatime. 'Hungry'?

'Where are we? I thought we were going back to our old house, Daddy.'

'We're in the Brecon Beacons, near a very high mountain called Pen y Fan. I often used to come here to train to be a soldier. How do you feel about playing soldiers with Daddy tonight?'

'No thank you, Daddy. I'd like to go home with you and Mummy, and it's dark outside, so we can't do soldiers.'

'That's the best time to play.'

'And it's cold.'

'Do you want to see what I've got for you?' Ben yawns and nods, squirming as he stretches in his seat. Alex leans back and undoes the buckle. 'There. I've just got to get it out of the boot.' Alex climbs out of the car. The cold hits him sharply, like a slap on the face. His breath fogs in front of him. The hard ground is shaley and slippery as glass under his leather-soled shoes. The boot opens and the light illuminates the black, unmarked bag. He unzips it and pulls out clothes, socks, gloves, scarves, hats and boots. He selects Ben's things and then opens the rear door and hands them in. 'Here you are, big man. Can you put these on? They'll keep you warm.'

Alex returns to the boot and starts pulling on his uniform. It's been a while since he's been in his green kit, but it feels natural and comfortable. With each item of clothing he can sense that he is becoming more and more the real Alex. The cold doesn't feel quite as cold, nor the barrenness of the landscape quite so threatening. He's done a 360-degree recce, but there are no lights. He has a military-strength torch with almost a 1,000-metre beam, and he knows it will pick up anything, or anybody, hiding in the rocks. Behind the tactical bag is a flat leather case. Alex touches it, as if to check that it is really there. Then he returns to Ben. He hasn't moved from his seat. He's obviously looked at the clothes, because they are scattered around him. The thick beanie hat on his lap, the padded combat jacket on the seat at the side of him. A boot in his hand. 'Come on, Ben. Look lively. We'll make a fire and have some food. I've got Coke for you.'

Alex helps Ben to get dressed. Once he's outside the car, with his boots laced, his hat in place and his jacket tightly belted, he looks older than his five years. Alex gets his phone and takes a photograph. He briefly considers sending it to Juliet, decides against it, and then thinks fuck it ... why not? So he pulls her out from contacts and presses send. Then he turns the phone off. Ben stamps his feet and waves his arms around. 'Dad ... it's really, really cold. Can I get back in the car now?'

'Don't you want to help light the fire, and put the tent up?'

'No. I want Mummy. I'm frightened cos it's so scary here. I don't like it.'

'Shut up and do as you're told.' Alex's voice is lower now, more of a growl. He has kindling and wood and charcoal. Everything that he needs to get a small fire going. He walks several paces away from the car towards a slight clearing semi-encircled by rocks. It will provide some shelter from the wind and the cold. 'Get over here ... where I can see you.' Ben stumbles over to Alex's side. 'You've got to stay close to me, shall I tell you why? Because there was once a little boy called Tommy Jones, the same age as you, and he got lost up here over a hundred years ago. And his Daddy couldn't find him.'

'What happened?' Ben asks quietly.

'He died. And they didn't find his body for a month. All alone, lost on a very high ridge. So you don't want to go wandering, do you Ben?'

Ben shudders. 'No, Daddy.'

Alex squats down on his haunches and has flames licking at the kindling in a moment. Ben watches the flames and rubs his hands together. 'There's a ration box in the front of the car, can you go and get it?'

'I don't want to go, Daddy. I'm scared of the dark. And I might get lost, like that little boy Tommy.'

'Don't be a sissy. Off you go.'

Ben walks reluctantly back to the car. Alex takes the case and opens it. He can put the rifle together blindfolded. Just a few clicks and twists, and the sight lined up in the right place. He has ammo in his pockets and a .308 rifle which can kill a man at over a mile's distance. It's comforting to feel the cold steel resting against his thigh as he sets it up.

Ben returns with the rations. Alex has a water pot in the boot. He's put charcoal on the fire and it should soon be ready to cook on. In the meantime he throws Ben a bag of crisps. 'Treat time, son.'

Ben can't open them without taking his gloves off, and he pulls them off with difficulty. Then he manages to open the packet, but it tips up and half spill out. 'Ben, for Christ's sake, what the fuck are you doing?'

'Daddy, that's naughty. You said the F-word.'

'You want to be a soldier like Daddy? You want to play big

boy's games? Then you swear like a big boy, OK? Listen, Ben,' Alex talks while he opens up the ration box and pulls out a silver bag of meatballs and pasta, 'when I was away ... you know, in Afghan?'

'Yes.'

'Little boys, just a bit older than you, they were fighters. Did you know that?'

'No.' Ben's voice is very quiet. So quiet that Alex can barely hear him.

'Hey Ben, do you want to know what I brought for you? I brought your guns to play with. Shall we pretend to be proper soldiers? Would you like that?'

'No!' Ben shouts. His voice is shrill with fear. 'NO, Daddy. I don't like it here.'

'Those little boys in Afghan, they didn't like it either, but they had to do what they were told. Otherwise bad things happened to them.'

'Pleeeeeeese, Daddy.' Ben's starting to cry.

'They didn't cry. So shut the fuck up.' Ben's snivelling is a fucking indulgence, just showing that he's been mollycoddled by his mother, made soft. Alex intends to sort it, like Alex was sorted at Ben's age. Alex can hear Ben's breath, ragged and uneven as he struggles to stop his tears. 'Come here, Ben. I want to talk to you, to tell you some stuff that you need to know, OK? It's amazing what children are capable of. People underestimate them all the time. Adults try and pretend that they're innocent little things, very different to adults, but actually they're not at all. Children are capable of doing everything that adults do. *Everything*, do you hear me, Ben?'

'Yes, Daddy.'

'There's no protection from the bad things that happen in life, the bad things that happen to people. Did children get spared in Auschwitz? What about the boy soldiers in Sierra

Leone? It's a myth that children are different. They're no different, they're just younger, that's all. And they're bloody effective, because they don't have the useless moral baggage strapped on to them that makes them stop and think.'

'Daddy I don't understand what you're saying, you're using really big words and I don't like this story.'

Alex puts his arm around Ben and pulls him in close. He thinks he sees a light flurry of snow beginning to muster around them. He can feel Ben's little body shivering. 'Let me tell you something else. It's not easy to turn men into killing machines. There's a lot of conditioning required, and you need to break down the levels of resistance. An unseen enemy firing at you from a mile away, with maybe a couple of walls between you as well, is not a difficult kill. You can't see eye to eye so it's not that real. Maybe someone you see walking around in a field, visible through a crosshair, isn't close enough for discomfort. You can't see whether or not they're a good bloke, and besides they've just been firing the shit out of you so it's a no-brainer. But someone a foot away from you? Someone unarmed? Someone you've eyeballed? That's when your killing resistance is at its highest – are you listening, Ben?' Alex gives him a squeeze but Ben still doesn't respond. 'You see, it's a good thing that humans aren't natural born killers because it is a good thing for humankind and it is ultimately uplifting and reassuring and comforting to know that one is not a natural born killer. And it doesn't matter that they're some fucking raghead insurgent, the point is that they're part of the SAME FUCKING SPECIES.' Alex cannot block the thoughts. And he can't stop the tears.

'You hear me, Ben?' Ben doesn't respond. Alex shakes him, but his eyes stay closed. The snow is beginning to settle now. 'Ben! Wake up, come on you're on stag, you can't jack on me, mate.' Ben's eyes flip open.

'Meatballs?' He likes the meatballs, but they're a bit hot, he says. Alex ignores his whingeing but hands him a can of beer.

'Eeeugh, tastes horrible,' he says.

'Knock it back.'

Ben takes a couple more swigs from the can. Alex belches. 'Can you do that?'

'Mummy says it's rude.'

'Fuck Mummy. She's not here.'

'I wish she was,' Ben says, quietly.

'We don't need her here, silly fucking tart.'

'I don't like you saying nasty things about Mummy.'

'OK. We love Mummy really, but I'm cross with her because she took you away from me.'

'She's frightened of you, Daddy. I'm frightened of you. I wish you and Mummy were back in our old house, and I could play with my friends. I wish we could do that. Can't we, Daddy? I'm cold, Daddy, and I want to go home ...' Ben's voice is a thin whine, and his teeth are chattering.

'Man up, Ben. I'm going to teach you how to shoot. Don't spill pasta sauce down you, or we'll think it's blood, won't we?' Alex laughs. Then he goes silent. 'Hey Ben, did you hear that?'

'What?'

'Shhh!' Alex tunes his ears to the tiniest little scraping but he thinks it's too loud to be made by an animal. It could perhaps be a deer, but it's odd for it to be so close. Alex's senses are on high alert so it's possible he imagines hearing things sometimes. But he hears it again. It sounds like a distant, rhythmic thudding, like heavy boots marching towards them.

'Ben,' Alex whispers, 'Get back to the car. Now!'

'No! I want to stay with you. I'm scared, Daddy, really scared. Please Daddy, can we go home now ...?'

'For fuck's sake, Ben, I said get back to the bloody car. Just do it.' Alex reaches out for the rifle. He hears Ben's sharp intake of breath. Alex takes a bullet from his jacket pocket and then slips the round into the chamber and closes the bolt. He braces his back against a rock and rests the stock of the rifle on top of his knee. Then the shaking starts. He feels clammy and sick, lightheaded. He forces himself to stand up, pointing the rifle in the direction of the sound. He can't see anything. He needs the torch. He pulls it from his pocket and switches it on, shining it all around. The powerful beam lights up snowflakes the size of cotton-wool balls, skirmishing chaotically on the gathering wind. It also serves to pinpoint Alex's position. He feels the sudden urge for a slug of whisky to calm his trembling. He could end up a gibbering wreck on the floor soon, and there's nothing he can do about it. He hears the scraping again. There's someone out there coming for him. An unseen enemy moving in closer, and he's a sitting target. His gut goes into spasm as if a knife has cut through his lower bowel. He feels bile in his throat, then he starts to retch and finally he vomits, shattering the silence of the night and telling whoever is out there exactly where he is.

'Drop the gun!' Alex pulls himself up, clutches the rifle, ready to aim in the direction of the voice.

'Who the fuck are you?'

'I said drop the gun.' Alex aims in the direction of the voice and pulls the trigger.

The sound of the gunshot fades and for a moment there is silence. And then a voice: 'Drop the gun unless you want me to blow your head off.'

Alex realizes he knows the voice. 'Price, you fucker. What the hell are you fucking playing at?' Suddenly the darkness turns green. Price has cracked a Cyalume. Alex can see Mark. He's armed with a pistol.

'Enough, boss. This is where it ends.'

Where it ends ... where it ends ... Alex takes aim; Price is only ten metres away. He could take him out before he raises the pistol. Maybe they'd take each other out. But then his hands start to shake again. He can't hold the gun straight. He can no longer do the one thing he was always so good at. 'What are you going to do? Shoot me? Because you know what, you'd be doing me a bloody favour, mate. So why don't you? Pull the fucking trigger, eh? What are you waiting for ... ? Go on, just do it ...' The rifle in Alex's hands judders so much he can barely hold it. 'Christ ...' he swears to himself, angrily. Despite the cold, sweat is pouring off his brow and stinging his eyes. 'Well?' he shouts. 'What's the matter with you? What are you, a fucking coward?' Alex drops the rifle to the ground, and then he falls to his knees. He puts his hands to his head, covering his ears, screwing his eyes up tightly, and then he slides his body down to the snow-covered rocks, unable to stop the convulsions knocking him about like fists on a punchbag. He's sobbing like a baby, and the pictures, the fucking awful pictures are there in front of him again. He's back there. Exhausted, frightened, exhilarated, but most of all shocked to the core at what he has just done. He's been to the edge of the abyss, looked into it and realized that he was staring at the evil inside himself. Alex can't hold back the tears. He takes ragged breaths. 'It just won't stop. It won't bloody go away. I just can't get that bloody kid out of my head ...'

And he hears Mark beside him, picking up the weapon, removing the bolt from the chamber. 'It's all right, boss. It's over. It's all OK.'

Alex hears his own voice, choked and ranting into the freezing night: 'He was screaming. We all thought the kid had taken a bullet after we'd been firing at Terry in the compound. We thought we'd shot the little bugger, remember? Boothe was in front of me. I yelled to him, 'Watch the fucking ground ...' and that was it, the last thing I ever said to him. I was on the deck, bits of Boothe all over me. That kid, he didn't move. He'd stopped screaming. I picked myself up and went over ... there was nothing wrong with him. He was a lure. Terry knew we were soft when it came to injured kids. Hearts and minds. The British don't shoot Afghan kids. And I looked in those big brown eyes, so fucking innocent, and I blew his fucking head off. In that moment of sheer blinding fury I took a kid's life. So what does that make me? I'm an animal. He wasn't much more than Ben's age now.'

'He lured Boothe to his death.'

'Yeah. But he wasn't fucking responsible. He was just a kid, just like Ben.'

Where is Ben, Alex?'

'Ben? In the car. I told him to go back to the car.'

'So he's all right. You're sure he's OK?'

'Yeah. He's fine.'

'So, is that whisky in that bottle? I could use a drink.'

Alex passes him the bottle and he takes a swig, then Mark sits down beside him. 'That kid. Yeah it was shit. But after everything that happened to us … no one can know what it was like unless you were there. And Boothe – he was one of the best. Something snapped inside you that day and somehow you've got to deal with it. I was worried you might do something stupid. There was a time when I thought I might … when I didn't think I could live with myself. But there's help out there. I just wish I'd realized that before I lost everything. When I look back I can't believe how tough I was on Zoe. I didn't want you to make the same fuck up with Juliet. We always looked out for each other, remember? Now I'm looking out for you. Why don't we go home and see her, eh? Take Ben back. I'm going to help you, boss. And it's too fucking cold to be out here. Let's get the little lad home. It's all going to be OK. Shall we go and find him? He's probably bloody terrified after hearing that gunshot. Christ, you could have blown my bloody head off. Lucky you're such a shit aim!'

Mark goes to the car. Then Alex hears him shout: 'Ben?

Where are you, big man? It's me, Mark. You hiding somewhere?'

Alex runs to the car and looks inside, at the back seat where he thinks Ben should be. Never could do what he was bloody well told. His mother's fault. No fucking discipline.

'Poor little chap must be petrified,' Mark shouts to Alex. 'Guess he's hiding somewhere. Ben … come on now, it's cold, and you're going to be safe. Everything's all right. There's nothing to be afraid of …'

The blizzard is thickening, forming a deadly shroud of freezing snow all around them, and around wherever Ben is. It deadens the sound of their boots and their voices, it covers their clothes and numbs their extremities. 'Christ, must be about minus three, I reckon. And the wind's picking up.' Mark calls again. 'Where's that torch?'

'I put it down and now I can't bloody see it. The snow's covered it.'

Mark cracks another Cyalume and it illuminates a large area, but there's no sign of life.

'Ben …'

'Bennnnnn …'

Their calls get more and more urgent. Alex is swearing at himself, shouting to himself, words that get snatched from his mouth by the wind. 'Christ, what have I done,' he wails to the night. This is all his fault. Again. All his fault. Everything – Juliet, the baby, the Afghan boy, and now Ben. Mark's right. He can't live with himself. He knows that he can no more live with his future than he can with his past. He lets out a howl of anguish. He goes back to the place where he and Ben were cooking and drinking their beers together, like men. He takes the 9mm Glock pistol from his pocket and pushes the muzzle against his right temple. *This is where it ends …*

Leabharlanna Poibli Chathair Baile Átha Cliath

Dublin City Public Libraries

EPILOGUE

Juliet finds it surprising how she can go through the motions of living: eating, sleeping; dealing with the endless domestic duties that the act of survival requires her to carry out each day. She feels as though she has become an automaton, performing the necessary acts but having had the ability to feel anything stripped out of her. She suspects it's a defence mechanism, this shutting down of emotions, because if she were to start to feel anything – despite what people have told her – she knows the pain would destroy her. Apparently it's all right to cry. If she wants to break down then that's fine, it's healthy. But she can't. Not now. Not after everything. She's always been good at distraction techniques, almost to the extent of dissociation, so it has been said by the so-called professionals: the various counsellors and shrinks she's seen over the years. It's how she's always dealt with the difficult things in life.

She finds Ben's bedroom a solace because it has always allowed her to pretend that things are really all right. It was her little haven. The tin soldiers, the painting of the cherubic young boy with his golden curls, the plump hippopotamuses rampaging over the walls, all the cheery things that can take her mind to a better place, where she can pretend for a short while that everything is just as it should be. She wishes that there was something more to keep her mind occupied, some clothes to fold and put away, or add to the laundry bin; perhaps some shoes to pair up, or pillows to plump and neaten, but Ben's room is immaculate. There is nothing left for her to do in here, other than to look around and commit every little detail to memory.

Juliet has used this house as a major distraction ever since they moved in; a distraction from her life, her marriage, herself, even from Ben. People might think she was mad to believe a house had the power to make everything all right. But she had, honestly, believed that it might. She had really believed that this house might have the power to heal them in some way. This house wasn't just bricks and mortar, it was the one thing that could save them. How could she have been so wrong? Because *apparently* it's the people living inside that make a home. Juliet's firm base had no more power to do that than a pile of masonry on a demolition site. Magazine features, smart nurseries, state-of-the-art kitchens, *apparently* it doesn't matter how or where you live, just so long as you are living with the right people, your people, the people you love. These are things that Juliet must learn so that she can move on, she's been told. But when you're lost at sea you cling to the one thing that might save you from drowning, don't you? You want something substantial and secure. This house was her life raft, and now she has to let go of it, along with the ghosts and the memories. She shuts the door on Ben's bedroom, crosses the landing and climbs the stairs to the bedroom she shared with Alex. So many ghosts and memories of the people they were reside in here. It is a room with a deeply unhappy feel, and there is an iciness that belies the warm April day outside. She throws open the window and looks down at the small garden below. Clumps of daffodils show off brazenly in the stark border, as if to say: "Whatever ... life goes on, you know. Just look at us." She turns back to the bedroom. Juliet hasn't slept in here since she returned. The bed is stripped, the mattress bare. She has moved all of her clothes out of here, but she still has to deal with Alex's things. She has been putting it off, unable to face opening the wardrobe, but she no longer has any choice, as she's running out of time. She must brace herself and get on with it. Even now, when she thinks of him it makes her shudder and feel mildly nauseous. To do what he did, to put Ben through all of that, she can never forgive him. Poor Ben. She feels her throat constrict, but she mustn't give in.

Focus and distract. She opens the double doors. 'There you are,' she says aloud. 'Alex Miller, officer and gentleman. Look at you.' She stands back and wonders what a stranger would make of this material representation of her husband, this legacy of Alex's shell, really nothing more than a sloughed-off skin. What evidence of the real Alex could be gathered from all of this *stuff,* the way *he* chose to present himself to the world?

She starts lifting things out, slowly and carefully at first, laying armfuls of suits on the bed: dark navy and charcoal grey, pinstripes neither too wide nor too bright. Shirts stacked in neat piles packaged and pinned in cellophane wrapping from the laundry service. Then his shoes: black leather Oxfords, brown leather brogues and chocolate suede loafers. His ties: silk, Hermès and Dior. More shirts: Turnbull and Asser, Thomas Pink; now Levi's and Diesel jeans, cashmere jumpers, dark and pastel. She starts pulling them out and chucking them with a mounting ferocity at the ever-expanding mountain on the bed. Clothes make the man, do they? Like the house makes a home? What a fucking joke. It's all a sham, a pointless fucking sham. You can dress things up, put on a showy façade, play the part – even don the uniform - but you'll never see the real people hiding behind it all. Alex's clothes, the house, it's all just camouflage to disguise the people inside who are, in turn, hiding from themselves, or so it seems to Juliet.

The clothes are all on the bed now. She will bag everything up and take them to Oxfam. It's a good thing that she's moving, otherwise she might see some of this lot walking around Waitrose. She's tired now, but she still has to deal with all the things that he stashed away in the bottom of the wardrobe. She gets down on her knees and takes a look. It's all very neat and organized, as she would expect. There's a black box file with a locking catch. She flicks it and it snaps open. Inside are dividers, neatly labelled in block capitals, 'CAR', 'INSURANCE', 'BANK', 'ACCOUNTS',

'PENSION', 'JULIET'. She pulls out the manila folder. She has a premonition of what she might find. She tips out the contents of the file onto the floor. There are photographs – the important ones – that he obviously felt should be with him in foreign places; the ones that would comfort him at times of stress and fear. There they are, the three of them: Alex with Ben on his knee and Juliet beside them, leaning into them, smiling. It's the little things that catch her. So much can be brought to mind by one little snapshot in time. Anyone looking on would think, 'A perfect little family. Lucky them.' Juliet hugs it to her because this is one of the few things she has left of her own little family.

There is a cheap airmail-style envelope, a 'bluey'. It is addressed to Mrs Alex Miller at their previous Army quarters. Juliet stares at it for a few moments and then picks it up. She examines the upright nature of Alex's handwriting, the handwriting of a ghost. She turns it over, strokes the paper, runs her fingers along the seal. Alex licked it, pushed his own fingers along the same crease. Inside this little slip of paper are Alex's words, addressed to her, unread and unseen since Alex composed them. Alex's voice from the grave, two months gone but he still has the power to tell her something new, to create a new memory. But it's so long ago, it surely bears no relevance any more? He was writing to someone else, a different Juliet, when *he* was somebody else. She takes the envelope over to the bed and sinks down on to the floor, resting her back against the bed. The twill of Alex's suit trousers touches her neck and she inhales the soft wool scent. Without realising what she is doing, she takes hold of the material and pushes it to her face, stroking the fabric. She puts her forefinger into the small gap on the crest of the envelope and gently teases it open. You have to be careful with a bluey, because you can easily rip it open in the wrong place. But Juliet knows what she's doing and opens it expertly. She stares at Alex's neat but tiny handwriting. It's dated: FOB, 8th July 2010

My darling Juliet,

First of all I pray that you never get to read this, because if you do it means that I'm not coming home to you and our babies. I am so sorry to cause you pain, my love, but I know you are strong, and you will have the courage to bear this, and to raise our children perfectly. Ben won't remember me, and I'll never get to meet our little tadpole. Six months now, darling. Not too long to go, and hope you are feeling well. I can't help thinking that posthumous babies are becoming a bit of a tradition in my family. Better make sure Ben gets a really safe desk job somewhere and don't let him cross the road, drive a car or do anything that puts him at risk. Remember I always used to tell you that being in the Army was really a low risk job, with a statistically low mortality rate? Doesn't feel much like that now, out here. It's not proper warfare, though. The other side don't play by the same rules as us, the bastards. And I keep telling myself that it will all be worthwhile, that we're doing a good job, but honestly? If you could see the raw bloody hatred in the kids' eyes when they look at you. Not sure we're doing so well at the hearts and minds initiative. Christ, this country's a head case and they're mighty sick of being occupied. Yeah, that's how they see us, not liberators, but occupiers ... but you know all of this stuff and it's not what's important. Only three weeks left on this tour at the time I'm writing this letter. Oh my darling, you can't imagine how much I'm longing to be home with you, to take you in my arms. I want to stroke that swelling belly of yours and feel our new little person wriggle and kick inside you. That thought comforts me and if it's one of my last thoughts, then it's a good one! Remember always that I love you and if I haven't always been the best husband then please forgive me. I know I was tough on you last R & R and I deeply regret that. Sweetheart I can't bring this shit home with me. When I'm with you and Ben I just want to forget this place exists. I've seen stuff ... done stuff ... that makes me wonder who I am, deep inside, like I can no longer recognise myself. I guess that's war ... being pushed to your limits and beyond. Beyond. I'm not a particularly religious man, but I hope there's something else, my darling. I want to believe when I put my boots on tomorrow that I'll be coming back to you. But if I don't, I know this sounds corny but I'll see you in heaven, my love. Take care of our little ones and most of all take care of yourself and thank you for giving me the happiest years of my life.

All my love, my darling, forever.

Alex.

PS You'll find all the boring stuff in the file at the bottom of the wardrobe, but you probably know that. And please tell Mum that I love her and that she was a terrific Mum!

Juliet carefully refolds the letter and holds it in both hands. These are the words of her Alex, the man she used to know, her loving husband. 'What happened to you, Alex?' she asks, aloud, 'where did you go to? How could this have happened to us?'

'Are you OK, Juliet? A cup of tea? A bucketful of wine?' Rowena is standing in the doorway. Juliet didn't hear her come up the stairs. She was too swept up in memories, good memories for once.

'Yeah. I guess ...'

'I've told the nanny to keep Ben for tea. She says he's happy playing with Cordelia if that's OK with you.'

'Is he all right?'

'I think so. He gave Cordelia quite a talking to about playing with guns. He said his Daddy accidentally shot himself and Cordelia ... oh you know what they're like ... she told him that she knew, and that she didn't want to talk about guns any more because her mummy had told her not to mention guns to Ben. Can't bloody win with these kids. Sorry.'

'At least he's talking about it. And one day soon he'll get to know the truth. But hopefully he can believe it was an accident for a little while longer.'

'Maybe it was? Maybe you can never know for sure.'

'Yeah, maybe.' Juliet sighs and pulls herself up from the floor. 'I found a letter. One of those "In the event of my death" ones. Written a long time ago. It was like the old Alex was talking to me, Ro. I don't know, somehow it makes me think of him differently. Does that sound weird? I mean, after all he did to me ... and to Ben ... like inside, somewhere, the old Alex was still there.'

'He was sick, Juliet, darling. You tried to do all you could to help him. And thank God that guy Mark found Ben before it was too late. Christ, when you think what might have happened. I guess mild hypothermia was a blessing, considering how bad it could have been. I just can't bear what you've had to go through. But I wish you weren't moving so far away.'

'Bristol's not exactly far away. And I can't stay here. All the memories, the people, the bloody house. We need a fresh start. You can come and stay. I've been thinking about the new house, thought I'd go for something a bit more bohemian to go with my new art student identity. Or maybe I'll go for all white everywhere and a Perspex floating staircase? It feels weirdly liberating that for once I don't have to have anyone's agreement, I can just do what the hell I like.'

'I can see I'm going to come to bloody Bristol and I won't recognise you anymore. You'll be poncing about in a kaftan chanting "om"', God forbid.'

'And you'll be buying your ready-made designer soups and hiding the cartons in the rubbish, and feeling permanently guilty about your work-life balance. Why does life have to be so damned complicated?'

'Come on, hon, let's go downstairs. I've brought a rescue bottle of white wine. Thought you might be ready for a drink.'

'I'm really going to miss you, Rowena. You know I can't thank you for all you've done. I just wish I'd opened up to you sooner about what was going on. It was all so terrifying, and I didn't want you to be involved … you know … to get dragged into the cesspit. Hey, I've offered to write a piece for the women's refuge website about internet security and what happened to me – anonymously, of course – and even if it only helps *one* woman it'll be worth it. I just want to make something good come out of all of this.'

'Ben. He's the something good, Juliet.'

'I know. Of course he is. My precious little boy. Geraldine says she'll pick up the school fees when he's old enough to go to boarding school.'

Rowena's eyes look as if they are going to pop out of her head. She slaps her glass onto the kitchen worktop. 'For fuck's sake, you're not serious?'

'No. Of course I'm not. No boarding school, and I don't care who or what he wants to be …'

'… as long as he doesn't join the fucking Army!' They chorus together.

'Juliet, you actually cracked a joke! Is this where the healing begins?'

'I hope so. I really hope so.' Juliet has tucked Alex's letter into her pocket and she imagines she can feel a warmth exuding from it. It was written by her Alex, the real Alex, and it doesn't matter that it comes from way back in the past because it's still real, it's still his words, his sentiments, his love; and she intends to use it as the foundation stone upon which to rebuild her and Ben's future.

NOTES

WHO ARE YOU?

I have a son in the Army. He has served in Iraq and Afghanistan and so I know what it is like to wave goodbye to someone you love; and much as you try to suppress the thought, you cannot help yourself from wondering whether you are holding them for the last time; or whether they'll suffer some horrific mutilation which will alter their lives forever. Now, as I write this, I can feel a tightening in my stomach, a sick reminder of 'putting on a brave face' and waiting until the last sighting of him before allowing myself to cry. I didn't really sleep properly for the entire time he was away; and I remember getting a phone call, coincidentally on the morning of my birthday, at the end of his tour: 'Hi Mum, I've just landed in Germany…' I burst into tears and couldn't speak because I was just so relieved and happy that he was safe. The best birthday present ever! I realized I had held my emotions in check until he was back, but then it was OK to let go. Needless to say I slept soundly that night!

My son loves the Army and let me confirm straight away that I have huge respect for him and for our armed forces; I am immensely proud of him and of what he does. Most people serving will cope with their experiences on tour in war zones, but I'm not sure that coping is the same as remaining unchanged. I remember when my son came home and I clumsily started to ask him about his experiences. He didn't want to talk about it at first. It took a few days for snippets to come out such as the fact that he thought, drily, it was a little bit unfair to have his first contact – i.e. being shot at – on his birthday. Bit by bit, other stories came out and it was only months later that he admitted the extent of the danger he had been in at times. I sensed he had changed. I felt I had said goodbye to a boy (albeit a 23-year old) and he returned a man, a little more self-contained, a little more worldly, a little more aware of the value of life, or lack of it.

Spending time in a war zone, thankfully, is not something most of us will have to experience, and without being there it is impossible to understand what it must be like. But as a mother I find myself drawn to anything that provides me with a vicarious experience of it. News items, documentaries, books – things that will help me to understand what our sons, daughters, husbands and wives are going through and the effects it will have on them both physically and mentally.

In January 2013 a young man called Jake Wood published a book called *Among You – The Extraordinary True Story of a Soldier Broken by War.* I heard Jake being interviewed on the radio, and also on television. The book exposed, first hand, what it was like to be on the front line, and the awful cost to a brave soldier who found himself – as a reservist – unable to cope, 'broken' through serving his country. I read his book; it is beautifully written and heartbreaking, and it inspired me to begin researching the subject of Post Traumatic Stress Disorder (PTSD) and combat stress, the hidden wounds, in depth.

I live in Herefordshire, home of what we proudly refer to as 'the Regiment', the elite SAS, and I spoke to several friends associated with the Regiment about the subject and was reassured that most soldiers love their jobs, carrying out their duties with professionalism and a finely developed sense of morality. Most come home undamaged and proud of the job they are doing.

So why do some people succumb to PTSD while others don't? And what can the armed forces do to detect an individual's vulnerability to the condition?

Recent research by the Association for Psychological Science focused on a study of 260 male veterans from the National Vietnam Veterans Readjustment Study.[1] Not surprisingly the study found that 97 per cent of sufferers had been exposed to traumatic events.

However only just under a third of these went on to develop PTSD over the long term; and of those exposed to the most extreme combat trauma, just under a third of those didn't go on to develop long-term PTSD. This suggested that there were other factors at work, needing to be identified, which could lead to a pre-disposition of developing PTSD. Childhood physical abuse was one; and another was the inflicting of harm on civilians or prisoners of war during combat. Bruce Dohrenwend, the author of the research and his colleagues stress that the recent conflicts in Iraq and Afghanistan are, like Vietnam, 'wars amongst the people' where there are risks of 'devastating violations of the rules of war.' Sadly there are many examples from recent conflicts which fulfill Dohrenwend's warning.

In 2009 a regiment of Danish soldiers was deployed on a six-month tour to Afghanistan. An award-winning documentary film, *Armadillo*, was made during that tour; and at the same time a psychological evaluation of a large number of troops, including these men, was carried out by psychological scientist Dorthe Berntsen of Aarhus University in Denmark, together with a team of Danish and American researchers.[2] The results of the two studies were similar. Most troops exposed to traumatic combat were resilient, either recovering quickly from any psychological distress, or having no symptoms at all. Of those who did suffer any long-lasting damage, a large majority were much more likely to have suffered psychological distress prior to deployment, such as physical abuse during childhood, and they often could not, or would not, talk about these past experiences. "We were surprised that stressful experiences during childhood seemed to play such a central role in discriminating the resilient versus non-resilient groups," says Berntsen. "These results should make psychologists question prevailing assumptions about PTSD and its development."

So these important findings seem to challenge the previously held perception that PTSD/Combat Stress is caused by repeated exposure to trauma during extreme combat; rather it may be more related to experiences of violence during childhood. Even more interestingly, 13 per cent of the Danish study that had exhibited symptoms of stress prior to deployment actually found their symptoms eased during their tour, finding social support and a sense of self-esteem, which they hadn't experienced before. However, upon return from combat their symptoms of stress returned.

Alex and Juliet are both victims of childhood abuse; two damaged halves of an imperfect whole. Alex is not meant to be representative of a soldier developing PTSD as a result of his war-time experiences alone; but as someone who was ill-equipped to deal with both the emotional and physical abuse suffered during his childhood, and who sought self-definition and security within the Army. Without his 'back story' he might easily have had the resilience to deal with his combat experiences. Both Alex and Juliet have an ill-defined sense of self, building up defensive layers in order to cope with the unresolved trauma from their childhoods. They create their own war zone and as the battles go on – as in most long term wars with an ill-defined objective - it is sometimes hard to tell who is the victim and who is the aggressor.

I admit Who Are You? is not meant to be an easy read. It has been a difficult subject to write about and some of the scenes are very uncomfortable. But I have tried, so far as is possible, to ensure that they are all based on fact; indeed, since starting to write this novel I have found it uncanny how much 'life has imitated art'.

In recent weeks – and days – PTSD has been very much at the forefront of the news. On the 12th May the charity Combat Stress marked its 95th anniversary by revealing a 57 per cent increase between 2012 and 2013 in Afghanistan veterans seeking help from them.[3] Knowledge and understanding of the condition was shown by Judge Peter Heywood in Swansea Crown Court last week when he granted leniency to Jonathan Dunne, stating: 'Our servicemen come home from the theatres of conflict and we consider that they are all robust by the very nature of their training. But, of course, seeing colleagues and friends fall is not easy and I suspect many of them clearly need psychological help.' The Sunday Telegraph on the 25th of May headed a feature article 'PTSD: The Bomb Waiting to Explode'. [4] If the book brings the subject of PTSD, its affect on the sufferers and their families to a wider and different audience, especially as the newly-released figures show an increase in the incidence of it as more soldiers return from combat, then I will have achieved everything that I set out to do.

I have been fortunate in being able to show the manuscript to some senior, but unnamed, sources within the Army and am grateful to them for their advice on authenticity, and for their endorsement of the facts.

Lastly, out of respect for our service men and women who are suffering from PTSD, I would like to stress that many have not suffered from any sort of childhood abuse, nor do they display violent tendencies. I want to finish with a few words from Jake Wood, which seems only fitting as he was there at the birth (little did he know it!).

"While childhood abuse is a recognized predisposing factor to PTSD, most veterans with PTSD, such as myself, will not have been abused as children – and therefore will not (or certainly should not) be abusive to their partners and children."

Elizabeth Forbes, 27th May 2014

[1] B. P. Dohrenwend, T. J. Yager, M. M. Wall, B. G. Adams. The Roles of Combat Exposure, Personal Vulnerability, and Involvement in Harm to Civilians or Prisoners in Vietnam War-Related Posttraumatic Stress Disorder. *Clinical Psychological Science*, 2013; DOI: 10.1177/2167702612469355

[2] D. Berntsen, K. B. Johannessen, Y. D. Thomsen, M. Bertelsen, R. H. Hoyle, D. C. Rubin. Peace and War: Trajectories of Posttraumatic Stress Disorder Symptoms Before, During, and After Military Deployment in Afghanistan.*Psychological Science*, 2012; DOI: 10.1177/0956797612457389

[3] http://www.combatstress.org.uk/about-us/

[4] http://www.telegraph.co.uk/news/uknews/defence/10853636/Post-traumatic-stress-disorder-the-bomb-waiting-to-explode.html

ACKNOWLEDGEMENTS

An enormous thank you to the following people without whom this book would not have been possible, and who between them helped fill in the potholes along the road to publication.

Paul Swallow of Cutting Edge Press, for being brilliant, supportive and patient, 24/7; for giving me the faith and encouragement to explore the 'dark' side, and who I am proud to call my dear friend. Broo Doherty of DHH Literary Agency who is the epitome of a writer's dream agent. Loyal and dear friend, counsellor, adviser; the patience of Job and a cracking sense of humour. No one could possibly work harder nor more generously.

Martin Hay and the team at Cutting Edge Press for supporting me a second time. Hatty Ash and her predecessor Saffeya Shebli for their great work on the publicity front. Alessandro Massarini for once more providing us with a stunning cover image. Sean Costello for his eagle-editorial eye. He is a joy to work with. Anira Rowanchild, my friend and ex-tutor for her unswerving honesty and encouragement. Clare John who gives feedback at the speed of light and who, as an Army wife, gave much needed encouragement at the outset of this project. Jake Wood, author of *Among You – The Extraordinary True Story of a Soldier Broken by War*. Two senior commanding officers for checking the military detail. My son for advice on military detail. Mandy at Eyetek Surveillance regarding spy cameras and tracking devices. Harriet Gordon and Deborah Herbert for advice on psychological issues. Anne Cater and BC@booksandswearing for their jacket quotes and support. Fiona Field, author of Soldier's Wives, who was herself a soldier, is married to a soldier, and has a son who is a soldier. To my friends on Twitter: the bloggers and fellow authors – new friends who are kind enough to share their tweets with me; and also to my face book friends who can bring a whole world of entertainment, chat and much-needed distraction into my garrett and who are saving the world from even more of my words.

My long suffering husband Jamie – my best friend in the world – and to my children Jamie and Poppy of whom I am immensely proud and who may be spared the ordeal of having to read their mother's words.

ORGANISATIONS FOR SUPPORT

If you have been affected by the issues raised in this book, the following organisations can help.

Mind – http://www.mind.org.uk/information-support/types-of-mental-health-problems/post-traumatic-stress-disorder-(ptsd)/#.U3C_p_ldVi0

Combat Stress – http://www.combatstress.org.uk/

SSAFA – https://www.ssafa.org.uk/

Royal British Legion – http://www.britishlegion.org.uk/

Samaritans – http://www.samaritans.org/

The NHS – http://www.nhs.uk/conditions/Post-traumatic-stress-disorder/Pages/Introduction.aspx

Refuge – http://refuge.org.uk/

National Domestic Violence Helpline – http://www.nationaldomesticviolencehelpline.org.uk/

Women's Aid – http://www.womensaid.org.uk/

National Centre for Domestic Violence – http://www.ncdv.org.uk/

NEAREST THING TO CRAZY
Elizabeth Forbes

"A wonderfully observed tale. Clever, compelling and utterly captivating."
Caroline Smailes, author of *The Drowning of Arthur Braxton*

"A clever unputdownable study of madness and manipulation."
Hereford Times

"Nearest Thing to Crazy took hold of me from the start and didn't let go until the end... This is a great book and it deserves all the praise it could possibly be given."
Jessica Patient, The View From Here

"A stunning debut novel that had me hooked from the very first page."
Sarah Taylor – Today I'm Reading

"Sometimes a book comes along that totally blows the mind... there is no doubt that this is going to be one of my Top Ten Books of the year."
Anne Cater – Random Things Through My Letterbox

"A distinctly dark heart beats at the centre of this story and it is when this darkness rises to the surface that it grabs the reader firmly by the throat... an energetic page turner which grips the reader early on and refuses to let go."
Dan Powell – www.danpowellfiction.com

"Stunningly intelligent plot that scares the absolute shit out of you and makes you question your sanity."
Book Geek

"I f***ing adored this book...It's one of those ones that make you want to grab the characters by the neck and shake them around a bit...will keep you gripped and guessing and questioning your own assessments of the story and characters all the way through."
Book C**t

NEAREST THING TO CRAZY

ELIZABETH FORBES

Published June 2013 • Paperback: £8.99 • ISBN: 9781908122582